Once Upon a
Quinceañera

Once Upon a Quinceañera

MONICA GOMEZ-HIRA

HARPER TEEN
An Imprint of HarperCollinsPublishers

HarperTeen is an imprint of HarperCollins Publishers.

Once Upon a Quinceañera
Copyright © 2021 by Monica Gomez-Hira

Library of Congress Cataloging-in-Publication Data

Names: Gomez-Hira, Monica, author.
Title: Once upon a quinceañera / Monica Gomez-Hira.
Description: First edition. | New York, NY : HarperTeen, [2021] | Audience: Ages 13 up. | Audience: Grades 10-12. | Summary: "Eighteen-year-old Carmen takes on a summer internship that has her reuniting with estranged family for an over-the-top quinceañera, reluctantly reconnecting to a long-lost ex-boyfriend, and finding happiness in the chaos"—Provided by publisher.
Identifiers: LCCN 2020035074 | ISBN 978-0-06-299684-8
Subjects: CYAC: Quinceañera (Social custom)—Fiction. | Family life—Florida—Miami—Fiction. | Entertainers—Fiction. | Interns—Fiction. | Dating (Social customs)—Fiction. | Miami (Fla.)—Fiction.
Classification: LCC PZ7.1.G652177 Onc 2021 | DDC [Fic]—dc23
LC record available at https://lccn.loc.gov/2020035074

Typography by Corina Lupp
Illustrations by Isabela Humphrey

22 23 24 25 26   PC/LSCH   10 9 8 7 6 5 4 3 2 1
❖
First paperback edition, 2022

To Hira, who made me believe it
To Anjali, who made it matter
And to my family, who made me

One

ONCE UPON A TIME, there was a sign.

Three, actually. Too bad Mami missed them all.

"That was your left," I yelped as we passed our turn. The humid, flowered streets of Miami slid by.

The wrong streets.

"Coño, this street has three different names, Carmen!" Mami glared at me in her rearview mirror. My fault. As usual.

Through six layers of sky-blue satin, my best friend, Waverly, muttered something about being late.

"Maybe we'll turn into pumpkins and I won't have to dance with a guy wearing an animal head," I said.

"Maybe start taking this seriously?"

Waverly and I worked as party princesses for a company called Dreams Come True. She usually played Cinderella, but since this was my first party, I didn't have a "usually" yet.

My buttercup-yellow Belle dress lay on my lap, as heavy

as a baby, still smelling like dry cleaning fluid. As soon as Waves finished putting herself together, she had to help me with this monstrosity. This was the most formal dress I'd worn since my baptism gown, because I didn't go to prom or have a quinceañera.

I'm not exactly the buttercup-yellow-satin, bluebirds-singing-around-her-head type. Satin means sweat stains. And if there are birds around me, it's because they're in the arroz con pollo I'm eating.

But here I am. Because I missed a few signs myself.

Miami Heights High School requires that every graduating senior take a life-planning class called Life Visioning. And a requirement of the requirement was an approved internship with a vetted local professional. Between two hundred and three hundred hours and a final project that had to be approved in advance. Not enough hours? No diploma. Unapproved project? No diploma. The administration thought that this would teach us persistence and responsibility, and, in an ideal world, give us the opportunity to discover our future college majors and eventual career paths.

This should have been a throwaway class—a guaranteed A that would let me sail across the graduation stage. That's what everyone said. Just tick the box and carry on.

Except . . . why not use the class as intended? I lobbied hard for my mentor match, a wedding photographer and videographer. It was the videography part I was excited about, because

I had dim ideas of maybe turning my fandom-video-editing hobby into a college major. I remember Mr. Velez raising his eyebrows at my sudden academic excitement. I wasn't normally that kind of student. I was an expert at doing the bare minimum. But this felt like it could be different. Like the hours I spent hunched over my ancient keyboard matching actors' faces with a perfect song lyric could pay off. Like it could *mean something*.

I feel dumb even admitting that now.

My boss, Edwin, I probably don't have to tell you, was not a happy, fulfilled artist. I have no idea how many mal de ojos he put on the various brides and grooms he worked for, but it must have been a lot. He also wasn't much of a mentor. His favorite topic was his own brilliance. And the exact shape of my ass.

Still, I'd taken a chance and shown him the final project I was going to submit. After he'd frowned through the whole thing, he'd said, "So jumbled . . . and why is it so blurry?"

"It's supposed to look dreamy."

"Well . . . that's a choice, I guess. I mean, it's for a high school class. Right?" Then he'd looked at it again. "Even for a high school class, though . . ." He actually rubbed his eyes like my video hurt them and sighed. "Honestly, Carmen, I expected you to take it seriously. Or did you just want to look cute at events?" He looked me up and down. "You managed that, at least."

He sort of made a move for me, so I ducked under his arm and decided right then that nothing could make me turn in that video. Or go back to working for Edwin. Ever again.

I was only forty hours away from fulfilling the time requirement, and Edwin wasn't big on keeping close track of the time sheets. So I declared myself done and wrote a paper to fulfill the final requirement. And yes, I *knew* that I wasn't supposed to change the project without approval, but papers were the universal currency of high school. Like paying with a credit card in another country. They'd grumble, maybe just give me a technical pass, but they'd accept it. It was *work*, after all.

But I probably should have run my brilliant plan past the teacher. Because he *didn't* accept it. Neither did the vice principal. Or the principal. Or the Board of Ed, not even after Mami took a day off from work to come with me to plead my case.

I offered to turn in the video, screw Edwin's opinion of it.

Except it turns out that Edwin had kept better track of my hours than I had expected. They all knew I was forty hours short. And, as I mentioned, there would be ice-skating in hell before I would make up those hours.

Which meant I was missing one credit in order to get my diploma.

Which means I'm technically not a high school graduate. Yet.

Funny how Life Visioning class was all about the visions and rules that *other people* had about my life and, since I didn't jump through their hoops, I was screwed.

The Life Visioning class HAD taught me one thing. I

didn't know what I wanted to do next, and I didn't want to waste money I didn't have figuring it out.

Luckily for me, between Hurricane Mami, Typhoon Me, and Tropical Storm Waverly, we managed to get the administration to agree to give me another chance to get my diploma. "You can work for Dreams Come True!" Waverly had said, and the school had agreed, after warning me that this was my LAST CHANCE. If I messed this up, I was stuck, no returns, no substitutions, no backsies.

"And I only need to make up the last forty hours, right?" I'd asked, hopefully.

Mr. Velez sighed and looked over his glasses like I was confirming every disappointing thought he'd ever had of me. "This is a completely different internship, so no. It's a second chance. A fresh start. From the beginning. And you need to turn in a final project that ACTUALLY gets approved."

Truthfully, it was fine. I didn't want to work for a princess party company, but I also didn't *not* want to. My best friend already did on weekends, and I could spend the summer sorting invoices for my diploma and writing a five-page paper about how the experience had changed my life. Simone, the new boss, hadn't liked that idea, though. She said, "Believe me . . . I can't even begin to express how excited I am to have an actual assistant in the office! Thrilled is an understatement! But . . . you can't really be a Dream behind a desk. The only way to *really* understand my business is to perform! And we'll record a performance of you as a Dream for your project!" Which meant working days as Simone's assistant (and I had just started that part of the internship), and nights and weekends as an official Dream, dancing and singing (once Simone had verified that I could actually do both) at the birthday parties of various rug rats.

Adorable rug rats, sure, but rug rats nonetheless.

At least I'd get paid for the performance part of it. Waverly made it sound like it paid a lot better than the Cupcake Chicas at the mall.

And that's why I was here, on the first Saturday afternoon in June, two weeks after I should have graduated, in the back seat of my mother's car, wriggling into a ball gown and pinning my wavy brown hair into a half updo.

"Thanks again for the ride, Ms. Mirella," Waverly said as she zigzagged the tie on the back of my bodice. We'd only been friends since the end of junior year, so she was still kind of formal with Mami. "My car is in the shop, and my parents are out."

"Yeah, maybe we'll make it to the party before the kid graduates from college," I grumbled.

"Listen, Carmencita, I could have made you take the bus. I have plans, you know, and I—" Mami said, then stopped as something caught her eye in the window.

Oh no.

We were driving past Coral Gables Park, a popular place

to take outdoor pictures. A troop of teenagers was there, all dressed up, the boys in tuxes and the girls in slinky maroon tube dresses and matching heels. And even though I couldn't see her, I knew that somewhere in that nest was a girl, probably dressed in a gown that looked like mine and Waves's, wearing a huge-ass tiara that weighed her head down almost as much as the twenty pounds of Aqua Net they'd put on her hair to keep it from frizzing in Miami's humidity.

A quinceañera.

"Mira, Carmencita . . ." Mami breathed out. "¡Que linda! Pero, maybe a few too many ruffles? You can barely see her head. She looks like one of those cozies that your abuela used to put on the spare roll of toilet paper in the bathroom." Mami honked at them and waved with a huge grin. Toilet Doily did a small curtsy back, and almost fell over. No one ever seems to practice the curtsying part in heels.

Waverly craned her neck past me to get a better look. I just stared straight ahead. I wasn't going to risk us missing the turn again.

Mami caught Waverly's interest and said, "Ay, Waverly, that's right! You hadn't moved here yet!"

I could practically hear the sad violin music in the background as Mami started her tale. "The story of Carmen's non-quince is an actual tragedy! It was . . . well, it was . . ."

"Actually, Carmen told me all about the canceled dinner, Ms. Mirella," Waverly said brightly. Bless her, thinking that

Mami could be stopped mid-rant just because you'd already heard the rant before.

"We were all so excited, Waverly. We'd rented a dress and hired a photographer to do a photo shoot on the beach in the afternoon before the dinner. Really planned to do it up." She glanced back at the party, now arranging themselves in a lineup like they were about to be brought in for questioning.

"Not *we*, Mami. Tía Celia. And when Tía Celia giveth, she can also taketh away."

"And whose fault was that?" Mami snapped, her voice bristling with indignation.

"Yeah," I grumbled, "you weren't too happy with her either, if I recall." Mami and Tía Celia's fights were always legendary, but THAT one . . . let's just say everyone on my block learned a few new curses that day. In two languages. Maybe three. I've blocked out a lot of it.

"Eh, Cecilia overreacted. Pero *tú*, Carmen . . . what you did *was* inexcusable." Mami twisted around so she could make eye contact with Waves. "And did Carmen tell you what she *did* to make my sister flip her wig and cancel everything?"

"Actually, Ms. Mirella—" Waverly began, still optimistic that she could derail the Mami Express.

"A party! She took her twelve-year-old cousin to a HIGH SCHOOL party! With drinking! And then her cousin recorded it and my sister found everything on her phone!" Mami waved a hand. "Did you know that? Or did my Carmencita tell you un

8

cuento al que le faltan muchos pedazos?"

Waverly looked confused, so I translated. "Mami is implying that I may have left out some crucial details."

"Oh, she told me everything, Ms. Mirella. And that she felt so guilty." She laid it on thick, even as she gave me big eyes that seem to say, *Maybe you did leave out some things.*

"I've already told you everything you need to know," I whispered to her.

Waverly's phone pinged with a text. She held it up to me and frowned. "Simone just says, *'Beast Late. New.'* Weird. She must mean Matt? Tran isn't new."

Mami sighed like she knew she was losing her audience. "Guilty should only have been the start of it!" Then *her* phone buzzed, thank the technology gods. "Speaking of . . ." Mami said before she silenced it.

Must have been Tía Celia. It wasn't a secret that she and Mami were talking again. But I didn't have to like it.

It wasn't even the canceled quince that still hurt. Or the canceled photos. It was the canceled people. People like Tía Celia, Tío Victor, my cousin Ariana, and her brother, Cesar, aka the "good" side of the family.

And I wasn't going to get into the boy I blamed for all of it.

Mauro Reyes. The host of the high school party in question. My dishonest former pseudo-boyfriend. My worst mistake.

I was saved from my badly wandering brain by the blessed

GPS. "You have arrived," she intoned in her perfect android voice.

"Finally. We're here."

Yes, my first party as an official princess. Beauty. Belle. Me.

Except thanks to the parts of Mami's history lesson that I couldn't drown out, I felt more like the Beast.

Not the one who was apparently running late.

He would be the one wearing the mask you *could* see.

———————

Cinderella had to pee.

This was not as straightforward as it sounded. My training was a jumble in my head, but I could remember Simone telling me over and over again that we were NOT to do anything to destroy the fantasy for the kids. And have you ever seen Cinderella pee? Exactly.

Still, I didn't much remember what Simone had suggested we say if we *did* have to pee.

I told Simone I wasn't ready for this party.

Waverly downed her second glass of "fairy tea," aka apple juice. "The kids are like little pushers, believe me, pushing drinks and slices of birthday cake and Cuban sandwiches and everything else on you," Waverly had told me. I hadn't believed her. I should have.

"Maybe you should say that Cinderella is trying to keep her tea consumption down. She's having trouble sleeping, and the prince is tired of her jumping him," I whispered to her, keeping my Belle-ific smile plastered to my face. I didn't blame Cinderella for overindulging—it was hot and gross and fairy tea was better than nothing when your tongue was sticking to the roof of your mouth. I'd only been here twenty-five minutes and already my too-long dress felt heavy with sweat and my feet were swollen in my four-inch heels. And let's not even talk about the funk around us that you could probably smell from space. Simone was supposed to double-check that the houses had air-conditioning, a must in Miami when you are wearing layers of satin and crinoline, but somehow, she forgot to confirm more often than not.

Apparently, princesses have to suck it up a lot of the time.

"Belle!" Cinderella said, choking on her tea. Then, in a lower voice, "Not. Funny." She twitched her blond bun toward a group of little girls, all dressed in miniature versions of our outfits and all watching us as though they had to dissect us later.

Cinderella shifted underneath her ball gown and glanced at the clock. "At least thirty more minutes of mingling, pictures, New Guy shows up as a surprise, last song, then back into our carriages," Waverly whispered to me. Or the city bus, since Mami had been a one-way ticket here. "And I don't think I'm going to make it." She was practically doing the pee-pee dance at this point.

"Oh my God, please don't leave me alone here. Just don't

think about water at all . . ." I clutched at her with my clammy hands.

I shouldn't have said the W-word, because she paled and practically mowed down two small six-year-olds to find the parents, who were off having their own party in the kitchen. Eight little pairs of eyes pinned me to the wall as if I were a butterfly, and my stomach fluttered like it was full of them. "Is Cinderella sick?" one of them demanded, her lip already stuck out and quivering. Ay, mi madre. I cursed Edwin's objectifying ass again and took a deep, shaky breath. Had Simone said anything about addressing questions about a sick princess?

If I didn't come up with something soon, these niñitas were going to riot.

"No!" I said brightly. "Of course not. Cinderella noticed a little rip in her gown and went to call some bluebirds to fix it!"

I held my breath as they stared, and I stared right back. Sweat trickled down my back and all of Simone's words played like bad Auto-Tune in my head.

I would run if I had to.

But then they nodded. *Of course* Cinderella couldn't bear to have a ripped dress, and *naturally* the bluebirds needed a GPS location and time to travel.

"Oooh," said another little girl, whose bright pink Sleeping Beauty gown was already stained by the fairy tea she'd spilled all down the front. "I wanna see!"

Shit. I looked around the room for rescue. Where the hell

was Waverly? Did these people have an outhouse? And where was Tran—the guy I'd spent the last two weeks rehearsing with? Had he tried to reach us on the phones we weren't allowed to have on us? Panic made my dress stick closer to my skin.

I heard the doorbell. Oh, thank all the saints. He was here. My Beast! He'd distract them.

I opened my mouth to tell our curious little Sleeping Beauty why she couldn't watch Cinderella's magical dress alterations, when suddenly a voice next to me came to my rescue.

"Cinderella would be so embarrassed if you saw her in her underwear."

Every nerve in my body was suddenly on red alert.

That wasn't Tran's voice. And it wasn't Matt's, either.

I knew it, but at the same time, I didn't.

Because it couldn't be the voice I thought it was.

No way could it be . . . but it was. Mauro Reyes.

 *Two*

I'M NOT (THAT) SUPERSTITIOUS, but my first thought was that I must have called him here with my car thoughts. Because Mauro Reyes hadn't entered my mind in ages, and suddenly . . . this? No lo creo.

For starters, Mauro didn't live here anymore and hadn't for years. (Gracias a Dios.) Considering how often he'd gone off about the Disneyfication of culture, blah, blah, I couldn't see him doing this job, not even for extra cash.

Mauro Reyes, son of famous photographer Oscar Reyes, would definitely never need extra cash anyway.

Richie Rich asshole.

But the real reason that it couldn't be Mauro was that none of Belle's stories ended with her knocking the Beast sideways for hooking up with her three and a half years ago, insulting her, lying about everything, and taking off.

So, you see, my logic was sound. Except that then the Beast muttered, "Uh . . . hi, Carmen. Wow. Um . . . yeah, sorry I'm late. Traffic," and damn it, I just KNEW that terrible voice.

"Uh . . . hi, Carmen" might be the only honest thing he's ever said to me. Maybe. Just the fact that my name had come out of *his* face made me want to double-check my birth certificate—to be sure that it wasn't a lie, too.

I looked toward the door, willing Cinderella to come back with a princess wave and steer us back on schedule, but I guess the bluebirds were taking their sweet time.

This was *so* not the moment for a reunion. Whoever was behind the mask didn't matter. I knew that I needed to stay in character. Mauro wasn't going to be the reason I screwed up my only chance of getting my high school diploma by the end of the summer.

Besides, I was Belle. These little girls deserved it, these mamis were paying for it, and el diablo himself could be behind that mask (though that might be an improvement, believe me) and I'd still playact love.

If I knew *anything* about him, I knew Mauro Reyes could *pretend* to feel anything. A mask would only help.

"Oye!" One of the aunts of Birthday Girl stumbled into the doorway and put her hands on her hips. "Why you all standing around for? Dance or something!"

Princesses don't glare, so I put on my sparkliest voice. "Who wants more cake?" Waverly had told me that I could get out of most bad situations as a party princess by offering cake. But the girls saw an opportunity for something new, and their eyes gleamed. "Yes!" they breathed out like one organism. "Dance, dance!" A few of them even sighed. The aunt raised her chin at me, and I could see the laughter in her eyes—the mojitos, too. Alcohol makes some people mean.

I looked at the Beast and shrugged, praying for the baldosa floor to open and swallow me up.

Because this was not good. Mauro had just started today. We'd never danced together, not even when we *were* together, and the waltz wasn't exactly something you could expect people to know off the top of their furry heads.

I turned to the Beast and gave him a deep curtsy, battle drums beating in my head. Because while I'm actually a pretty good dancer (Mami would have kicked my ass if I weren't . . . she considered it one of the most important parts of being a Latina), it wasn't like I could lead myself in a waltz. Especially not while wearing heels and a too-long dress and making sure I didn't end up headfirst in the flat-screen TV.

Thankfully, the Beast bowed deeply, strolled forward, and took my hand like we'd been doing this all our lives. Simone's training certainly hadn't said one word about how to act if your ex showed up dressed like a cross between a French soldier and Chewbacca, so I concentrated on the mask—because at least THAT wasn't him.

Under the mask, he could be anyone! Right?

Who was I kidding? Three and a half years later, and the pressure of his hand on my waist tumbled me back into the high school darkroom. My body knew this wasn't Tran, and I couldn't tell if Mauro was feeling anything at all.

Mauro Reyes wasn't supposed to be here in this house, or here working for Simone, or even here in Miami—holding me tighter in his arms than any guy who hated me had a reason to.

I gritted my teeth in a smile and waited for the waltz music to start and for this to be over. Ideally, my alarm would go off and this whole thing would just be a too-much-tres-leches-cake-at-dinner-fueled bad dream.

Except then Birthday Girl's cute big brother put on a CD and what blared out was a little more Daddy Yankee and a little less Uncle Walt (Disney, that is). What was I supposed to do? Start grinding in my ball gown? With Mauro? *That* wasn't going to happen. No high school diploma was worth that kind of humiliation.

Mauro didn't miss a beat, though, throwing up his hands and bouncing up and down. I just . . . stood there for a second. No way was I shaking what my mami gave me in front of Mauro and a bunch of six-year-olds. So I settled for wiggling my shoulders a little and kept smiling. Always freaking smiling.

"Ay, mija, that's not dancing!" one of the tías shouted, and the others laughed and started giving me encouragement in two languages. "Gotta get closer . . . un movimiento sexy!"

They acted out the moves in case I needed a visual aid.

When the abuelitas started to drift into the room on their cloud of talcum powder and curiosity, the brother quickly put on a merengue. Mauro immediately started the quick, jerky two-step, pulling me even closer while I pushed him away. People started to laugh.

It may have been three and a half years later, but he was still bad luck. Mauro was playing with me; he wanted me to join in, one-up him. Even though I couldn't see his face (and *hated* that he could see mine), I could feel that he was laughing underneath his furry head. Enjoying watching my reaction, the asshole. But I couldn't afford to screw around. My future literally depended on me not kicking him in the shin.

Not that it wasn't tempting.

I gave Birthday Girl's mother a smile that managed to be happy *and* pleading at the same time, and she clapped. "OK, Miguel. Enough is enough. Put the right song on, por favor."

He shook his head like we were ruining his fun and put on the Disney one.

The dulcet sounds of "A Whole New World" started up. Now the little girls who had giggled when we were dropping it like it was hot howled in protest. "NOO! That's from *Aladdin*!"

He shrugged. "So? It's Disney, right?"

They rolled their eyes in unison. "It's not the right STORY! You can't put them in the wrong STORY! It doesn't make SENSE!"

The mami, tired of her son screwing things up, sighed loudly enough to be heard next door and then changed the song. "Tale as Old as Time" filled the room. Mauro, who had been whipping and bouncing three seconds ago, and doing a not-terrible merengue two seconds ago, turned to me then and gave me another perfect, elegant bow. I curtsied back, even as I panicked. I was hoping we were done with the dance portion of the evening. One of the abuelos, apparently thinking that we were still taking requests, shouted out, "Bah, put on a good salsa!" Birthday Girl's dad laughed and shook his head. By now, the other parents from the party had come in from the kitchen and the patio, all teetering on the same good mojitos, smelling of lime and pan con bistec.

Luckily, I'd made myself sit through the whole Disney movie oeuvre as soon as I got this internship, so I knew the scene in question. I looked away coyly, and then put my hand delicately on Mauro's arm. This was formal and pretty and totally wrong for us. I didn't like feeling *shy* around Mauro, of all things.

"This is so awkward," I muttered through my smile.

He cocked his lionesque head at me. "Don't worry, I know how to waltz. I dated a debutante once. Unless you mean awkward for another reason?" He was just daring me to say something about our past. Our stupid, meaningless past.

"It's awkward like those movies where the actors have to kiss five seconds after meeting," I told him.

"We're not kissing, though. Are we?"

Ugh, why did I have to bring up kissing at all? I willed myself to be a robot, to only speak in character.

"Fine." He gave a dramatic sigh. "I promise not to ravish you on the dance floor. Unless the girls ask for it, of course. Gotta give the kids what they want."

He started whirling me around in time, and then I couldn't think about anything but making sure I didn't go skidding across the floor like a rag doll. Dance-wise, I had to admit, he was always in control. Solid. Mauro had always been on the scrawny side of skinny. Still, the arm I was holding on to was strong. Even stronger than I had expected.

Have I mentioned how much I hated having these thoughts at all?

In the movie, Belle and the Beast are dancing in a gorgeous EMPTY ballroom, serenaded by the teapot chick. That was not our situation. The Florida room wasn't small, but it was packed with eight little girls who were whirling around us, like drunk little backup dancers. They were crashing into each other and into us. Meanwhile, the parents hadn't done much more than move the oversize recliners against the wall. The coffee table was still there, close to the center of the room. Still smothered by about a million photos of the family at the beach, at weddings, at random parties a lot like this one. Still perfectly level with my knees.

Oof. A munchkin plowed directly into my side.

"Wow, you took that hit like a linebacker," Mauro said, admiration in his voice. I couldn't see his face through the mask. I gritted my teeth through my princess smile and said nothing at all. I could hear the abuelos, already bored, muttering in Spanish. But the grown women were strangely enthralled.

"Ay, que lindo! Reminds me of my quince. Oh, to be fifteen again," one of the mamis sighed to another.

But Drunk Tía wasn't fooled. "Óyeme, isn't this a love story? Don't you have to, you know, LOVE each other? It's like you're dancing in different rooms!" She wiggled her fingers at us, like she was flinging some love dust at us. Birthday Girl's mami laughed and nudged her playfully. My hands twitched. I wanted to shove someone. Guess I'm not cut out for that fairy-tale life.

"They don't get romantic until he becomes the prince!" one of the three Ariels pointed out. "He's not sexy till then."

Sexy? I thought these kids were, like, six.

"Naw," said a fellow little Belle. "He was hotter as the Beast, THAT'S when they fell in love. Him being a prince was, like, TOTAL Ken doll." She looked at Mauro and said, politely, "No offense."

"None taken," he said in a laugh-choked voice. Finally, FINALLY, the damn song ended. I was ready to drop another curtsy to him and then to the girls, when he surprised me by dipping me and lowering his masked face to mine, I guess to make the little shipper who loved the Beast AS a beast happy.

Thank goodness for the plastic and hair between us. I clutched his arm, making sure to dig my nails in there a bit. If he could go off script, so could I.

The girls screeched with delight. At least they seemed happy. So did the parents, who had brought out a pitcher of sangria and were now dancing together, exaggerated versions of our waltz.

Birthday Girl glanced at them. Her face clouded over. It was an expression I recognized. The adults were taking over. She could feel her birthday slipping away.

Damn it. No. I wouldn't let that happen. Not on my watch. But before I could do anything, Mauro stepped in front of her and bowed. "Princess, may I have this dance?"

She squealed and clapped her hands. He began to whirl her around, evoking several high-pitched little girl shrieks. All the mamis stopped and sighed. A few whipped out their phones to memorialize the moment of extreme cuteness.

Cinderella finally reappeared next to me. "Uh, that doesn't look like Matt."

"That's because it's not. Thanks for leaving me out here alone, by the way."

She shrugged. "When nature calls, even Cinderella must answer. Besides, I caught a bit of that dance. I liked the method acting. Playing Belle pre-romantic furry feelings? Respect the choice."

I ignored that. "You were gone awhile. You OK?"

"Yeah, this is a new costume and I couldn't get the clasp undone. I think I peed on it a little bit."

Note to self: Try not to play Cinderella any time soon.

We began to unobtrusively clean around the room. Hoping to make a quick getaway and let the parents handle their little sugared-up chiquitas.

Thank goodness my first party hadn't been very elaborate, no face painting or animal balloons. Just fairy tea and misery.

Cinderella clapped her hands. "Oh MY! Tee-hee, look at the time! It's time to get back to the castle. The prince gets SO worried."

"Then Belle can stay 'cause the Beast is already here," one of the Rapunzels pointed out. She put her hands on her waist.

"And he JUST got here."

A papi smothered his laugh. Must have been his little angel.

Cinderella's smile wobbled for a moment, but unlike me, she was a pro. "We all have to make sure to get back to Fairy-land together!"

"Is it like catching the train to Hogwarts?"

"Something like that," I assured the girl. "And if we don't get back soon, why, Lumière might torch the whole place! You know how he gets."

I don't know how Cinderella managed to look smiley and demure and STILL shoot me a warning look, but she did.

As we were saying our goodbyes (and Waverly was in the kitchen collecting our fee plus, please lord, any tips), Birthday

Girl gave me a huge hug and buried her face in my neck. Her cheeks felt sticky against mine. She smelled like buttercream.

"I love you, Belle. I love you forever."

I knew she wasn't talking to me, just the character I was playing, but my eyes stung anyway. They were unexpected words to hear. Her parents watched me warily, like they wanted to make sure I wasn't going to whisper to the kid that this was all just pretend.

They didn't need to worry. I wouldn't crush this kid's dreams. Life would do it to her soon enough.

"Happy birthday" was all I said, my voice feeling a little shaky. "Feliz cumpleaños, little princess."

"Jessie, quieres más cake?" her tía called. Jessie pulled away from me and patted my little yellow satin purse. "Bye!"

"Bye." I waved and sighed.

Time to head back to the not-so-fairyland of my real life.

———————

When we were safely out of view of the party house, Waverly turned to Mauro and said, "You aren't Tran. Or Matt." She crossed her arms and waited.

"Uh . . . not the last time I checked," Mauro said, giving her that smile that I still remembered. The teasing one where it felt like he was including you in the joke.

"Um, that was your cue to introduce yourself. Here, I'll demonstrate." She held out her hand and gave him a Princess Sparkle smile. "I'm Waverly, aka Cinderella, and this is Carmen."

"We've met," I grumbled.

"Repeatedly," Mauro said. And then shifted the furry Beast head to the crook of his other arm and held out his hand to her. "I'm Mauro. The once and future Beast."

I couldn't help it, I snorted.

Waverly raised her eyebrows at me. "Why am I getting the feeling you two know each other?"

I said, "Barely," at the same time that Mauro said, "Very well, actually."

I could almost see the gears behind Waverly's blue eyes turning.

I'd told Waverly about Mauro exactly once, a late-night whispered confession earlier this year when she'd asked me about my worst breakup.

I'd left a lot out, though. Like, you know, his name. He was just "the photographer."

The night I told her the story, it was still so easy to fall back into remembering. Barely a blink and there I was. Back at the party. The See and Be Seen Party.

If I could find him, if we could talk, maybe we could find some understanding. I hated that he thought I was someone I wasn't. Someone who would brag about a promise that I hadn't even wanted him to make. He needed to know that I didn't even care about whether his father took pictures of me or not.

Ariana was going to confess. That's why I'd risked bringing her here. But I wanted to talk to him first.

I hadn't even thought about what I might find when I got there.

I made my way toward the back of the house. His father's bedroom. I'd never been here.

Voices, inside. Mauro's and another.

A girl's.

A part of me wanted to go stomping in there, shouting, throwing shit, right?

But it was like I was frozen to the floor.

Mauro. His shirt off, pants unbuckled. On top of another girl. A blonde. I couldn't see much of her, and whoever she was didn't matter. What mattered was who she wasn't.

She wasn't me.

"Hey . . . uh . . . you planning on walking home?" Mauro asked me. I'd walked right past the Dreams van, caught up in the toxic movie replaying in my brain.

Oh, how I would have loved to have done just that. But I knew Simone was expecting us back at the Shack, and I wasn't about to drag my Belle dress through the dusty Kendall streets.

I swept past him and got into the van. I'd never been inside it before. Props lay in heaps around us—extra gloves and bunches of silk flowers and bags of bright-colored plastic beads and party favors. A wire rod was propped against the back door, for us to hang our costumes on when we weren't wearing them. It all smelled a little like watermelon candy.

I didn't even ask how Mauro had gotten access to the Dreams

van, considering that as far as I knew this was his first party, too. But that was Mauro. He could talk people into things. Lots and lots of things.

"Are you Simone's long-lost kid or something?" Waverly asked. "I've never seen you before, and she's letting you drive the van? No one drives the van."

Mauro grinned from the driver's seat. "Simone's a friend of my father's. They used to work together. I go to Berklee College of Music in Boston, but I didn't get into any summer programs so here I am, crashing at her place this summer." Our boss, Simone Travis, had worked runways back when she was young, before she'd decided that her fortunes lay in making Dreams Come True (literally and figuratively).

And *music*? Since when? I remembered that he played the guitar, but he had always been all about his photography.

"Your dad is a model?" Waverly asked him, and gave me a sidelong glance, like, *That explains so much.*

"No, he's a photographer. Oscar Reyes." And then he waited, like he'd probably done all his life, for the other person to recognize the name and start fawning.

"Huh." And just when I was about to gloat that Waverly obviously had no idea who he was, she said, "He's the one who was on *Modelista*, right? The Miami season!" She turned back to me. "Is that when you guys knew each other?"

"He went to our school," I said. "For a little while. Before you transferred in."

"Yeah," he said, meeting my eyes with a smirk. "And Carmen and I—we also had photography in common."

"I guess *photography* held your interest for as long as it held mine." I shrugged.

A few seconds later, a text.

Waves: Wait—photographer? Is this—

Me: Yes. And I promise to tell you later.

That was all I needed to say. Waverly narrowed her eyes at the back of Mauro's head, already on my side.

"Well, anyway," she said in a very change-the-subject voice, "that family totally stiffed us!" She started stripping out of her stank ball gown and pulling off her wig, revealing her closely cropped red hair. "Did these people not realize that tipping is customary, like at a restaurant? We are SERVICE PROVIDERS!"

"Maybe they didn't think a Cinderella who went tinkle deserved twenty percent?" I shimmied out of my dress and felt the air-conditioned coolness finally hitting my skin, blasting against the sweat that had collected there. I pulled the pins out of my heavy Belle hair, shaking it away from my face. Ah, sweet freedom.

Mauro shifted us into traffic.

God, it was surreal to have him here, being a part of this. Looking so different. The Mauro I remembered had long wavy black hair, always pulled back in a careless ponytail. He wore loose black clothes on his lanky frame. This Mauro had short hair, messy but on purpose. His clothes fit now. They had something to fit to. The memories kept seeping into my head like smoke. Me lying on my bed, texting him and laughing at his snarky replies. Him and me sneaking off to the school darkroom in the middle of the day. That was our shared hobby. He took photos, and then we pretended we desperately needed to develop them every day so that we could hook up.

At a light, he started to pull off his bulky Beast costume, leaving him in just a T-shirt and his costume's tights.

Yeah, those arms that I had felt before . . . they weren't because of the costume. Neither was the flash of abs I saw before his shirt settled back down.

Muscles. When did he get those?

I didn't even realize I was staring until Mauro glanced in my direction and our eyes met and held. Usually after a few seconds of stare-off, guys look away. Mauro didn't. His light green eyes were unsettling. I swallowed and blinked first.

None of this made any sense. Mauro didn't live here, and Dreams wasn't the kind of job you moved to Miami for. So . . . was Mauro filling in for someone? Doing Simone a favor? Was God himself punishing me for not working hard enough in high school to avoid this whole horrible situation?

I was leaning toward that last one. And I was ready to sacrifice a chicken or goat or whatever the santería people recommended in order to fix it.

My phone buzzed.

Waves: You OK?

Me: Sure.

Waves: Because you are staring.

Me: It's just weird.

Waves: Are you going to talk to Simone?

Me: No. Hopefully the last house will say that we sucked together and I'll get to play Jasmine instead.

Waves: Do I need to throw a glass slipper at his head? I will totally throw a glass slipper at his head.

Mauro looked back at me for another second, before he slammed on the brakes and swore at an old man who'd just blown the light.

Thanks for the distraction, viejito.

Me: Don't throw it. He's driving. But keep it handy.

Traffic meant that the van was creeping along, barely getting any closer to the Shack than it had been ten minutes ago. So we sat, letting the soundtrack of other people's cars fill the space. The silence felt like standing at the front of a classroom trying to solve a physics problem, knowing the teacher wasn't going to let you go back to your seat till you came up with the answer.

And you were never going to come up with the answer.

"OK, fine . . . about Carmen and me . . ." Mauro burst out.

"Nope! None of my business," Waves said immediately.

"Right. Can I just say some words in my defense?"

"She just said you don't need a defense," I snapped. Not like he had one, anyway.

"Is that why she's glaring at me like she wishes my head would catch fire?"

It was true. Waverly had no poker face.

"So, yeah, to answer your unasked question, Waverly . . . Carmen and I dated my sophomore year, her freshman year, and—"

"We didn't *date*," I corrected him instantly. "We hooked up occasionally, in the darkroom at the high school—"

"Yeah, and then we had a misunderstanding . . . one that she mentioned to the wrong people—"

"You aren't seriously talking about the damn photos, are you? Because if you are . . . a ese cuento le faltan muchos pedazos!" My blood pressure was rapidly climbing past Disney princess–approved levels.

"Hey, I know what that means now!" Waverly said, pleased.

"And then I had a party and even though we were fighting, she came anyway and—" Mauro continued.

Waverly whipped her head toward me and said, "What is it with you and parties? No wonder you didn't want to be a party princess!"

"Not just any party. THE party. My twelve-year-old cousin, a red Solo cup, twerking, and video evidence."

"And I don't know how any of that was my fault. Neither of you were supposed to be there!" Mauro pleaded, trying to look innocent. And failing.

I shrugged. "It was your party. It was your house. Your alcohol. Your underaged friends. See and Be Seen, remember? She took it literally." And really? It *wasn't* his fault. Not that part of it, anyway. I'd been the one who'd told Ariana about the pictures to begin with, and I was the one who'd brought her with me in order to make her confess to Mauro that *she'd* been the one who had mentioned (online! for the whole world to read!) that *Modelista* photographer and Colombia's favorite son Oscar Reyes was going to give *me* a photo shoot as a quinceañera present, because his son was *so* crazy about me.

I was such an idiot to think that any plan involving Ariana would work.

And that was before Tía Celia went through Ariana's phone and found the video evidence of the party. La Virgen de la Caridad del Cobre, the Holy Mother herself, couldn't have saved me after that. Tía Celia canceled my quince dinner and my predinner beach pictures (the only *real* photo shoot I actually had scheduled), and no amount of Mami hechando chispas could convince Tía Celia to change her mind.

Not that Mauro needed to know any of that.

"Still, Carmen, cops? You had to involve the authorities in our breakup?" He met my eyes in the rearview mirror. "I mean, I know it was you."

I wasn't admitting to shit.

So many eyes on me, and none of them kind. I sat next to some of those people in class, but it didn't matter. They believed that they belonged there, at Mauro's house. And they believed that I didn't.

I'd heard it all.

"Did you see who is here tonight?"

"Yeah, Carmen Aguilar . . . still panting after Mauro like she has a chance."

"Bueno, she did . . . in the darkroom, anyway . . . The light of day is different, especially when she started running her mouth about his father. She should have kept using her mouth for the other thing."

And then both of those people died.

Not really, but a girl could dream.

I should have been keeping better track of Ariana. But at that moment, I was just grateful she wasn't anywhere near me. At least she hadn't heard what people really thought of me.

That I was a slut.

That I was a fame whore, hooking up with Mauro because of his famous father. And the worst crime of all—that I was stupid, because I'd actually trusted that Mauro wasn't running a game on me.

I didn't bother to look to see who was talking about me that night. Because it truly was everybody. Even people who didn't know me. Maybe especially them.

But I knew who I really was. And at that moment? I was a girl . . . with a phone . . . who could call 311.

Suddenly, I could feel all of it, buzzing in my throat like angry bees. It wanted out. It wanted me to give voice to it. But

I couldn't give Mauro the satisfaction.

I could feel how flushed my face was, so Waves could definitely see it. Which is probably why she said, "ANYway, it's all ancient history, right?"

"Absolutely," I said, without hesitation. "Dusty, decrepit—"

"Dead," Mauro said.

"Destroyed," I fired back.

"Done and dismal—"

"All the D-words," Waverly said.

"I can think of a few more," I muttered.

I saw Mauro smirk in the mirror.

Waves: You better tell me everything you should have told me before.

Me: I did tell you.

Waves: Yeah, well . . . here's another D-word for you: details.

 <u>Three</u>

A FEW OF THE Dreams were already waiting for us at the Shack when we got there, but not our fearless leader, Simone Travis.

Waverly held up her phone. Her weather app was bright red. "This weather is not fit for humans." She stuck her hand into a bowl of chips and started crunching. Jessica, the girl who plays Snow White, plopped down next to her and joined in.

I couldn't even think about food. That was what one-hundred-degree heat did to me.

"She's probably just stuck in traffic, like I've been all day," Mauro said, reaching into a basket of apples that were props, not food. He'd figure it out soon enough.

Jessica smacked his hand away. "I don't know who you are, but those are MY apples, and if you eat them, I'll have to kill you." She smiled so angelically that Mauro grinned back, uncertain. Then she dropped the sweet face. "I mean it, jerkface."

Leila watched Mauro. "Have I missed you at practices? Are YOU the new Tran? To go with our new Belle?" I glared at her for putting that thought out into the universe. Just as quickly, she waved her hand in his direction. "Know what? Never mind, don't care."

"Don't take it personally, new person," Matt said, putting his hand to his heart like he was wounded. "She lives to cause pain." Matt was our resident Every Prince, down to the wavy blond hair and piercing blue eyes. Not my type, but apparently Disney's. His one sadness in life is that he will never get to work with Leila, who always plays our Jasmine because she can rock that belly-dancing outfit better than the rest of us.

There is *someone* I know who would be a perfect Aladdin, but no way would I ever bring Alex Sharma into the Dreams family.

He was mine. Or he would be soon.

I let myself think of him for a split second: floppy dark hair, shy smile, soccer body. *Hmm, maybe I should try to use this new manifesting power for good.*

After a second or two, Leila stood up like she'd had enough. "OK, seriously? Who calls a 'super important meeting,'" she said, making the finger quotes, "and then doesn't show up?"

On cue, Simone came rushing in, carrying a bunch of dry cleaner bags with costumes inside them.

"Sorry, sorry!" She dropped our outfits on the chair closest to the door, all pink and puffing. I stood up, ready to grab her a water like the good assistant I was training to be, but Mauro was already at the minifridge, holding one out to her. How the hell was he already so comfortable here?

She held the bottle up to her forehead and gave him a grateful smile. She sat down and faced us all with eyes dancing, like it was taking all her strength not to break into song.

Simone Travis kind of WAS a Disney character. Cinderella's mom, if not Cinderella herself. Becoming the owner of Dreams Come True was really just her way of becoming fully self-actualized.

She looked around at us, eyes twinkling. "This is going to be the BEST, most eventful meeting the Dreams have ever had!"

Leila crossed her arms and said nothing. I kind of agreed with her already.

Simone's smile faltered, but just for a second.

"Now, normally I would leave the introductions to the end because people are more important than parties, BUT . . . it looks like we have ANOTHER new addition to the Dreams family! That's right, Carmen, you aren't the baby anymore! Everyone, I've acquired a new roommate for the summer, and already trapped him in indentured servitude. Thank goodness I'm such a great teacher!" She grinned at Mauro. An inside joke. "And this is all incredibly lucky, considering Tran just let me know he'll be spending the summer in Vietnam with his family. So . . . Mauro's actually doing me and the Dreams a huge, huge favor and I endlessly appreciate him and I'm sure you all will, too. And that's probably more than enough prologue for all of you, so, everyone . . . this is Mauro Reyes!"

The last little bit of hope I had that this was a nightmare of some sort died. The whole summer stretched ahead of me. It was only the first Saturday in June. Summer officially ended on the Fourth of July, right? Meaning Tran would be back soon?

Simone was still talking. "His father is one of my oldest and dearest friends, and I've known him for literally ever. In fact, I first moved to Miami while Oscar was working for *Modelista* a few years ago!"

Waverly was practically doing an interpretative pee-pee dance next to me, she was trying so hard to catch my eye.

It's not my fault that my nails were so fascinating.

"Please, don't talk about changing my diaper." Mauro groaned.

"Talk about it? It's documented on film. Just ask Oscar."

Mauro ignored that and faced the rest of the Dreams. "Hi. I'm looking forward to dressing like an overgrown stuffed animal all summer long with you. So, thanks for having me." He glanced at Simone. "I'll stop there, before you explode into a cloud of glitter."

"OK, you got me. I can't hold it in any longer!" She turned back to us, and I swear, she *might* have been leaking glitter already. "The other big news is—"

And just then, my phone started to blare "Tale as Old as Time." Waverly had put it on my phone as a joke when I'd started here. I fumbled through my inner pocket until I silenced it, my face burning.

"—that I got a call that—"

Barely even friends. Then somebody bends. Unexpectedly.

My phone, again. I jabbed at it, put it on silent for sure this time. Simone frowned. I mouthed back, "*Sorry.*"

"We've been hired! And it's not just ANY job. Oh no, my dear Dreams. It's a quinceañera. AND not just ANY quinceañera. It's going to be the biggest one that South Florida has ever seen! At the Biltmore! I know that we mostly do children's parties, but I've been researching, and this is an excellent time for us to expand our audience! We'll get to do a completely different kind of performing! The exposure we'll get from this could take our business to the next level. I mean, it sounds like this family knows pretty much *everyone* in the Latinx community here in Miami!"

I snorted at that bit of exaggeration. That's something everybody's mami would say. But in spite of myself, I was getting excited. Not that I didn't think working with kids was fun, but at least working at a quince would give me a chance to meet people who were taller than my knees. Maybe male people. Maybe *hot* male people.

Plus, these parties could be serious blowouts—I've been to

many in my time. It wouldn't exactly suck to get paid to party at the Biltmore. I've never been to a quinceañera there. I've never run with that kind of crowd.

Well, except when Mauro . . .

That's the closest I've come.

"What kind of performing will we have to do? Will we be in character?" Jessica asked.

Simone did a salsa step in place. "A combination of Latin dance and hip-hop. I've already got so many ideas! And no . . . you'll just be your own glorious, talented selves." Leila snorted at that.

"So, like a baile sorpresa?" That from white boy Matt. He shrugged at all of our startled looks. "I've been a chambelán before. Born and bred Miami boy."

Simone clapped. "More like additional entertainment. Apparently, the surprise dance is what the court does, and Celia hasn't told me yet what she and Ariana plan to do about that. Just that they want it to be a Dream Come True and that means US!"

Wait. Celia?

Ariana?

Record scratch.

Oh no.

No, no, no.

There may have been a lot of Arianas in Miami, but Arianas with mothers named Celia?

I knew who had just booked Dreams Come True. For a quinceañera. At the fucking BILTMORE.

My manifesting power was working, all right.

But apparently, it was stuck on suck.

Because the company I was working for?

Had just gotten booked for my witch of a cousin's quinceañera!

I went out the back door for some air while Simone filled everyone else in on what I already knew. That we'd be forced to perform at least once, if not multiple times, for the two most awful people in Miami.

Ugh, depending on what Tía Celia has in mind, we may have to actually perform *with* Ariana's corte.

And then I remembered that Tran was gone, and as a result so was any chance that I'd be paired with anyone but Mauro. I mean, Simone could give me another part in the next couple of days if I had a stroke of extremely good luck.

You can forgive me for not being terribly optimistic about that happening.

Mauro and now Ariana. Surely the school would understand *why* I couldn't do this anymore. I'd show them the video I'd made for Edwin. I'd rewrite the paper, in my own blood if I had to.

Because *maybe* I could have handled a summer stuck with Mauro. But that, *plus* Ariana and the whole Garces family?

I could feel the sweat on my back, hot and then cold. I kept moving, like I could outpace the stupid situation I was now stuck in.

Ideas came with every panted breath. I'd get another job, and then my GED. It would still count as a high school diploma. It would still be . . .

It would still be exactly what the family expected of me.

To say that I wasn't exactly considered Einstein by my nearest and dearest was an understatement. It was more like they expected me to screw up even the most basic things.

The only one in my life who believed in me was Mami. Mami, who had fought for me when the school told her point blank *why* I wasn't graduating. Mami, who defended me when the rest of the family lowered their expectations yet again . . .

Mami, who had now, for a fact, reconciled with Tía Celia.

Benedict Mami.

I stopped pacing and sat down, hard, on the back steps of the Shack. Those phone calls I had ignored—the timing—it all started to make a sick sort of sense. Even the quince we'd driven past earlier. All a damn sign.

I pulled my phone back out. Three missed calls. All from Mami.

The hope that she'd had nothing to do with this was evaporating into the humid air.

I called back. The phone rang. "Oh, Carmencita, there you

are!" she answered in a high-pitched voice that made her sound like a guilty tween. "I was worried—"

"Did you know about this?"

I could almost hear her lashes fluttering through the phone. Her tell. "About what?"

"Mami, *seriously*? I don't know what you were thinking, but there's no way I'm working for Ariana! How could you even— after everything that's happened?"

"Carmen, cálmate! No seas tan dramática!" She sighed, all dramatic herself. "Sí, OK? Yes, your tía and I—you know we've been talking, and it's really best for everyone—"

"No."

Another sigh, tinged with frustration, like she couldn't believe I was being so dense. "OK, you want the truth? Fine. You remember last winter? When you were in the hospital? And we had those insurance problems—"

"You told me it was all fine. You told me that—" I stopped. Suddenly, I realized exactly how it had been made fine. Mami was right about one thing. I was being dense. Those bills hadn't just magically disappeared.

"Pero it's not about the money, which I've almost totally paid back, by the way. It's just . . . seeing you in the hospital . . . I realized life is too short to be separated from la familia."

I rolled my eyes. I'd had mono, not Ebola.

"I have to do this quince because we owe Tía Celia money?"

"No, no, of course not. You have to do this because you are working for that company all summer. For your diploma."

I winced. The fence I was staring at felt like a pretty good metaphor for my current situation. I was trapped.

"But it would be a good way to show, tú sabes, your appreciation," she continued, her words tumbling over each other to try to convince me. "And to finally reunite the families. Which is what your abuelo y abuela would have wanted!"

"What Grandpa and Grandma would have wanted is suddenly so urgent almost four years later?"

"Anyway, I was going to tell you in the car today but you—"

"Oh, please! You just wanted to rehash my whole non-quince for Waverly! You want to make nice with the Garces family? That's fine. Just leave me out of it."

"Ay, Carmencita, they are your family, too! And your tía and I have been talking about this for a while. It was always the plan. This is the perfect time. And better late than never."

"Better never than never, because I'm never doing this. I'll ask Simone to find a sub."

"Oh?" Mami paused here, delicately. "It's just that, well, I got the impression from Celia that she is *very* excited to have *you* dance at the quince . . ." She let the words dangle. And when I wouldn't bite, she continued. "It's a good opportunity for the Dreams. You know that your tía is willing to tirar la casa por la ventana for this party."

Yeah, she'll throw the house out the window all right. And

she'll drop Simone if I don't go along with her plan. Just like she dropped me.

"It's finally Ariana's turn."

Ha. It'd been Ariana's turn since she was born.

"You'd be indispensable, Carmencita." I heard Mami loud and clear. I had no choice. I was a Dream for the summer, and the Dreams would be performing at my cousin's quinceañera.

Damn Life Visioning class.

The last thing I heard before I hung up was Mami saying, "Carmen, people change! Forgive! Give them a chance!"

I grunted. "People change? Ha. Not these people." Then ended the call.

In my experience, people who say, "I've changed!" really just mean, "Learn to ignore all the shit I'll continue to do to you!"

"I agree," a voice called from the doorway. "People do change."

I put my head in my hands. Case in point.

Of course Mauro was standing right behind me, with his eavesdropping ass.

"I must have missed the part where any of this concerned you." I was proud of myself for keeping my voice almost normal. I'd betrayed myself enough today.

As per usual, he didn't take the hint, and he sat down next to me. "Naturally it concerns me. I just discovered that I'm about to be a part of your touching family reunion."

I stood up. "Somehow I doubt that. I'm sure Oscar will

come around and let you join him in Zimbabwe, or wherever the hell he is."

He looked away. "I told you, I do music now. He has other assistants."

"Oh yeah? Lucky him." I started to go back into the Shack, but then he grabbed my ankle. I froze. Oh, if my fairy godmother existed, THIS was the moment to give me nuclear-powered eyes. I glared enough that he got the message, though, and pulled back.

"I have to talk to Simone."

He stood up, brushed his hands on his thighs. "And I'm going to help."

"I never said I needed your help!"

"Except that we're apparently coworkers now." He pointed to me and then himself. "Unwilling ones, so let me make sure Simone knows that. It's not like I want to be stuck with you any more than you want to be stuck with me. So, you can get paired with that blond dude in there, and I'll definitely have other choices." He grinned, the dimple I remembered deepening in his left cheek. "I mean, I always do."

Well. There was something I hadn't expected. That Mauro himself would want to give me an out.

Of course, it could also be a way to make me look difficult in front of Simone. Because any choice between him and me wouldn't exactly go Team Carmen. Simone had never changed my diapers.

"I never said I couldn't work with you. Or on this quince. Nothing happened between us that would make me go to Simone." I forced a laugh and got in his face. "You're just a point in a long line," I said in the kind of low voice that implied everything.

I'd wanted my words to make him feel small, forgotten. But all he did was shake his head, a smirk on his lips that didn't reach his eyes. "Fine . . . we won't talk to Simone. For now, guess I'm your Beast. Perfectly cast."

I tried to brush past him but miscalculated, and suddenly we were sneaker to sandal toe. And the fury inside me shifted, replaced by the sudden memory of his closeness, his hands on my bare skin.

No. Not this time. For starters, I knew him now. And that knowledge was enough to keep me away. Far away.

Definitely.

For the sake of my manicure and my belief in nonviolence, I let myself out of the backyard, slamming the fence door for good measure.

The bus would be my coach. Considering they take about two hours to arrive, maybe I'd cool off by the time I got home.

Except that my coachman was waiting for me at the stop.

And she wasn't going to let me cool off alone.

―――――

A few hours after the meeting at the Shack, Waverly picked me up for a special trip to Goldman's Deli by the beach. My favorite.

After we'd ordered (my beloved Reuben for me, a Rachel [a Reuben with turkey and coleslaw] for her), she tapped her fingers on her place mat like a drumroll. "OK. Sustenance acquired. Now talk."

"Nothing to say." My Coke glass was sweating, a perfect circle. I moved it again and again. Made the iconic Mickey Mouse head.

She pursed her perfect lips. "After everything you DIDN'T say in the van? Girl, please."

I sighed. "First of all, could we keep the fact that Ariana is my cousin between us?"

Waverly looked confused. "People are gonna find out anyway?"

"They are, but . . . let me have a few more glorious Ariana-less days."

I was going to light a whole botanica's worth of candles and pray that this would all somehow go away.

Waverly looked like she was going to argue, but then she nodded. "Putting off the inevitable is just going to make it a bigger deal, but . . . you do you, I guess. Now . . . talk."

"OK, fine, back to the party. My cousin wasn't even drunk. She'd probably had like, what, one or two sips, tops! She was showing off to a bunch of high school kids and stupidly filming herself."

Waves raised an eyebrow. "One or two sips. But wasn't she, like, twelve?"

"Whatever. Nobody forced her."

"Why don't you start at the verrrrrrrry beginning?" Waverly said invitingly.

"Well, the doctor told Mami, 'It's a girl!'"

She narrowed her eyes.

I grinned. "OK, fine, fine! I met Mauro early in my freshman year. He was a sophomore. We were paired together on a psychology assignment in part because our birthdays are so close—I'm November 18, he's November 22. I didn't think much about him—"

Lie number one, for those keeping track at home.

"—but obviously, he thought about me. He used me as an example of something in a psych discussion. Ms. Weir told him to take his crush outside."

He hadn't. We'd taken it to the darkroom.

"Huh. Seduction through classwork. That's not a thing that I ever would have thought would work with you," Waverly said.

I could feel myself stiffen. Waves always said that she understood why I hadn't applied to college (even before the Life Visioning incident), and that made me feel, I don't know, understood, I guess. Like, college isn't for everyone. And not everyone goes directly there, like do not pass go, do not collect $200. But then she said stuff like *that*, and it made me feel like she thought I wasn't very smart. And maybe I'm not as smart as she is, but I'm not an idiot.

Which, yeah, this story wasn't going to help with that perception.

"Anyway, we started hooking up, nothing serious, just the darkroom and texting and occasionally getting pizza together—"

"Which sounds exactly like *dating*—"

"—except it wasn't."

"Your choice or his?"

I dragged my fingers through the Mickey Mouse head until it was just one big smear.

"Both, I think." My mind played a few moments back to me. Mauro's hands on my waist, fingers spread until they warmed my skin. The way his lashes fanned out on his cheeks as he closed his eyes when he moved closer to kiss me. Me, wondering if we'd ever come out of the darkroom, and what everyone would say when they saw the weird, mysterious new guy and me.

I wasn't a mystery; I wasn't much of anything at school.

I would watch him, wondering if I should take anything about him seriously. I knew I wasn't the only one, and mostly, I was OK with it. We weren't exclusive. And I wasn't going to be the one to blink first.

"Both," I said again. "Neither one of us was looking for anything more serious."

"That's not how he made it sound, though—" she said.

"And then, I don't remember how, we started talking about quinces, probably because our birthdays were coming up, and I told him that mine was basically just a dinner, and he said his father could take pictures, which was a big deal, because Oscar Reyes was always photographer-famous, but then he became reality show–famous. It was, like, *too* big of a deal, so I told him no, at first."

"*It's a dumb dream,*" *I confessed on the phone one night. "Like . . . maybe in the big dress with the tiara, and the corte, and the limo, I'd look different to people. The kind of people who see my C average, and my neighborhood, and my family, and assume my only future is either as a baby mama or working the pole. And I mean, those things are fine if you want them, but like, I want to think I have more choices, you know? So . . . there would be the big party and the photos, and then Junior would appear and tell me that he was sticking around. And then we'd have the big father-daughter dance and a million flashbulbs would go off.*" *I laughed self-consciously. "Ugh. So stupid, right? Like a quinceañera is some magical night that can change your future or some shit. It's not like I'm even having a party. And even if I had been, Junior wouldn't have come. He wouldn't have even known about it.*" *Junior, my sperm donor, had never really been in my life. But it still hurt a little. Especially on birthdays. Especially then.*

A silence stretched between us, and I squirmed inside. Why had I told him all this? Because I had to tell someone.

Someone who I wasn't related to.

Someone who didn't know Junior.

Someone who didn't worry about the future.

"*Not stupid,*" *he said finally. "It's not stupid to want a big, meaningful celebration, and to want your father there."*

He'd told me a bit about his own father—about how he wasn't around that much, mostly. Busy with his models and filming Modelista. *Which is why I was so surprised when he'd said, "I know it's not a big fancy party, and it's not like having your own father there, but . . . my father could maybe take a few fancy quinceañera pictures for you. Like, not right on your birthday, but . . . eventually."*

I rolled over on my bed and stared blankly at the ceiling. I played it off, but feelings were clogging my throat, making it hard to speak. "I get that you feel sorry *for me, but why should Oscar?"*

"It's not because I feel sorry for you! It's just because . . . C'mon, Carmen . . . let me do this for you."

"Yeah, but . . ." I thought about Mauro and his father around the rest of my family, and I didn't like that it made me feel nervous. Yes, I'd like to see myself through Oscar Reyes's lens, but I didn't want to have to see Mami and the rest that way. I wasn't sure I'd like what he would see.

"I couldn't pay him," I said instead.

I could hear the smirk in his voice when he said, "I'm sure you could find a way to make it up to me."

Waves snapped her fingers. "Earth to Carmen. Where did you go?" She cocked her head at me. "A million miles away just thinking about it . . . and you claim you weren't even dating," she said flatly.

I looked toward the door, careful not to meet her eyes. "Like I said. It was just moments in the darkroom."

"Clearly not just. I mean, didn't he say he was doing music now? He quit the entire activity! Maybe the darkroom was too tainted after you."

"Oh, please. That's just Mauro. He's always halfway to giving up. Believe me, I wasn't special. And he made sure I knew it."

She scrunched her lips together like there was so much she wanted to say, but instead she just looked at me and waited.

The water that had been Mickey's ears evaporated—like nothing had ever been there at all.

"So, I accepted his supposed offer, and I actually let myself get excited about it, despite the fact that we didn't have a date set yet, and Mauro himself never brought it up again. And I told Ariana."

Tía Celia and Tío Victor were the ones paying for a small quince dinner for me at Ladrio's on South Beach. Just our two families. Pictures right before on the beach in a rented dress. Still, it was extravagant. Much more than Mami could have afforded, and I was grateful.

Plus, I had a photo shoot from Oscar Reyes to look forward to. My secret gift. Eventually.

"Even though I'd told Ariana to keep it on the down low, she put it online. Some people from school saw, and before I knew it, the whole school was talking about it, and laughing at me. Apparently, I wasn't even the first girl who Mauro had made that kind of offer to. Oscar's magical camera, ready to make any girl feel like a star. But I was the first one who took him seriously enough to brag about it." I hugged my arms, remembering the chill of the stares in the hallway that Monday at school. I'd gone from being an invisible freshman to being, well, a girl who was apparently so full of myself that I was like a piñata at a five-year-old's party. About to be knocked down.

"But that's not fair!" Waves protested. "You weren't the one who said anything."

"Yeah, they weren't real concerned about that part of it." I took an unwilling breath. "Anyway, Mauro freaked out that people were talking, and that people might think that I was special to him or something. He got pissed off and told me that I'd misunderstood him, he'd never promised me shit, and that we were over."

Waverly's face was a thundercloud. "Wow. What an absolute DICK."

"Another D-word," I said.

"DICK," Waverly said again, and banged a fist on the table as an exclamation point.

"Uh, I'm going to put the food down now, if that's OK?" The server balanced the tray, a concerned look on her face.

"Oh, it's fine," Waverly said cheerfully. "Boy problems. Hers."

"In that case," the waitress said, "don't bang the table too hard—you don't want to be bruised up when you go after him." She grinned and set the Reuben in front of me.

As soon as the waitress left, Waves was right on cue. "So Mauro backed all the way out of the photos. And your non-relationship."

I sighed. "Can't we eat first?"

She just looked at me.

"OK, fine. He was all, 'I should have guessed your reason for hanging out with me. It wouldn't be the first time some girl was after me because my father is famous. Don't bother coming to my party this weekend. It's not like you'll be getting anything out of it.' Which, again, everything had been HIS idea."

Waves winced.

"And, well, you basically know what happened after that." Except my brain refused to follow my mouth's lead and took me through the lowlights.

"Mauro . . ." whined the blonde. "How do I know I can trust you? So many pretty girls in Miami."

"Pretty girls? Empty heads. In a few years, they'll all be baby mamas. Or be working the pole."

My own words in his mouth. My own worst fears used to get into some girl's pants.

I didn't notice my fist was curled around my knife until Waverly gently pried it off.

"So that party . . . that's when people at school decided the rumors had to be true. I was only a freshman, but now I was *that kind of girl*, and I would stay that way." I put my hands up. "And that party is exactly where I decided I didn't give a shit

55

about any of it. I didn't have anything to prove to any of those assholes."

"So you've been single for three and a half *years* because of Mauro?"

I shrugged. "Mauro was out of mind pretty quickly. I was just done with relationships, even pseudo ones." Boys had other uses.

"So, basically, karmically, you *deserve* Alex. It's the only way to even the scales."

Ah, my Waverly. How could I question your loyalty to Team Carmen? "Thanks, but I don't think that's how it works."

My crush on Alex Sharma, junior and soccer star, had been the one thing I couldn't bullshit myself about last year. He was the only one I really wanted.

Ever-constant Waverly argued, "That's how it SHOULD work."

"Back to the problem that actually matters: Can you think of any way to get me out of this? With Ariana and with Mauro?"

She scrunched up her forehead, staring at her plate. Then she looked up at me and sighed. "Quit. Get another job. Beg Velez to let you do your senior year over. Or get your GED."

We looked at each other for a second.

"So, no," I said. "We can't think of a way."

"Not good ones, anyway."

"OK . . ." I played with the edges of my sandwich. "It's just a few months, right? I can do ANYTHING for a few months."

She chewed on a fry pensively. "I don't know. I mean, this is a lot worse than Edwin, and look how THAT turned out."

"Hey," I protested, "I'm older and wiser now. And also? I'm not going to let Mauro and Ariana ruin another important thing for me."

No, three months wasn't going to break me. I wouldn't let it.

 # Four

I FELT THE WAY a prizefighter would feel by the time I got home. The way I'd felt in middle school when Lorena Cardenas found me after she'd heard I'd hooked up with her boyfriend, Tonio.

FYI, he hadn't been worth the beatdown.

Adrenaline and black feelings tore through me. I wanted to fling shit around the room until everything was destroyed and none of this was real.

Except then I'd be the one who was left with nothing. Again.

Out of habit, I started my computer and watched as the viejita wheezed to life. One of the things I'd wanted to do this summer was buy a new laptop, the kind that moved as though it was reading my mind.

I bet Ariana has a device like that.

I put my head in my hands, my poor Dorothy ass gripped by

memories and lousy facts whirling through my head like a tornado. Missing graduation; this stupid princess job; Junior, my sperm donor; Ariana, covering her eyes as her mami canceled my coming of age . . .

Mauro's coldness when he accused me of using him for his father, making me feel like I'd begged for something that he had offered to me.

The party. The blonde. And then Mami and Tía Celia screaming at each other, the kinds of insults you can only hurl when you know exactly where the sangre will flow from.

Mami knew I'd screwed up, but she was Team Punish-Her-with-Something-Else. She would never have taken away my quince. Ever.

She hadn't been the one holding bank, though. And all the words in the world wouldn't move Tía Celia. She was like the Tin Man. The one without a heart.

Speaking of the heartless, there was Mauro again. Whatever we'd been doing before hadn't involved hearts. Other body parts, sure (not the main ones, though—we never went that far).

Mauro had no heart, no courage. OK, fine, he had a brain. He'd managed to get himself into college, although how much of that was him and how much was Oscar Reyes and his *Vogue* and *Modelista* fame, I didn't know.

My computer finally blinked into full wakefulness, and I opened the last thing I'd been working on. The video I'd shown Edwin. The one I'd chosen *not* to turn in a month ago.

Images flowed to life then, all colors and movement. A love story, something I thought he'd appreciate, considering his wedding business.

Ha.

After another second, I shut it off.

I couldn't see it anymore, the original inspiration. All I could see were the things he'd said were wrong with it. Which was basically everything.

And I didn't know how to fix any of it.

There was only one remedy. I needed to start a new project.

I quickly loaded in some clips from a show that I loved, *Cascadia Falls*. Trying to see if I could use them to tell a whole new story. My favorite character was Veronica, who lingered in the shadows while the more popular Tina crooked her finger and got everything she wanted, like she was a magnet drawing the whole world to her. Veronica was right to hate Tina, who always batted her eyelashes and got away with everything that Veronica couldn't do. Veronica couldn't have juggled two brothers, Dorian and Charlie—not without the whole town hating her. But somehow Tina had done so and was still seen as the sainted victim! And don't get me started on the switched-at-birth story line that proved Tina was Niles MacDougal's real daughter! Especially since Dorian had already proven his love by defying his rich uncle Andrew to be with Tina. Niles practically turned a cartwheel when he learned that he wasn't related to Veronica after all. Like it confirmed his blood was OK all along.

It wasn't fair. And in my video, it wasn't going to happen.

Honestly, Veronica's big issue was that SOMEONE needed to be in the shadows so Tina could stand in the light. Veronica and Tina had grown up together, and Veronica was seen as the flawed first draft of the second girl child, who had emerged all perfection. So I took her through a story line where *Veronica* proved them all wrong (through her own actions, even, not using a deus ex rich daddy).

No more suffering that malcriada. No more second best.

Bonus: I'd have her get the guy, too.

It's amazing how flexible the clips could be, how different they could seem, depending on the timeline, the music, the lighting, the speed of cuts, the way I made a lyric linger during a closeup until words and images were married. All run through a filter that made everything beautiful.

That's what I always love to do with my videos. Show the real story that was lurking underneath the obvious one—make an effort for the characters who the writers themselves couldn't be bothered with. Because girls like Veronica, girls who weren't rich, who weren't blond, who weren't santicas—they deserved the occasional win, too.

My brain hummed contentedly while I cut footage, moving and dropping and deleting. It was the closest thing to total flow I'd ever experienced. It was like sitting at the beach and watching the waves come in, only I could control them—their height and their speed.

I gave that girl on the screen my history. She was the one who was there in first grade when Josie Velez made fun of Mami's flip-flops when she picked me up. "Welfare chanclas," she had called them. The girl on-screen said, "That's right. Guess I'm lucky she took the curlers out of her hair, too." She had the right response when five-year-old Ariana had asked where my papi was: "Which one? Ask Mami. Depends on the day." She cringed the way I had in high school when some kid said I gave good head. "Is that what I found in my mouth the other day? Coño, I thought that was a toothpick!" My strategy was to always take the bullies' own words and make them worse—as if I was proving them right—until they got uncomfortable. Then they'd stop.

I blinked at the screen again. Ran the timeline. Not bad. You almost couldn't even tell that it was a mash-up.

I watched it once more. Beginning to end. Everything was the way I wanted it to be.

Veronica was the girl in the spotlight.

And then, I deleted it.

———————

I got home from the Shack the next day and found happy Cuban chaos. Everyone crowded on our run-down couches, reaching out for cups of cortaditos and cookies that Mami had arranged on a tray. Like two queens had come to visit. Which I suppose they had.

Mami looked over at everyone and beamed. My very own

Benedict Arnold, making nice with the same people who had broken my heart. Hers, too. And someone new—a dishrag with legs watching her with puppy-like adoration. This had to be none other than new love interest Enrique Fernandez, who was on the express ramp to meeting the entire familia. May God have mercy on his soul.

If I had to describe Enrique, I'd have to be looking at a picture to do it. And I mean, *looking*—like, if I put it away for five seconds, I wouldn't remember anything about him. He resembled every other middle-aged Cuban guy in Miami: paunchy, receding hairline, pasty skin. Guayabera shirt and a gold crucifix that was too tight around his thick neck. Surrounded by a cloud of Paco Rabanne cologne.

Not normally Mami's type, but who knows how long she's been betraying me and what else she's been hiding.

No one could miss that Mami and Tía Celia were sisters. The same light-brown eyes that crinkled when they laughed, like they were doing right now. A left dimple that found its twin on the other one's right cheek. The button nose that cursed my own face. They hadn't been in the same room in years (that I knew of) and you could tell they were making up for lost time, talking over each other, voices getting louder, accents thicker. Mami's hair was short, an auburn color found nowhere in nature, and Tía Celia's was softly waved, expensively tinted, and blow dried away from her forehead, which was definitely tighter than I remembered. Enrique watched them, fascinated, eyes going from one to the other like they were a tennis match.

Tía Celia was waving her hands around, all the better for her two-karat diamond solitaire to catch the light. Sitting down, her body looked generous, like Mami's, actually, even though Tía Celia draped hers in a loose A-line linen dress and Mami squeezed hers into spandex.

And right next to my tía, sitting up very straight like she was being interviewed by Oprah, was my little cousin, Ariana. Except the skinny tomboy with scabby, bony legs was gone. In her place, I saw Tía Celia from twenty years ago—long wavy hair, winged eyeliner flicking her eyes like a cat's, gracefully crossed ankles. The only part of her that still had the personality that I remembered was her faintly pouted lips, glossed in magenta.

She stopped mid-lean toward a pastelito and raised her eyebrows at me. Daring me to do . . . what? Yell? Throw down?

Tempting.

"Bueno, Carmencita! Finally!" Tía Celia stood up, arms already outstretched.

I just looked at her until she dropped them, with a self-conscious laugh and meaningful glance at her sister.

The jasmine-and-rose perfume she always wore hit me like a punch, and that's what almost made me tear up. Because I'd been mad at Tía Celia for years, but before that? There was my whole LIFE, right? I mean, it's not like I expected her to like me BETTER than her own daughter or anything, but . . . I was her sobrina. I was her sister's only daughter. We'd all been deep in each other's business my whole life, and after one mistake, I was just . . . gone.

That was all it took.

Yet she still smelled the same way she had when she took me to buy my first bra at nine because Mami thought I was making it up when I said the boys were beginning to bother me, at school and on the streets. Tía Celia had been the one who had nodded at me while I sniffed through my recital at the table, and she'd taken me to Macy's right after school the next day.

But that was before she decided that I had screwed up one too many times and that there was no chance for forgiveness. A lost cause at fifteen.

She'd smelled like jasmine and roses that day, too.

"Look at you, Carmencita. All grown up!"

"Time will do that," I said flatly.

Mami gave me a look and then stood up, tugging Enrique up to join her. "Carmen, I'd like you to meet my friend Enrique. He's an *entrepreneur*." The little purr she put on the word "entrepreneur" meant that Mami was about to start reading about stocks and bonds, or widgets, or whatever the hell Enrique bought, sold, or made.

And "friend"? I guess life had taught her to be careful about how to introduce men to family, especially when Tía Celia was around . . .

I sized Enrique up quickly. He was definitely the type who

would want me to talk to him in Spanish.

"What's up," I said, holding out my hand. Which he took. And kissed.

"Se parace a ti completamente, Mirella. Bella como tú."

Ugh. That kind of shit worked on Mami. Telling her that I was gorgeous and still making it all about her. Mami tossed her head back and laughed. "Pues claro! She's my daughter. But she gets her temper from her father!"

Everyone did that strained sort of laugh and I winced. Really? Bringing my long-lost loser of a so-called father into this? Nothing about him was funny.

"Nice to meet you," I said. I forced myself to look around the room. "Well, if you all would excuse me—"

But no way was Mami going to let me go. "No excuses, Carmen. We ALL have SO MUCH to catch up on! Plus, I made a fabulous dinner, and you WILL enjoy it."

Spoiler alert: I would not.

Oh, the food was delicious. Mami had outdone herself and made moros y cristianos (my favorite Cuban bean-and-rice dish), pollo al ajillo, tostones and maduros. She was still in the "auditioning to be a good girlfriend" phase. She always passed with flying colors.

Still, seeing Tía Celia and Ariana crammed around our uneven Formica table with the wiggle, trying not to compare it with whatever chef setup they had at home? That made everything taste like sawdust in my mouth.

I faded in and out of the conversation, which was mostly about how Mami and Enrique had met. Apparently, he saw her every time he went to the bank, until he was brave enough to ask her out. (Isn't that stalking? Aren't there laws against that?) Out of the corner of my eye, I could see my cousin picking at the food like it was offending her.

"And the rest is history," Mami crowed.

"Doomed to repeat itself?" I muttered. I hadn't been talking about Enrique, but I could see the tops of his ears turn red, which made me feel bad for a second. Although it could just have been the steam rising from the food he was shoveling into his face.

Ariana caught my eye and smothered a smile. I looked away. We weren't at "share an inside joke at the mamis' expense" level yet.

"Luckily, not *all* history repeats itself," Mami said, with an arch look in my direction. "We're breaking the quince curse for this familia!"

Tía Celia's smile didn't quite reach her eyes. "Que curse? There's no *curse*, Mirella."

Mami threw her head back and laughed. "Between what happened at your quince and Carmen's lack of one, I'd say we might feel a little differently."

Oh. My. God. Was she really bringing it up? My mother needed a therapist, like, stat, for her intense and unstoppable masochism!

Tía Celia's quince, *twenty years ago*, was where Tío Victor and Tía Celia had fallen in love. Not at first sight, because he'd seen her plenty—wait for it—*while he was dating my mother.*

Of course, by then Tío Victor and Mami were done, and she'd moved on to Junior.

Still, though. Tío Victor should have been off-limits forever. But that? Is not what happened. And it is a thing that we dare not name. I was actually wondering if the universe, or at least our living room, was about to spontaneously combust.

"My quince was perfect, and you know it," Tía Celia began, sounding about ten years old. "And as far as Carmen goes, if she hadn't—"

"ANYway," Mami interrupted her. "Like I said, it's all history."

"But we need to learn from history," Tía Celia said.

"Yeah. Learn to let it go."

Wow. This was working out so well already!

While Mami and Tía Celia chattered and passed the heaping plates around, the phone in my pocket buzzed. Mami was usually as strict as hell about devices at meals, but she wasn't paying attention. So I balanced it on my lap under the table.

A phone number I didn't recognize.

Hey, Simone was looking for you. I told her I saw you leave. She said to check in with her sometime this weekend.

Great. Mauro had my phone number now. Thanks for

sharing my info with my worst enemy, Simone.

Ariana glanced at me, curious.

Well, *one* of my worst enemies.

And I just wanted to say . . . I'm sorry that everything
took you by surprise. Me, I mean. This is a surprise to me, too. To see you again after so long
was super surprising.

And I feel like I just wrote the word "surprise" way too
many times. Or variations of it.

Surprise. Sur-prise. SURPRISE!

"But it all worked out perfectly! Good things coming from
bad! All of us together again. Carmencita done with high school!
Getting ready to celebrate Ariana's coming of age!" Mami just
kept going, like if Mary Poppins was a steamroller.

I sighed. I could see the connection. A lie about graduation
leading to a lie about a family reunion.

Ariana took another spoonful of chicken. "Actually, it's Ari
now, Tía."

Tía Celia and Mami shared a look and then my tía hauled
out an enormous wedding magazine and squealed. "Y look! We
can figure out some ideas to take to Doña Thomasina!"

The phone buzzed again.

Hello? Do I have the right number?

Me: I'M IN THE MIDDLE OF AN AWKWARD FAMILY
DINNER.

I looked up from my furious typing and saw the table had

gone dead silent. Shit, had I said that out loud?

"Carmen Maria—" Mami began.

Ariana stood up. "So delicious, Tía, really. I've missed your cooking! But, you know, Carmen and I have so much to talk about." She yanked me up. "I'd love to see your room."

Once we got inside and closed the door, I said simply, "Here's my room."

She rolled her eyes. "It was the best I could do under pressure."

"Yeah, it's never been your strong suit."

"Or yours," she retorted. "Which is what caused the last three and a half years of grief."

THAT got a laugh out of me. "Me? *I* caused it?"

She shrugged. "Obviously."

That wasn't even worth the response. "So why the Dreams?"

"This wasn't *my* idea. This was all Mami and Tía Mira. But . . . hell, the whole quince is for Mami anyway, so this is just typical." She shrugged again. "It was the best compromise."

Glad my misfortune was the "best compromise" for them.

"Mami and Tía Mira get to reunite, you dance at my party without me having to ask you to be in my corte and you saying no. Because if that happened, Tía Mira and Mami would be forced to stop talking AGAIN because of your little tantrums."

Wait. MY little tantrums? Was that what we were calling canceling my entire quince celebration?

Meanwhile, Ariana ignored me, nosing around my walls like she belonged here. I blessed my tradition of never displaying any picture I wouldn't want to explain to the FBI.

"I've seen hotel rooms with more personality," she commented.

Honestly, it was either punch her or text Waverly. So that was what I did.

Me: Waves, you have GOT to rescue me. Unwanted
     family reunion in aisle one.
Waves: Sounds bad. Give me fifteen.
Me: I know I said no more Bay, but . . .
Waves: Damn, must be worse than I thought. Give
     me ten.

"Ooh, he's cute," she said about a picture of me and Tran taken at a practice that I'd stuck in my mirror a few days ago and forgotten about. "Is HE going to be at my quince?"

Tran had clearly known something I hadn't. "Not unless he's doing it on video chat. He's in Vietnam this summer."

She giggled. "Wow. He must really have wanted to get away from you."

I closed my eyes. Breathed in. Held it. Mami's last boyfriend, Tony the yoga teacher, would be so proud right now. Too bad Mami had ended it once she'd mastered the headstand.

"Anyway," she said. "We won't have to say two words to each other if we don't want to."

My God. Was she always this naive? Had she been smarter

when she was twelve? "Seriously? Do you really think that Mami and Tía Celia schemed all of this for one night only?"

She frowned. "You're blowing it out of proportion. It's a one-night performance. You'll have to come to, like, three rehearsals or something. Tops. That's what Mami and I agreed to."

Oh, how I wanted to believe her. I was already stuck with Mauro for the summer. I didn't deserve Ariana, too.

Then, she *opened the door to my closet and peered inside.* My mouth dropped open like a fish's. Who the hell did she think she—

"Hey, what's in that box?"

I slammed the closet door. "And here is where we reach the end of your journey." Just then, I got a text from Waverly.

Waves: Downstairs.

"All right, Ariana, guess I'll see you later. I wish I could say I was looking forward to it, but unlike the rest of the family, I don't like to lie."

"Wait. You're just leaving me here? Alone?" Ariana was finally dropping the cool girl act. "Can I come with you?"

I laughed. People really didn't change. "Seriously? I might have to work a few nights for you, but believe me, I have zero desire to spend time babysitting your ass. Especially since we all know you don't like to behave."

At least she had the grace to look embarrassed, but only for a second.

"I can't believe you are still BLAMING me for— I was

twelve. You can't BLAME me for believing what YOU told me!" Ah, there she was. The little brat I remembered so well.

"You're right. I blame myself for trusting you and believing you wouldn't turn around and ruin everything for me," I said, ushering her out of my room and closing the door firmly behind me. "Luckily *I* learn from my mistakes."

And with the sweetness of her pissed-off face and the last word behind me, I waved to my relatives and Enrique and vanished.

Five

MIAMI IS KNOWN FOR its banging club scene. I mean, little kids in Croatia probably know that when you want to have a good time, Miami is better than most places on earth.

The problem with that, though, is that all the places you want to go to in Miami are places where they never let people our age in. Unless your name is on a building downtown or in the credits of some hit Disney Channel show. So we had to take things into our own hands.

Waverly glanced around. "Looks like every underage kid in the city had the same idea tonight."

The guy at the door nodded at us as we edged our way to the front, the vibrations from the music shaking through me. I know it's dumb, but it felt good to be recognized, even though we hadn't been here in a while. Like we'd been missed.

The inside of the place looked like someone had cleared out a space in their storage locker for dancing. When I got tired (often) or the music got boring (rare), I liked to wander around and figure out what kind of life would have space for all these random things. I couldn't imagine living in a way that made an old cigar box guitar *and* a broken snow blower (really? in Miami?) make sense.

She waved to someone almost as soon as we walked in. "You gonna be OK for a bit?"

"I don't need a babysitter."

"Uh-huh. Just tug your pacifier if you need me. Or, you know, text." She gave me a little hug before the crowd swallowed her up.

I was surrounded by people pressed against each other. There were faces that looked familiar, somehow, but I didn't know if that's because I'd really met them or because people our age were all starting to look the same.

But then I saw Louie Amador, and he definitely only looked like himself. Like if a tiger was a teenage boy. And the look in his eyes told me he was hunting.

I tried to melt back into the shadows, but he grabbed my arm. "Carmen," he said, voice all fake husky. "Just the person I was looking for." He was swaying a little bit. The Bay didn't serve alcohol, so people pregamed before coming here. Judging from the way he stank, Louie's pregaming was more like the World Series playoffs.

"Keep looking." I started to pull myself away.

"Aw, what's the problem? This isn't about Alex, is it?

C'mon . . . you and Alex?" He gave an ugly laugh. "What? I'm not supposed to know? You're not exactly subtle. *'Oh, Alex . . .'*" he said in a singsong. And then in a slightly deeper voice, he added, *'Oh, Carmen . . .'* My kitchen was like a fucking telenovela set! I almost felt bad for interrupting, but I had to keep my boy unmolested." He spit up laughter at his own dumb joke, and I kept my face a cool blank breeze. That's not what had happened, but if I admitted anything, I'd be giving him the truth. And he didn't deserve it.

"Aw, come on, Carmen." He stopped and steadied himself against me. "You know me. I can keep a secret!" He put his arm around my shoulders. Ick. "See? Now you can relax. So it's good that you saw me tonight. It must be fate."

"Yeah, well, I believe in free will. Goodbye." I finally twisted free and pushed him away. His Coke splashed back on his white shirt, making a brown stain that looked like South America.

"Bitch!" He started to wipe at his chest, making it worse. "Still waiting for Alex to make up his mind? You gonna be waiting a long-ass time. He doesn't need secondhand goods! Especially now!"

"Careful," I said to him as I walked away. "That's definitely going to stain."

I managed to pull off the "whatever, loser" walk-away. I held it together as long as the bathroom, which amazingly enough was free. I shoved my way in and kept my knee pressed against the door for privacy. How many chickens was I going to have to sacrifice to get this mal de ojo off me? Because this bad day was turning into an even worse night.

His words about Alex echoed in my brain. *"Especially now"? What the hell does that mean?*

I didn't want to give his words any space in my head. Because I doubted highly that he and Alex sat around talking about their love lives, anyway. Louie just wanted to hurt me because I wouldn't get with him.

Louie was full of shit. But . . . he knew. I banged my head softly on the stall door. He fucking KNEW. He knew about my feelings for Alex. And if *he* knew . . .

Oh, don't get me wrong. Like Mami always said, guys were like buses: maybe you'd have to wait around for one, but one would show up eventually.

Still, after Mauro, I knew in my heart that none of them were going to matter. Until Alex Sharma. Alex, with his sweet smile and piercing black eyes and soccer bod.

Except he'd always had a girlfriend, and Alex wasn't the kind of guy to cheat. Wanting Alex was like wanting the moon. In fact, I was proud that I did, like it proved that somewhere, somehow, I still had good taste. Mauro and the others had me doubting that.

There had been a moment, though, at Louie's end-of-the-year party.

That's what Louie had seen.

I stared at myself in the mirror. Maybe the person giving me the mal de ojo . . . was me.

Screw that. I put my lipstick back on, outlining my lips in red until I felt like myself again. I wasn't here to be miserable. I could do that at home for free.

So, Louie was my third thing. I could handle that.

Lucky for me, problems don't come in fours.

———————

Music does something to me, works its way under my skin and twists me all around until everything is alive. There was something familiar about this music, the way it snaked itself over and under me, but I wasn't here to think.

I closed my eyes and pressed back against the wall of sound. There were people around me, but they were just another part of the wall.

It wasn't long before I realized that another guy was determinedly dancing near me. And miraculously, he wasn't anyone I knew. His face was smooth, shaved. Pale. The colored lights threw parts of him into shadow, breaking him up and putting him back together. Preppy college boy. His clothes fell on him the way they do on rich people.

He leaned into me. "I'm Paul."

I nodded and kept on dancing. Because Paul, I am not here for you. That's not what tonight is about.

He got close to me again. "I like how you dance. You're a good dancer."

I nodded again, because OK.

"Will you tell me your name?"

I smiled up at him. And said, "Ariana."

It's so good, that moment right before you kiss someone, seeing the way they look at you. Like you are the only person in the whole world. Like they'll die if they can't touch you. Paul's brown eyes flicked to my mouth, to my eyes. And stayed.

It was good. It was so easy.

Too easy.

Too bad I didn't want it.

"I have to go," I whispered. Surprised at how dry my mouth felt.

Paul's eyes were still soft, unfocused. "Huh?"

It felt good to know I could do that.

It just wasn't enough.

"I mean, I have to find my friends."

He started to lower his head to mine. "I'm sure they can wait."

"No, I mean . . . no. I don't want this."

His head jerked back. "What?"

"I mean, thanks for the dancing, Paul, but . . . I have to go."

"Ariana . . ."

I started to see red for a second until I remembered he was talking to me.

"I don't get it . . . I thought we had something there." His whining only proved that I was right.

"Yeah. Dancing."

"Oh, come on, girls like you . . ."

"Hold up." I pushed him away, hard this time. "What?"

He looked surprised, like I was saying words he'd never heard before.

"Like, you know . . ." He gestured down at me. "Chonga type."

"*Chonga type?*" I hated hearing the words come out of my own mouth.

"Yeah . . ." He looked confused. "You know, right?"

Oh, I knew. I just hadn't heard that term in forever. Chongas were Latin girls who wore tight clothes and were tacky as hell. And who were considered wild and easy and (insert convenient stereotype here).

I rolled my eyes. "It's the twenty-first century. Get a new insult."

He smirked. "Truth hurt?"

"No, but her fist might." Another voice. Male. I didn't even have to look over. Because of course it was Mauro. My messed-up fate.

Paul put his hands up. "Hey, she didn't say she had a boyfriend."

"So, if she didn't have a boyfriend, then it would just be OK to stand here and insult her?" Mauro asked, quiet. Furious.

Paul was glancing over his shoulder, like he was afraid we were going to pull guns or something and turn him into a cautionary tale.

"Just . . . go away. Please." I was so tired.

After taking a last glance at us, Paul took off so fast I could still see the outline of his Abercrombie & Fitch shirt.

"And remember," I shouted after him, "a real chonga would have kicked your ass!"

I could feel Mauro trying to come up with something to say. Not just anything, the right thing.

This already felt so, so familiar.

I started to walk past him, but he put himself in front of me. After everything, I appreciated him not touching me.

"I was fine. You didn't have to come charging in on your white horse." He smelled like sandalwood and sweat. Just like he had in the costume.

"Hey, I wasn't doing it for you. If you ended up killing him, they'd probably shut the Bay down. Since I'm trying to get a DJ slot here, that would be terrible for my career. And it's not the Bay's fault that guy is a total troglodyte."

I didn't say anything, and not just because I only sort of knew what "troglodyte" meant.

"OK, you are mute, and this is awkward." He ran his hand

though his hair, and the familiar gesture sent a dart through me. For a second, I was fifteen again, standing in front of the school darkroom and waiting to see him loping down the hall, his camera strapped on his back, occasionally banging into his guitar.

"It doesn't have to be," I said finally. The place was full of people, but there was no one nearby who could get me out of this situation. Maybe if I set off a flare?

"Great. So how do we make that happen? Ignore everything from before?"

"Nothing happened."

"Wrong," he shot back, his voice low. "I remember you." He pointed at me with his index finger. "You remember me." He turned the finger to point at himself.

He was very close. A different type of close from when we were at work. The kind of close where the air around me buzzed and bent. The club swirled around us.

I took a breath. Stepped back for air. "I just remember a lot of making out that we hid from everyone." Cocked my head. "To say nothing of broken promises . . ."

"I already said I was sorry about that!"

"Did you? My memory of you is so, so faint—"

He looked down at the floor and sighed. "OK, maybe I thought it. I thought it a lot, though."

"Considering I don't live in your brain, that doesn't exactly count."

"What if I say it now?"

"It would make exactly one of us feel better, but that was always your MO, so go for it."

He sighed again. "Look . . . maybe I overreacted. To what I thought you did." The words sounded hesitant, foreign in his mouth. "But we both made mistakes."

I laughed right in his face. "The only mistake I made was that I let myself feel bad about your bullshit. I mean, I was only fifteen, but I still should have known better. You always did. You knew that once you mentioned the pictures, I'd stick around, and that's why you were so pissed to be proven right." I saw the way his mouth tightened and, yeah, it felt good. "But I mean, we're over it, right? It's not like you were the love of my life. So, cálmate, OK?" Those were the words I finally needed to say, out loud, to him. I needed to slam this door right in his face. And the way he brushed back from me, I knew it had worked. Por fin.

It was like the music agreed with me because it switched to my favorite song. Perfect for walking away with the last word.

"Good talk. Go and sin no more," I said dismissively, feeling better than I had in days. "Have fun DJing and see you at work."

And that was it. No more haunting from the Ghost of Darkroom-Makeouts Past. I was finally free.

 # Six

SINCE WE'D ALL BEEN trained to curtsy and twirl around in a waltz, it was difficult for some of the Dreams to make the leap to salsa, meringue, and dropping it low.

Simone played us a few videos of other quinceañera dances—for inspiration, she said. "But we're doing so much more than that! I have so much more in mind!"

Too bad that what she had in mind didn't seem to go with what people could do with their bodies. Moves that should be fluid and sensual were puppet-string jerky. And it was just too damn hot for us to be dancing so close. The clouds hung low, as thick and sluggish as we felt. You could smell the coming rain, and we all wished it would come and give us an excuse to stop.

Simone sighed, and her sigh said, *I thought I hired professionals!* Yes, professional costume wearers, tea party facilitators, and tantrum soothers. Not reggaetón experts.

"Again!" And so we did it again. And then more.

Eventually, I started to get the hang of it. Bless Mami's dancing genes. And soon Waves and Leila joined me. The only thing we couldn't quite do yet were the lifts. We weren't strong enough to lift each other. But the three of us were still having fun—dipping and twirling and swaying, making Simone's moves bigger, sexier.

Best of all was who WASN'T getting it. Mauro. The smooth waltz we'd done together at the party was clearly a fluke. And it was fun to watch him flailing (and failing). Because Mr. Good at Basically Everything just didn't seem to know how to handle sucking quite so hard.

I mean . . . he was practically tripping over his own feet, robotically swaying like someone had left his on button pressed and the battery was running out. And it was pissing him off.

Simone had been working with him for the past half hour, and he wasn't any closer to being able to move the way she wanted him to.

"And left foot, pivot, right foot, pivot, spin me, rock forward, rock back! And then . . . backbend, up, sway, sway, lift me!" That clearly did not compute for Mauro on any level and he just stopped. Simone blew her sweaty hair off her forehead and clicked the music off.

"Maybe we should take a break?" Jessica suggested, her normally pale face lobster red. She was also having trouble but watching her wasn't as painful. Like, there was a dim hope she might get it someday.

I saw Simone and Mauro talking intently. She flung her hands around, while Mauro shook his head and shook his head again. Simone said something and gave him a pleading look and I saw the exact moment he relented with a single nod. Then he stomped into the Shack and slammed the door.

Waverly plopped down next to me and jerked her chin in the door's direction. "So . . . HE'S not having a good day!"

"Nope!" I couldn't quite keep the glee out of my voice.

"Did you know he couldn't dance?"

I shook my head. He'd danced well enough at the party even before our waltz, but lots of guys could bounce to the beat. That didn't mean you could learn a full-on partnered Latin dance routine. "I'm actually kind of surprised. Don't musicians have to have some rhythm? He should have stuck with photography. And, I mean, not to be stereotypical, but maybe he takes after the non-Colombian side of the family?" All I knew about Mauro's mom was that she was a model—and she wasn't Latina.

She nudged me. "So many opinions. And how do you explain me, then? Full Scandinavian, right here!"

I shrugged. "Eh, you grew up here!"

My phone buzzed along the side of my leg. *Tale as old as time . . . True as it can be . . .*

Waves raised her eyebrows at me, and I shrugged and went off to the side of the Shack.

"Hello?" I rubbed the back of my sweaty neck. How did

someone get sunburned on a cloudy day? Miami sun was insane.

A burst of noise and static greeted me, followed by a muffled curse. Then, "Hey, Carmen? It's Alex."

My heart put the words together before my brain did, and started doing Simone's whole routine, right in my chest. My entire body flushed as red as my neck felt.

"You there?"

I gripped the phone harder against my ear. "Yeah, yeah. Alex, hi!" OK, what was that high-pitched shit coming out of my mouth?

"I'm sorry for the noise . . . I'm in the car, making deliveries." The Sharmas owned an Indian place called the Papadum Palace.

"No problem!" OK, could the squirrel in my throat please hit puberty?

"Anyway . . . I can't talk long . . . but are you busy?"

I looked around at the clump of Dreams waiting for Simone to call them back for practice. Mauro had come out of the Shack and was leaning against a tree. Every now and then he glanced my way. And looked sour.

Good. Maybe he'd quit.

"Carmen . . . you still there?"

"Yeah, yeah, of course!" My voice was back. Victory! "I have a second . . ."

"Then I'll make this quick. You want to hang out tonight?"

And then it was like the backyard faded into a watercolor

and the only solid thing was the phone in my hand. The connection between me and Alex.

"Um . . . *yeah*! I mean . . . yeah. What are we doing?"

He laughed. "Nothing too exciting . . . maybe a little mini golf? Maybe some coffee or something afterward?"

"I suck at mini golf," I said, and then kicked myself. Way to be negative!

But he laughed. "I promise I'll take it easy on you." His voice was muffled by the sounds of the car and the traffic around him, but did I still hear . . . flirting? Was Alex Sharma actually FLIRTING with me?

"So . . . is it a date?" he continued. A DATE. His word. Not mine.

My whole body was smiling. "Yeah, just text me the details when you're done driving."

"Excellent. See you tonight."

"Yeah. See you."

As soon as I clicked off, I looked around and saw that the Dreams were all staring at me. Waiting to start. Waves's eyes were practically telegraphing novels, while Mauro's were narrowed.

"If you are *finally* ready, Carmen . . ." Simone said. "Pair up with Mauro, please."

Oh, I was definitely and *finally* ready—*to have something good happen to me, for once!*

"You look pleased," Mauro said sourly as we went into the

beginning pose, my hand loose around the side of his waist.

I grinned back. "What can I say? I love to dance. It's the heritage of my people . . . and yours, I might add. Partially."

"So chatty, too."

"Complaining?"

He spun me into a complicated right-then-left spin. It actually wasn't half bad.

"No," he said, when I returned to his arms. "It's actually good to see you smile for once."

The only way he could have made my smile bigger at that moment was to quit the Dreams altogether, but unfortunately, it seemed like he was finally getting the hang of it. Some of the moves, anyway.

"You don't have to hold me so close," I griped.

"Am I?" he asked, all innocent, even though I was practically flush against him, back to front. "Simone said what I needed was to feel the dance." His breath tickled the sweaty curls on my neck. I could smell his sandalwood cologne mingling with my vanilla perfume. Together they made something strange.

Once I put a little daylight between us, I made sure to hook my ankle around his, causing him to stumble.

"Then feel *the dance*," I said. "Not me."

And then we settled down and concentrated. Or tried to. He was still shaky on big parts of it, and the angrier he got, the worse he moved.

"You know . . . unlike me, you don't have to do this," I said sweetly, after he botched another bit of complicated salsa footwork. "You can always quit. Save yourself."

"Believe me," he muttered. "Nothing sounds better right now. This isn't what I signed up for. But . . . Simone asked. So I promised her I'd stick around. And I don't break my promises."

"Well . . . that's new."

His hand pressed into the small of my back, and I arched away from him into a modified backbend, pushing my hips closer to his. Then I slowly swayed back up on a four count.

He froze, his eyes locked onto mine. There was anger in his eyes, but something else, too. I shivered, my skin recognizing something I couldn't find words for. Moving this way with him was very different from doing it with Waverly.

And then my phone buzzed between us. And buzzed again. I pulled away and checked it before Simone could glance our way.

"Same person as before?" he asked. All casual. Like he hadn't been eavesdropping. "Andy? Aaron?"

"Alex. And yes."

"Huh." Mauro twirled me into the final pose of the dance, holding my leg up against his waist with one hand.

It would have been so hot with someone else. Like, someone who could actually move without looking like he was running every step past a committee.

I let myself daydream about me and Alex, just like this . . .

"Hey." He snapped his fingers in front of my face. "Simone

wants us to start again." His voice was a snap, too.

This wasn't working. Which was actually wonderful. Once Simone saw that . . . she'd separate us. Especially if she wanted to impress my tía and cousin.

Or maybe we'd fail miserably, and I'd manage to avoid Ariana, too!

I mean, Alex had just asked me out. On a DATE. Miracles were in the air! Anything was possible!

Again. And again. I kept waiting for Simone to make the call. But she never did. We'd hit the wall and tunneled all the way under it. We were getting tired and worse.

Moods started to stretch and snap around me. Mauro's most of all.

But not mine.

Until Mauro almost dropped me during the final lift of the dance.

"Hey, what the hell?" I said, sitting down hard on the grass.

"Get your head out of the damn clouds," Mauro muttered, his face dark.

Ha! Mauro was definitely not having fun. Let *him* bitch to Simone. Let *him* look like the difficult one. All I had to do was continue to be my charming, dancing self.

"You're so right," I said, my voice miel sweet. "I mean, I DO have plans." And then I waited a delicious beat. "Maybe Alex and I will go dancing. After all, he's *much* better at it."

Seven

I STOOD IN THE middle of my bedroom, piles of shorts and jeans and jean shorts stacked on the bed. My favorite going-out song was blasting, four girls talking about how they were invincible. And hot.

Tonight, *I* would be invincible. And hot.

As long as I found the right outfit.

This was not as easy as it sounded. My mind drifted for a second to Ariana at dinner the other night, how she'd looked pretty and polished in a plain black T-shirt and A-line skirt. I could do something like that . . .

But why the hell would I want to look like Ariana?

I put my hands on my hips and stared at myself in the mirror, at the person I'd seen a million times. And usually, I liked what I saw. So did the guys who saw me at the Bay, at the mall, walking down Ocean Drive. If I had a dollar for every

"Oye, Mami" I've ever heard, I could probably pay for college. Or move to Europe.

Óyeme, pues. Was this what I'd become? Pumping myself up with the memory of street piropos? Yuck.

Besides, one of the reasons I liked Alex so much was that he wasn't like that. He wasn't the "lean out the window and shout" type. In fact, he usually tried to shush Louie and the other soccer players when they pulled that shit.

But that didn't mean that I didn't want to make him *want* to say something.

Inspiration struck. Black fitted skinny jeans, a white T-shirt, and . . . a teal scarf. I pulled my long hair up into a high ponytail.

Ariana and her mother weren't the only ones who could pull off Audrey Hepburn, Latinx style.

Mami glanced up at me as I walked into the room and smiled. "Where are *you* going?" Someone screamed on the TV and her eyes snapped back there. A crumpled *Wall Street Journal* sat forgotten next to her.

I was still furious at her, but it was hard to hold on to that in the face of Alex. I was willing to declare a truce for one night, because he was basically world peace.

"Oh, nowhere special." I dragged a finger on top of the side table. "Going to play mini golf with Alex."

THAT got her attention. "Alex . . . as in Sharma? As

in"—she put her hands under her chin and gave a dreamy sigh—"THAT Alex? All-of-senior-year Alex?"

"The very one." I fought a smile and lost. "And I've never sounded like that."

She hopped up and hugged me. "Well then, congrats, mija! I knew you were full of it when you kept telling me you were just friends."

I pulled away. "We still are. It's just mini golf."

"Golf doesn't make ANYONE smile like that, except maybe Tiger Woods."

I laughed, and the doorbell rang. I ran for it, ignoring Mami frantically shaking her head. I was probably supposed to run into my room and pretend like I'd totally forgotten our date.

In other words, lie.

I wasn't starting our night like that.

Alex stood in the doorway, in a blue polo shirt and crisp black jeans. He looked uncertain, until the moment he saw me.

"Carmen, wow, you look—"

"So do you." I grabbed his hand and called over my shoulder. "Bye, Mami!"

But no way was she going out like that.

"Alex!" she trilled out. "Nice to see you!"

"Hi, Ms. Aguilar." He grinned back at her. "We're going to play mini golf. You wanna come with us?"

I could feel the smile on my face wobbling. But Mami laughed and shooed us out. "You kids have fun now!"

After the door closed, I rolled my eyes at him. "What would you have done if she had said yes?"

Alex whispered, "I got nervous. It just came out."

"Nervous? Did you have some kind of scary mini golf flashback?" I teased.

"No," he said, looking serious. "I just saw you."

It was a gorgeous night for mini golf, the sultry kind of weather that defines Miami. Unfortunately, everybody else Alex had ever known apparently felt the same way. Before long, we were playing with Louie and his flavor of the moment, Yesenia, and Rob the goalie with his boyfriend, Aiden.

So much for me having a montage-worthy date with Alex.

"Ha! Hole in one, in your face!" Rob crowed on the last hole.

Louie muttered and slapped a five-dollar bill into Rob's outstretched palm. Aiden grinned. "How about we use that for a victory latte?"

Louie rolled his eyes. "Man, screw that. Let's go to Palacio and get some cortaditos."

Yesenia said, "Wait, I thought you said you were taking me out to dinner."

"You know they sell food there, babe."

Yesenia shook out her long black hair and sighed. "Oh no. You said this was a DATE, not a . . ." she said, looking at the rest of us with distaste, "a *hangout*. I'll catch a car home." And she stomped off. Louie stood there like a sitcom character waiting for his laugh track, and then he shrugged and took off after her.

"The sad thing is," Rob said, "that she'll still hook up with him later."

"And she's depriving herself of a delicious cortadito on top of it," I added. "Just losing all the way down."

Alex laughed and put his arm around my shoulder. I still couldn't quite get used to that feeling. "Actually, we're gonna have to stomp off, too," he said. "Carmen has to go home."

Once we were in the car, I turned to him. "I never said I have to go home." I had my Dreams shift during the day, and my first Ariana practice at night. But none of that mattered more than what was happening right now.

He grinned and started the car. "Good. Let's go get some coffee. Alone."

Dadeland Mall on a Friday night was full—full of parents rolling squirmy toddlers through the crowd, stuffed shopping bags threatening to tilt strollers over. Full of older people looking to get out of the heat and into one of the massage chairs while they sipped their food court cafecitos. Full of packs of teenagers, side-eyeing each other in curiosity and competition. The thick smell of department store colognes mingled with the humidity that hung in the air despite the air-conditioning that kept the entire mall roughly the temperature of Iceland.

Unfortunately for me, Dadeland Mall was also one giant mixed signal. I didn't think of Dadeland when I thought about romance—I thought about Mami and me swatching lipsticks at the MAC store, or Waves and me splitting a cinnamon roll as big as our head.

And he'd said that he'd wanted to get some coffee. Alone. This wasn't exactly alone.

Still, I didn't necessarily mind an audience. Some independent proof that I wasn't editing this out of some different, worse reality.

And then he took my hand, and held it.

Dadeland was seeming more romantic by the second.

We wove through the crowd, occasionally smiling at people who looked familiar. I'd only been out of school a few weeks, but already people were fading into vague memories. Being here with Alex made it easier to pretend that I'd had his high school experience instead of mine. At least I was done with it.

We found a corner table, half hidden by a giant potted palm, and Alex went to get my cortadito. When he got back, there was a lot to do. We had to arrange the cups, just so. Make sure we had enough napkins. Keep the stirrer off the slightly sticky table.

"I told them low sugar, like you always do. Was that OK?"

I took a sip. It could have tasted like vinegar and I would have nodded. Luckily, it was perfect.

"So . . ." he started, stretching out the word. "What's new?"

That was the problem. Too much and nothing.

"Um, well, I have to . . . I'm working as a party princess all summer. You know, kids' parties? Someday my prince will come? Like Waverly?"

He smiled. "Talk about perfect casting."

I could feel my cheeks getting warm. That's the kind of thing only he could say without making me want to roll my eyes. He sounded so sincere.

"And after summer?"

I shrugged. "We'll see." Except I couldn't see anything but the guy sitting in front of me. Life plans could wait. "What about you?"

"Oh, you know . . . school. Trying to get a soccer scholarship. I'm in a friend's fancy birthday party this summer."

"That must be catching—I'm working a quinceañera that's really a sixteenth birthday."

"Actually, yeah. That's what she called it, too! Any pointers you can give me?"

Yeah, follow the Life Visioning rules and graduate, so you don't have to suffer afterward. "Uh, I'm not really that involved. It's just work." I definitely wasn't going to get into the Ariana thing. They probably knew of each other at least—some soccer party somewhere.

Ugh, how the hell had Ariana entered my brain? I didn't need my summer to revolve *more* around her.

He kept smiling at me, glancing away, and then smiling again.

I'd been waiting for this all night. But now that it was just the two of us, my mind felt blank. Every idea that I may have had burned away before it could make it to my mouth.

The edges of my thumbs were raw from me pulling the skin off.

Maybe we should have gone to the Bay. Then at least we could dance away this awkward energy.

"Hey," he said abruptly, standing up, like he felt the same way. "I'm gonna go get a cinnamon bun. Want anything?"

I wanted *everything*. Still, I shook my head. And watched him walk away.

Oh well. I could use the time.

Siri, how does someone talk to a cute boy?

———————

I scrolled through my phone, distracted, but not finding much of an answer. A fly started to buzz around the back of my neck, my ear. I absently swatted it away.

And touched a hand.

"That's some delayed reaction." Mauro slid into the seat facing me and plopped two shopping bags down. "I was already wondering how to escalate. Maybe sting you?"

I groaned. "Ay, Dios mío, why are you everywhere?"

Mauro smiled. "Working." He patted one of the bags.

"Errands for the Great and Mighty Simone. Why are you here? Wi-Fi down at your house?"

I opened my mouth to give him the roasting he so richly deserved. Before I could spit fire, though, Alex came back, balancing a tray with a bun and two bottles of water.

He looked at Mauro, who looked back. Neither of them smiled.

"Everything OK?" Alex asked.

"Everything's perfect," I said, grabbing one of the waters. "Mauro was just leaving."

"Actually," Mauro said, pulling up a chair, "I've been craving one of these buns." He picked up a fork. "Mind if I take a bite?"

Before either of us could answer, he'd speared a piece and shoved it into his mouth. Ugh. Maybe he'd choke on it.

"I'm pretty sure you can afford your own," I said tightly, pulling the cinnamon bun out of his reach. "And wouldn't you rather have your own table? Far away?" I nudged his fork away like it had cooties, which, obviously, it did.

He shrugged. "Nah, I'd rather spend my evening with friends, just like you two are. It's good to see friends enjoying themselves, celebrating their friendship." He paused. "Arlo, right?"

I rolled my eyes.

"Alex. So . . . you work with Carmen?" Alex asked.

Mauro grinned. "The Beast to her Beauty."

I kicked him under the table.

Alex said, "Yeah. We were just talking about her new job."

"Oh, so then she told you we just got hired to work a party that will involve months and months of practices? We'll be practically joined at the hip all summer!"

"All the more reason to have some time AWAY from you," I said through my teeth.

Mauro ignored that. He reached into one of the bags and pulled out a bundle of towels, T-shirts, protein bars, water bottles, dry shampoo, sweats, socks. "In fact, that's part of the reason I'm here." Tights. Leotards. "Picking up supplies." Wait. None of our routines needed a feather boa! At the look on my face, Mauro shrugged. "Hey, it was on the list, no explanation, and I didn't ask." He shook it in front of me. "But clearly, it's gonna be a long, busy summer. So many practices. So many parties. So many feathers."

If I didn't engage, he'd get bored and go away.

"You got the 'long' part right, anyway." My mouth had clearly not learned the new plan.

"So." Mauro turned to Alex. "That's me. How about you, Atticus? You joined at the hip with anyone this summer?"

"Alex. And I'm pretty much married to soccer all summer. We're trying to make the state championships again—"

"Huh. Fascinating. Well, this has been lovely, but I need to check in with Simone. She'd mentioned something about a mesh T-shirt for me, and I need to talk her out of it. Unless my summer partner has a different idea?" I'm lucky my head didn't snap off with the sheer force of my negation. "Oh well. Enjoy your evening. And Carmen?" He leaned in close. "I'll check in with you later."

"Nobody wants you to," I muttered, but by then he was gone.

As soon as Mauro walked away, Alex shook his head and laughed. "I never had anyone have so much trouble remembering my name."

"Yeah, Mauro forgets a lot of stuff." I wished I could erase him from my own mind. And I could only hope he was kidding about mesh anything. *Please, universe, hear my plea.*

Alex leaned toward me, offering me a piece of cinnamon roll on his fork. "I figured you wouldn't want his fork." Gratefully, I took the bite, conscious of the romance of him feeding me. "So . . . is that what work is like?" he asked.

How weird would it be if I just . . . kept this fork forever?

"The job is OK. The partner, though . . ." I shuddered with the horror.

Out of the corner of my eye, I could still see Mauro, balancing his bags and pretending he wasn't staring.

"Cheer up . . ." Alex said, leaning forward and dangling another piece of cinnamon roll in front of me. "I've heard mesh T-shirts can cut off circulation."

I took my bite, and then held my hands up like they were scales. "Possibility of cutoff circulation versus actually having to SEE him in that?" I waggled my hands. "Tough call."

Alex laughed. "You know . . . even full-time jobs are usually about forty hours a week."

"Meaning?"

"Meaning . . ." he said, holding my hand loosely on the table. Visible to anyone who might be looking. "There's still plenty of summer to spend with . . . people who aren't your work partner."

I was amazed that the whole table wasn't vibrating with the sheer force of my pulse.

"That's the plan," I said, trying to put a world of meaning in my words.

But he wasn't looking at me. He'd glanced back at Mauro, who was sitting about two tables away, pretending to be engrossed in his phone.

"Well, looks like your partner knows that." He grinned. "Even if he doesn't like it."

"Here's hoping he kept the receipts for Simone." I offered him a piece of cinnamon roll on *our* fork. "At least then we can return everything when he quits."

"Oh, I don't know . . ." He looked serious. "Maybe you all can keep the boa."

Eight

I HADN'T EXPECTED TO hear from Mauro after I got home. Correction, I hadn't *wanted* to hear from Mauro after I got home. I had important things to do. Like celebrate an absolutely perfect night, complete with a cinnamon roll and a cortadito and the most beautiful fork ever manufactured. Finally, finally, something was going my way. Not even old baggage could ruin things.

MrtB: Sorry.

Apparently, we'd now graduated from texting to direct messages in Discord. Technology betrayal. Maybe the push I needed to delete my account. I turned my phone upside down until it buzzed again.

Damn.

MrtB: No excuses. I was as bad as that troglodyte from the other night. So much for trying to demonstrate I've changed.

MrtB: Come on, Carmen. Talk to me. Yell at me.

MrtB: We can commiserate about the next bunch of months together. You can curse the heavens. And me.

I could ignore him.

MrtB: I know I deserve it.

But wouldn't ignoring him just make him feel like what he did mattered? After tonight, Mauro Reyes was a nonevent in my life. He was my Dreams partner. I could keep that separate from my private life. Well, now that I was going to HAVE a private life.

DivaCee: Yeah, you do.

MrtB: She lives!

DivaCee: What, did you think I'd died of happiness?

MrtB: . . . and I think I threw up a little in my mouth.

DivaCee: Then my work here is done.

MrtB: . . . just ONE question and then we'll never speak of it again.

DivaCee: Mauro, we work together, fine. I can make my peace with that. But. There are boundaries. Walls. The Great Wall of Carmen.

MrtB: ONE question. One QUESTION. 1??? Una pregunta?

DivaCee: If I say yes, will you stop?

MrtB: Maybe.

DivaCee: Fine. ONE. 1. Una.

And then my screen started scrolling A names. Andrew.

Adam. Arlo. Arnold. Over and over. Honestly, I was impressed at the effort it took him to avoid "Alex."

DivaCee: You might have missed one.

MrtB: Seriously, though, Carmen. THAT'S ALEX? All the frown emojis in the world can't contain my sadfeels.

DivaCee: Wow. Guess you finally remembered his name.

MrtB: I mean . . . "married to soccer"? All his brains are probably in his feet.

It would be so easy to log off.

But I couldn't let that last remark about Alex slide.

DivaCee: You are going to hurt yourself with that reach.

MrtB: Frankly, I'm disappointed in your diminished standards.

Oh no. Not tonight, Satan.

DivaCee: Yeah . . . how dare I like someone who treats me with consideration and respect.

MrtB: Should I be offended that you are suggesting . . .

DivaCee: Yes. You should be offended, always. Can we move on now?

MrtB: I can if you will.

DivaCee: From this conversation? Gladly.

MrtB: Why are you up?

MrtB: Working on a vid or something?

I stopped, genuinely surprised that he remembered. I don't even remember when or why I had told Mauro about my little hobby. Probably because he'd had his photography and his guitar and everything else, and I'd had nothing. I'd expected him to make fun of it, but he'd actually taken me seriously. He'd given me feedback and even helped me upgrade my computer to a faster editing program.

DivaCee: I have NO idea why I ever told you about that. And no, I don't do that anymore.

I winced, grateful that he couldn't see my face. I didn't want him to have the satisfaction of knowing he'd hit my sorest spot of all.

MrtB: So there are TV couples out there not having their romance set to music? Love is dead.

DivaCee: Or . . . I found a better outlet for my passions.

Edwin's voice hissed in my ear for just a second, before I pushed it away. He'd ruined enough for me. He wasn't going to get to ruin tonight.

DivaCee: And can we maybe drop this?

MrtB: O . . . K. But can I at least say that I'm honored that I'm still the only person who knows your inner geek? Your secrets are safe with me.

DivaCee: . . . because you don't know any of them.

MrtB: False. I know about your romantic videos. (Love Hospital! Sorry, I'll drop it now.) I know about your passion for Jewish deli (and where's the loving musical tribute to THAT?). I know about your cousin, and how you'd rather be eaten by a shark than perform for her (but you don't want to give her the satisfaction of quitting). I know you don't really want to be talking to me right now, especially after tonight, but I'm just too damn entertaining.

He was right about one thing. I *didn't* really want to be talking to him.

But if I stopped now, he'd have the last word. And it would be him complimenting himself, and assuming I agreed.

DivaCee: 1) Videos are no more. 2) No shame around the pastrami, dude. 3) Quitting was never an option, quince or not. And the less we mention my cousin to people, the better. 4) You continue to have too high an opinion of yourself.

MrtB: Uh-huh. Yet here you are.

DivaCee: A slave to technology. And pleading the Fifth.

MrtB: . . . you mean like when you called 311 to report my party?

DivaCee: I plead all the amendments that would protect me right now.

MrtB: You can unclench. I don't hold it against you. Anymore, anyway. My See and Be Seen Party was certainly a crime against humanity, civilization, decency. To say nothing of the rumors of underaged debauchery. A twelve-year-old drinking and dancing—quelle horreur!

He was playing it off like a joke, but I'd heard about what had happened after the phone call. Oscar had sent Mauro to St. Timothy's Academy in upstate New York.

At the time, calling 311 on his party had felt like the right thing to do. I didn't think there would be any consequences beyond him getting grounded. But . . . damn, boarding school? It didn't matter how furious Mami and I could get with each other, she was my mother. She'd never *send me away*. For the first time, I felt a twinge of guilt in my stomach.

MrtB: My father, after losing his shit but before shipping me to parts unknown, told me to take this as a lesson that Hell hath no fury like a woman scorned.

DivaCee: I think you mean a woman who was doing her civic duty and alerting Miami's Finest about the dangers lurking in their streets?

MrtB: You don't feel a teensy bit of remorse? You brought a bazooka to a knife fight. We probably could have come to some sort of peace. If I'd stuck around, of course.

DivaCee: Fine. Thanks to Alex, I'm feeling generous this evening. I may have overreacted. A bit. Don't get me wrong, you treated me like utter shit, and deserved my wrath, and possibly community service, but you also deserved to remain local.

MrtB: So magnanimous. I can barely recognize the virago who haunted my teenage dreams.

I grinned unwillingly. It was definitely an improvement when he was virtual.

DivaCee: You are still a teenager. Barely.

MrtB: Then I guess the haunting should be present tense.

OK. Clearly time to cut this conversation off. Because nothing about us was present tense, except work.

DivaCee: And we've reached the end of the night.

MrtB: Aw, c'mon. This is the first conversation we've had since I got back that hasn't felt like war. Ironic, considering the evening.

DivaCee: Only because I'm not physically in the room with you. The Great Wall of Carmen. Good night.

MrtB: Fine. Night.

I was half asleep when my phone buzzed again.

MrtB: And Carmen? Challenge accepted. ☺

I didn't want to think about what that meant.

But talking about videos made me . . . want to make a vid. Before I could talk myself out of it, I opened my software.

I let myself forget everything, set up a timeline, and started dropping my favorite show clips and effects in.

Started to scroll through my music, looking for the perfect song to capture this almost perfect night.

And, like always, I felt like I'd come home.

———————

The next morning, I felt exactly like Cinderella must have the day after her ball. Desperate for some Bustelo and quiet time to think everything over—twice.

I'd need all the memories from last night to get me through

today. In just a few hours, I'd start my summer as a dancing monkey, performing in Ariana's honor.

I knew my diploma would be worth it in the end. It just didn't *feel* that way right now.

"I've been waiting for you all morning!" Mami exclaimed as soon as I slumped into the kitchen and pulled open the fridge. "La bella durmiente! Good morning, sleeping beauty!" She waved her cup at me. "I stopped at Palacio today and picked up your favorite. Café con leche la azúcar del café."

Tempting. Still, I made a point of turning my back to it and starting a new cup in the machine instead.

"You're still mad at me," she said, her voice flat. "I thought after '*Alex*'"—sighing in a bad imitation of me—"that we were good again."

"Just because I'm happy about something else doesn't mean I'm over any of this." I kept my face straight, but memories of last night were making the corners of my mouth creep upward. I couldn't stop it.

"Oh yeah? Look at you pretending to be pissed at me when I can see that whatever happened last night went WELL!" Mami laughed, then side-eyed me. "But it better not have gone as well as it might have gone, because you know I don't encourage that. Not for my only daughter, who should know better—"

I glanced meaningfully at the mandals in the hallway, and then raised my eyebrows at her. She tossed her head. "I am a grown-ass woman—"

"So do as you say, not as you do?"

She put up her chin like she was going to fight. Then laughed. "Exactly." Her face got serious. "And I don't only mean about men. Although maybe I'm finally a good example." She waved a wrist at me. A gold bracelet shimmered there. "From Enrique!" She sighed like she was imitating my feelings about Alex. Except she wasn't kidding. "He's so generous, Carmen . . . It's been so long since—" She stopped at the look I could feel on my face. This was becoming so familiar. Some guy was going to be the solution to all of our problems. Some guy was going to treat Mami the way Tío Victor treated Tía Celia. Some guy was going to make us all equals.

Except it never happened, and the thought that Mami might be keeping Enrique around to impress Tía Celia (when Enrique wasn't even THAT impressive, honestly) just pissed me off. Mami deserved better.

"Oh, Carmencita . . . I know you are mad about your cousin's quince, pero tú sabes que la familia es para siempre—"

Yeah. Always making you feel like shit. "I don't believe that." She looked shocked. "Sorry, Mami, but maybe my life is better without some people in it." Too bad they apparently were *all* back.

"And you think canceling a dinner and a few pictures is reason enough to decide that?"

It had meant more than that, and she knew it.

"Maybe not, but that doesn't mean I want to celebrate Ariana like everything is fine, like nothing happened at all!" Oye, she'd been back in my life for less than a week, and I was having the same conversations I'd always had about Ariana. *Carmen Maria, you are the oldest. You need to protect her. Forgive her. It's not her fault. She's your little prima hermana.*

"And let's not forget the things I've forgiven Celia for, in order to keep a relationship with my sister." Claro, of course. Quince number one. The founding story of the feud.

Mami's forgiveness depended so much on whether she had someone of her own. Just now she did, so history could be a charming backstory.

It never lasted.

"Maybe quinces between our two families aren't supposed to be happy occasions," I said instead.

Back up went the stubborn chin. "That's why Celia and I thought this was brilliant. It's fate. This quince will give you and Ariana plenty of time to get to know each other again, forgive each other. Right the wrongs. Make the two families into one."

I grumbled. "And then we all lived happily ever after. Yeah, right."

She slipped her arm around my waist. "You're a fairy-tale princess for the next few months. So make it happen."

The doorbell rang, saving me from having to answer and crush her dreams.

"Waverly to the rescue," I said, and swung the door open.

Except it wasn't my best friend standing there. It was Mauro.

"You aren't Waverly," I said, like a dumbass.

He raised his eyebrows at me. "Sorry to disappoint you. I think I heard that she was babysitting some . . . albinos or something? She's going to meet us there."

I shook my head. "Amoebas. She's at the lab." Waves's mother had managed to get her a three-times-a-week day job at the university to help her stand out among all the other premeds in September. She was so busy now that if we hadn't been Dreams together this summer, we probably wouldn't have much time together at all.

"Is she afraid they'll throw a wild party while she's gone?" He gave me a slow smile.

"Long as you're not there, I think they're safe." I could feel my own mouth tugging in response. Last night's chat had gone a long way to making things feel a little bit more normal between us.

Mami smothered a laugh. Shit. I'd forgotten she was standing right there.

Mauro looked up at her and I could tell the moment he slid into Nice Boy mode. "Buenas. Carmen didn't mention a sister."

I groaned. The oldest, cheesiest line in the book.

Mami obviously loved that book, though. "Carmen, you never told me about your friend," she purred, looking Mauro up and down.

"Mauro, Mami. Mami, Mauro. Let's go."

Except then she frowned. "Mauro?"

And then I waited, because I'd told Mami about Mauro. Not a lot (Ariana had been my confidante back then), but enough. If she remembered, I'd have to walk to Ariana's because Mauro would be ashes on the floor.

But Mauro was going to get away with it and live another undeserving day, because all she did was giggle and hold out her hand, which he kissed like a quince chambelán.

I hope that when I get older, I retain my ability to see bullshit when it's coming my way. Even when the carrier is somebody's idea of an attractive man.

"OK, bye!"

She held me back. "Carmencita," she whispered. "Remember everything I said."

"Quinces are bad luck and it's my job to reverse the spell. Got it."

"Seriously, mi amor—just . . . be open, OK? In your heart, not your mouth."

I rolled my eyes. "It's a party. Just work."

"You know it's more than that."

"If I think like that, I'll never do it."

Mami looked at me another second.

"And I want to hear more about this one. He looks . . . interesting."

I shut the door before she said anything else.

# Nine

MAURO SLUNG HIS ARM over my seat as he reversed the car and got out of the parking space. I held myself still until he moved.

"You know, we don't have to do this. I can put on the head, take my rightful place as the king of the jungle, and bring home the fruits of the hunt," he said.

"We're dancing, not hunting. And didn't you tell me once that you faint at the sight of blood?"

"The other animals don't have to know that."

I rolled my eyes. My stomach dipped uncomfortably as we started going down the familiar road to Ariana's house.

Except that I had no idea what would be familiar once I got there. It had been three and a half years.

As though he'd read my mind, Mauro said, "People can change in almost four years, you know. I'm sure they have. I mean, you have."

"I haven't really changed."

"You have, you know. I mean, just on a superficial level, you are even more gorgeous now. Objectively." He kept his green eyes carefully on the road, so I couldn't read his expression.

I rolled my eyes. "I am not Mami. I cannot be flattered into submission."

He glanced over. "What? You don't believe me?"

"It's just . . . 'ooh, you're more gorgeous.' Seriously? I mean, when did you get so . . . generic?"

He looked offended. "I am *not* generic."

"Well then, I'm not a blow-up doll, you know? Telling me the same empty things every guy tells every single girl in the world isn't going to impress me. You should remember that," I said, crossing my arms over my chest, "for, like, whoever you date next."

"O . . . K?"

I clenched my hands. "It's not my fault you AND my cousin are both suddenly back in my life. Believe me, it's not like I've spent the last three and a half years thinking about any of this!"

We reached a stoplight and Mauro held up his hands. "I didn't say you had. But, like, people *do* change, Carmen. You can't expect the worst from me—and from everyone you know—forever. I mean, would you want us to do the same with you?"

"I'm NOT saying—" But then I stopped because, yeah, I was. I let out a breath. "I think people talk big about changing and being different, but when you push just a little bit, they go right back to who they always were."

He shuddered. "That's a scary thought. No growth. No surprises. Just trapped in the feelings we'd always had. Forever."

". . . and I think I'm done with the tour of your head, thanks."

He laughed. "I wouldn't wish being in my head on anyone. Not even you."

"I thought you said people could change."

"I have changed. My brain has found new and alarming ways to torture me." He gave me a sidelong glance. "You, for instance."

"Me?"

"Let's just say you've managed to bleed back into my brain alarmingly quickly." Anyone else saying something like that, you'd think, *oh, kind of sweet, maybe?* Mauro just sounded pissed off.

"You make me sound like a disease," I said sarcastically.

He closed his eyes for a second, opening them again just before the light turned green. "Look, I DON'T know you. I'm admitting it. I never know what's going to come out of your mouth. Except it's never what I expect. Even this conversation . . . I'll be thinking about it later, wondering what I could have said or done differently. That's how it *always* was. I was *always* trying to impress you because I found you so . . . impressive. And I hated it. I mean . . . that's part of what happened between us. I could never win with you. Not ever." He shut his mouth suddenly, like he'd gone a lot farther than he'd planned.

"Impressive," I repeated.

I mean, I wasn't Mami. I wasn't going to just believe something because it flattered me. Believing something at face value was a bad sign. I forced myself to remember the things he'd done that contradicted what he was saying. The things I'd seen and overheard at his party. "That's interesting, because the way I remember it—"

"How about instead of remembering, you listen to what I'm actually saying right now." He pulled into a parking spot and turned toward me, his face surprisingly serious. And then I was the one to look away.

"People say a lot of things. You of all people know that. What matters is what people do, and what they have done, and that's how you know what to expect," I said.

I fidgeted with the seatbelt. The air in the car felt heavy, like it was pressing me in the wrong direction. I rolled the window down.

"You know, Buddha said that you can change ten thousand years of darkness by lighting a candle," Mauro pointed out.

I looked outside. Ariana's house—we'd arrived.

"Yeah, well." I got out of the car and leaned into the window. "Buddha never met the Garces family."

———————

I learned to swim in that pool. Had my first kiss under the big palm by that fence. Staged Barbie fashion shows with Ariana on that big glass table. Sat reading while Abuelo and Abuela listened to their *Arte Religiosa* radio show, my leg wiggling to the rhythm of the words. I'd doodled the names of my crushes in my notebooks there. The air still smelled like the cedar mulch my tío liked.

My feet still knew exactly where the salmon pavers were, and avoided the boring gray ones.

Tío Victor turned around and right away started nagging my tía about the time. "What the hell took you so . . ." Then he saw me. ". . . long?" Tía Celia gestured to me, and there was something in her face that wasn't happiness. She watched my tío closely as he ran over to me, picked me up, and spun me around. "Carmencita Maria, no lo creo! I don't believe it! Where the hell have you been? Is your mami here?"

OK. Why were these people pretending that they HADN'T cut us out of their lives when I was fifteen?

I mean, I knew that part wasn't Tío Victor's fault. He'd always had to be careful, which is what happens when you date one sister and marry the other. He knew he always, always had to be on one side. Which usually wasn't the one I was standing on. But still, it wasn't as though not seeing him had been my choice.

"So!" He clapped his hands together. "Ariana called you? That's wonderful, mija!" Whatever Tía Celia and Mami had cooked up, he hadn't been in on it.

"Um, not exactly?" I looked at Simone, who was busy setting up the music player and wasn't looking at us. "I work with Simone. I work for Dreams Come True."

His smile faded. "But . . . work?" He looked at my tía, who

quickly said, "It's not exactly *working*, Victor—"

"But she said—"

My older cousin Cesar loped up to me then, while his parents argued. "Sup, Carmencita." He grinned, and then gave me a hug, slapping my back. "It's good to see you, loca." I'd missed my cousin, who I hadn't spent any real time with since the falling out three and a half years ago (except a few awkward online chats that had faded from memory quickly). My beef had never been with him, but just like Tío Victor, he'd chosen the easiest way. He'd chosen to follow Tía Celia and Ariana right out of my life.

Still. It was impossible to be angry at Cesar, so I didn't even try.

Ariana flew in then, already apologizing, moving so fast her hair looked like it was caught in a breeze. "I'm sorry, I'm sorry . . . practice ran so late and then we got stuck in traffic . . . I'm ready to get started, promise . . ."

And then another voice. One I *definitely* didn't expect to hear at my tía and tío's house. "Hey, Ari . . . there's no room in your driveway so I parked down the street."

"Oh my God," Mauro muttered. He placed a hand over his mouth when he saw who it was.

Because it was Alex.

Alex Sharma.

From such dates as *just last night*.

At Ariana's quince practice.

Ten

A MILLION QUESTIONS BUZZED around me like mosquitoes. First among them, *Why the hell is Alex Sharma at my cousin's quinceañera practice?*

After that, ones like:

What had last night meant?

What did *this* mean?

Did anything in the world mean anything anymore?

My breath came in shallow pants. Alex looked as surprised as I did, eyes darting between me and Ariana, probably wondering how the hell he'd managed to land in the same quince that I was working.

It would've been hilarious if the truth of it wasn't so fucking tragic.

Had Alex ever mentioned knowing Ariana? I felt pretty certain I would have remembered that.

Sometime in the chaos, Waverly had come in. She stood

next to me in solidarity, trying not to stare at Alex. I could relate.

It took me a second to realize that the small clutch of people standing around the yard were the whole corte. It must have hurt Tía Celia that the only people here who weren't Dreams were Olivia, Gus, Alex, and her son, Cesar. The Dreams were the majority. And even with us, we were still short one guy. Ariana's corte was basically just a bunch of paid performers who couldn't have picked the quinceañera out of a lineup.

Well, except for me. And possibly Mauro.

Who kept glancing at me, and then at Alex, like we were a calculus problem he couldn't understand.

My God. I couldn't believe this! Without meaning to, I'd just given Mauro the ultimate way to torture me all summer long. All he had to do was pretend to feel sorry for me.

It was just one date, I told myself.

But I'd told Mauro how I felt. He'd seen me and Alex together.

And now Alex was in *my cousin's corte*.

I glanced at my tía and tío. This was insane. *History was repeating itself.*

My inner Mami was going crazy, pointing at Alex and waving her finger around.

No! I had to ignore her. The answer was obvious—Alex had become friends with Ariana somewhere along the way and was doing her a favor. His presence didn't mean anything more than that. He was just in the corte. He didn't have to be her personal chambelán or anything. He'd even mentioned being in a quinceañera party for a friend turning sixteen. And he hadn't sounded like it meant anything special to him.

Meanwhile, Ariana was being open and friendly with everyone, including the other Dreams. She was the perfect hostess, a mini Celia.

If I'd been a mini Mami, I'd be throwing back a glass of something strong right about now.

Forget that. Tonight had an explanation, and as soon as Alex and I had a chance to talk, I'd hear it.

This didn't need to be as bad as it looked.

It didn't.

Simone cleared her throat and said, "Well, um . . . welcome, everyone! I am Simone Travis, owner of Dreams Come True, and my team and I will be assisting with the party, as well as, um, performing. Mrs. Garces invited us to come and perform before your first rehearsal, just to provide a taste of what she can expect from us. Of course, Ariana and Alex will be the ones doing the traditional court dances, and I'll be helping you with those as well. Anything we can do to make this the best experience possible, just let me know . . ." Her voice trailed off.

I'd been to a million of these parties. Half the time the chambelanes aren't boyfriends. They're family friends or long-lost cousins fresh off the boat or guys your mami dug up through the grapevine. It doesn't have to mean anything.

Still, the boy I was crazy about was going to spend all summer helping my cousin get ready for her ball, and I was going to play the entertainment.

There was probably a word that described that level of awkward. But I didn't know it. In either English or Spanish.

"Well, everyone, maybe we should start by introducing ourselves? I'm Simone Travis, which I already said." Then Simone pointed at me. "And this is Carmen Aguilar, my assistant and all-around right-hand woman. If you can't get to me, you'll have to go through her." Polite laughter. Tía Celia looked satisfied, like Simone had just confirmed my indentured servitude, had made clear that I was the help. I couldn't quite trust my voice, so I just waved at the group. I had planned to tell Simone about Ariana being my cousin, but this practice came up so fast . . . and I hadn't seen any damn reason to tell Alex at all.

Then Simone clapped. "So, now the star of the show—the birthday girl in question!"

Ariana blinked at her and scanned the rest of us, her eyes carefully not meeting mine.

"I'm Ariana. Um," she said, glancing again at Simone, who nodded in encouragement. "I know it's called my quinceañera party, but I'll be sixteen years old. Thanks for being here." Weird. She seemed almost . . . shy? She leaned into Alex. I could feel something tighten in my neck.

"What can I say?" Tía Celia said, with a syrupy look at Ariana. "I needed her to wait the extra year—just wasn't ready to see my little girl become a woman!"

My own modest quinceañera would have happened when I was fifteen. Because clearly by then, no one saw me as an innocent little girl.

After a second, Alex cleared his throat. "Uh, and I'm Alex. I'm . . . uh, seventeen, and I'm the birthday girl's date for the evening, and I guess for the next three months?" He tilted his head toward Ariana in a way that maybe someone else could have found adorable. Ariana gave him a glance and a flirty smile. My stomach twisted into a pretzel.

So, he *was* her chambelán. And not in name only. I dug my nails into my palms. Little red half-moons bloomed on them.

A tall blonde shook out her hair and said in a low voice, "I'm Olivia. I'm a dama. The MAIN dama. I go to school with Ariana." She looked at me and opened her mouth like she wanted to say something else, then shut it again.

Olivia. I vaguely remembered her. She hadn't been blond the last time I'd seen her.

Then someone who had changed so much that I actually HADN'T recognized him spoke.

"I'm Gustavo. Gus. I'm another chambelán." He looked embarrassed.

Gus was a friend of the family—and he was always underfoot. A four-eyed, pudgy loudmouth who never went anywhere without a Matchbox car, who could be persuaded to cause a distraction while the rest of us ran from whatever trouble we'd recently caused.

The only thing that the Gus I remembered had in common with this one was the name.

Pudgy Gus now had a swimmer's body, eyes as blue as the ocean (now visible thanks to . . . contacts, probably), and thick, wavy black hair with a little streak of white (which, come to think of it, had been there since he was born).

Why couldn't I just run up and hug him? I *knew* him.

For whatever reason, I felt nailed to the floor. The tension was so thick, I could cut it with a knife.

The idea of turning tail, taking the GED test, and being done with all of this made a play for my brain.

But then Ariana and the rest of the family would have yet another reason to look down on me and Mami. I wouldn't give in.

My cousin Cesar took center stage, the way he always does. "Hi. I'm Cesar. I'm her brother," he said, pointing at Ariana, who rolled her eyes. "And HER cousin." Then he pointed at me.

Alex turned with Cesar's finger and froze, staring at me while the last piece of realization clicked into place in his brain. The rest of the Dreams kind of stared for a beat. Simone's eyes widened like she was debating whether it made sense for her to be utterly furious with me. Guilt pricked me, because this information didn't have to be a big deal, but I'd turned it into a reality show reveal. I'd just been trying *so hard* to get out of this whole situation . . .

Waverly was right. By not telling everyone at the beginning, I'd been the one to make it weird.

I felt my cheeks go super hot. The moment seemed to stretch into infinity. Then when I couldn't take it a second longer—

"And, uh, I'm Mauro. I'm a Dream for the summer. You can see my work at your local kids' party, the Bay, or a furry convention." People actually laughed. Except for Ariana, whose eyes flew to mine. Her own little shock. Mauro. She remembered.

Tía Celia clapped her hands and there was silence again. "And . . . that's it for introductions!"

"I'm not having a full court," Ariana confessed. "I couldn't come up with *that* many people." Her voice wouldn't have sounded out of place chatting with small woodland creatures.

Jessica nudged me. "A full court? What does she mean?"

"Traditionally, it's seven guys and seven girls. Some people go all crazy and actually have fourteen on each side, and then the fifteenth couple is the quince and her date."

"Wow." Jessica shook her head. "I've never been so happy to be white."

Waverly poked her. "That sounds racist, especially paired with your translucent skin."

Jessica poked her back. "That's not racist; it's goth. Idiot."

I shushed them both, especially since Simone was looking right at me. Time to start being a right-hand woman.

"Well! That's everyone, I think!" Simone said. "Let me start by showing you all a little of the routine." She glanced at Tía Celia. Then she grabbed Matt and nodded at Mauro, who turned on the sound system. We got into position. I closed my eyes and pretended we were back at practice. I hated that I was nervous, but this felt like a combination of a final exam and waiting to be picked for a team in gym class.

Mauro tipped my chin up. "Hey, just look at me. All right?"

His eyes pierced through mine for a second. I blinked back the tears that were for some reason prickling at the corners. "OK," I told him.

Mauro got us into the beginning of the dance, which started with a tight embrace. He may have made it tighter. I tried to put a little daylight between us, but Mauro didn't let go.

He counted us off, and then, without the music, we started, moving into the salsa that started the number.

I was still pissed about Alex being here, so I put a little sparkle into my dance, knowing that it would piss Ariana off that she couldn't move like me. I forced myself to let go of my issues with Mauro and just dance like he was all I'd ever wanted. And Mauro actually kept up, mostly. Waltz, salsa, reggaetón. He must have practiced—probably with Simone. The robot was gone.

I caught a glimpse of Alex. Damn, if Ariana had any sense, maybe she'd wonder why her chambelán was looking at me like I was cheating on him.

Wait.

What if this stupid quince actually brought Alex and me officially together? Oh man. That would be the most perfect karma *ever*. Not only would it make up for the disaster of my own quince, it would avenge the quince harm done to Mami, too!

Cosmic fairness!

Mauro and I were still not totally in sync. We couldn't quite relax into the moves—it was like my body was braced for him to hold me a little too hard or to step on my foot or something. And you can't dance well with someone if you feel like you don't trust them.

He spun me off into the individual part of the dance. Ariana stood, her arms crossed tight. But I saw Alex relax a little. Until I ran to Mauro and he lifted me high into the air!

I made it back to the ground without bruises.

And Alex looked like he was going to puke.

We went into our final pose, my head tilted up a little bit. Mauro's eyes drifted over my face, and I didn't want to think too much about what he saw there.

I blinked when the group started clapping. For a second, I'd almost forgotten where I was.

To say this was not the friendliest crowd was not an understatement. And at least one of the people here knew my history with Mauro. Hold on. Could Ariana find a way to use that against me? I didn't know.

Somehow, I got through the whole routine with only a few minor stumbles. Gus and Olivia looked mostly impressed. And Simone looked ready to levitate. "That's what we'll be performing at the party. Of course, by then it'll be totally flawless. We'll make sure jaws drop after every dance at this quince!"

Tía Celia clapped twice and said, "After all that, I think some snacks are in order! I'll bring them right out!" She nodded at Ariana. "Can you help me?" Then she went in through the patio door without waiting. Ariana glanced up at Alex and gave him an uncertain smile, then followed Tía Celia into the house. And for the first time, Alex was alone.

Looking right at me and *not* smiling.

Mauro glanced at him, and then at me. "Everything OK?" Even the damn cleft in his chin looked like it was gloating.

How could he ask me that? He damn well knew everything was not OK.

"Fine. Just need to use the bathroom."

The Dreams, Gus, and Olivia were all in line for the bathroom closest to the backyard. But I knew how to find the one in the house. Dubious perk.

I closed the screen door softly behind me and turned toward the bathroom in the hall.

But then I heard Ariana say, "I know I agreed to do this. But . . . I don't want her here. Why do I need to share my night with her at all?"

I held my breath.

"Ariana Victoria, you've been blessed with a lot of things in this life, and part of coming of age is learning to share with people who have less than you." Tía Celia gave a heavy sigh.

Wait a second. If anyone was sharing anything here, it was me!

"But it's my party—and everyone will be looking at Carmen! Like always!"

Typical Ariana. Must have been novel for her to compare herself with me and have me be the winner for once. Even if I couldn't quite balance myself on Mauro's hands during the backbend yet.

But I couldn't savor my victory, because I was still stuck here. With Ariana. And Alex.

"And Cesar hasn't even picked a dama and—"

"You know what the solution is for all this, Ariana. It works out perfectly," Tía Celia said.

"No, Mami! That was never the deal. I agreed to Carmen PERFORMING . . . and now I'm even second-guessing that!"

I made sure to stay ducked behind the door, but I could see Tía Celia leaning forward. "Mira. You are right. Carmen and her Dreams WILL be the center of attention at your quince . . . unless you *all* do that dance. Perform together, and there will be no doubt who the star of the night is. And mija, it's sweeter to shine bright around certain people."

That was some straight Cinderella stepmother shit right there.

"But I said NO to her being a dama—" Ariana whined again.

Hold up. Tía Celia wanted Ariana to invite me to be in her corte? My stomach must have churned loudly enough to make a noise because suddenly Tía Celia looked up and right at me.

Ariana looked at the floor like she wanted to fall through it, but Tía Celia didn't even have the grace to look embarrassed. But then again, why should she? I was just the help here, right? And I was the one eavesdropping.

"Oh, Carmen. You all did such a wonderful job! Reminded me of Mirella and me, back in the day." She smiled.

I didn't smile back.

"In fact, it gave me a brilliant idea. Could you please send Simone in here when you get a chance?"

Mm-hmm. Like the help, I'd been dismissed.

The corte was sitting on the ground—as though they were the ones who had just done a five-minute dance routine in ninety-degree heat. The ones I knew, Olivia and Gus, kept sneaking looks at me. I planted myself next to the resting Dreams.

Waverly started in right away. "So, does Ariana know that Alex—"

I shook my head. She gave me a low whistle. "Awkward."

Exactly.

"I have a feeling this quince is about to get a whole lot weirder," I said, rubbing my temples to fight off a sudden headache.

Jessica made a face. "I don't like the sound of that."

Ari looked embarrassed as she and Tía Celia came back out, but she was the only one. Tía Celia looked as smug as a cat with a caldero full of cream and Simone looked thrilled.

Tía Celia waited until she had the crowd's attention. "I think we can all agree that the performance was amazing!" She started to clap, loud and showy, until the corte joined in half-heartedly.

"And I realized . . . we have a tiny, incomplete corte, and an AMAZING dance group . . . why not put them TOGETHER? You can *all* perform an amazing baile sorpresa and all the other dances, too."

Tía Celia probably hoped for a little more enthusiasm than the total silence she got. But she barreled forward. "Simone will teach you all this dance and you can fill out the corte—"

Ariana looked up then. "Actually, Simone . . . I think maybe we could just stick to the, you know, traditional dances, and call it good." The court was nodding. I could see why these were all Ariana's people.

I was surprised when Tío Victor, of all people, was the one who interjected.

"Ariana, we booked *three months* of rehearsals." He smiled at Simone. "In advance. I'm sure Simone will choreograph the perfect dance for you all to learn in that time."

I almost snorted. Tío wasn't hurting for money, but that didn't mean he wanted to see it wasted, either.

"Yes!" Simone gave everyone a tight smile. "Definitely! We'll have you all whipped into shape in exactly the time we allotted! With the Dreams crew's help, you all can do it! In fact, why don't we start right now?"

My boss definitely had a way of looking at the bright side. Stony eyes stared back at her. Dreams and corte, united in disbelief.

"Yeah," Alex said, giving me a quick look. "I think we can probably learn it. C'mon, guys! Think of the views! This party will totally go viral." He did a little step spin and almost fell over on the grass, which was probably on purpose. Typical Alex, trying to put everyone at ease. The girls giggled, and the guys groaned.

"Let's break up into small groups! I'll put you each with one of my cast members, and they'll take you through the choreography." Simone was already pointing us to different corners of the yard.

Which is how I ended up stuck with Ariana, Alex, Olivia, and Gus.

Fabulous.

I took a deep breath and said, "Um, so should we just start breaking it down into pieces or what?"

Ariana said, "Talk your boss into something simpler." It was the first thing she'd said to me, practically, since I'd gotten here. An order.

"Not likely. She put a lot of work into this dance, and really, it's not THAT hard. Didn't you know the kind of stuff she does?"

She shrugged. "No offense, but it's not like I wanted to hire you. I mean, *Dreams Come True*?"

Alex said, "Um . . . can we just go over a few of the steps?"

I wasn't sure if I could get that close to Alex in front of everyone without showing every feeling on my face. And there were people who didn't need to see any of them.

But it would look strange to say no.

So I nodded and took his hand. I could feel that mine was slick with sweat. I wished there was a way that I could wipe it on my shorts without looking weird. Then I decided to just go for it. I wiped off my hands. Alex kind of curled his lip in disgust.

Kill me now.

We got into position, and I could see Ariana over his shoulder. She was watching us closely, her lips pressed flat like she had to hold some words back.

She knew something was up. She had to.

And a part of me was glad. Because let her see that I wasn't anybody's charity case. And that I wasn't going to be the only one who was going to suffer through a whole summer's worth of practices.

Ugh. *Relax, Carmen. This is temporary.* I mean, eventually we all die, right?

Looking into Alex's eyes was a mistake. Especially since he wasn't exactly trying to hide what was between us, either.

Luckily, once we got moving, I had to concentrate on guiding us through the steps, slowly and then faster.

Dancing with Alex was completely different from dancing with Mauro. Every step felt fluid, connected, like we were sharing a story that we couldn't quite put into words. And my whole self wanted to be there.

Toward the end of the dance, when I was bent backward, I could see Mauro watching us. He looked about as happy as Ariana. Probably because Alex was getting the steps down a hell of a lot faster than he had. Even his lift was more confident.

We finished the dance to silence, broken only by our own hard breaths. Ariana came toward us and tucked her hand through the crook of Alex's arm. Claiming him.

Gus was already eyeing me. "I really think I've got it. I just need to maybe try it with you. Tú sabes, muscle memory. That's what my baseball coach says."

"Ay, Gus, stop sliming all over Carmen," Ari burst out. Then she looked at me, and almost smiled.

It felt like an olive branch, and for a second, I wanted to take it. But then Alex leaned over and whispered something in her ear, making her giggle.

"Let's just start at the beginning." My voice sounded rough even to my ears. "Partner up."

About an hour later, I leaned against the big palm tree by the fence and drained a bottle of water. I worked my finger into one of the fence planks, searching for the spot where I'd carved my initials.

Yup. Still there.

Suddenly, a shadow blocked the sun. Ariana loomed over me, a tight, uncertain smile on her face. "Can we talk?"

I don't know. Can we? The thought came right to my mouth, but I stifled it and nodded. "Talk."

She twisted her hands behind her back, the way she always did when she was uncomfortable.

"Um . . . I just wanted you to know that I'm not going to tell anyone about Mauro. I can imagine how hard this is for you." Oh, could she? She waited a second for, what, a confession? Then started again: "Because I know Mami would absolutely freak out and, like, demand that Simone fire him or something . . . if she knew."

I shrugged, giving her nothing. "OK."

"But at the same time, if you *want* me to do you the favor and tell everybody, I guess I can do that, too. Consider it my down payment on a happy quince."

The thing I most wanted to happen from the last person I wanted to make it happen. "And why exactly would I want that?" A *down payment* for Ariana's happy quince? Fuck that noise.

She looked at me like I was exceptionally dense. "Uh,

because of everything that happened to me around *your* quince."

"Happened to *you*?"

"Well, yeah . . . I mean, I shouldn't have even been at that party . . . Something horrible could have happened! I was scared! I was there to help *you* out, and you left me alone!"

"Except you never actually helped. And you didn't exactly look terrified in those shots all over your socials," I pointed out. Reasonably.

"I was too dumb to be scared back then."

"Finally, we agree on something."

She huffed an annoyed breath. "Is this the way it's going to be this whole summer? You being a bitch to me and me just having to suck it up because Mami and Tía Mira want this so badly?"

I put on a deeply concerned face. "I know! How dare Tía Celia give you this huge party and a chance to stick it to me for three months?! You are such a victim here . . . just like you were four years ago when Tía Celia canceled my dinner and everything."

"You were more upset about everything that happened with Mauro than you were about the dinner," she said quietly.

I stood up. "Wow. I'm glad I have you back in my life to explain how I feel about things!"

"I'm just saying . . . you screwed up your own quince, so don't for a second think I won't be watching that you don't screw up mine. You and that bad luck charm of a partner.

Although at least Mami already covered the deposit on *my* pictures."

"Everyone ready to get back to work?" Simone. A good reminder that this was just that, and only that. Work.

"You know," I said to her as I started to walk away, "you and Mauro will probably really get along. He likes to blame everybody else for his mistakes, too."

Eleven

BACK IN MY ROOM, I lay on my bed, holding my empty diploma cover in my hands. Tracing the fake gold lettering and tilting it in the light. Regal red fake leather, heavy with fake accomplishment.

It all looked so legitimate. As long as you didn't look inside.

My stomach was tangled up in knots. Screw Ariana and her cursed party. Screw her somehow worming her way into Alex's life.

The only messages I'd gotten since we got back were from Waverly.

CatchTheWave: Anything?

DivaCee: Nope. ☹

CatchTheWave: Are you going to text him?

DivaCee: I . . . don't know. ☹

CatchTheWave: If you don't stop sending me sad

faces, I'm going to go over there and kick whatever ass you didn't dance off.

In spite of myself, I grinned.

Then my phone rang. Waverly—to commence the ass kicking, no doubt.

"Hi, Carmen. It's um . . . me." Not Waverly. Alex. In the car again. "Can you talk?"

"Can *you*?" I blurted out.

"Yeah, why else would I call?"

"Oh yeah. True."

Silence.

"Anyway. We need to talk. Can you meet me by the gazebo in about twenty minutes?" Not exactly the same invitation I'd recently accepted.

"Yeah . . . sure. Bye."

Ariana was entangled with all of it now, and I didn't want her there. Hell, I didn't want her anywhere, and suddenly she was everywhere.

And I couldn't edit her out.

––––––––

The gazebo wasn't far, but it was pretty late. I'd hoped to borrow the car, but Mami had just left with Enrique. (Question to remember for later: Why didn't *his* ass have a car?) So I was walking.

The closer I got to the gazebo, the faster my feet moved,

the faster my pulse beat. The easier it was to push everything else—Mami and Tía Celia, Ariana, Mauro, the quince—out of my mind. Mami's voice in my mind: *Mira, que estás desesperada!* I *was* desperate, damn it. Desperate to get on with it already.

Good things supposedly come to those who wait, and oh, I had waited for the past year. Endless frogs kissed. I was ready for the prince!

I could see him standing there, shadowed against the peekaboo moon, spotlighted and then disappearing.

And yeah, I've seen the movies. Wasn't he supposed to meet me halfway? But he stood frozen.

So he was nervous. That was OK. He's a freezer. I'm a mover. That's one of the reasons why we work. Will work.

Finally face-to-face. There were so many things I wanted to say and wanted to hear. More than the silence around us, anyway.

I got closer to him, watching his face, waiting for the moment when his expression said, *Too much.* And wondering if I knew him well enough to know when that would be.

"Hey," I said softly.

"Hey." The breeze picked up, whipping his dark hair into his eyes. He was still very carefully keeping a little bit away from me.

This *definitely* didn't feel like last night.

"I could have come to get you." He dug his hands into his pockets.

"Walking was OK." I wondered how long we'd discuss transportation.

"So . . . you and Ariana." He looked at me. "Why didn't you say anything?"

"I had no idea that you even knew her," I told him.

He frowned. "Yeah, well, I do."

I took both his hands in mine and tried not to notice how chilly they were. "My cousin and I are not friends. We're not close, we're not anything, which is why you didn't know about me potentially working her party. Because it's just a job."

"Except . . ." He looked away. "She asked me to do this for her. To be her date for this party. This is a big deal."

And then I saw it. A twist of his mouth, a guilty look he blinked away.

He liked her.

"Why did you want to see me today, Alex?" Thunder rumbled a warning in the distance.

He sighed hard. "Believe it or not, it's not about Ariana. I mean, yeah, we're friends, and I think you should give her a chance because—"

"Because she's obviously so willing to give me one?"

"She's a good person," he said.

If my eyes had rolled any harder, I'd have gotten a calambre.

"OK, so . . . good. You've put in your pitch for my saintly cousin. Can I go now?"

"No. I mean—like I said, this isn't about your cousin. It's about your new partner."

That tore a laugh out of me. "Mauro?"

"Yeah. At Dadeland, I saw the way he acted like he owned you. Just . . . be careful. I can tell what kind of guy he is. You are too good for him."

"That's it? That's why you asked me to come here? To give me a warning to be careful of Mauro?"

The idiot actually had the nerve to look confused. "What else did you think?"

I was blind. With anger, with disappointment, and with the fact that he was standing in front of me, feeling none of it.

"Um, *last night*?"

He flushed. "Last night was . . ."

Before he could finish, I put my lips on his, just for a second. The musky scent he always wore mixed with the rain-heavy breeze and overwhelmed me.

He froze. He did not kiss me back.

Calling myself every single kind of idiot, I pulled away. "Oh my God. OH. MY. GOD. I truly cannot believe that I did—"

"I'm sorry . . ." He tugged my chin up gently, so that I was looking at him again. "You are beautiful, Carmen. This could have been fun. I just think with Ariana and you . . . it would be awkward."

Someone should tell him that it had worked out just fine for Tío Victor.

I stood up very straight. "So you said what you had to say. You choose her. Fine."

He smiled sadly. "Carmen, I've spent years watching you with guys. None of them ever stick around long enough to matter. Besides, your cousin? That's family. That's forever. You don't want to mess with that."

I shook my head. "No, this is all bullshit. These are all excuses. Warning me about Mauro? Kumbaya-ing about Ariana? Please. Just admit you don't want to be with me when you can have my cousin instead!"

He looked like I'd slapped him. But he didn't say I was wrong.

He took a step toward me. "Let me drive you home. I wanna stay your friend, Carmen."

The dreaded F-word. Friends.

I didn't have a comeback; I couldn't strut away with swagger. It was like True Carmen was tied up in a basement somewhere.

He took my wrist. "I never meant to hurt you . . ."

"Then don't," I said softly, hating myself even as the pitiful words came out of my mouth.

But, of course, he already had.

"If you want me to drop out of the party, I will."

"Fine," I said, shoving my phone into his hand. "Call her right now and tell her that. I'll wait."

He stared down at the phone, but he didn't look like he was going to call anybody.

I grabbed it back. "Figures." I spat the word at him as he watched me walk away.

 *Twelve*

AND, OF COURSE, THE Miami sky chose *that* moment to dump itself all over me. The clouds that had been streaking past us the whole night came together in one huge thunder burst and sheets of rain smothered me as I ran away.

My feet kept time with my racing heart, but I couldn't outrun the sick feeling in my gut. I'd thrown myself at him. I'd leaped, thinking I'd be caught. But I'd fallen flat on my face.

He could say whatever he wanted—that it was about Ariana, Mauro, or my long list of guys.

Ben in tenth grade until Valentine's Day.

Carlos before junior prom.

Jose for two weeks at the beginning of soccer season.

Louie at that ill-fated bonfire. (And he gave me mono.)

And the others. After Mauro, exactly all of them had mattered the same. Which was not at all. Not until Alex.

I thought he'd understood. I was wrong.

I got a calambre in my leg and a stitch in my side at the same time and sat down hard on the concrete sidewalk. Panting, furious with myself, with Alex, with the universe. I wished I could sit there like that forever, covered by the waves of rain that seemed like they would never stop.

Until headlights swiped over me and stilled.

"Carmen? What the hell? Are you OK?"

I looked up.

I didn't want to be rescued. And for damn sure not by Mauro.

He leaned out of his car window. "Hey, get in the car."

I shook my head. He turned on his hazards and got out of the car, ducking a bit when the rain crashed onto his head.

"Are you hurt?" He held out his hand to pull me up.

A car trailed its horn past him, annoyed, as it went around. Mauro ignored it, his eyes looking panicked.

"Carmen?"

Another car honked. He wasn't going to leave, so I got up and went to the car.

"Just drive." I closed the door and leaned my wet head against the window, the heat of my breath blurring against the coolness of the AC.

And in a very un-Mauro-like move, he said nothing. Just started the car and drove away. We were like that for about a block, and then he pulled into a parking spot and killed the engine.

I expected him to make a smart-assed remark, but instead he just pulled me into his arms.

I didn't want to be there, but . . . I didn't make any moves to leave. We breathed in time for a second.

"I'm sorry. I'm getting water all over your car," I muttered.

"Not really high on my list of worries right now, but thanks." He shifted me a little bit, so that I could see his face. "What happened?"

"It's nothing."

"Because you always go for a run in a rainstorm and then sit on the ground and cry?"

"It wasn't raining when I left the house!" I pulled myself away. "And I wasn't crying!" He was close enough to see the truth on my face, and that was a problem.

"Carmen, come on. Pretend that nothing ever happened between us and talk to me. You know you want to." He leaned forward. Open. Ready to take whatever burden I was ready to hand him.

"You know I wouldn't dump all over a stranger."

He considered this. "OK, point taken. Pretend I'm a guy in your psychology class, and we've been paired on a project together . . . about, um, the Stroop test."

I closed my eyes for a second, remembering Mauro's impassioned argument about the Stroop test in the psychology class we'd been in together. We'd seen the word "red" written in the color green and shouted out "GREEN." Then he'd used me as an example of someone you'd call the wrong name, because you didn't quite know what you were seeing.

That was the first time I'd followed him to the darkroom.

"Can we just . . . drive?"

He shrugged and started the car, pulling into the deserted street.

We listened to music without saying anything. The music sounded familiar and not. And then it ended, and it was back to the silence.

"What was that?" I asked, just to fill the dead air.

"Music," he said in his usual way, but then glanced at me. "What did you think?"

"It was OK. Good, even."

He sighed. "That was my last project in school this year. My final."

"*You* made that? Wow, then I think it was REALLY good."

"No, it wasn't. You were right. It was just OK. That was part of the problem. Everybody at Berklee is good. Most of them are great. OK doesn't cut it."

"But . . . I thought that was OK for a professional. For a student, it's great."

"There are no students at Berklee. Just pre-professionals."

"Then it sounds like your kind of place," I said without thinking. He smirked.

"I have been a little . . . self-assured. I'm beginning to see the value of being a neophyte. That means . . ."

"I know what it means," I snapped.

"I know you do. I just wanted to get that reaction."

"You know, pissing me off doesn't ALWAYS make me feel better." Except I did feel a little better. Less tragic, anyway. Damn him.

He grinned like he'd heard my thoughts.

"School isn't going super well?" I asked.

"If it were, I wouldn't be here. I'd be there, in the summer program I applied to. The one that turned me down," he said, fiddling with the volume.

"Ouch. Your first time?"

"What's that supposed to mean?"

"I mean . . . you usually get what you want."

He stared straight ahead. "Not always."

"School stuff. Artwork. Your photography."

"I don't do that anymore. I discovered music production."

I remembered the open happiness on his face whenever he talked about photography, our hands in the fixing liquid together, swishing the blank paper until the magic slowly emerged.

"But . . . you loved photography."

He gave me a little half smile. "Maybe I just loved using the darkroom."

More flattery. And I still wasn't buying it. "No. That's bullshit. I remember your pictures. They were amazing."

"I just . . . wanted to do something else. And look, I managed to prove you wrong." After a beat, he added, "I showed you that people can change."

"No. Things got difficult so you moved to a backup. That's not exactly much of a change for you."

He snorted. "Not a backup. I was always just messing around on my guitar, but I didn't start with music production until after I transferred." He stopped there, stared at his hands. "And I realized that I'm no Oscar Reyes. After a while, I got tired of him telling me that. Especially since I knew he was right. So it was either keep banging my head against the wall with photography or try something new. Luckily, music liked me back." When I didn't say anything, he said, "And come on. I was good enough for high school. But high school stuff isn't real."

"Considering I wasn't that good at anything in school, that should make me happy. But your stuff . . ." I thought about my own video editing. *You aren't bad, but you don't have much of an eye, and that can't be taught. Be realistic. Better you realize that now. I was great in school, and look at me. A wedding photographer.*

I was so lost in the echo of Edwin's words that I almost missed when Mauro asked softly, "So what really happened tonight?"

"Oh, OK. I get it. If I ask about photography, then you get to ask about Alex?" Then I could have bitten my tongue off because I'd just opened the door myself.

"Oh. Anthony."

I gave him a look.

"Carmen, come on. Are you freaking kidding me? Sitting out in the middle of a monsoon weeping because of . . . Aaron?" He sounded so disgusted it almost made me smile.

"I. Wasn't. Weeping. And it wasn't a monsoon. It was just Miami summer. And his name is Alex. Which you know."

"OK, fine. I'll stop. It's Alex. But I mean . . . seriously. What do you SEE in him?"

Alex's face swam into my mind. Big brown eyes framed by eyelashes any chica would kill for. A dimple that teased his left cheek. Straight black hair that flopped into his eyes. Sweetness . . .

"Besides the obvious," he said flatly.

"Alex is just . . ." I shook my head. "He's what I want. He's WHO I want. And I thought he wanted me, too."

"Oh. He does," Mauro said, turning his blinker on and merging onto a busy street. "He wants you, but he also wants to keep seeing himself as this nice, sweet guy. The kind of guy who would NEVER be shallow enough to fall for a girl's . . ." He glanced at me. "Assets."

"He is not shallow."

"Oh no. Alex is a paragon among men, I get it."

I crossed my arms. "He IS."

"You are delusional."

That was close enough to the truth that it stung. I turned back to the window.

Mauro pulled onto another side street and parked again.

"Hey . . . I'm sorry. Maybe I'm not the best person to talk to about Alex . . . and you."

"You wanted to talk," I muttered.

"He's just . . . a regular guy. And there are a lot of us."

Except that Alex would never do or say the things that Mauro had at his party. Not that I had to say it. I mean, I had gotten over that a long time ago.

"Really? Are you saying that Alex would never send mixed signals to keep you around him while he nobly hooked up with your cousin?"

"He's not hooking up with my cousin!" Except his face, though, that guilty flush when I'd mentioned her.

I put my face in my hands. "Oh God. Of course, he's going to hook up with *her*. They're perfect for each other. Like attracts like, and Alex and I aren't anything alike."

"You say that like it's a bad thing."

"Isn't it? He's sweet, and kind, and smart, and . . ."

"Boring."

"You don't even know him."

He glanced over at me then, a look on his face that I couldn't interpret.

"What?"

"I can't believe I am going to suggest this, but . . ." He tore a hand through his hair. "Look, it's obvious Alex feels something for you. And he obviously doesn't like me. So you can use that to your advantage."

He stopped and locked eyes with me. "Use me."

I froze. "What?"

"I mean . . . Alex already thinks that we're, I don't know, about to pick up where we left off or something. I saw the way he looked at me at practice. And at Dadeland. We don't have to DO anything," he added hastily. "Just . . . don't disabuse him of that notion. He doesn't have to know how you REALLY feel about me." He glanced down at the steering wheel.

I thought about it. I had kept our fork, after all. I was invested.

"OK, no. I don't play games like that."

"That's the beauty of my plan. There is no game. His mind will do ALL the work." He looked away. "Trust me."

I narrowed my eyes at him. "What's in it for you?"

"It's doing you a solid." He grinned. "Plus, guys like Alex deserve to be messed with."

Yeah, no. Still not buying any of this. I just looked at him and waited.

"Fine. I get it. You don't believe me." He lowered his voice to a rasp. "I called you. So many times. Even a few times after I started St. Timothy's. I wanted to explain." He leaned toward me. "You never called back. You never even gave me a chance. I want to make it better between us. Call it . . . wiping the slate clean. I'm sorry about the way things ended between us. The pictures. Everything."

The rain started up again, so hard and so fast that it blurred the outside world. The only thing that was clear was him.

"I want to help you. I want you to have what you want. Even if I personally think it sucks." Mauro leaned forward, black waves falling over his forehead. Without thinking, I smoothed her hair back, the way I always used to.

He grabbed my hand and held it. The air in the car shifted, because this wasn't the Beast touching me the way he had a million times already. This was Mauro. And this was a touch I remembered, fingers stroking the back of my hand, once, twice. I could feel my heart start to pulse in time to the thoughts racing in my head.

I tugged my hand away. "I don't want your help."

"Carmen, I—"

"Just . . . leave me alone. I'm serious. We're working together, but don't think it's ever going to be anything more than that. Because I know *you*. And I don't like you."

I saw the exact moment Mauro pulled on his Mauro mask. He shrugged and shifted the car back into drive. "No problem. Just making sure you had enough time to pull yourself together."

"Yeah, thanks. I'm pulled."

I had Mauro drop me at Waverly's instead of back at home. As soon as I rang the bell, Waverly popped into the doorway. She took one look at my face and sighed. "What did he do?"

I was struggling to hold myself in check. "I guess I always knew this was the way he felt."

"Start from the beginning, please." She dragged me inside. Out of the corner of my eye, I watched Mauro speed away. Waverly caught it, too.

"Wait. Was that Mauro?"

"This is about Alex," I said, even though I was still a little shook after that moment with Mauro in the car. I had a million reasons to ignore what I'd felt, the first one being that I knew better. Of all people, I knew better.

So why was I still feeling his touch on my hand?

"Well, yeah, I figured as much."

"Typical Mauro. Wrong place, wrong time." I slumped down at the kitchen table. Waverly shoved a cup of chamomile tea at me. I took a sip and grimaced. "Rum and chamomile don't mix."

"I work with what I have."

I told her the whole story, then took another long sip, the nasty taste a perfect symbol. "He likes Ariana. Alex, I mean. And, of course, I can't quit. And I can't tell her why I can't quit. Which means she wins either way. She always wins." I thought about Mami and Tía Celia, about the way Mami was always trapped in a one-sided competition she'd already lost.

"You should have taken Mauro up on his offer," she said, taking another long sip of her tea.

I gave her a look.

"What? He deserves that shit."

"You clearly made these things too strong."

"No, really. Think about it. Alex gets all primal and realizes the two of you belong together. Mauro falls hopelessly in love with you again and loses, which is only fitting karma considering what he did before. Win-win." She looked smug, like she'd just proven a theorem, and then took another long swig.

"Again? Oh, please. Mauro never fell the first time." I thought about the look in his eyes in the car. I'd always figured that after we stopped hooking up, I slid out of his mind. It was weird to think that I might have lingered.

She tapped her chin slowly. Pensively. "That's exactly it. This asshole owes you." After another second, "Plus, I think Mauro is absolutely right. Alex will fold like a cheap lawn chair."

"And . . . you're cut off," I said, taking her cup away from her.

"It could work. It probably *would* work. But . . . you're resisting." She slanted a look at me. "I wonder why?"

"Because . . ." I waved my hands around. "I mean . . . OK, Waves. Go home. You're drunk." I put my head down on the table. "Ugh, have I mentioned how much I'm going to miss you? How much I miss you already?"

"Well, this is my home. I am currently here. And I am

wondering why you aren't agreeing with me on this." I heard her parents start to move upstairs, so I drained the teacups in the sink and shoved her into her bedroom.

"Come on. I don't need to give your folks any more reasons to think I'm a bad influence."

She lay back on her bed, already beginning to look drowsy. "Oh, just do it, Carmen. Might as well have a little fun while you're working this party. It might end up being the best thing that ever happened to you. If it IS a contest between you and your cousin, wouldn't it be nice to win this time?" She snuggled into her comforter.

We stopped talking for a bit, and eventually I heard her soft snores.

Glad the chamomile was working for one of us.

# Thirteen

WE DID HOURS AT the Shack the next day (and helped book some ACTUAL kids' parties. I never thought I'd be excited about that).

Then it was back to the quince mines.

As I was walking into practice, Mauro gave me a sidelong look.

"So?" he asked. "Shall we forgive and forget my offer? We friends?"

"No."

"I mean, you're worried. I get it. I'm overwhelming. Unforgettable. Irresistible. Regretfully, I understand." He shoved his hands deep into his jeans pockets.

I tapped my chin. "What is more negative than no?"

"Fine," he said. "Not friends. We'll simply stand next to each other a few times a week."

"And sit." I gestured to his car. "Don't forget sitting." But I couldn't keep the smirk off my own face.

He held out a hand. After a second of looking at it, I took it.

Waverly came outside then. "Hello? We're getting started. Bond on the dance floor. You need it," she teased.

"In order to move as one," Mauro responded, "we have to celebrate the birth of the ideal of the Platonic relationship."

Waverly cocked her head at me. Something about the way Mauro said the truth made it sound like a lie.

I watched him as he walked away, the way his jeans hung a little low so that I could see the muscles in his lower back. His shoulders were broad, straining against his faded Truth Squad T-shirt.

And then my mind decided to have a little fun without me, in the form of a weird mental movie. Me and Mauro in the back of the van, him touching me, easing my tank strap off my shoulder. My hands stroking his face, feeling a hint of stubble scratching the tips of my fingers. My skin feeling like a million sizzling nerve endings, like the way the sun dries every drop of ocean water individually on your skin.

What the hell? Was "platonic" some weird trigger word that Mauro had managed to plant inside my brain?

I blinked, trying to get the image to go away before my face started to flare into redness. Because I didn't even think of Mauro like that anymore. Like, at all. I mean, no. His ass needed to stay an ancient darkroom hookup. Strictly vertical.

Now to make sure my stupid body understood the wisdom of my experience.

I shook it off and stalked off toward the backyard and the rest of the group. And especially away from him.

———————

Most of Ariana's corte was already there (I knew that technically we were all one now, but it was pretty obvious still who was in the OG court). One of the guys turned around, and I got a good look at the smirk on his face. Louie. Ugh, seriously? Since when? Ariana was really scraping the bottom of the barrel if *he* was the only guy she could find to make us an even number. Could this get any worse?

Everyone turned to look at me. I may have said that last part out loud.

His smirk grew even wider. "Always happy to see you, too, Carmen." And then he leered up and down at me. "Definitely always nice to see you."

Next to me, I could feel Mauro getting tense.

I pulled out my sparkle training and smiled so wide at him, it probably looked like a threat. "Hi, Louie!" He stepped back, uncertain.

When I glanced over at Alex, his eyes were round apologies.

Simone broke us back into groups and, joy of joys, I had Louie in mine.

"Since I just got here," he started, "I might need some private instruction."

Not for the first time, I wished Simone's dance included some more physical separation. Like, one person in Miami and the other in Moscow or something.

I'll say this for Louie. He was a quick learner. After about twenty minutes of spins, twists, step lefts and step rights, and swiveled hips, he pretty much had the basics. I let go of his sweaty hands with relief.

"OK, everybody! Now . . . let's have a run-through and see how it goes!"

It . . . did not go. Like, at all. People who I could have sworn knew what the hell they were doing, like Cesar and Olivia, were suddenly crashing into each other like we were playing bumper cars or something.

Simone clicked off the music and sighed. "People, people! It's not enough to know the steps, you need to know where you are in relation to other people!"

And maybe that was the problem. We didn't have much of a relation to these other people.

Tía Celia was sitting on the sidelines, sipping a glass of iced tea and frowning at Ariana, who was looking back at her like, *I told you!* Ariana had avoided me throughout the practice so far. Maybe she'd actually grown a conscience about the ugly stepsister chat she'd had with Tía Celia? Eh, I doubted it. She was probably just preoccupied with impressing Alex and worried that I'd convinced everyone to ruin her quince on purpose.

But then she looked at me and I realized that I might have been right the first time. She looked as uncomfortable as I felt.

And for a second, I almost felt something like sorry. Tía Celia and Mami were the ones who'd engineered this. Ariana hadn't wanted this either, and now it had the potential to mess up her big day.

Even if she "shined sweetly" in front of me, the overall effect would still be clearly small-time. And the Garces family never did anything small.

Ariana flicked her eyes around us, her mouth tight.

She always managed to get her way. Maybe she would with this as well, and the Dreams would be able to exit stage left . . .

Hope flared in my chest, but then I looked at Simone, who was sparkled out, head drooping, staring at the dried grass that poked through the pavement.

Damn it. I was actually going to have to *help*.

I clapped my hands. "OK, you guys . . . let's play a game!" *Game?* Where had that come from?

"A . . . game?" Ariana wrinkled her forehead. "Really?"

Simone sighed, and nodded at me. "Practice can be officially over for tonight." When she walked past me, she whispered, "Good idea."

"Yeah! Um . . ." I ran through my brain, scanning for an appropriate party game that wouldn't give Tía Celia and Simone the vapors.

And then I got it.

"How about Twister?"

"Twister," Ariana said to me, her voice flat.

Now that I'd put it out there, I had to sell it, carajo.

"Yes! You still have it from before, right? It's a great idea! We learn to work together, move together, give each other space."

Gus winked. "And we get to get REAL CLOSE."

Olivia smacked him in the arm. "Like we weren't doing that while dancing?"

"Yeah, but . . . this will loosen us up. We don't have to think about steps or anything!"

Alex stretched his arms over his head. "I'll just have you know that I'm a grand master at Twister. Ask anyone!"

"Oh, please," Mauro scoffed. "You've been lied to all your life, my friend."

Alex cocked his head. "Did I miss when we became friends?"

"You seem to miss a lot of things," Mauro said smoothly.

Ariana and I went inside to find the game. "You sure this is a good idea?" Ariana said. "Those guys already sound like they want to make it a duel or something. Please tell Mauro not to be a jerk."

"Like I can tell Mauro anything. They're just trying to figure out who's the alpha gorilla."

She gave me a sidelong glance. "And who do you think that is?"

"Since it's your party, I guess I should say you."

"I don't think I like the idea of myself as a gorilla."

"Still, they want to think they're jockeying for our attention? Let them. Hopefully it will loosen them up. It's like dancing with a bunch of a robots out there," I said.

Ariana laughed. "Yeah, Alex can dance, but there were a couple of times there I thought he was going to steer me into the street."

I'd noticed. At least a couple of times, it was because he'd been looking my way, first when I was with Louie and then with Mauro.

Without thinking, I went into the side closet where Ariana and Cesar always kept extra toys and games.

"Looks like you still remember," Ariana said softly.

I shrugged. "Eh, that's where most people would keep them."

This was a job. Ariana wasn't going to con me into a family moment. Especially since I knew how she and Tía Celia *really* felt about me being there.

We went back outside, Twister tucked under my arm.

Ariana read the rules of the game while Gus, Cesar, and Matt set up the plastic mat on the ground, weighing the edges down with rocks from Tía Celia's garden.

"To make sure nobody wipes out the board. Keeps it fair," Gus said seriously.

Ariana frowned at the paper. "I'm . . . not sure this is going to work, people. I mean, it says no more than four people should play. One to hold the spinner and ref and three to maneuver."

"Are the Twister police going to come for us if we do it wrong?" I asked her.

"No, but . . . they had to have a reason, right?"

I looked around the yard. "Everyone OK with being Twister rebels right now?"

Nodding all around.

Satisfied, I said, "Then I appoint myself spin-master." I started to grab the spinner from the box, but Alex said, "No way . . . this was YOUR idea! You get to watch us fall all over each other and what, laugh from the sidelines?"

"Much as it pains me, I think I agree with him," Mauro volunteered.

"Way to have my back, Beast," I muttered to him.

"I DO have your back. I just also want to have your left foot on yellow and right hand on green."

"OK then." I looked around. "Who volunteers to be spin-master?"

Surprisingly, Olivia grabbed the spinner out of my hand with an expression that made me feel like I'd done my one good deed for the day.

We decided the best way to work with such a big group was with teams. Ariana's team was Alex, Leila, Mauro, Gus. Mine was Waverly, Matt, Louie, Jessica.

Cesar decided to sit it out to keep the numbers even (and probably because he didn't love the idea of crawling all over his sister and cousin).

"Right foot, yellow!" And right away, I saw why the game was for just a few players. The spots weren't made for so many hands and feet at once. But everyone was laughing and balancing as much as they could.

I pulled my hair up off my neck into a topknot, and saw Alex looking at me. I could feel his eyes on my hair like he was touching it.

"Here's hoping we don't get another yellow," I said.

So of course, we did. And now we were REALLY crowded.

"I did say we needed to get to know each other," I laughed. I had Alex's leg stretched like a booby trap in front of me and Mauro's arm nudging me off my own spot.

Another spin. Left arm, green. And that's when people started to go down. Gus got so tangled with Jessica I thought we were going to need the Jaws of Life to pull them apart.

Another spin. Right arm, yellow. Ariana shrieked as she wobbled and fell right into Alex, but amazingly they both managed to stay upright. I glanced away, which threw my own balance off, sending me right into Mauro. Our faces were so close that for a moment I could see the flecks of gold in his green eyes. So close he could have moved barely an inch and kissed me.

I adjusted my ass so fast I ended up on the ground. I was out.

Ariana's leg was in the air, and she couldn't hold the pose. She crashed into Alex so hard that she sent them both to the ground. He rolled over with her in his arms.

Ugh.

Then I heard screaming. Alex had Ariana over his shoulder like a prize and was headed for the pool. "No, no!" I looked at Cesar, but he was laughing at something Waverly was telling him. Tía Celia saw, but she just shook her head and smiled, probably happy that her daughter was finally having fun with this quince thing.

Once they splashed into the pool, it was open season. Olivia said, "Finally!" and ran in. Soon almost the whole court was in there, laughing and shrieking.

I sat on the grass and watched them. Mauro came up next to me. "So, looks like your idea worked. Everyone is getting up close and personal."

"Yeah." I rubbed my neck. "I noticed." I held out my hand. "Congratulations on being Twister champion. I should have come up with a prize." My mind flashed to that moment when we were so close on the Twister board.

I wasn't going to be able to get through this summer if my stupid head didn't cooperate.

"The honor is prize enough." He looked steadily at me. "You actually do like him, don't you," he said.

I shrugged. "Sucks to be me."

"Then I'm sorry." And he really did sound sorry.

"Thanks, actually."

"I know it's annoying to see it right in front of you." He tilted his soda bottle and took a long swig. "It's just four months."

"Three." I fanned my fingers out for emphasis. "A blip in the grand scheme of things."

"A fleck of dust in the universe's unblinking eyes," he added.

"A molecule on a fleck of dust." I sighed and held up my bottle of Postobón Manzana.

We clinked.

"'Tis better to have loved and lost, than never to have loved at all,'" he said softly.

"That's bullshit," I countered.

He stopped for a second. "How about, 'It's good to have loved, it's better to BE loved back, and anyone who says differently is a lying liar who lies.'"

I clinked his bottle again. "Word."

We took long sips. I groaned. "Is it always going to feel this sucky?"

"Nope," he said. "Sometimes it feels much worse."

I laughed against my will. "Maybe you are taking this truth-telling thing too far. We're into the cheering-up portion of the night."

He grew serious. "Remember, you're Belle. A girl who can break a spell."

"I'm not having very much luck," I said, jerking my head toward the pool, where Alex and Ariana were still frolicking.

"Eh. Maybe that's part of breaking the right spell." He looked at the pool, too, his eyes reflecting the glow of the water. "Screwing around with the wrong one first."

"*Screwing Around with the Wrong One First* is going to be the title of my autobiography."

"I'm afraid to ask you what you think mine would be," he said.

"Yeah, you probably should be." I laughed again. "How about *I Was a Beast, Inside and Out*?"

"You can do better than that."

"*I Deserved This Spell*?"

He put his arm around me companionably. "Better. Getting better."

Reflexively, I shrugged him off. But I realized I actually *was* feeling better. "Hey, thanks. Really."

He smirked. "Hey, we'll always have professional courtesy. And additional terms and conditions." He held out his hand.

I took it. "Here's to faking it."

One a.m., that night.

MrtB: Hey, Carmen.

I rolled over in bed. I really needed to remember to set my damn phone to Do Not Disturb.

DivaCee: Why are you messaging me?

MrtB: I think the reason we find pairs so attractive is that we're covered in them. Like, two eyes, two ears, two arms, two legs . . .

DivaCee: It's 1 a.m.

MrtB: Were you asleep?

I looked at the phone. Did I want to answer? He did have a point. About the pairs thing.

DivaCee: No, I'm awake.

MrtB: So . . . maybe if humans had ONE eye or something, we'd find THAT the standard of beauty.

DivaCee: We only have one mouth though.

MrtB: True.

MrtB: Thanks to the internet, maybe physical standards will change . . .

DivaCee: Except we can still see people online.

MrtB: But that can all be digitally altered. I mean, you do editing. You know how that works.

DivaCee: Good night, Mauro.

MrtB: It makes sense, though. Just think about it.

MrtB: Would you be more interested if I had ONE eye? Or THREE? Hypothetically?

DivaCee: Night, Mauro.

I smiled and slid over the Do Not Disturb button.

Now that I was awake, the siren song of video editing called me. The way it usually did after Mauro got my brain buzzing.

If I found a good sci-fi show clip, I could probably test that three-eyes theory.

Hypothetically.

Fourteen

IT WAS NOW THE last week of June and the end of the beginning. Eight weeks to go. Regardless of how it had started, we were now one happy corte, amen. A lot of the internship office work now involved stuff about Ariana's quince—dealing with the vendors was a responsibility Tía Celia had been happy to dump on us. I became Simone's Google whenever a piece of quinceañera tradition got tricky, and the interpreter between Simone's brand of crazy and my family's. It didn't take long for Simone to realize that me being related to the quinceañera and her family was a great thing (for her).

"Carmen," she cooed, "you are my secret weapon."

Yeah, a weapon who only aimed directly at herself.

Whatever, so long as I stayed busy and professional, I didn't have time to get dragged into anything personal. And that's how I wanted it. Three practices a week. I could do this! Even if I did have a ringside seat to my little cousin's blossoming romance with Alex. They were pretty much openly flirting, Ariana coyly taking any excuse to touch him. And him pretending to be grumpy about the whole thing, while his eyes laughed at her. It was sickeningly adorable, and there were some nights I'd get home and flop facedown on my pillow.

Alex was still friendly and sweet toward me, still watched me sometimes while Mauro and I danced (although he might have just been trying to make sure he knew the routine). The whole thing made me feel like I'd only imagined the way he'd looked at me at Dadeland before he knew Ariana and I were cousins.

At rehearsal, Simone paced around us. Stopped us again and again. One of the big problems people were having were the lifts. Simone had envisioned this triumphant march around the dance floor, all of us arched into the air and carried by our partners. Except it turned out that while the girls were beginning to trust their chambelanes to swirl them into spins on the ground, they were emphatically NOT HAVING IT in the air. The guys groaned like they were lifting sofas up three flights of stairs whenever they had to pick us up. "No, no . . ." Simone sighed. "She's not a sack of potatoes," she said to Louie.

"Tell her that," he said through gritted teeth. Olivia wriggled out of his arms and smacked him on the way down for good measure.

"I'm sure we can make it work!" Simone trilled, the edges of her sparkle fraying.

Since Mauro and I were still not entirely perfect on the lifts, she had Waverly and Cesar demonstrate it again.

Yeah, something was up between the two of them, too. Waves was holding out on me. I looked at her and mouthed, *"Welcome to the family."* She turned as red as her hair.

As soon as practice ended, Mauro turned away from me and whistled for the group's attention. "Hey, everyone? I've got news. I'll be a guest DJ at the Bay this Saturday night. So be there or be . . . elsewhere, I guess . . . in three days."

The group found some energy, applauding and whooping it up, even Louie. The Bay was our second home, one of the few places people our age could hang out and dance, and to have someone like us actually get to DJ there was a big deal.

"Aw, I'm touched," Mauro said, his face all lit up. "I guess I'll see you all there."

I turned to grab some water, and he asked, "So, um . . . you going?"

"Well, you just made it a work thing," I said. "So, I guess."

"Yeah, but . . ." He looked away and tugged on his shoulder. "It's not. A work thing, I mean. And . . . I really want you there."

"Sure, I'll be there. Maybe all people need to nail the lifts is a night at the Bay."

———————

"You sure you don't want me and Enrique to come?" Mami asked on Saturday, teasing. "You know, class up the joint a little bit?"

I was drowning in fabric, putting on a new slouchy silk tank top I'd bought just for tonight.

"Just the fact that you used the word 'joint' kind of kills the class points."

She laughed. "Don't worry, the last thing we want to do is to head off to a teen club. All those bleeps and blaps." She shuddered. "Give me a good salsa any day." She helped me straighten my shirt and frowned, shaking her head. Then she stuck her head in my closet until she pulled out a silvery sheath I'd worn to yet another quinceañera last year. "How about this?"

I wrinkled my nose. "I think maybe too much. This is a work thing," I reminded her. "I'm just going to support a colleague."

Mami threw her head back and cackled. "Colleague. That's hilarious. He's not the VP of human resources, Carmencita! He's a cute boy who looks at you like you glow in the dark. Mamita, you'll only be young for a little while. Always wear the silver sheath."

"Words to live by. Thank you so much for your input."

"They've served me well," she said, shaking the dress in my direction. It caught the light in a way that made me consider it.

Clothes, like words, mean things, and I didn't want to go to the Bay blaring out *Óyeme, I'm ready to date, mate, and celebrate!*

Still, though. So pretty.

A brief flare of something like hope got turned way up for a second when I looked in the mirror. The dress felt like possibilities. Maybe whatever was going on between Alex and

Ari would melt like fog in the glare of me in that dress.

Then a shiver of something like guilt came over me. Coño. She was still my cousin. This was not who I wanted to be.

Still, it wasn't like I owed her anything.

I slipped the dress on. Wearing a dress wasn't a crime. I couldn't control what *other* people did just because *I* decided to wear something. Right?

I shook my head. I was being ridiculous.

I was about to pull it off when the doorbell rang. It was Waverly, picking me up.

Mami threw her arms around my best friend and dragged her to my bedroom door. "Waverly, please tell my stubborn daughter that this dress is *perfect* for tonight."

Waverly leaned against my door. "She's right, you know."

"Suck-up," I said, sticking my tongue out at her.

Mami laughed and practically pushed me out the door. "Go shine, mi linda. And if something-something happens . . ." She wiggled her eyebrows at me.

"Tonight's about Mauro, not me," I said firmly, but I kept the dress on.

"That dress says you are probably wrong about that," Waverly argued with a grin.

———

We sang along to the radio loudly while driving to the Bay. It was a perfect night, the humidity turned down low and stars peeking in and out of the palm trees as we drove. It felt like I'd made a decision, wearing this dress.

Tonight was about knowing nothing would happen with the right guy, so why not see what kind of fun could be had with the wrong ones? High school was over. It was a new time, which deserved new guys. All I had to do was see them.

"You think Mauro's any good at this?" Waverly asked me. "Or is tonight going to be about pretending not to be drowning in secondhand embarrassment?"

I thought about the music he'd played for me in the car. I remembered him picking out chords on his guitar, teaching himself to play by ear.

"Knowing Mauro, there's no way would he have invited all of us if he wasn't good at it."

She pulled into the parking lot and slid into a space.

"That's probably *why* he invited us," she said. "We're literally professional party people. We're definitely going to make him look good tonight."

"Don't make me regret coming," I muttered.

From outside, we could already feel the vibrations of the music. I couldn't tell what was playing, just that it was loud. Perfect.

"Look at these people. Here's hoping we don't break the fire laws tonight."

Waverly smiled. "Maybe we can just bend them."

We found the rest of the corte, already in line. Ariana came up to me and threw her arms around me. I stiffened, surprised, until I smelled the hint of rum on her breath. Shit. We all knew whose ass would be blamed if Ariana got caught drinking (again). Hint: not hers.

I glared at Alex, who was standing over her shoulder. He shrugged and mouthed, "*Olivia.*"

Ari pulled away from me and giggled. "Don't worry—I've already switched to water!" She shook a teal Hydro Flask at me as proof. "Plus, it was just ONE mojito and Olivia and I split it!"

It must have been a glass the size of a quart of milk to get her to hug me.

I pried her arms off me while she continued babbling. "It's so weird to see you again! Like . . . a person! And so much of you!"

Correction: a *gallon* of milk.

I'd had so much angst about the dress I was wearing, but she wasn't too covered up herself, wearing a low-cut spangly tank top that on her looked stylish but not slutty. The Grace Kelly thing must be in the genes.

The new guy at the door nodded at us as we edged our way to the front. Then he did a double take, and his whole face changed. "Mirella?"

Then he shook his head and grinned. "Nah, can't be. Not unless she's gone back in time. But you gotta be . . ."

"I'm her daughter," I muttered, well aware of everyone looking at me.

"Wow, you look just like her. Mirella. Wow. All us guys thought . . ." Then he grinned. "Junior would kick my ass if he heard that. You Junior's little girl?"

I shrugged, because I was, and I wasn't, and the truth was way too complicated. "I'll tell my mother you said hello, Mr. . . ."

"Hernan," he said. "We used to hang at this pool hall in Hialeah. She probably won't remember, though. She only had eyes for Junior. Shit, though, he was just plain crazy." He chuckled. "Tell that loco I said hi too . . ."

Ariana piped up, "Oh, he's not around anymore." She looked at me, eyes open wide.

I recognized the look on her face. Tira la piedra y esconde la mano. And I wasn't going to let her throw the rock in my face. Not this time. I yanked her past Hernan before she spilled the rest of my sordid family history. Let Hernan remember Mami and Junior differently. I wished I could.

The other Dreams were already there, camping at a clump of tables at the edge of the dance floor, purses flung all over the chairs, shoes shoved under the table. People had gotten started early.

Ariana danced a little bit in place, and then started to tug on Alex's arm. "Let's show off all this practice!" She opened her eyes wide to me. "Wow, Carmen. Mauro is like . . . a professional. That's SO hot." OK, so she was going to play it like she *hadn't* been about to spill my family business at the door? Fine. I could pretend, too. I did it for a living.

"What, did you think he would suck?"

She wasn't wrong, though. If I hadn't known who was DJing, I would have assumed it was someone real. The beat was hypnotic, thudding against my chest, the treble like fingers. Touching me everywhere.

I looked up at the slightly raised DJ platform, at Mauro, head cocked to one side, wearing a set of those oversize headphones around his neck, moving a little bit to the beat. He hadn't seen me yet. There was a cluster of girls crowding around the booth, waiting for him to notice them. Maybe a few more than usual. He definitely didn't need us to make him look good tonight. I started to dig through my purse for money to cover a Coke.

Ariana nudged my shoulder. "I think he's looking for you."

Mauro was scanning the crowd. And then stopped, right on me. The lights reflected in his eyes, making their usual green strange and glowing.

He smiled, shyly. I was surprised when the breath I took tingled, just like the old days. I told myself it was probably just the same force that pulled those girls to the DJ booth. The obvious, that he was the hot new DJ.

Except I knew him, good and bad. So what was my excuse?

I moved to the dance floor. Let the music push and pull me

where it wanted me to go.

And it wasn't just me. The floor was packed with bodies, people who didn't know Mauro. People who were just here to have a good time, and he was giving them one.

I remembered the way he'd talked about Berklee, about not feeling good enough for it. Tonight would show him he was wrong. And then he'd be insufferable again.

I danced my way through the crowd, until it parted and became one person.

"Shouldn't you be up there?" I asked him.

"Technology means I can be everywhere." His lips were twisted in their usual smirk, but I could see a hint of genuine happiness.

"All that drama up there with the headphones and everything, that was just for show?" I was trying to get back to our usual. But this didn't feel usual; it felt like the old days, when seeing him was a heart beating in my throat.

"I wanted to see you. Say hi." His voice went low, a husky whisper.

"Hi," I said, trying to keep my voice from doing the same thing. And failing.

"Want to dance?"

Such a simple question to make me feel such a complicated way. Like I wanted to give in to whatever was happening. And then like I was letting myself down.

"Aren't you on duty?"

"I thought I just explained that. It's not like being a cop."

"Well, we're not on duty right now, either," I reminded him. "You dance with me three times a week, at least."

"So . . . maybe I want to dance with you again. Off duty."

He took my hand and we nudged past the crowd until we found a bit of space. We started to move. Not as Belle and the Beast. Not as part of a quince court. Just as us. For the first time.

And, truth, it felt seriously weird. Like if I looked and then he looked, it would feel meaningful. And it would just be me. I would be the one feeling too much. Again. I couldn't go to that place with him again.

I could feel myself moving toward him, pulled by something stronger than I could fight.

Then he slid his hand to my waist, and in his touch, I felt the darkroom. I felt the way he made me laugh as the Beast and during our late-night online chats.

I felt the See and Be Seen Party.

My heart hammered against my chest because I remembered it, this very-specific-to-Mauro feeling, like I was underwater and desperate for air. The music felt like it was pressing us together. He moved closer, his hand sliding to my lower back now. Pulling me closer. I shivered. I could hear the song in the background, a woman's voice incredibly high, a note stretched out like longing. Like danger.

For one moment, I forgot everything he was and everything

he'd done and everything he'd ever been to me.

Until a pair of eyes became distinct in the crowd. Steady, brown, and staring directly at me. Alex. And just like that, I was brought back to myself.

Mauro noticed me stiffen and glanced over his shoulder. And when he turned back to look at me, his face had hardened, trying for its usual smirk. And failing.

"I have to go," I said, already pulling myself away.

"Yep. Duty calls."

––––––––

We stayed until the annoyed Bay management started flashing the lights. I couldn't remember the last time that had happened.

Whatever Twister had started for the group, tonight had reinforced. A casual onlooker would never be able to guess that we weren't all Ariana's BFFs. Olivia and Leila had their arms around each other, rapping some popular song, off-key. They sounded drunk, but I knew it was just the effect of this really great night. Courtesy of Mauro.

We milled around outside in the parking lot. "So!" My cousin bounded up to me. "Where to now?" I could smell more than just one mojito on her breath. I looked at the water bottle in her hand, a different one from earlier. She flushed and looked away, and then made a point to hand it to Olivia and grab her own bottle back.

"Uh, home?" Cesar told his sister. "Mami never said you were allowed to stay out all night."

She put her hands on her waist. "The big brother thing would be so much more effective if you didn't have Waverly's lipstick smeared on your cheek."

Ha! I'd been right! I filed that away until I could think through how I felt about it.

He grinned sheepishly and rubbed his cheek. "Still, I promised Mami."

"And you should never break a promise to Tía Celia," I reminded her.

"What's she gonna do, anyway?" Ariana spun around. Was I the only one who could hear a slur in her voice? "Cancel this quince too? This is nothing like yours." She snorted. "It's bigger than all of us now."

Probably not bigger than Tía Celia, though.

Mauro came outside after packing up his gear. Ariana threw her arms around him. "You were AMAZING! Someday, I'm gonna be able to say that I knew you when."

Alex rolled his eyes. But Louie clapped Mauro on the back. "I still think you're a dick, but good job, man."

Mauro grinned. "Thanks. You're a dick, too."

"So," Ariana asked again, her eyes wide and looking at all of us. "What next?"

"Home," Cesar said firmly.

"But . . ." Her voice got wheedling. "You can see Waverly anytime you want. But Alex and me . . ."

"Not the most persuasive argument," Cesar said, smiling tightly. I was with him on that one.

"We can go to my house, you know. I have a pool table," Gus piped up.

Ariana looked skeptical. And I had to agree with her. "Your house? There's no way."

Gus looked offended. "You'll see."

Which is how I ended up following this night to a second location.

Aren't there warnings about doing that?

And there's probably a bonus warning about sitting next to someone who you came very, very close to kissing about two hours ago. Someone who you knew you had to avoid at all costs.

A blinking neon MISTAKES MADE HERE sign would not be out of place.

Or a simple IDIOTA, NO!

Maybe that had been Hernan's job tonight. To remind me that I didn't just look like Mami, I carried her inside me. That desire to beat my moth wings against a destroying flame—it was genetic. Like Mami and Junior. That was not a history I needed to repeat.

But for a second, I'd been tempted.

Mauro kept his eyes firmly on the road. Cesar and Waverly talked over the sulking figure of Ariana, sitting firmly in the middle of them in the back seat and taking the occasional angry pull from her water bottle. "Stop pouting," her brother said for the fifth time. "He didn't fit in the car."

Meanwhile, I stared out the window and watched the neighborhood go from familiar to strange. The houses got closer together, interspersed with panaderías and bodegas. Fewer three-car garages and way more makeshift car parks, cement lines buried in the grass.

If I had to classify Gus's house, I'd put it somewhere between Ari's small mansion and my townhouse. It was tucked in the Crossings, a neighborhood west of Kendall, on a block full of small one-floor houses with plastic flamingos strutting on tiny parched lawns.

"My moms isn't home, but if y'all make a mess, you are staying here to explain it to her," he said as he jiggled the stuck key in the lock.

I couldn't see how she'd see that things were any worse. Pizza boxes stacked in the corner with a pile of mail and paperbacks that looked like it was going down at any second. Laundry baskets full of funky clothes on top of the couch.

Gus stopped for a second, as if seeing everything for the first time, and then shrugged. "Sorry, everybody. Mami's been busy."

"What about you?" I asked him. "You live here too, right?"

He shrugged again. "I don't do that kind of stuff."

Ariana met my eyes, alarmed. "Admit it," she said to him. "You brought us here to clean, didn't you?"

Gus laughed. "Let me pull out the pool table."

"Pull out?" Mauro shook his head. "That does not sound promising."

Gus didn't say anything, because he'd already burrowed into a room that looked like that TV show where people suffocate in old newspapers and get eaten by their cats.

Then he emerged, carrying what looked like a Monopoly box. He put it down and exclaimed, grandly, "Our pool table!"

Everyone looked at it. It . . . well, it WAS a pool table. For mice, maybe.

"We gonna play or not?" Gus said.

So we settled on the floor (I saw Olivia lay a Bounty down before she sat) and started to play pool like it was marbles. Cesar whispered something to Waverly, who smiled and then followed him outside.

Loneliness washed over me. Waverly was still here, but with whatever was going on with Cesar, she might as well not be.

She was my best friend. But now, she was a part of them, too.

I wasn't crazy about that.

Louie was sprawled alongside the couch, ignoring Olivia in favor of his phone.

"Have there ever even BEEN this many people in your house before?" she bitched at Gus.

"Hey, maybe ask Carmen's hood friend for directions to that pool hall in Hialeah next time," Gus shot back. I glared at him. Traitor.

Olivia turned to me like a cat who'd smelled a new mouse. "Yeah, what ABOUT that, Carmen? He sure remembered your mami fondly." She laughed in a way I didn't like.

"Mami told me once that Abuela and Abuelo sent the police to that pool hall looking for Tía Mirella and she and Junior had to sneak out the back," Ariana said cheerfully.

I willed my cousin to, kindly, shut her freaking mouth.

But her mouth stayed open, and shit kept emerging from it. Shit about my family. And my so-called father.

"Yeah, Abuela and Abuelo figured that Junior had some outstanding warrant or something, and that would be a good way to get him away from Tía Mira's life." She glanced at me. "Not that I think it would have worked. Tía Mira is pretty stubborn."

Louie looked intrigued. "He sounds hard-core. Did you ever know him, Carmen?"

"Yes. It happened when we had our first sit-down with the Five Families. We did that instead of going to Disney World." I turned back to the table. But Olivia didn't get the hint.

"What *about* his family? Like, did they know about you?" she asked. I winced at the implication, even if it wasn't wrong.

"His family in Puerto Rico had money. Like, a *lot*." My cousin was loving being center stage with chisme from my life.

"But still, Tía Mira was a catch—gorgeous—and even though Junior was loaded, he was still kind of a criminal. The black sheep." Ariana lowered her voice but made sure that everyone could still hear every word. "Drugs, right, Carmen? So sad. That's probably why it made sense for him to go home." She took a swig out of her water bottle like she wanted to savor the suspense. "But then . . . he never came back."

I tried to think of hushed forests, smiling babies. But the volcano inside me was groaning awake.

She continued, "Mami told me the whole story because she says it's important not to make the same mistakes."

I stood up. "Oh, you mean like sharing my private business in front a bunch of people I don't know?"

She rolled her eyes. "These aren't a bunch of people!" She leaned against Alex, who I noticed was very carefully not looking at either of us. Coward. "This is my corte!"

I laughed. "Half of which your mami rented!"

She stood up then, too. "Like you."

"Yeah. I wouldn't be here otherwise."

"Oh, please. You are just jealous, as usual, because my parents can give me something that your mom can't. Tía Mira started with the same things that Mami had, same upbringing, same everything. But she picked the wrong man."

"Who's jealous now? You just can't stand that the door guy remembered my mother so well that he picked me out of a crowd years later. Not my fault you all fade into the damn woodwork and we don't." I tried to sound like I was proud of that, because I knew I'd hit it. I'd hit the nerve, the reason she was being such a bitch right now.

Ariana tossed her hair. "And who is this *we*? He remembered your mother, not you. *She* was memorable, all right, but definitely not for the *right* reasons."

Alex said, "Um, maybe we should just get back to the game?"

Red blood was swimming in my vision. Whatever sense I had left was telling me to shut my own mouth, to turn around and leave these people, and then to call Simone and quit, like, now.

I got really close to her. "You really think Tía Celia stayed away from us because I took you to that stupid party? Or because she couldn't stand the competition? For her OR for you?" Ariana gasped like she couldn't believe I'd gone there. But my chonga mouth was on fire now, and I didn't care who heard. "No, Mami chose the right man. She just didn't know her hermanita was going to steal him from her. Because that's what you all do. You take things. You ruin them. Like my quince."

Alex looked up. "Hey, Carmen, damn, take it easy. Calm down."

"What quince?" Ariana tapped her chin. "Oh, you mean that little dinner? Please. And you couldn't even afford that without *my* parents! It's not my fault you messed everything up for *yourself*. I mean, you should be used to it by now. It's who you are. Who Tía Mira is. Like mother, like daughter." Her face got redder. "Know what? I'm going to tell Simone and Mami that you need to be gone. I don't care what they say. I'm done with you!"

"Yeah, you do that. But remember, you started this."

Ariana and I stared each other down, like a dare.

Waves and Cesar came inside, laughing, until Waves saw my face and nudged him. Mauro was right behind them.

Ariana's eyes flicked to me, and then to him, and her lips curled.

"Like I said: like mother, like daughter."

Fifteen

FINALLY, I WAS ALONE. Finally, I could take a freaking breath that wasn't filled with rage.

But the walk was having the reverse effect. I wasn't calming down. I was revving up. Replaying every grievance. The greatest hits of Carmen Sucks, But Luckily, We Have Ariana.

Screw Alex for jumping to her defense. Screw Mauro . . . just in general. I thanked God and all the saints that I hadn't given in to the moment on the dance floor.

He probably agreed with them. He'd thought the worst of me when we were together, that I was using him and bragging about it. That I was a liar.

Now look at me. I wasn't in school and wasn't going to be. I was the daughter of the cautionary tale Tía Celia used to scare her daughter into perfect submission. A collection of the worst clichés people believed about girls like me.

And soon I was going to be out of a job and without a high school diploma.

A few minutes later, I heard footsteps. "Hey, wait up."

"Go away, Mauro."

He finally jogged up to me. "I did go away. And now I'm here."

"Where I don't want you."

He stopped, breathing hard. "Hey, I get that you're pissed. But Carmen . . . You know she just wanted to hurt you, right?"

"Why are you still here?"

He stiffened. "I'm here because we're friends."

"Really? Or because you were right all along?"

"What the hell are you talking about?"

I whirled around to face him, and he looked so innocent, so caring, it actually made bullshit tears come to my eyes. What the hell was wrong with me that I could still look at him and not hate him for showing me to myself?

I started walking away faster. But he kept up.

"Cesar told Ariana off big-time after you left. Said that if she says anything to their mom about you, he'll be forced to tell her not only what she said, but also about the mojito she drank tonight," Mauro said, like we were just chatting. "And whatever else was in those bottles."

"Glad to know someone has my back," I muttered. Ugh, I hated that a tiny part of me was hopeful. Considering all the bullshit I'd already gone through this summer, I wanted to come out on the other side with my diploma. And for all my big talk, I knew that if Tía Celia complained, Simone would have no choice but to get rid of me.

Even if I didn't know whether I'd be able to dance for one more minute in front of Ariana, I wanted it to be my choice if I quit. Because something should fucking be my choice.

"Waverly, too. She thought you might need a bit of time before she came out."

"So why didn't you follow her example?"

He ignored me. "And last I saw, Gus was losing his shit with Olivia, told her to get the hell out of his house, that she could call a cab. I think Louie ended up driving her home."

"Great." Meanly, I hoped that I'd managed to ruin Ariana's quince the way she'd ruined the one I never got to have. There was a beautiful symmetry in that. But then I thought about Simone, and the guilt pricked my eyes.

And that was before I thought about having to look Mami in the face and tell her I'd ruined her family reunion, and by the way, I wasn't going to get my diploma after all.

I *was* the one who always ruined things, after all.

"I just wanted to let you know," he said.

"Good, you let me know."

He shoved his hands into his pockets. "I'm . . . I'm sorry about what Ariana said about your father. You never told me all that."

"And why would I, Mauro? Exactly when were we at the 'deep family histories' stage of our non-relationship? I only knew about Oscar because you liked to flash his name like a Mastercard."

"Carmen, why are you mad at me?"

"I just . . . I don't want to get into it with you tonight. Seriously. Just go. You are great at that."

"I'm not leaving you like this."

"What? You need me to supply a blonde first?"

"Wait, what?"

A reckless meanness took over me. The outline of anger was already there. It was always there. I just needed to fill it in. "You thought I was a liar and a user, right? That I bragged about pictures that you never promised, and that I stuck with you because of them? Right? That was all bullshit, but—"

"I don't know why I said that. I knew even at the time that—"

I continued as if he hadn't spoken.

"—that prophecy you laid out for the blonde at your party? You said I'd end up with a bunch of kids, right, Mauro? On a pole? I heard you! You took my own words, my own fears, and used them to make her feel special!" My voice was getting more hysterical. "And look! Here I am! I don't even have my fucking high school diploma! I couldn't even do that! I'm not going to college. And you heard my cousin. I'm a *cautionary tale*, and you got yourself the fuck away before I infected your life too much with my chonga ass!" In the distance, I could hear a car backfire, a door slam. I was being loud. Fuck it, I was tired of trying so hard. Maybe this was who I was. Maybe all these years, when I'd one-upped the people who insulted me, maybe it was just because I knew the truth. The doorman recognized me. The product of Junior and Mirella. DNA doesn't lie.

"Carmen, I swear, I—"

I laughed. "Please, don't swear. We get a lot of thunderstorms, and you're not worth being struck by lightning over."

"Carmen, please—"

"Please, what? 'Please, Carmen, don't remind me about how I felt about you, and have ALWAYS felt about you'?"

A voice from one of the houses. "Shut the hell up, or I'm calling the police!"

I opened my mouth to scream back, but Mauro dragged me off. "I know you wanna prove what a badass you are right now, but maybe you DON'T want to get a record tonight on top of everything else?"

"You better let me go!"

He did, so fast I stumbled into him for one second.

And that was all it took.

He put his arms around me and that knot I was holding on to with both hands, that easy, lifesaving Mauro-hate knot inside me loosened, and I finally couldn't stop myself with anger anymore.

He didn't say anything for a long while, just let me cry it out.

Finally, I slouched out of his arms and started walking.

"Carmen," he started softly. "I'm so sorry. I'm sorry about your father, and your idiot cousin, and I am ESPECIALLY sorry that I said something I didn't mean years ago that I don't even remember. I wasn't talking about you, honest."

"You expect me to believe—"

"I mean . . . I was just saying bullshit to impress Kristy, just anything. I was thinking with my stupid dick, OK? And yeah . . . you were on my mind. I just . . . I knew it was already done, *we* were already done, and I was trying to pretend like it didn't hurt like hell."

"Why?" I asked. "It's not like anything between us even mattered. You made sure I knew that."

"C'mon, Carmen. Even at the time, you must have known that was bullshit." He tugged a hand through his hair and sighed. "I didn't WANT to like you. I didn't want to like anybody. Screw around, be a man. That's what I was supposed to do. The Reyes way. When I asked my father to shoot your pictures, at first he said no because he didn't have the time to do a good job and he didn't want his name on anything subpar. Then he admitted that he didn't *want* to make the time . . . not for one of my 'little hookups.' I told him that you were special, but he just said, 'Yeah, before or after you offered my services? Don't set the bar so high, Mauro. Don't use me to impress this girl, because then for the rest of your relationship you'll wonder if you ever really measured up.' And the thing is . . . when it got

199

all over school, it was like, Oscar was *right*, you know? Right again. And I hated him for that. And I hated you."

I sat down on the sidewalk, stunned. "You decided . . . you made all these offers and then took them away and then had all these realizations and I was just, what? The blank screen? At least when I went to the party, I was going to TALK to you. But I guess it's easier to be in a relationship by yourself."

I stopped myself. It was the first time I'd admitted out loud that whatever we'd had before then could be called a relationship. Whatever else it was, it was that.

"I'm sorry. It's not like I knew much about relationships back then," Mauro said softly.

"Yeah, like my cousin just informed the world, it's not like my parents were these big role models of romance, either. But I still knew better than that. I knew better than to shit all over someone because I cared about them, and because I was afraid that they might care about me."

". . . And did you care?"

"It doesn't matter. Because I don't now."

He looked down at his hands, and then back at me. "Carmen. I'm so, so sorry. I didn't mean what I said at the party. Not in general, and DEFINITELY not about you. I never even thought about those words again, because they were such bullshit. I hate so much that they've been in your mind, because they shouldn't be. They weren't ever real. Not when you said them, and definitely not when I did."

I thought about tonight. About Ariana's snide, true words, and the way everyone had reacted to them. Maybe Mauro was telling the truth. He hadn't given the words a second thought.

But they'd still come from him.

Sixteen

SOMEHOW, WE'D ALL SURVIVED the first eight days of July. Ariana and I were pretty much on a need-to-speak basis, and surprisingly enough, we didn't need to speak all that much. Ariana had done me the favor of having a "bad cold" (ha) the day after the Bay, so she missed practice. Too bad she made a remarkable recovery the next day.

I kept waiting for Simone to tell me that the family had demanded my dismissal, but nothing ended up happening there, either. Cesar had managed to save me. I didn't want to look too closely at how.

Slowly, the dancing itself started getting a little better, which was all Simone cared about. And if Tía Celia noticed that we weren't exactly having a blast at practices, she didn't mention it.

The other thing that happened was that Alex and Ariana became official. A part of me wanted to burst her bubble, to watch the rainbows drain from her eyes when I told her that Alex had known me first, had picked me first, if only for a night. But—my feelings for Alex had sifted through my fingers, like something that had happened to someone else.

Anyway, I'd said everything important I needed to say to Ariana at Gus's.

Just when I was beginning to worry about the lack of steady princess parties (and tip income), Simone informed us that we were booked for two parties, back to back. The first with Leila and Mauro and me, and the second one with Waverly and Matt and Mauro and me.

It was a relief to be off 24-7 quince duty, if only for one day.

"I don't see WHY I always have to perform alone!" Leila said, as usual. "It just makes me feel exposed, and like the kids aren't as excited to see me!"

"Jasmine is a popular princess in her own right—plus, you'll have us," I tried.

She picked at a loose string on her belly-dancing bottoms. "I just don't see why Simone can't find someone for me."

"It's a kid's party, not Match.com."

"You know what I mean." She jerked her chin at Mauro. "You get a man," she pouted.

We were all in the van, our gear spilling out of the bags around us. Simone liked us to have everything perfectly organized, so that even if we got into an accident, the police would notice how well placed all the props were. I think it was her version of wearing clean underwear.

"OK, Leila, fine. You want to trade for today? You win." I figured that if we showed up with Aladdin instead of the Beast, the kids would still be fine. It was ALL about the princesses. And truthfully, it would be nice to have a Beast-free party. I still wasn't sure how I felt about everything Mauro had said outside Gus's house. We'd admitted something to each other, that those darkroom moments had marked us. What he'd said to the blonde, though . . . I'd been carrying those words in my head for so long—in a way, they'd changed me more than the relationship with Mauro had.

If I dropped the words, then all that was left of us was the rest of our history. Which was complicated. And also, not necessarily history, thanks to this job.

Like I said, I needed a break.

Leila frowned. "I don't know if Mauro could manage to play Aladdin."

Mauro looked back at us in the rearview mirror. As usual, he was driving. "I'm not a tradeable piece of meat, you know."

We both ignored him. "He's so tan at the moment, his skin color could go either way. Put him in the costume and the kids would be happy," I pointed out.

"It WOULD be nice to get out of my Beast head for a day," Mauro mused. Or maybe he just needed a break from me, too.

Leila pondered it for a hot second.

"OK, let's go back to the Shack and pick up the Aladdin clothes."

Once we'd done that, we pulled over into a Pollo Loco parking lot and stood outside while Mauro changed from his Beast outfit into the Aladdin outfit.

To say we got a lot of attention is an understatement. Guys were openly slowing down and drooling over Leila, but they didn't seem as surprised by her as by me. I guess that Jasmine's clothes were a little bit closer to what Miami girls usually wear compared with a full buttercup-yellow satin ball gown.

"Hey, Your Highness, you like balls? I can show you mine!"

"Ew. Do they really think that's going to work?" Leila asked, staring down another idiot who almost crashed his car into a dumpster, he was ogling her so hard. "Why do they think they have to say anything?"

"Because if they don't say anything to us, we might get the idea that it's OK for us to just stand here and exist, dressed however we want, without their input or permission or anything."

Leila turned to me quickly. "That's . . . actually really profound."

Mauro came out then, and the boy looked REALLY good in just a vest. It only accentuated the definition in his arms and broad chest.

I looked away. I needed to not have any broad-chest thoughts complicating shit further.

A few girls passing by hooted and whistled at him, and he bowed.

"Mauro, I had no idea you were hiding all that under your costume," Leila drawled. "We're going to make a stunning pair."

"What do you think, Carmen?" He turned around. "Do you like the Beast more or Aladdin?"

"I like whoever is going to get me to this party. We're going to be late."

The little girl who opened the door had the widest, bluest eyes I'd ever seen. I would have called her a china doll, except those are usually white, right?

"Belle," she breathed out. She glanced at the other two, but I was obviously the main attraction, especially since she was wearing a little replica of my dress. A rhinestone tiara rested tilted on her braids.

It was time to sparkle. "Why, you are a beautiful princess as well!" I said, fluttering and fanning out into magic spirit fingers. "Happy birthday, Tonya!" And then I giggled.

She stepped to the side and dropped a pretty nice curtsy. *I should give Simone this kid's number.*

"Please, come into my castle."

The castle turned out to be a two-bedroom apartment, which was a smaller space than we were used to. I looked around the tight living room and was already mentally changing the dance that Mauro and I do to make sure we had enough room.

Except I didn't have to do a dance after all. Since Mauro was playing a different part today.

Mauro and I had only been paired up for a month and a half, but it definitely felt weird to go through the party without him. Especially when he and Leila danced, and got (almost) the same amount of applause that we usually did.

Tonya tugged on my skirt and I bent down to her. "What is it, Your Highness?"

"What about the Beast?"

I glanced at Mauro, who was helping Leila give out some goodie bags, then whispered back to Tonya, "No Beast today."

"Oh." She fidgeted with her dress. "I just . . . I mean, I wanted to see the Beast, you know? I tried to get my cousin Arthur to dress like him, but he didn't want to."

I took her hands. "Tell you what. Let me go and see if I can get in touch with the Castle. Maybe I can call the Beast and see if he can stop by."

She ran off to her mother, calling excitedly about the Beast and stepping all over her gown.

I could see how much this family had stretched itself to give Tonya her fairy tale. And it felt good to make it extra special for her. Because no one should have to be realistic all the damn time. Especially when they're seven.

I called Mauro over. "I think you should put on your Beast costume now."

"You miss me?"

"Not even a little. But Tonya really wanted to see the Beast."

He grinned. "Cover for me."

After he sneaked away, I told Leila the plan. She smirked at me. "Couldn't go one party without your boyfriend, huh?"

"Hey, we're just doing what Simone always says. Making Dreams Come True."

"This little coy romantic thing you are working is adorable," she replied. I started to argue, but then her face got serious. "Just . . . don't take it too seriously, OK? It would suck to have to break in another new Belle."

The next night, eleven p.m.

MrtB: Look at me, online at what anyone would consider a decent hour. Definitely deserving a full conversation. Unlike the silence I've faced for the last week.

I stared at my phone.

Did Mauro and I have anything left to say to each other? We'd finally talked about the See and Be Seen Party. He'd apologized, explained. We could get through the summer now. The Pax Aguilar Reyes.

Things could stay exactly the way they were.

MrtB: So . . . where do we go from here? I mean, it's only July 10. We have until Labor Day. We're working together. We're dancing together. I thought we'd moved past the should-be-awkward stage at record speed. Delayed awkward doesn't sound great.

MrtB: And we could keep going the way we were—where you pretend to hate me.

DivaCee: Pretend??

MrtB: And I cajole you into admitting that I'm not actually the Antichrist . . .

DivaCee: Jury is still out on that, too . . .

MrtB: And it could be fun—during a summer where I didn't think much was going to be fun.

MrtB: But . . . I don't want to pretend anymore. I don't want to do a routine (I mean, besides Beauty and the Beast and the quince dances and . . . shit, we do a lot of routines . . .). I want to be friends. For real. Maybe that's what we screwed up the first time. We skipped friends and went straight to hooking up.

Yeah, that was because back then I hadn't been looking for a friend. And definitely not one who made me dizzy to hit that darkroom every day. I remember having that feeling during the class before lunch, that pull on my skin, like it was already straining to find him.

But things were totally different now.

MrtB: So . . . I guess what I'm asking is . . . can we have a do-over?

DivaCee: To be friends?

MrtB: Absolutely. New friends. Complete with that new friend smell.

DivaCee: That just got creepy.

MrtB: Duly noted, with apologies. With our history, it makes sense to get it right.

DivaCee: Since we never did before.

MrtB: Exactly.

Could I do this? Could I let the party go? His accusations? The things he said?

MrtB: Um . . . a little verbal affirmation would be great here. Even a 😊 or a 😃 or a 👍 since new friends wouldn't exactly know how to read weighty silence online.

DivaCee: Fine. Friends-ish. And all the emojis that entails.

MrtB: Friends-ish? It's a start. I don't know if that comes with the new friend smell though . . .

DivaCee: Yeah, don't make me regret it.

MrtB: I already did once. So I won't.

DivaCee: What does it say about our history that I understood what that meant?

MrtB: Second time's the charm!

I stared at the chat for a while after he logged off. What exactly had I agreed to?

Whatever it was, it flooded me with a sudden burst of energy, the perfect feeling for a little recreational video editing. It had been a few days since I'd wanted to. A week, probably.

I didn't want to think about that connection too much.

 Seventeen

"BONJOUR, MA BELLE," MAURO said as I climbed into the van. We weren't rehearsing today—we were on our way to a dress fitting. Mami and Tía Celia had been going through magazines feverishly since mid-June, but they refused to show me their final decision. I had hoped that having Mami involved would mean that I wouldn't have to dress up like a cupcake, but considering typical quince fashion, my hopes, they weren't up.

"Not in the mood." I sighed.

"For?"

"French." Or watching my cousin dazzle the world in a custom-made gown, playing coy and pretending to be overwhelmed by all the attention that everyone was paying her. Gag.

"Would that be ALL things French? As in . . . no to French toast, to French dressing, to French bread, to French . . ." And he dangled a bag from the Argentinean burger place in front of me. I could smell the fries and reached for the bag, but he snatched it back.

"But they are French fries . . ."

"They are Argentinean fries. And if you don't hand them over, you'll be pulling back a bloody stump."

He let me have the bag and gave me a sidelong look while I gloried in my favorite shoestring potatoes, just the perfect amount of salt.

"This is amazing," I said, munching away. "I promise I won't eat all your food."

"As if I'd risk sharing my fries with you. Those are all for you."

"Oh." I looked back down at the bag. "Thanks."

"You're welcome."

I ate and he drove, and we didn't even talk for a few minutes.

"So . . ." he finally started, still staring at the traffic. Maybe that was why things always flowed better between us online or in the car. No eye contact. Still, our two-day-old Official Friends-ish Experiment was going well. And it brought starchy perks, too.

"Has the magic potato done its work?"

I licked my fingers. "I am willing to open negotiations between us and France again."

He grinned. "Excellent, ma Belle."

"Don't push it, Beast."

"Hey, think of it this way. We're almost halfway done with this quince thing," he said.

"That means more than halfway left," I retorted.

He laughed. "Ray of sunshine."

We got to Doña Thomasina's salon on Calle Ocho. Tía Celia's Lexus was already parked outside.

I turned to Mauro. "What are you going to do now?" Because he hadn't had to be here at all; the guys were wearing traditional tuxes that matched our dresses. But Mami and Waverly had come straight from their jobs, and I had desperately needed a ride.

He shrugged. "Pan con bistec. Want one?"

I thought about the dress, and the bag of fries I'd just inhaled. "Probably not."

The shop door tinkled as I went in. Tía Celia, Mami, Ariana, Olivia, Waverly, Leila, and Jessica were already inside, sitting on white poufs that looked like mushrooms. Everything was draped in a soft white fabric that shimmered every time someone moved. It felt like the whole room was floating. "Pero que corte tan grande!" Tía Thomasina had said, spreading her arms wide, when we'd trooped inside the first time, and Tía Celia had puffed up with pride and neglected to mention that more than half of us were employees.

Doña Thomasina was legendary in Miami. She'd been

doing this so long that she'd even made Mami's and Tía Celia's quince dresses.

"Why can't we just go to Dadeland and hit Nordstrom or something?" Ariana had asked when Tía Celia had made the announcement before we went in to get our measurements taken.

Tía Celia had looked scandalized. "Because Doña Thomasina is TRADITION," she sputtered. "She's the best!"

"And she costs it," Tío Victor had added grimly. Lately, he'd looked a lot less excited about everything. And was spending a lot of time at the dealership.

"She's worth it," Mami had declared, and that was the end of the discussion.

She might have been legendary, but Miami real estate being what it was, her shop was a small storefront tucked between an Ecuadorian restaurant and a souvenir cigar shop hazed with plumes of blue smoke. It was like those stores in Harry Potter, where you couldn't tell the magic that lived inside.

Doña Thomasina came out of her office when I arrived, with six dresses draped in plastic over her shoulders, skirts overlapping and whispering as she moved. She was a petite, dark-skinned woman, who wore a flamboyant Marilyn Monroe wig all the time. She spoke in whispery, sugar-sweet Spanish until you said something she didn't like. Then the steel entered her voice. But she was always happy to see us. "Doing the dresses for generations of the same family? La cosa más linda de mi vida," she'd swear, her wrinkled, bejeweled hand over her heart.

"Bueno! Everybody here?" She glanced around. "Then estámos ready!" Four seamstresses materialized from the walls and started tugging on me and Ariana. "La dama principal y la quinceañera primero," they said. I tried to disentangle myself from their hands. "I'm not the dama principal," I argued. "Olivia is."

Doña Thomasina shrugged. "Eso es lo que me dijeron." That's what they told her.

Three guesses who "they" were.

Ariana stood next to me, biting her lips and fidgeting and scratching her mosquito bites. She did not look like the girl who would become a woman in The Dress. Out of long-buried habit, I smacked her hand away from her bites.

"They'll scar," I reminded her, just like I had a million times.

She looked at me, surprised. It was the first time I'd spoken to her willingly since Gus's house.

I let the seamstresses pull me into a dressing room and shut the door. "Um, I can undress myself. Thanks." When they didn't even react, I repeated myself in Spanish.

They nodded at me with pins in their mouths.

Quickly, I yanked my shorts and T-shirt off. They draped the dress over my head, and for a second, I was floating in a salmon chiffon cloud in the sunset. Then they buttoned up the back and tied the sash.

And I got a good look at myself.

I could see that they weren't quite done; there were some loose seams and threads. But, ay Dios mío, this was the most beautiful thing I'd ever had on my body, and I was including people as well. Crossed panels of lightly layered chiffon made up the fitted bodice, with a modest V-shaped neckline edged with strings of pearls and crystals. The skirt fell gracefully to my knees, and it looked like I was forever standing in a soft breeze.

I stepped out of the dressing room and Ariana let out an honest gasp. "Oh, cuz. You look BEAUTIFUL."

I must have, because she hadn't called me "cuz" in years.

It was a floating, magical, expensive thing. And I was glad that Tía Celia had offered to pay because this was so not what I'd thought it would be. Everything for Ari's quince just kept reminding me of how small my imagination really was. When you had the money, you needed to have the big-dreaming mind to know how to spend it.

And I didn't have it. Not the mind and definitely not the money.

"Almost perfect," Doña Thomasina muttered through her mouthful of pins. She crouched down and began taking in the sides a little bit.

I thought about all the little girls at their princess parties, staring at me in the Belle dress and dreaming of the same thing for themselves.

That's how they get you. They sell you the dream. Even a

girl like me, who should know better.

Mami teared up when she saw me. "Que linda! You look JUST LIKE ME!"

She wasn't wrong, but typical Mami, turning a compliment about my looks into an affirmation of her own. Then she leaned her forehead on mine and said, "I finally get to see you in a quince dress. Just like I've always wanted." Then her eyes started to twinkle. "Y Alex se va a morir cuando te vea! He'll die. Good! Let him see what he threw away."

"Ay, please, Mami . . . no one is going to die." I tilted my head and looked in the mirror. OK, maybe I was hoping *some* people would die. Mauro floated into my head just then, and I shut that shit down like Fort Knox.

Doña Thomasina and her workers were everywhere, little whirlwinds of pins and scissors and needles. Things getting taken in, and occasionally let out (cue Tía Celia's disappointed pursed lips).

And then Ariana stepped out of her dressing room, and everything stopped. I knew that if anyone died that night on Labor Day weekend, it wouldn't be because of me.

She'd gone a nontraditional route, in a light brown dress with chocolate-brown embroidery throughout and delicate, winking crystal beadwork, instead of the usual pink-and-white meringue. It looked classic, with its fitted sweetheart bodice and chiffon skirt, where the color faded from dark to light in an ombré effect. It fell delicately around her in a gentle A-line swell instead of a giant bell like so many other quince dresses.

The skirt was hushed and swishy around her, and the delicate roses embroidered around the hem looked like they'd grown there.

This was the kind of dress that someone would remember wearing all of their life. It was made to remind the rest of us that we were average, even though two seconds ago we'd been strutting around in here like we were awesome.

Mami had a saying, one she usually intoned after she'd put on a bunch of songs from the nineties and had a couple of glasses of wine: "La envidia te come."

Envy eats you alive.

I could feel the teeth sinking into me.

Tía Celia opened the door and gestured frantically for someone to come in. Tío Victor entered the shop, looking doubtful until he saw his daughter and his eyes lit up.

I thought, then, about Junior.

But what was the point in that.

Doña Thomasina and her minions were going around the room, handing out tissues.

I closed my eyes. Ariana was going to have the quince every girl wanted. The one I hadn't let myself even dream of. And when it was over, she was going to get to keep the dress.

When I opened my eyes, I saw Tía Celia looking at me with a little smirk. Savoring the exact moment when I had looked at Ariana and remembered not to get too above myself.

Or maybe she was just looking at me the way she always had—half pitying, half gloating, the way everyone in the family looked at me.

Now I had a dress from Doña Thomasina, too. But it wasn't a quince dress. It was one of a crowd. She had made quince dresses for everyone else in my family. Except me.

I'd been skipped.

Envy took another deep bite of my heart, and when I looked around me, all I could see was everything I'd never had a chance at. Maybe everything I'd never even deserved.

"I think the dress looks better in motion," I blurted out against the dark turn my thoughts were taking. I took out my phone and shouted at Ariana, "Spin around!" Obligingly, she did, and I recorded her, in color and in black-and-white.

My cousin, all beautiful possibility and shining star, getting everything she wanted.

Eighteen

GETTING INTO OUR QUINCEAÑERA outfits for the first time changed things. The quince stopped being some event off in the far distance and became real. And there was a really good chance we were all going to look like idiots if we didn't nail these performances.

"Remember, kids, the internet is forever!" Simone trilled to scare us into doing our moves one more time, one more time, one more time.

It was the third week of July.

No way would this kind of grueling schedule have flown in most other cultures. But for Latinx, this is a big part of our heritage. And it was expected that once you were "honored" by being chosen by a quinceañera for her corte, you'd suck it up and bask in her reflected glory on her special day, be immortalized in her pictures, et cetera, et cetera.

It was just hard to see much glory in anything when it was

100 degrees outside, and about 200 percent humidity.

Which might explain why conversations were a little short today, and why even Olivia had screamed at Ariana after Ariana tripped and caused Alex to stumble straight onto the ground with her.

"Hey, calm down," I told her. "She's got that step down. She's just tired."

"If she just DOES IT," Olivia said through her teeth, "then we can all go home. To our ACs."

Tía Celia looked alarmed. "Maybe we should find a way to practice inside?"

So another ten minutes went by as she and Mami (who'd stopped by on her way to pick up Enrique) rearranged the furniture in the Florida room while we sat, slumped, in the hallway, drunk on the cool air.

Finally, the room was ready. The phone rang and Tía Celia and Mami wandered over to the kitchen. Simone stood up and grinned at the group. "This is already going to be the best baile sorpresa this year. Let's make it the best one of all time."

At this point, the only surprise was that we hadn't killed each other yet.

Amazingly, we managed to get through it well enough that Simone said we were done for the night. I slid down to sit on the floor, my back against a wall, and took a long swig of my now lukewarm water. Mauro plopped down next to me.

"You need more sleep, anyone tell you that before?"

This was turning into a running joke, because Mauro's insomnia usually meant that he'd message me a bunch of random shit in the middle of the night. Shit that I should have been able to ignore. But somehow, I keep getting drawn into discussions about things like the possibility of alien life, and how we wouldn't recognize them if they walked among us, especially if they'd watched Earth media before invading. (Which gave me some ideas about Enrique.)

I groaned and shoved him away. "Too tired to deal with you. Go away."

"I'm just training you to be able to stay up all night when I go back to Boston in September," he said.

I felt a hollow dip in my stomach at his words, like when you miss a step on the escalator and come close to falling.

"Um, hi, Mauro." Olivia, looming above us. She sounded almost shy, which surprised me because as far as I could tell, she operated on two modes only: bitchy and totally devoted to Ariana.

"Hey," he said. When she didn't say anything, he prompted, "Hi . . . again?"

She dug her toe into the floor like she was planting herself. "So, um. Can I ask you for something? You know, a favor?"

He straightened up a bit. "What?"

"Well, it's Ariana's birthday. Uh, obviously," she said, rolling her eyes a little at herself. "Anyway, I was wondering if you could take some of the videos I've taken of Ariana and our friends and stuff and print a few pictures from them?"

Mauro pondered this for a second. "Nope, I actually can't do that."

Her face got hard. "OK, sorry I asked." She started to stalk away.

"But I know someone who can do something better for you!" he called.

"Like what?"

"Edited video. You know, to music."

"That would be perfect!" she said eagerly. "You can do that?"

"Nope!" He jerked his head in my direction. "She can."

Oh shit. He did not.

Olivia looked like she shared my feelings completely. "Her?"

"Yep. She worked for a wedding photographer before she worked here." He sounded like a proud mami bragging at Costco. "She's been doing it for a while."

"He means, I HAVEN'T done it in a while," I corrected. "Maybe you should ask someone else."

Now she looked away. "I was hoping to get someone to do it, you know, as a gift."

"Then that's perfect! Carmen *is* her cousin, you know."

Olivia nodded, slowly, like this was new information. She finally turned to me. "So . . . you'll do it?"

"What kind of footage?" I asked, stalling.

She looked impressed that I'd called it that. "Mostly on my phone, but some of her games and stuff I took with my dad's Canon Rebel."

"I don't know. I mean, my laptop is ancient. I could barely run the old software on it. The new Vegas Pro would destroy it . . ."

"Not a problem," Mauro interrupted smoothly. "You can use my equipment. I'll download whatever you need."

"Seriously?" Olivia said, her voice higher-pitched with excitement. "Oh my God, Mauro . . . THANK YOU! You are the best!"

She ran off. She hadn't even bothered to thank me, and I was supposedly the one who was about to do the work.

"Estás loco" was the first thing I said to Mauro as soon as she left. "She's going to want professional quality, not some vidfic girl who wants Veronica to be with Damian on a show! My videos are all about trying to show how things COULD be and SHOULD be. I highly doubt anyone wants me to do that with Ariana's life. Not anyone who likes her, anyway. And do you really think I want to spend MORE of my time finding ways to celebrate my annoying cousin, who I'm barely speaking to? Like I'm not doing enough already? You of all people should know how I feel about this. Like I need another reminder of all the shit Edwin said to me, which is why I'm stuck here with you, by the way? Plus, you know it's going to suck, and then it will be one more thing they can hold over my head to make sure that I know I can never do anything right, especially compared with my perfect cousin, and anyway you should have FUCK-ING ASKED ME, I am literally sitting right next to you . . ."

The steam was curling through my body and coming out of me and I could feel myself getting more and more pissed. Metido, where nobody wanted his ass . . .

"You're right. I'm sorry," he said.

"How exactly does 'sorry' help me right now?"

He held up his hands. "Look, I know I should have asked you. But I knew you'd say no."

"And that didn't maybe give you pause?" I glared at him.

"Not really, because that's what you do. You say no to stuff like that when you should say yes. And I remember those vid-eos. The topics were, um, OK, *maybe* kind of dumb, but the editing was sharp, especially considering the software you were using. And I remember you loved doing it. And if I know you, you've only gotten better since your freshman year. I mean, I'm not lying. Simone told me that you DID work for a wedding videographer."

I wondered what else Simone had told him. He knew about the diploma. Gus's whole neighborhood did, thanks to our epic scream-down in front of his house.

"It was just a hobby." *That I've been doing secretly all summer, usually after we stop chatting online.*

"Not that I even believe you, but so what?" He gave me his most ingratiating smile. "Don't think of it as celebrating

Ariana. Think of it as more time for us to hang out, bang out the video, make fun of your cousin and her friends. I mean, literally *everybody* wins!"

I grumbled as I gave up. "Ugh, why do you always get your way?"

He turned serious for a moment. "You know I don't." He looked intently at me long enough that something in my insides started to shift.

Then he put his arm around my shoulders and added, cheerfully, "For starters, everyone knows Veronica belongs with Charlie."

———————

Waverly burst into the Shack a few hours before Wednesday practice. I was trying to put Simone's receipts into files—easier said than done when her files had names like "?" Literally, just a question mark.

I was happy for the interruption, but Waves should have been at *her* internship, babysitting her amoebas as they split into . . . more amoebas.

"Oh my God, what's wrong?" I asked her immediately.

She laughed. "You know what I love about you most? Your positivity!"

"Well, I am positive you shouldn't be here. So what's up?"

She fanned out a series of envelopes and waved them in front of me. "It's just that I *got my official shopping list for J-ville!* Wanna go to the mall?"

I glanced at the piles of paper. "I'm pretty sure Simone needs me to finish this."

"And I'm pretty sure that Simone will understand that this is a momentous shopping excursion needing the full participation of my very best friend."

"Um . . . why don't you go with Cesar? I'm sure he wants to spend more time with you."

This was clearly the wrong thing to say. Her eyes narrowed. "I spend plenty of time with Cesar, and this is something I wanted to do with YOU. You remember. You? Me? Best friends? We do stuff together?"

"And now you do stuff with Cesar." I couldn't quite keep the bitterness out of my voice. She was *my* best friend, and it did feel a little like she had gone over to the enemy when she started dating him. Especially since we never really talked about it. Not that she needed my permission or anything.

And if I was honest, the last thing I wanted to do was help her buy stuff that meant she'd be leaving for good.

"I've invited you to come out with us before. You should get to know him again, Carmen. You might like him."

"I DO like him. And I know he likes you. Go forth and go to the mall. Take him to lunch or something."

"No," she said slowly. "This isn't about Cesar. This is about college. You know, Carmen, you are the one who chose not to go—"

"I don't even have my diploma yet!"

"Which you didn't know would happen, so you could have still applied and then deferred. They would have worked with you."

"And how do you know that? Oh, could it be because *your* parents work at a college? And can afford to send you?"

"I'm getting aid to J-ville," she muttered.

"Which they knew how to get for you." I pointed at the papers in her hand. "I'm happy for you, I am—just because I can't go right this minute doesn't mean anything."

"No, it does," she said softly. "It really does." She hugged her mail to her chest. "It means . . . I got you this job. Because I support you. And it sucks that you can't do the same for me. Not with J-ville. Not with Cesar. I love you, but . . . you suck at being there for people."

And with that, she flounced out of the Shack, the little bell on the door ringing like a cheery wave goodbye.

"Simone," I called out past the lump in my throat. "Can I have a long lunch?"

———————

Oh, *not* to go to the mall with Waverly. Hell no. Not after the tantrum she just threw at me. I mean, I *was* trying to be supportive. Hadn't I kept my mouth shut about her and Cesar even after she said NOTHING to me about it? Hadn't I listened to her go on and on about extra-long twin sheets and Bed Bath & Beyond coupons and her new roommate from DC?

No. Cesar could have her ass.

I just needed to get out of the Shack for a little bit.

I walked through the neighborhood, and thank God I knew it well by now, because I was blind, having the argument with Waverly in my head again, only winning this time.

Except the more I walked, the more another voice, quieter, started to seep in. Like, maybe Waverly had a point. About the school thing. It wasn't that I was jealous, but . . . OK, maybe I was a little jealous. In the traditional meaning of the word. I knew I was going to lose Waverly to school. She'd find people she liked better; she'd come home in the fall like the college kids always did, with big words and bigger egos.

And she'd realize she was too good for me and always had been.

I'd never really had a best friend until Waverly. I'd had Ariana, I'd had Mami. And a long time ago, I'd had Mauro. But a best friend? That took a lot of trust that I didn't want to give. It took a lot of letting people know you—the real you.

It took a lot of giving them that part of you, and then watching them walk away.

I put my hands over my face. Dios mío, Waverly was right about everything, and I had to apologize. My call went to her voice mail. I tried a text.

> Me: Hey, you were right. I'm sorry. Let's go shopping! Cafés con leche after—my treat. You can even bring Cesar if you want.

But it went unread.

I blew air into my bangs and looked up. Somehow, my feet had brought me to a mall (another reason I prefer walking to driving—would a car have known where I needed to go?). And look—a Bed Bath & Beyond. I could pick up the damn extra-long sheets, maybe in a hideous pattern we could laugh at when she called from school. Which I knew she would do. Because unlike me, Waverly knew how to be a best friend.

And tucked next to the store was a cute little boutique, the kind that had those mini canvases with messages like "You got this!" Waverly loved that stuff. I quickly found the perfect one—"We are the scientists, trying to make sense of the stars inside us," Christopher Poindexter—and paid. It still didn't feel close to enough, though, so I kept browsing.

I was staring into a crystal ball when a voice at my shoulder said, "You casting a spell with that?"

Great. Ariana. "No," I sighed. "If I were, you wouldn't be here."

"Um, I guess I deserved that." For some reason, Mauro entered into my head. The echo of him saying close to the same thing at the Twister practice.

"Is Tía Celia with you?"

"Nah, she's at the bath store. She wants to get all new stuff for the bathrooms before the family comes in for the quince."

"Cool. See you at practice."

She picked at a mosquito bite on her leg. "Actually . . . it's good that *you* are here. Can I talk to you?"

"As long as you quit doing that."

She gave me the ghost of a grin. "Nice of you to care."

"Just a habit."

"Carmen . . . I've been thinking about you ever since we were at Doña Thomasina's . . . trying on the dresses. It was something that I always saw doing with you but, like, with us as *friends*. And you should have had that moment, too, and . . ." She waved her hands and fluttered her eyelashes and waited for me to rescue her.

Oh no, not this time.

After a second, she sighed. "I'm sorry about what I said at Gus's house—I can barely remember all of it, but what I do remember?" She winced. "It sucked and I was wrong. And you were . . . I mean, fine, you were right. Something about seeing that doorman talk about Tía Mira and you . . . it just bugged me."

"Because you can't stand not to be the center of attention for five minutes?"

"Oh, please. When am I EVER the center of attention when you are around? This quince is more about you and the Dreams than me . . . you are helping Simone plan and choreograph and—and . . . I didn't want you in it because I knew this would happen. You'd end up being the star and I'd be hidden behind you at my own damn party!"

Me? The star? Ha.

She took a deep breath. "And you should be the one to feel guilty, not me! You abandoned me—"

"What?"

"I was *twelve*. You were my idol. And then I made *one* mistake and—"

"Hold up. I did not abandon you. If anything, you and your mother—"

"Just . . . please. *Please*." That *please* would have cost me at least a spleen. But I still watched her, unsure. "Can we just . . . not hate each other anymore? I don't want to go through the rest of my quince like this. We still have five and a half weeks to go!" She nudged a little closer to me, and the reflection blurred us into each other. "I really am sorry." She peered into my face. "Aren't you?"

"You girls gonna get that?" An older woman wearing a long satin cape walked up to us.

I put the crystal ball back down. "No, thanks. I don't think it works."

I left the store without another cute gift for Waves (bad friend) and hoping Ariana would go back to Tía Celia (bad prima). But she just followed me to the middle of the complex, where there was a cement fountain shaped like an angel, pennies carrying so many wishes scattered like sequins around it. She trailed her hand in the water.

"Remember when we used to come here in, like, August, and stick our feet in because it was so hot?" I said.

"Yeah, but then we'd get screamed at because Mami and Tía Mira couldn't go into stores until we dried."

"Especially since the stores crank the AC like they're trying to make snow." I hadn't thought about that for a long time.

Ariana turned to me. "Carmen . . ."

"Yeah." I trailed my own hand in the water.

"This would be the time to tell me that you are sorry too and that we're cool."

I couldn't quite force those words past my lips, so instead I said, "I haven't quit your quince and . . . I don't want to throw myself into traffic every day. Maybe just every other."

She laughed and flicked up some water at me. "Progress!"

I was deer-in-headlights frozen for a second. Then I said, "Oh, you are SO going to regret that!"

She cupped water in her hand and flung it at me.

"OK, OK, it's ON, little cousin!"

"Still big enough for me to kick your ass!" She started double cupping the water, throwing it over my hair and T-shirt. By this point, we were both laughing so hard we were hiccuping.

A security guard came over to us, already looking pissed off. "Hey, hey! You two! Stop! You are making a huge mess!" He looked me up and down. "You are DEFINITELY old enough to know better!"

Ari and I tried to look repentant. "Sorry, sir."

He puffed up. "Just . . . get out of here. Go!"

We turned the corner back toward Bed Bath & Beyond and slid down the wall, cracking up.

"Is this the baptism of our new relationship?" she asked, gasping with laughter.

"Yeah, the kind where we have to bring in the authorities."

She leaned her head on my shoulder for a second. And I let her. "Following in their footsteps. The mamis would be SO proud."

———————

Later that night, I stared into my screen, just like I did almost every night. But I wasn't scanning Mauro's words, for once, or flipping through a romance.

Instead, I was staring at a splash screen for FIU. Florida International University. It wasn't the maple-leafed campus of my TV dreams, but it was . . . a start. Something close to home, something affordable. And they even had a video production program. Like I said, a start.

Because Waves was right. It was too easy for me to think that no one would ever work with me on anything. Easier than asking.

But maybe I was tired of taking the easy way out. Maybe it was time to force the world to reject me, instead of rejecting myself.

It was just research. Preliminary research. I didn't know what I wanted. But I knew I was finally ready to start looking.

My fingers only shook a little as I clicked on "Request more information."

Nineteen

I DROPPED OFF THE sheets and the canvas quote by Waverly's door with a note. *Did a little shopping for your time in J-ville. The sheets actually weren't that hard to find.*

And then I waited. If she forgave me, she'd say something. It wasn't like Waverly to play hard to get once she'd decided about something.

One of the many ways we were different.

I didn't have long to wait. As soon as I got to Ariana's for practice, Waves threw her arms around me so hard I almost fell backward. "You bitch. You made me cry with the heartfelt emotion of your note."

"What? They *weren't* that hard to find."

She grinned. "I forgive you. And to celebrate—you, me, and Cesar, hanging out and spending time together! Tonight, at the Grille down on Ocean. Just the way it's going to be for the rest of the summer."

"You make that sound like a threat," I muttered as Simone clapped for us to get into position.

"Oh," Waves said, tossing her head as she went to find Cesar, "it is."

Something about being out to dinner with Waves and Cesar made me start watching them like we were on a nature special. Behold the grizzly bear and the lion. These powerful titans have developed a rare and special friendship—but no one else should dare to get too close.

"And then the amoebas started their division, exactly to plan. And it was so exciting—like, I was partnering with nature herself or something!" Waverly said excitedly. The Grille was the kind of place that ended up on the glossy cover of the magazine they put in hotel rooms. Cesar must have been *really* trying to impress Waves.

Cesar grabbed a roll, and then made a face. "Ever since I started dating you, I'm afraid to take a bite out of anything, for fear that I'm destroying a whole civilization of organisms or something. Like I'm Godzilla."

"That's because you are such a sweetheart," Waverly said, grinning at him. I expected him to front being a tough guy, the way he usually did, but instead he ducked his head a little, a pleased smile on his face.

The smile of the lovestruck.

I checked around for escape routes. Sometimes, I'd heard,

they were behind you.

But then they toned it down, and we spent the rest of dinner talking about summer jobs (Cesar was working, reluctantly, at Tío Victor's dealership) and movies we wanted to see.

Even though they weren't being mushy anymore, it was obvious to anyone with eyes how into each other they were. Waverly was fluttery, always leaning toward him. And Cesar— usually Cesar's smile was more of a smirk, like he thought everything was a joke. But around Waverly, his smile was genuine, and he threw his head back and laughed.

It was just nice to be around them. Mostly.

After dinner, Cesar said, "Hey, let's go down to the beach."

I figured he was just talking to Waves, so I said, "Cool— have fun, you guys!"

NOW the Cesar smirk was back. "I meant you too, loca."

So that was how we all ended up walking along Ocean Drive as the sun set.

"You know, if we were in LA right now," Waverly commented, "this would truly be spectacular. Because the sun sets in the west, directly over the water there."

"Eh, I like this," Cesar said, stretching his arms wide to indicate not just the beach, but the line of cars that snaked next to it, playing everything from cumbia to reggaetón to black metal.

She snuggled into him. "They have music there, too, you know."

But it couldn't be like this. I mean, there are Latinx in

LA, claro, it's practically northern Mexico, but Miami . . . we saturated this place. Cesar and I understood that, felt that in our bones, in a way that Waves maybe didn't.

The salt air tingled on my cheeks, and I could smell the garlic wafting from the restaurants up and down Ocean, combined with the scent of coconut from everybody's suntan lotion.

It was sweet of Cesar and Waverly to stroll with me on the beach, considering how romantic the whole situation was.

I felt like a charity case.

DivaCee: Trapped on a date.

I hit send and then immediately regretted it. I'm not sure why I had messaged Mauro at all.

MrtB: Give me a place. I'll show up with a bat and ask no questions.

I laughed. Waverly glanced at me for a second, and then she and Cesar sped up, just a touch.

DivaCee: I'm the third wheel, actually. I'm with Waverly and Cesar.

MrtB: That's great!

MrtB: Well, better than the alternative.

DivaCee: And what would that be?

"Uh, Carmen? Are we interrupting something?" I tucked my phone away, guilty. But Waverly shook her head, a smile widening on her face. "No, you go back to your conversation. Cesar and I are going down to the water."

DivaCee: Shit. I think Waves knows I'm talking to you.

MrtB: Is it a secret?

DivaCee: No . . . I mean, not exactly.

MrtB: I don't know if I should be honored or offended to be your dirty little secret.

DivaCee: Depends. Are you dirty?

MrtB: Why don't you come over and find out?

I could almost hear him saying that, in the low, raspy voice he used when we would meet up in the darkroom.

And where did THAT thought come from?

DivaCee: Uh, actually, I think I'm going to enjoy this lovely sunset over the water with my cousin and my best friend. Talk later.

MrtB: K. I'm always here.

MrtB: Also, technically, while the sunset is at the beach, it's not over the water because of the whole East Coast/West Coast thing.

I laughed and logged off, then ran to catch up with Waverly and Cesar. Ready for Waves's snark about my phone addiction.

Except I didn't have any smart answers for her. Because I didn't understand it myself.

If I was addicted, maybe it was time to go cold turkey.

———

Midnight:

MrtB: So . . .

MrtB: Tonight sounds like it was fun.

DivaCee: ☹ I mean, I'm happy for Waves and all. I just

wonder . . . she's going to school in Jacksonville. Cesar is here. Summer is halfway over. What's the point?

MrtB: Does the heart need a plan? Must love have a point? Also, maybe Waverly's heard of these wonderful things called cars . . . or trains . . . even buses.

DivaCee: Not the same. I wonder if they'll be OK.

MrtB: Define OK.

DivaCee: Stay together. Stay happy.

MrtB: Then probably not.

I rolled over on the bed. Something about his smart-ass answer put me in the position of being the defender of true love and shit, which, obviously, was not my usual.

DivaCee: You weren't at this dinner. They were all over each other. It was sickening.

MrtB: Eh, limerence. Crush time. Gather ye rosebuds. That shit never lasts.

DivaCee: It must last for SOME people.

MrtB: Yeah? Name them.

The seconds ticked by, and I could only come up with a few names.

DivaCee: Tía Celia and Tío Victor. And Waves's parents. So maybe they have a better chance because they've seen it growing up.

DivaCee: Not like me. Junior and Mami. The whirlwind, only to settle down and find him gone and us covered with trash.

DivaCee: Metaphorically, of course.

MrtB: Believe me, I get it.

I'd always wondered why Mauro lived with Oscar and not his mother, but I'd known enough not to ask. Years of having to hear questions about Junior had taught me well.

DivaCee: Yeah.

MrtB: Wanna talk about it?

DivaCee: . . . ?

MrtB: Your superhero origin story. Your parents.

The cursor blinked through the silence.

DivaCee: Not much to tell that you didn't already hear that night at Gus's.

DivaCee: Junior . . . he's Puerto Rican and lived there. Miami was a place where he could take a vacation.

DivaCee: He and Mami, it was like . . . fast and furious. She was on the rebound from Tío Victor. They used to date before he hooked up with Tía Celia.

I waited a second to see if he'd have any reaction to that bit of family weirdness at all. When he didn't, I kept typing.

DivaCee: Junior was exciting and flashy and he had money. So they hooked up and she got pregnant with me and . . . he went home. And I don't know if the plan was for us to go over there. I mean, he knew about me. I was born before he left. He was back and forth for a bit. Then I guess he just . . . forgot us. And he was gone.

I had that inner squirm of sharing too much and wishing I could take it back.

MrtB: I'm sorry, Carmen.

MrtB: Believe me, I understand.

MrtB: Have I ever talked to you about my maternal situation?

DivaCee: I never wanted to pry.

MrtB: I'm volunteering. So! Story time. My mother was a model, and my father was a photographer, so you'd think it was perfect, right? Not so much.

MrtB: Oscar was a womanizer, and Stella wasn't going to take that. So she left him. But it was like he had left her first, and it didn't matter that they were living in the same house. They weren't together in any of the ways that matter.

MrtB: Anyway, Oscar got his first *Vogue* cover for Italia, and he turned that into a lot of European work. We'd been traveling so much and I fell behind in school. It was eighth grade. I figured I'd stay home with Stella—she was adamant that I go with Oscar. She said it would change my life, and it did. When we got back, she was gone.

I could almost hear his voice right now, the defensive deadpan, like his life was something he'd seen on TV. I knew he needed for me to believe it.

I knew that voice because I'd used that voice. And I needed the same thing.

I kept my own tone casual, even as my heart ached with a strange feeling. Sympathy for Mauro.

DivaCee: Wow. Did you ever see her again?

MrtB: Not really. I mean, I did, but . . . I just couldn't be her son in the same way. Then she got busy with her work, and I started high school, and Dad got *Modelista* and we moved here.

MrtB: I asked her once why she had left me with Oscar, and she said he needed me. I guess that meant she didn't. Anyway, from then on Oscar was full of lessons about "how to be a man." And lesson number one was that a man didn't need anybody. Especially not a woman.

I remembered Mauro's cold eyes when he told me that I shouldn't bother going to his party at all, because I wasn't going to get anything out of him.

He'd already learned his father's lessons well.

MrtB: Not like he was abusive or anything, more like . . . he was angry about Stella. I was angry about Stella. But I also thought if I were like him, I would never have to feel that way again. So . . . that was the year I figured I'd go all out in my Become Oscar plan. Follow his advice. New school. New life. Sophomore year.

DivaCee: Good plan.

MrtB: Not so much. In hindsight.

MrtB: So, yeah, I'm one of the few people I know who can say he has a deadbeat mom.

DivaCee: That sucks. You didn't deserve that.

MrtB: Yeah, well. Neither did you.

MrtB: I've never told anyone that before. Thanks for listening. Er, reading.

Silence. I ached with something I couldn't put into words. It wasn't just sympathy. It was sameness.

MrtB: Getting back to Waverly and Cesar . . . if it's doomed, it's doomed whether they are in the same room or on opposite continents.

DivaCee: I don't know . . . There's a reason why people say "out of sight, out of mind."

MrtB: They also say "absence makes the heart grow fonder."

DivaCee: Or we could just be taking this all way too seriously. I mean, it's a summer romance. That's a thing too, right?

And I linked him to "Summer Nights" from *Grease*.

MrtB: Exactly. Summer loving, had me a blast. If everyone were always obsessed about endings, there would be no beginnings.

DivaCee: Well, here's to no beginnings, endings, OR middles then.

MrtB: ☺ And that's why I'm happy we're friends, Carmen. Just when I think I've gotten as morose as possible, you manage to out-bleak me.

 *Twenty*

AT THE END OF the next practice a few days later, Olivia pressed a few DVDs into my hand. *"Footage,"* she mouthed. Ariana was standing a little away from us with Alex (as usual), but she still eyed us curiously. I nodded and shoved them into my backpack.

Once I got home, I went into my room and started booting up my old-ass laptop. I knew it would take the pobrecita a while to wheeze into life, so I wandered into the kitchen, where Mami was slicing into a stack of mail and sighing. She looked up and tried to smile when I came in.

"Bills?"

"Well, let's just say it's not invitations," she said, pushing everything away and patting the table in front of her. "I need a break. Siéntate."

"Where's Enrique? He need a break, too?" Oh, if only . . .

She laughed. "Don't sound so happy. He's coming . . . he's

just running some errands, picking up some dinner from La Carreta." She faltered. "You want me to call him and get you something, too? It's just that you haven't been around much lately . . ."

"No, it's OK. I'll be in my room working on something anyway."

"Working? On what? Something for school?"

"Nope. A favor."

"For? No, wait . . . let me guess." She did a quick drumroll on the table. "Ariana's quince. What do I win, Don Francisco?"

"Wow, you are like Walter Mercado, Mami."

"It's strange," she mused, tapping her chin like she did when she was about to get all deep. "One quince tore us apart and one will bring us together."

"That your fortune cookie for today or what?" I said, teasing her while I nosed around in the fridge.

"And it HAS brought us together," she said, ignoring me. "How are YOU, though? We haven't had much time to talk lately. You've been so busy with the quince, and I've been with Enrique." She paused and blushed. So unlike her. "I still can't really believe that it's been this easy, tú sabes? Like . . . Celia and I are really BOTH working on this. We actually talk through our disagreements without screaming about everything we've ever done to each other. So *this* is what adulthood is like." She gave a short laugh and shook her head. "But . . . don't think that I don't get that this is weird for you, to be around everyone again. I've missed Celia and Victor and Ariana and Cesar. But did you?"

"Not like you cared about how weird it was before," I reminded her. At least she pretended to look guilty.

I ignored the question about missing everyone because she had to know how much I *had* missed everyone. Especially Ariana. Even if I wasn't sure how I felt about Ariana right now. Sometimes I could look at her and remember the way we'd been, and I'd want so much to get back to that. But then Alex would sling his arm around her, and something would steel itself around my heart. I didn't even *like* him anymore, really. I'd learned how to turn my heart off when I saw that something was impossible. But . . . it still burned that he'd fallen for her so easily, when I'd wanted him for so long.

"It's complicated." I shrugged and grabbed a banana from the counter. "It's OK so far. But, like, let's see how things go after this party is over."

"That's my question, too, mija. What happens after. Not just with the family. Con tu vida."

Then I got it. Mami wanted to make this one of Those Talks. One where I'd give her something to hold on to, something that told her that, yes, I actually had plans beyond playing pretend Belle at parties.

Too bad that I didn't *actually* have those plans yet.

"I know it's summer," she kept going, "but it won't be

forever. Once you get the diploma you so richly deserve, you need to start thinking about jobs, school, and everything else." The words *Don't Be Like Me* were flashing above us like a neon sign, but neither of us actually pointed to them.

"I know" was all I said.

She heard in my voice that I didn't exactly want to travel down this road with her tonight, so she said instead, "Tell me about this favor. Nothing illegal, right?"

"Well, first I make Ariana a fake ID and then . . ."

"Carmen Maria," she warned. "Not funny."

I laughed. "No, it's a . . . kind of video. Olivia gave me some footage, and she wants me to edit it."

"You know how to do that?" She sounded surprised. "Did one of your boyfriends teach you that?"

"No, believe it or not, I actually had an interest and taught myself how to do something with my own inferior lady parts."

"Fresh mouth," she said, and tapped me upside the head. "So show me." She followed me back to my room and stood over me while I opened the program.

"Uh, maybe you should let me watch this first." Ariana and I had been burned by parental viewings of our extracurriculars before.

"Why? I'll see whatever is on there at some point anyway, right?"

"That's why they call it editing," I said pointedly.

She threw up her hands. "Lucky for you I don't have the patience to start that thing up." She winked. "Unless it's for a very, very good reason."

Note to self: Change password.

Mami was still on the *Chicken Soup for a Teenager's Soul* advice kick. "Look, Carmencita. I know that whatever you are doing now feels like it's going to be the one thing that matters forever, but not everything from now deserves to go on into the future with you, tú sabes? I mean, Ariana, sure. Your friends, of course. But not everything." She paused. "Like, Alex . . . now that he's with Ariana, maybe he needs to be cut loose." She fiddled with her bracelet. "I haven't told Celia, you know, about them."

I thought about the way Alex and Ariana were together at practice.

"Tía Celia doesn't know?"

Mami smirked. "Celia is the reigning queen of only seeing what she wants to see. And believe me, she doesn't want to see that. ¿Y que? You think I want Celia to know her daughter won over mine?" She poked me. "Kidding! He's just a boy, no prize."

"Well, thanks, I guess. Nice of you not to stand in the way of true love." I said it sarcastically, but she took me seriously and squinted her eyes.

"Don't make me reconsider . . . I did it for YOU, mija. Not him. Or her. Or them."

"It's ancient history."

And that's when she looked at me, and her eyes knew everything, the way they always did when she really *looked*.

"You're only eighteen . . . how ancient can it be?" Then she pulled my head onto her shoulder. "You are so much like me. So stubborn. Piensas que lo sabes todo."

"Any more life advice?" I didn't move, though. It hadn't been like this for months.

"Um . . . don't get pregnant. Go to college. Don't eat all the arroz con frijoles they give you in restaurants—they just want to fill you up for cheap."

I laughed. "Who are *they* exactly?"

"And don't ignore what's right in front of you!"

"And what is that?" I asked.

She rolled her eyes. "Ese Mauro tiene potencial. You know I'm not the most forgiving person, but . . . that hasn't always served me well. Look how much time Celia and I have wasted! I'm enlightened now!"

"Started yoga again?" I teased, but her words still struck home.

So! She did remember Mauro!

Sonofa . . .

I thought about the conversation Mauro and I had had the night of my date with Waves and Cesar. About Junior, about his mother. Our stories were in each other now, and we were unlocked. The filter over everything I knew about him changed. Our story had to be re-edited.

"Mauro and I are just friends."

Those eyes that saw everything narrowed. "I think you've already forgiven him, and it's pissing you off big-time."

She was about to say more when the door opened, and the usual suspect bellowed out, "Mirella! Dónde estás? The feast has arrived, and I got your favorite bizcocho for dessert!"

Mami stood up, smiling. "Oh, and tell your *friend* that if he doesn't let you sleep, the least he can do is bring you some café con leche when he sees you."

"He does," I said softly.

Her eyes gleamed. "That's why that one is a keeper."

I tried to get Mami's words out of my head while I watched the footage in front of me, but I couldn't concentrate. Part of the problem was that Olivia had given me EVERYTHING she'd shot for what seemed to be the last couple of years, and a lot of it was her and Ariana giggling over some joke that nobody bothered to share with the camera.

My body decided that what I needed was a nap.

What I got was a weird dream.

Mauro in a Truth Squad T-shirt, tracing lines into my hand. The simple touch flooding me with tenderness, and something else, too. "So, finally, you made a choice." A pause. "The aliens would prefer pairs." And then he was laughing, and I was laughing, too, as I reached toward him, tangling my other hand in his tousled hair as I pulled his face to mine. The warmth of his breath heated my skin, and the moment shivered between us. I traced my thumb along his lips and strained to get closer to him. But it wasn't enough. And then I woke up pissed off and turned on and terrified. Because it wasn't a nightmare, and it wasn't a lie.

Shit. Mami was absolutely right.

Exactly the worst thing in the world had happened again.

Only so much worse than before.

And I knew I couldn't go back to sleep.

Twenty-One

SO DID YOU THINK that once I'd figured out my idiotic attraction was back, I'd use all my wiles (and they were considerable) to get Mauro into bed so I could get it out of my system?

Hell no. If the Mayo Clinic had had some sort of protocol for purging unwanted feelings, I would have followed it to the letter. No way would indulging my stupidity help it go away.

Instead, I distracted myself.

First, I cleaned my room from top to bottom. Then I deleted the playlist he'd created for me online (well . . . disabled it). I took the Polaroid of us at practice that Waverly gave me the other day and stuck it deep in a drawer.

Then I went back to the footage Olivia had given me and logged it with grim determination. I studied it like Olivia was going to test my ass about the final score when the soccer team from Our Lady of Rich Bitches played Sacred Mastercard Academy last year (it was 3–2 and my cousin scored the winning goal). Every time my concentration flagged, I pinched myself. Somehow, without me noticing, Mauro had become the base level of my thoughts, and I was chatting with him in my head all the time.

This shouldn't have been a problem. I had one stupid dream about a hookup. I've also dreamed about hooking up with Harry Styles (don't judge).

But. My mami had spoken. So extra measures were necessary.

I even carefully, carefully stoked the ultimate fire—my old feelings for Alex.

Dangerous, but worth trying. I'd deal with the repercussions later.

Except the way I felt for Alex could not be stoked. There were no embers left to inflame.

And tonight I was going over to Simone's to work on Ariana's footage with Mauro.

———————

I was nervous and angry about it when I rang her doorbell. Mauro threw the door open. "Hey, you," he said, a slow smile curling on his face like he knew exactly how I'd just spent the last few hours.

"Is Simone here?"

His smile faltered. "Um, no. She had plans. I told her you were coming over, though."

"You needed to *clear me* with Simone?"

"No, but . . . No. You OK?"

"I'm fine," I snapped.

"Aw, c'mon. You're not holding a grudge anymore about me volunteering you, right?" If I still had a functional brain, I'd be holding on to *all* the grudges. Alas.

"It'll be fun," he said, and put his arm around me, pulling me toward his bedroom. I stiffened, and he dropped his arm.

Mauro's room was sparse, except for the corner devoted to his computer and speakers and his haphazard pile of discs and headphones and papers. A picture of us as Belle and the Beast was tucked into his mirror, at eye level. A postcard from NYC and another from Barcelona were immediately above and below it.

I put a flash drive in his hands. "This represents the last week of work. I watched everything and edited it down to this. We just need to download and render it before we start."

"Well, actually," he said, fishing out another freaking flash drive. I eyed it.

"Please tell me that's not what I think it is."

"I am afraid it's probably exactly what you think it is."

I groaned. "More?"

"Olivia said this is the stuff she's shot around rehearsals."

"Great. No wonder they can't learn anything."

He slipped the flash into the drive and immediately Ariana's face filled his screen.

"Here we go again," I muttered. I settled myself into his

chair, trying not to think about the fact that this was exactly where he probably sat while we chatted in the middle of the night.

He turned me around. "I'm sorry. Again," he started, leaning over me a little and looking at me intently. "I just figured that things were OK enough with your cousin, and . . ." Here he smiled self-consciously. "I thought it would be a nice way for you to catch up with her life and . . . know her again. Second chances." He rubbed his cheeks until they were red. "I'm sentimental, sue me."

It would have taken so little for me to reach out to him, to touch him. And I'm (pretty) sure that he wouldn't have resisted.

"Maybe . . . we should just get to work?" I turned away from him.

"OK . . ." But he kept leaning over my shoulder, pressing keys.

I shuddered. This was never going to work.

"Can you get off me, please?"

Without another word, he got a chair and settled next to me.

I tried to ignore Mauro's closeness while I stared at the screen. My own face, hard and uncertain, as my family danced far away. Everybody playing Twister, me landing so close to Mauro that our faces almost touched. Alex twirling Ariana by the pool, where she slipped and almost fell in.

"See? He's gotten better, too. He's not a hazard to himself and others anymore. Still a tool, though," Mauro said.

"Ay, enough. I'm beginning to think you are the one in love with him." I watched a clip again, making notes on the seconds I'd be shaving off and what transitions I wanted to slide in.

"Love. Huh." He typed hard after that and didn't look at me.

We worked in silence for a bit, and I started to lose myself in the rhythms of the process. Play, pause, mark entrance and exit points, drop in the timeline, render, smooth with the tools, insert transitions, select effects and filters. This app was a gigantic improvement over the last ones I'd used, on my computer and even at Edwin's, and it worked as fast as thought. It was satisfying to make something, as long as I kept my mind off who I was making it with.

Except that we'd forgotten one of the most important steps. I hit my forehead. "Coño, Mauro . . . I forgot!"

"What," he said, distracted, frowning at a bit of corrupted clip.

"Hi, we need music!"

"Oh shit. Yeah." He frowned again. "What are her favorite songs?"

"How the hell should I know?"

"What were her favorite songs before?"

I thought of the reggaetón anthem everyone was dancing to back then and shook my head. "I don't think my tía would appreciate seeing Ariana's life narrated to the dulcet tones of 'Mueve Dat Ass.'"

He laughed and started humming it. "No, I guess not."

I went back to cutting clips while he virtually rummaged through his many files, looking for a song that could work.

He found some clips of me singing as Belle. I shook my head. "Totally doesn't fit into the mood of the vid. Plus, I sound fuzzy."

"You sound good, but I agree with your first point."

While I worked, I started singing a cheesy Vegas rendition of Alphaville's "Forever Young." He cocked his head to one side. "Maybe a little on the nose. But . . ." He grabbed his guitar. "Try it a little more wistful chanteuse and a little less seventies Elvis." He sat cross-legged on his bed, the guitar balanced on his lap, the strap pulled taut on his shoulder.

This was the most textbook seduction ever.

And it wasn't a seduction.

We were friends. Nothing more. He knew that.

He strummed softly until he found the key. Then looked up at me expectantly.

"Uh, I don't know all the words," I stammered.

"You aren't really going to make me do everything, are you?" He groaned.

I didn't answer.

"Fine. You and your cousin owe me forever. Just jump in whenever I hit something you recognize."

He started to sing, and I could feel my stomach tighten. I held my breath hard because if I let it go soft now, then everything would go soft. I would go soft.

"You're never going to be able to sing if you don't let your-self breathe," he commented. Then he started again, looking up at me every now and then through the hair that had fallen onto his forehead. I followed his lead, somehow, and got through the song.

Our voices mingled. He even managed some harmony.

It was . . . beautiful.

We were silent after the last note. Mauro reached over and pressed a button on his keyboard. "Not bad. Well, it's an idea, anyway."

It was impossible that he didn't see how I was feeling.

Without another word, we went back to the timeline and the footage, watching my cousin growing up like one of those time-lapse movies. Watching her with Olivia and her other friends, stretching before a soccer game, pushing the camera away, laughing during a supposed study session. Watching her with Alex.

It felt weird to see so much of her without me. I had missed a lot.

I didn't realize that I was rewinding and replaying the same scene of Alex and Ariana—a scene where they sat at the base of the palm tree in Ari's backyard. They weren't talking, but she had her head on his shoulder and he was playing with her fin-gers, held loosely on her knee. I was trying to time it perfectly to the lyric "Youth's like diamonds in the sun/And diamonds are forever."

Mauro reached past me and clicked it off. "That's it. You're cut off."

I stood up and stretched. "How close are we to done?"

"You tell me."

"I can't tell you anything right now. I don't think I could tell you my own name."

He held up three fingers. "How many fingers am I holding up?"

"A part of a hand." I giggled, and then stopped myself. I don't giggle off princess duty. Ariana must have been seeping into my brain.

"Maybe you should lie down . . ."

". . . five minutes," I said, and flopped down on his bed and almost immediately fell asleep.

The first thing I realized in the morning was that it wasn't my bed. It smelled like pine needles and soap and coconut oil and sandalwood.

The second thing was that I wasn't alone.

Oh, I was alone in the bed, but I could see Mauro lying on the floor, on a pile of sheets and pillows, like he'd planned to make himself a nest and fallen asleep before he'd managed it. He could have slept in his bed; I was out like a light and I wouldn't even have realized it.

But he hadn't. And that fact filled me with a tenderness that felt like regret.

And yeah, I admit it. I let myself look at him, all soft in sleep, his eyelashes curled impossibly long on his cheeks, his hair rumpled and messy. Old familiar feelings crowded inside me, fighting with new ones, threatening to spill out and do something incredibly stupid. Like reach out. Like touch him.

My hand started creeping toward him on its own.

Except that just then, I realized the third thing. The most important thing.

Mami. She was going to kill me. The only question was whether she'd wait until I got home or hunt me down.

I hopped out of bed and started gathering myself together. No time to leave a note—Mauro would figure out where I'd gone. I scrolled through my texts and missed calls. Two texts from Mami, and then nothing.

What did that mean?

Halfway down the stairs, I heard a voice.

"Mauro? Should I make coffee?"

Oh shit. Fourth thing. This wasn't Mauro's house—it was Simone's.

"Carmen, would you like some more coffee?" Simone held the pot out to me, her face a mask of politeness that I'd only ever seen used on our most difficult clients. It was like Awkwardness itself was sitting with us at the table; it would not have surprised me if Simone had offered Mr. Awkward some bacon and eggs. "I know it's not café con leche, but—"

"No, it's good. I mean, thanks."

I still hadn't texted or called Mami back, which meant I was pressing my luck into the next galaxy. Since I was dead anyway, I might as well have the World's Most Awkward Breakfast with my boss and my ex.

Mauro and I were very intentionally not looking at each other. I couldn't stop thinking about last night. Him, holding the guitar and singing. Him, snuggled on the floor so I could have the bed. Him, him, him.

Ugh, he was like a song permanently stuck in my head.

"No, thank you." I stared down at my plate. Scrambled eggs of shame. Toast of trepidation. Bacon of . . . OK, bacon is always welcome.

Mauro's eyes flicked from me to Simone, and then he put his fork down with a loud clatter and said, "Simone. Nothing happened."

"I didn't ask!" she protested.

"You didn't have to," Mauro said. He grabbed another slice of bacon, like this was totally normal. "We were working on something for Ari, and it got late, and she was too tired to go home." Just all matter-of-fact, like nothing else could have occurred to him. "She fell asleep on the bed. I slept on the floor."

Simone looked appeased, if still a little suspicious. "Just . . . Look, Mauro. I know things aren't great between you and Oscar right now, but he is my friend and he's already trusting me enough to have you stay here—"

"And you know he wouldn't give a rat's ass about Carmen spending the night here, except to give me crap about sleeping on the floor."

"Oh, I don't think—"

"—anything but the best about my father, I know, I know." Mauro rolled his eyes. "But believe me, I know him better than you do."

Simone smirked a little. "Somehow, I doubt that."

Which of course meant I was dying to ask her more about Oscar. But that conversation was going to have to wait because Mauro was sawing at his omelet like he was performing pissed-off surgery on it.

Not seeing a lot of promise in that direction, Simone turned to me. "And I called Waverly this morning, Carmen, but she'd already checked in with your mom and told her you were with her."

"How did Waves know?" Best friend telepathy?

"Cesar told her that your mom called his, looking for you."

Wow. "I'm amazed she didn't demand to speak to me."

Simone's face turned pink. "Um, Waverly made it sound like she was maybe . . . interrupting your mom and, uh . . . when she called your house."

Oh my God. Brain bleach needed in aisle one.

She cleared her throat. "Still, I feel compelled to say—"

Mauro looked up again, and she held out her hand.

"Stop. It's my job as the adult here. Now . . ." She looked at both of us. "I'm not blind, and I know something is happening between you two—"

"You are blind," Mauro said, shaking his head and reaching for another piece of bacon.

Óyeme, he didn't have to sound so vehement about it.

"But whatever is happening, I just want you both to be sure. Carmen, I feel responsible for you—I'm your summer mentor, after all! But I also care about you, both of you, and workplace romances—"

"Are a bad idea," I finished for her. "Which is why we're not having one."

Ha! Two could be vehement. Vehement felt good, even, *especially* if it got under his skin. But Mauro just nodded.

"And if I find out anything IS happening, especially here, under my roof, after I promised Oscar and Miami Lakes High that I'd be responsible for you two?" She slammed her hand down on the table, hard, making me jump.

But Mauro just gave her a lazy smile. "Simone. You can trust us."

Simone glanced at me and I nodded.

His bare toes under the table brushing against mine shouldn't have felt like an invitation. Not at all.

Because Mauro had just made it abundantly clear.

Nothing was going to happen.

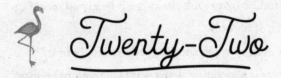

Twenty-Two

I'D BEEN AVOIDING MAURO all afternoon. I had to let this thing burn itself out. Then everything would go back to normal.

That was, if we lived through our latest Dreams gig.

What was that, you might ask?

Well, Tía Celia thought we were *so* incredible and *so* professional that we were just perfect for a sales event at Tío Victor's car dealership.

"Find Your Happily Ever After in a Brand-New Minivan!" screamed a banner hung across the whole building.

I'd give her points for creativity, if I wasn't so certain she was totally *relishing* my servitude.

Meh—points for creativity anyway.

"I swear, Simone is trying to kill us," grumbled Jessica, whose Snow White dress was the warmest of all, a velvet that looked (and smelled) like it was trying to roast her alive. "What happened to the air conditioner rule?"

"Oh, there's an air conditioner," said Matt, sounding almost as bitter as Jessica, which, for him, was Halley's comet–level rare. "It's just inside—*where the owners are*." He tugged at his Prince Charming collar and looked up at the thick clouds that had gathered over us, glaring at them like they were offending him personally. At least he wasn't wearing a giant furry head. I'd expected Mauro to play Aladdin today, but he'd shown up in his Beast gear.

And about a half hour after we got there, a Miami downpour came straight from the sky and flattened the balloons that Tío Victor and his crew had hung up. Whatever helium was in them was no match for the storm, and once it cleared, the balloons sat on the ground like tired, pouting toddlers.

There were a lot of those, too.

Tío Victor had advertised the family-friendly event and the families had come. A win-win for the dealership and Dreams Come True. People had scurried into their corners while it rained, but in Miami rain never lasts long, and the monsoon was over in a few minutes. The sales staff chatted with the adults under tents that boasted cold drinks and sad-looking snacks.

Simone came over to us then, looking cool in a linen shift dress while we disintegrated in our costumes.

"You all look amazing!"

We muttered stuff that probably didn't sound like "thanks."

"I know it's hot, kittens, but these are families! With

children! Children who have parties! If we make an impression here, we'll get lots of new clients!"

Mami strolled over to me with Enrique, who was now, more often than not, in tow.

"You look beautiful, Bella." She kissed me on both cheeks.

"Belle. And thanks. Why are you here? A new car for me?" I asked, half hoping.

"Yeah, when you can pay for it! No, Enrique wants to look at a car. Victor better give us the friends and family discount!"

Simone walked over. "Carmen, it's almost time for you to sing."

Mami looked happy. "You are singing, mija?"

"Yeah."

"Break a leg!"

Enrique came out of his haze. "Si, mija, break two!" I rolled my eyes.

I'd decided at the last minute to switch to a solo: "Belle." Singing "Tale as Old as Time" with Mauro right now would have been too awkward.

I finished and was happy to hear a little bit of applause and cheers from the kids.

Ariana wandered by with Alex. "You sounded great!" she said. "And I actually mean that."

I pushed my hair out of my face. "Thanks."

Mauro walked over to me then, his mask still over his head. "Didn't Simone tell you that we were singing 'Tale'?"

Ari looked wide-eyed at Mauro. "You know, you look really convincing."

He ignored her. "Carmen, why have you been avoiding me?" I could feel him glaring at me through the mask.

"Um, character names, remember?" I pasted on my Belle smile.

"Fine, *Belle*, you seem to be spending more time away from the palace lately."

I shrugged. "I didn't want to sing 'Tale' today."

"You and I are a package deal, Belle, and if we want to get hired, then maybe we should perform together. Otherwise, why the hell am I here in this damn heat, dressed like a furry?"

"Ask Simone that!" I shot back.

"I'm asking you that!"

"And I don't have an answer!"

Shit, our voices had gotten louder and louder and now we were attracting a nice little crowd. Simone was staring at us, her face frantic. Tío Victor looked like he was going to run us over if we cost him any sales.

I forced a laugh. "My dear Beast, please do not raise your voice at me."

He stomped off.

Ari's eyes followed him. "Wow, he really gets into character!"

I pulled my hair off my neck and took a long, deep breath full of humidity.

"Yeah."

A few minutes later, Mauro's voice rang out. Except he wasn't singing anything from our movie. No, he was up there with Leila. He'd changed into Aladdin's costume (he must have sneaked into the office) and was singing the first notes of "A Whole New World."

With Leila.

I imagined my face as the expressionless emoji—straight lines for my eyes, and another for my mouth, a perfect picture of Zen detachment.

"Can I talk to you?" Ari again. She pulled me to the side until we stood alone. (I could still see Mauro and Leila, talking to a gaggle of parents who'd surrounded them after their song. Not that I was paying that much attention.)

I forced myself to focus on my cousin.

"I have a favor to ask you. And you aren't allowed to say no."

I narrowed my eyes at her. So much for our truce. "Because I work for you? Because, honestly, Ari—"

"No, because it's really, really important to me. It's something I've wanted to ask you for a while, but I couldn't let myself because . . . you know . . ." She tilted her head. "Will you . . . sing at my quince?"

Well, that wasn't what I had expected.

"Sing?" I scanned my brain and drew a blank. "Sing what?"

"Duh. 'Mi Niña Bonita,' of course."

Of course. The traditional father-daughter dance song, all

about how much the father had wanted a boy until he had a daughter and discovered what love truly meant.

Maybe not my favorite song in the world.

"I don't know." I stalled, chewing on the inside of my cheek. "I mean, isn't that usually sung by a man?"

"Yes, but . . . I think it would be so much more meaningful from YOU. Please, Carmen?"

I narrowed my eyes at her. "This is a long way from 'you'll be the star' and 'you'll suck up all the attention' and 'this is *my* quince.'"

She flushed. "This IS my quince. And, I don't know. Maybe I'm finally growing up."

"Ha. So what's the plan? Pig's blood from the ceiling or something?"

"Wow, that took a dark turn." She laughed. "No . . . this is a bona fide offer. An evolved offer."

"Well, I'm not UNtouched. But . . . it's not a great idea." I thought about Tía Celia. I thought about all of those eyes—watching Ariana and Tío Victor, sure, but also me. Standing there. Singing words I—I wasn't sure I could handle.

I could already see myself there, disappointed and disappointing.

"Ariana . . . I really appreciate the offer. But I think I should stick to dancing."

Ariana-the-brat flashed briefly over her face, but then she just looked sad.

"I can't make you reconsider?"

"Think of it this way. It's my gift to you. The old Carmen would have taken the chance to sing and ruin everything."

She flinched. "You know I don't actually believe that, right?"

Maybe she didn't. But I did.

There wasn't much for us to say to each other after that, so Ariana drifted back to Alex and her posse. I'd made the right choice, saying no to her. So why did a part of me feel like running up to her and taking it back?

Ugh, everything just felt wrong today. I wished I could talk to Mauro, but he was a big part of what was wrong.

I just needed to concentrate on my job. It was my turn to take over face-painting the kids, especially after Waverly got tired of being at the station and face-painted the anarchy symbol on a very excited six-year-old. Who I guess was now ready to fight the power.

Tío Victor was hustling extra hard. I knew from whispered conversations between Mami and Tía Celia that the quince was definitely turning into The Thing That Ate Their Bank Account.

"Where's the Beast? Where's the Beast?" Two little five-year-old twins tugged on my skirt like I was hiding him down there or something.

And that was a very good question. We'd become a mutual avoidance society. Every time I saw him across the dealership, he made a point to turn away. When I walked near him, he made sure to concentrate on whoever was standing near him. And not me. He'd started the day as the Beast, but apparently he wanted to finish it as Aladdin. Which told me everything I needed to know.

A terrifying thought crossed my mind. Oh my God, what if he knew? What if he could tell clearly what I was feeling, and he was trying to avoid having the Friends Talk with me. Ironic, because we'd already had that talk this summer. More than once, even. But back then, I'd been sure about how I felt.

Unlike now, when I was all over the damn place.

Was that why he was acting like this? Because he knew he'd already hurt me once, and he wasn't enough of a beast (ha) to enjoy the idea of doing it again? Especially now that we'd found our way past Fake It Till You Make It?

I mean . . . we HAD found our way, right? Shit, nothing felt solid right now.

Meanwhile, the little girls were still standing in front of me, all big Cindy-Lou Who eyes. Waiting for an answer. "Um. He's—"

"Right here," the Beast said in a deep voice.

"Right here," I echoed, trying to keep the surprise out of my voice. He'd changed back.

Of course, the girls wanted a picture with us, and then they begged for a picture of just me and Mauro, "looking romantic, please?!"

Mauro came over to me and obligingly put his arms around

my waist, leaning his Beast head on my shoulder. It was like a prom picture, except, you know, with a giant furry head. His hands were barely on me, though. It was like a photo negative of the way everything had been all summer. He'd wanted to be near me. It was his idea to message through the nights, his idea to be friends. Now it felt like he couldn't get away fast enough.

After the phones flashed and the kids got one last hug, Mauro and I were alone.

"Excuse me," he said, very formally, voice a little muffled through his mask. "I have to go mingle."

OK, that was it. I had to take the Beast by the fur and finish this.

I moved to the left just as he did. Then when he shifted to the right, I did, too. It looked like we were dancing without touching.

Because touching was the thing I was desperate to do. And desperately afraid to do.

"If our little minuet is over—" he began.

"OK, you need to stop avoiding me when I'm avoiding you!"

He cocked his head. "That doesn't even make sense."

"Yes, it does! Because I know why I'm avoiding you, but you have no reason to avoid me, and if you do, then you need to *stop avoiding me* and just SAY IT." I crossed my arms. Maybe I sounded crazy, but somewhere in that sentence was something that I needed him to understand.

Just as soon as I understood it myself.

He pulled me into a corner where the guests couldn't see us and took his Beast head off. "OK, that's it, Carmen. You need to know the truth."

My heart started hammering, low and hard, somewhere near my stomach.

"Look, if—" I started.

"I just mean—" he continued.

"I already said—" I followed.

"Will you let me talk?" he finished.

"Believe me, I get it. I get how things are. I DO. I don't need it. We are cool. Beyond cool. Ice cold. Really." I started to walk away.

Mauro just looked confused. "What . . . wait. Carmen . . . I . . . Huh?" Then he shook his head. "Wait. You think? Oh, Carmen. You are so wrong. Like . . . canonically wrong."

Oh.

OH.

"Would it be better if I knelt down?"

"Not unless you want Mami and Tía Celia stampeding over here with a shotgun, a priest, and a stroller."

"Stroller?"

"They'd want to cover all the possibilities." My voice shook.

"Then I'll tell you standing up. Carmen . . . I . . ." He put his Beast head on the ground and tugged a hand through his hair. "OK, now I don't know what to say."

But I knew. I looked at him and suddenly I knew that I'd

been wrong. Maybe I'd always known, but I'd been afraid to believe it.

So I stood on tiptoes, my dress a bell around me, and I kissed him.

And he kissed me back, so long and so hard that the air grew still and far away. It took moments for sound to resurface around me. I finally let myself touch him, my fingers in his hair, trailing along the back of his neck, holding on to his shoulders to steady myself. Our lips knew everything we'd been trying to hide. I blinked my eyes open, for just a second, almost afraid to look directly at him, in case this was another lie. Another dream. Or the wrong person.

But it wasn't. It was Mauro, and everything finally made sense.

A voice interrupted us. A little girl had somehow found her way around our corner. "Mami! Look at the Beast, he ain't got no head, but he's got Belle anyways! Ooh! They're kissing for REAL!"

Our lips broke apart for a second, and he touched his forehead to mine. "I got Belle anyways?"

"Transformed by true love," the mami answered her little girl.

I answered Mauro's question with another kiss. A kiss that was real.

Simone had always warned us about staying in character.

And I guess we had done just that.

I didn't know it was possible for people to clap sarcastically. But eventually a few staccato sounds broke through and I came back to myself. I could see some of the Dreams and corte over his shoulder, their mouths hanging open in shock. Waverly shook her head, but a knowing smile teased her mouth anyway.

"So," Mauro said in a raspy voice, his forehead on mine, his hands cupping my face. "So."

I didn't say anything. I needed to think about what had just happened, in front of the Dreams and the corte and the random people who probably hadn't expected a floor show with their 3.5 percent APR loans.

Don't get me wrong—I wasn't *upset* about what had happened. It had felt like finally breathing deep after breaking through the surface of the ocean following a long swim. Avoiding Mauro and sidestepping all my feelings had been so much freaking work, and at least now I knew I didn't have to do it anymore.

Except now I had to brace myself enough to explain everything to everyone else.

It was the beginning of August. We had one more month of summer together.

Our timing had never been great.

Waverly and some of the corte approached and pulled me away from Mauro, lured by the irresistible chisme. "You better start talking, or did Mauro take your tongue away?" Waverly's smirk told me that she was way too pleased to have been proven right to give me any grief about what had happened.

"What?" I tried to look as innocent as someone can when their lipstick is smeared halfway to their earlobe.

"Um . . . for starters, the fact that the guy you SWORE you hated just grabbed you and kissed you like at the end of a telenovela!"

"I grabbed *him*. And I DID hate him. Before."

"Ha, bullshit," Olivia said triumphantly.

"So what about now?" Leila asked slyly.

I opened my mouth, all ready to give her a smart-ass Carmen comment. But what came out was a way more hesitant "I . . . don't know."

"You don't know," Olivia said flatly. "So . . . you can kiss a guy like THAT and you aren't even sure what it means?"

Thanks, Olivia, for reminding me who I've always been.

"Yeah," I said simply. "I guess I can."

Waves pulled me to the side. "Look . . . are you sure this is what you want? It's Mauro. And you guys have a history that's not so great."

"I know . . . but . . . I just can't seem to help myself," I confessed.

Waves grinned. "Then by all means, carry on. But let me know if he ever needs a shoe to the head. I wear glass slippers and they hit hard."

Mami found me then, her eyes alive with interest. "Carmen-cita, WHAT just happened here?"

Segue time. "Ariana asked me to sing 'Mi Niña Bonita' at the party," I informed Mami.

"Really?" She frowned. "That's a man's song, though."

"She said it would mean more coming from me. But I said no."

Mami put her arm around my waist. "Why don't you tell me all about it on the ride home? ALL of it." She grinned. "Start with the kissing parts."

Twenty-Three

MrtB: I thought I was going to get to drive you home.

I was instant-replaying the kiss in my head from every angle, complete with color commentary.

"Well, Biff, points for assertiveness, his tongue action is strong . . . oops, teeth knock, that's GOTTA hurt . . ."

Alone in my room, I could admit what I couldn't say to anybody at the event today.

Of course I knew what the kiss meant. Or could mean. Claro que sí. And you know how sometimes you get what you want, and it doesn't live up to your expectations? I mean, I remembered how things used to be between us. Pretty damn good.

(Until they sucked.)

But today? Today was better than I remembered, the kind of better that worried me. Because it could be so much better than it used to be. And because I knew it couldn't be anything but temporary.

DivaCee: My mom and her boyfriend drove me home. Even my fingers feel stiff, formal.

MrtB: About that . . .

MrtB: Ignore the awkward segue . . .

DivaCee: That's going to be on our tombstone.

MrtB: Do you mean . . . declaring our physical deaths (and thus implying that we're going to be together till death do us part) or do you mean the death of our relationship . . .

DivaCee: . . .

MrtB: I am getting the sense you don't want to talk to me right now.

DivaCee: Because . . . I'm typing to you?

MrtB: OK, look. We can call it a moment of mutual weakness. You were overwhelmed by me without my head on. Sweat carries pheromones. It's an occupational hazard. Really.

DivaCee: I really don't want to do this on-screen.

MrtB: But on-screen is where I'm a Viking!

DivaCee: unwilling LOL

MrtB: I don't want you to be unwilling.

DivaCee: I wasn't.

MrtB: See, this doesn't have to be awkward at all.

DivaCee: As long as we never have to see each other again.

MrtB: Which could make the parties logistically challenging.

DivaCee: Technology has come a long way . . .

MrtB: Like, for example, I am typing this outside your door.

DivaCee: Bullshit.

MrtB: Look outside.

I ran to my window. The Dreams van was parked in front of the house.

I looked down at myself. A faded Minnie Mouse T-shirt from when Tony the yoga teacher took Mami and me to Disney (I'd saved it from the Great Tony Purge) and boxer shorts with llamas on them. A ponytail. And my legs could have used a shave.

Ah, screw it.

I pulled the door open. Mauro stood there, in a plain white T-shirt and black jeans. And he was carrying daisies. My favorites.

"Hi," he said softly.

And so I kissed him. Again.

The flowers got squashed between us as he pulled me closer to him, so close I could feel his heart beating against my chest. It wasn't calm. Neither was I.

"Carmen," he started, and then gave up.

A whole empty pool of our wanting each other was in front of us, and no matter how much we kissed, it was like we could never fill it. My fingers twined in the hair on the nape of his neck, learning again how fine his hair felt there.

I don't know how we got into the van, but we ended up there, lying in the back on a bed of crushed costumes and satin gloves and kid-party props. His hands left trails of knowing on my skin, goose-bumping with something better than memories. I wanted everything. Right now.

I ran my hands along the bottom of his back, tugging his T-shirt up.

From my haze, I felt him tense up.

"Wait, Carmen, wait . . ."

I stopped.

He looked at me, green eyes unfocused. "Um, that's not why I came over."

I wrapped my arms around myself.

"God," he said, rubbing the back of his neck, where my hands had been a few moments before. "Believe me, I'm . . . not . . . but . . . we should talk."

"We should," I said, running my fingers along his knee, a spot I remembered he'd always liked.

"I can't while you do that."

"So . . . talk."

Instead, he started kissing up my neck toward my ear. I shivered.

"That's . . . not talking."

"And we should," he breathed. "Talk, I mean."

I forced myself still and waited.

"Just . . . this summer, getting close to you again . . . it would have been the best thing that's ever happened to me, even if this hadn't ever happened. The best."

I couldn't have stopped my smile even if I'd wanted to. "Same."

He pulled away from me for a second and smirked. "What? No smart remark? If I'd known all it took was to kiss you . . ."

"Don't get used to it. This is all just for now. Very temporary," I said.

"No. Not temporary. Permanent. This is." He started to pull me down on top of him again.

I couldn't help it; I started to crack up. "Is that right, Yoda?"

He laughed, too. "Do, or do not. There is no try."

"You are such a geek."

"That's why you are crazy about me."

"Oh yeah? You better remind me exactly how crazy I am about you."

And then he did.

After what felt like only a second of kissing, I leaned against Mauro, who had propped himself on the back door of the van. Our legs tangled together. His fingers curled with mine.

"So . . . Carmen . . ."

"So . . . Mauro . . ."

"Not to be all formal, but . . . are you going to make an honest woman of me?" he teased, nibbling on my neck.

284

I shivered. "That would be counterproductive."

"I mean . . . so . . ." Something weird was threaded through his words. Nerves.

I turned to face him fully. "Mauro. Talk," I invited, pulling away a little so I could concentrate without the smell of his sandalwood cologne distracting me.

"Just . . ." He looked down at our hands, still touching. "What exactly are we doing?"

And there it was. The question I hadn't exactly wanted to answer.

"Well, about five minutes ago we were making out hardcore in our boss's van."

He gave me a dimpled grin. "You know what I mean."

"Of course, I know." I sighed. "This is August. In September you are going back to school, and I'll be here."

"Neither of those are absolutes," he pointed out.

"Uh, you aren't going to skip school for some hookup."

"It's interesting that you saw that as the only possibility," he said. "Plus, I think we both know this isn't just some hookup."

"Except we don't know WHAT it is."

"Which is what I'm asking."

I started to hum "Summer Nights."

He shook his head. "Please. Not *Grease*."

"They had the right idea!"

"Except everything else in the movie totally contradicts the point of the song since they couldn't get over each other, and plus she ended up going to his high school and wearing tight pants," he said.

I waved that off. "Anyway, we have at least . . ." I counted on my fingers. "Four weeks. Thirty days."

He groaned and put his head on my shoulder. "Not long enough."

"Then let's make sure to make every second"—I looked directly at his lips—"count."

He leaned into me, and before I lost myself again, I muttered, "Terms and conditions apply," into his lips.

"What did you say?"

"Just . . . look, this is the kind of situation where people can get hurt if they don't plan ahead."

He leaned back now, a smirk plastered on that beautiful mouth. "So. A plan."

"Rules."

"Oh," he said innocently. "Like how I should always be sure to run my fingers along—"

"Not those kinds of rules!" I said hastily. "Just . . . you know. Four weeks. Fun, friendship—"

"Are we really going the F-word alliterative route here?"

I smothered a laugh. "And NO hard feelings."

He grinned. "You are making this WAY too easy."

"Exactly. Because rules."

He rolled his eyes and held out his hands. "Fine. Four weeks of fun, friendship, feelings."

"That's not what I said," I protested.

"I know," he said, already leaning over me. "That's just what I heard."

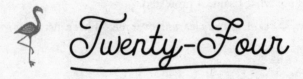 *Twenty-Four*

AY, THE "I TOLD you so's." Not just people saying it (and believe me, they did say it, so many freaking times) but also the smirks when we danced together, when Mauro kept his fingers enlaced with mine even between routines, when he slung his arm casually over my shoulders. Even Simone had come around, the smile on her face proof that she'd always expected this to happen eventually, in spite of her earlier warning. Nobody cared that we had rules. The Dreams and the corte had finally found common ground. Making fun of us.

"It's like the lion lying down with the lamb," Jessica said, laughing.

"I don't want to think about what they do in the bedroom." Olivia shuddered at that, to more hooting laughter.

"Pics or it didn't happen," Louie drawled. Leila hit him on the shoulder.

"Then it's never going to happen," I said.

Mauro held a hand over his heart. "Ouch! Never is a long time."

Ariana and Tío Victor were practicing the vals, the traditional father-daughter waltz. The rest of us were on a ten-minute break. Mauro and I were sprawled out on the grass, our legs intertwined. I turned my face up into the sun. After the jumpiness of the past two months, I realized I felt completely at peace. Not pushing, not planning, not staring jealously at anyone. Just . . . happy.

"How come *they* don't have to break out into six different traditional dances?" Mauro asked me.

I tickled him with a grass stem. "Because no one wants to be getting freaky with their dad!"

"Not all Latin dancing is freaking," he scolded. "Have you learned nothing from this process, woman?"

"Oh yes, please, enlighten me about my cultural norms, mestizo." I leaned my chin into my hands, eyes wide like an anime girl.

He put on his professor voice. "Proximity makes a difference, and I do live with my father, so—"

"Not even you can make that make sense."

He laughed and started to inch his face closer to mine.

"Sorry to interrupt," said Alex, looming over us and not looking particularly sorry at all. "Just . . . Olivia wanted to know how it's going on the video," he continued, determinedly looking only at me.

"Almost done!" Mauro said cheerfully. "You know, whenever we stop making out long enough to work on it."

I punched him in the shin.

"It will be done in a few days," I said.

Alex ignored him. "So, great . . . I'll let her know."

But he didn't make any move to leave.

"Do you . . . have any other questions?" Mauro prompted.

Alex looked at me all disappointed before he stomped off.

Simone clapped to get everyone's attention, and then reminded us, "This is the home stretch, everyone! And you looked GREAT today, really! All that hard work is finally paying off! Four more weeks!"

Four weeks. That's a long time. Right?

———————

One-thirty a.m., four days later.

MrtB: You know, I like this thing we've got going.

DivaCee: Sleeping, yes. I like it, too. Especially when you aren't messaging me in the middle of it.

MrtB: Just saying. I could take a semester off . . .

DivaCee: Oh, please. Don't use me as an excuse to avoid hard work.

MrtB: Hey . . . YOU are hard work, you know.

DivaCee: But I don't grade you.

MrtB: Why don't I believe that?

DivaCee: Because you are a smart boy. ☺

MrtB: I'm going to miss . . . Miami, you know. The

sunshine. The palm trees. The . . .

That's as sentimental as we let ourselves get. Terms and conditions, remember?

DivaCee: Miami is going to miss you, too. And you know what misses me? My bed. Good night, Mauro.

MrtB: Dream of me.

DivaCee: Meh. You wish.

But I probably would.

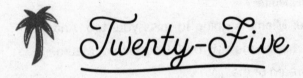

Twenty-Five

IT WAS A FEW hours before practice, and we were trying to be responsible. To make some more headway on Ariana's video.

"We've been working for hours," Mauro declared after much less time than that, getting out of his chair and stretching his arms above his head. His shirt rode up, giving me a glimpse of the black band of his boxer briefs, and just like that, I totally agreed.

Ariana's video could wait.

Before long, we were in his bed, his hands running up and down the length of my body, his shirt pulled off. My hands smelled like his shampoo after I pulled his head closer to mine, every kiss feeding the need for the next one. We tangled in his sheets, our own cocoon. It was our way to stop time.

Until Mauro's tablet started chiming.

He groaned against my mouth. "Ignore it. They'll stop."

And I tried.

But it just kept going and going, and finally, I surrendered. "The sooner you answer, the sooner you can hang up."

Mauro rolled off me and grabbed the tablet. "This better be important—"

"Dude!" said a voice from the tablet. I heard laughing in the background. "We are ALWAYS important! Are you up to no good?" A guy about Mauro's age, with dark hair, dark eyes, and tanned skin. He would have made a good Aladdin.

"Ahmed!" Mauro's voice relaxed, and I rolled my eyes. Clearly, time had started again. "Where ARE you guys?"

"The Caymans!" The screen swerved around and I saw a couple more guys and two girls sitting behind a low table full of cans and half-empty glasses in a white room with tropical décor. "What do you think?"

"Looks good!" Then Mauro turned the tablet toward me. "This is Carmen." I waved.

"Looks good!" another voice echoed, and then a head popped into the frame. A blond-dreadlocked head. Mauro laughed. "Dreads! I can't believe you did it!"

The tablet was yanked toward another person, a girl, a tanned Latina with a platinum pixie and a diamond nose ring. "I told him not to! Dreadlocks? On a German guy? Isn't that, like, total cultural appropriation? I mean . . . I'm not saying it's a relationship deal-breaker, but I'm not NOT saying that, either . . ." Then she focused her eyes on us. "Hey, nice to meet you! Carmen, right? I'm Yo. Please tell Dylan his hair looks like shit. Do it in solidarity of brown people everywhere!"

"Umm . . ." I began, searching my brain for the one cell where I stored diplomacy.

"I can already tell she's too nice for you, Mauro," Ahmed declared, and Mauro smothered a laugh. Then Yo poked her head back in. "YOU tell Dylan what you really think, Mauro. You are definitely not as nice as your girlfriend."

"Nice" didn't feel like a compliment. It felt like it was two steps away from "dumb."

And Mauro hadn't called me his girlfriend.

"I refuse to answer on the grounds that I'd like to have a peaceful living experience in the fall," Mauro said.

Ahmed snorted. "Most of the lack of peace was YOU, my brother," he started, and then he glanced at me. "But . . . perhaps that's a conversation for another time."

"Tell us about YOU, Carmen," Yo started. "You know, I grew up not far from you! Homestead." Then she laughed. "Homestead to Harvard in a single bound! Well . . . Berklee, anyway."

Dylan laughed. "Oh no . . . that's her 'let me tell you about the struggle of the proletariat in the arts' voice."

Yo whirled around to him. "I do NOT have that voice! What is that voice even?" And after another second, "And anyway, who does it benefit to pretend that class is not a thing? The ruling class, aka you assholes."

Ahmed said, "Yeah, poor you, here in the Caymans with us—"

"Just because I'm wise enough with my money to afford a splurge now and then—"

"—and you won that first-year prize, too. That probably helped. Plus, the summer program was paid for." Summer program? The same one Mauro hadn't been accepted to?

Yo ducked her head. "Yeah, maybe that, too . . ."

"And if you were truly broke, you'd be applying your genius toward law or finance or something, not music production—"

Yo pointed at the boys. "The underbelly of the elite, Carmen! They act like all we're good for is McJobs—"

"Uh, is this why you called me?" Mauro asked.

Ahmed grabbed the tablet back and held it so that we could see only his face. "Nah, mostly we just wanted to say wish you were here in a slightly more personal way than with a braggy Insta. Come down for the weekend!"

I heard a bunch of WOOs in the background.

Mauro shook his head, laughing. "I got commitments, my brother."

Ahmed raised his eyebrows. "We're using the C-word already?"

"I mean WORK," Mauro said, maybe a little too quickly. "You know what that is, right?"

He grinned lazily. "Not during the summer. School is hard enough. We're not all Yos."

"Hey!" Yo called from the couch. "Don't invalidate my efforts!"

"He's complimenting your brilliance, sweetheart," Dylan shouted at her. "Take a fucking compliment!"

The screen jerked and started to bounce. We were in motion, looking around what was obviously a gorgeous villa, with overstuffed white mattresses, chiffon curtains fluttering in a tropical breeze, and a glimpse of a sandy beach and dazzling blue ocean just beyond. Steps from where they were. I could practically smell the Sol de Janeiro Bum Bum Sol Oil.

"Still not convinced?" Ahmed asked. "Hell, bring Carmen, man! We've got plenty of room!"

More room than my townhouse. Possibly more room than Ariana's McMansion.

Mauro grinned, but shook his head. "We really *are* busy, but thanks, man. Another time."

Ahmed gave an exaggerated sigh. "I tried! Oh well . . . Carmen, hopefully we'll see you up in Boston sometime?" He sounded enthusiastic in his vagueness.

"Yeah . . . sure."

"Awesome! OK, I'd better go make sure these assholes aren't setting fire to anything—this place is booked under my dad's name! Ahmed out!" And the screen went dark.

We were both quiet for a second.

"So my friends are . . . a lot," Mauro said finally.

"Yeah."

"They're not usually that bad," he said, wincing, as he pulled me into his arms. "Blame it on the alcohol . . . or sunstroke . . . or . . ."

"They had the Entitled Asshole filter on their tablet and forgot to take it off?"

He laughed, and then his eyes went straight to my mouth. "So . . ."

And then he kissed me, and I tried to focus on that, on the way his mouth felt like the only true thing in the world.

But I couldn't quite get Mauro's friends out of my head, especially Yo.

The way she came from here, and had managed to get so far away. Belong so completely to another space.

Mauro sighed and pulled away from me. "OK, talk."

"It's nothing."

"It's never nothing."

"It's just that . . ." I sat up, straightened my shirt. "I'm sorry I'm keeping you from that beautiful villa."

"Believe me . . . there's no place more beautiful than wherever you are."

I rolled my eyes, but I couldn't stop the smile creeping up on my lips. "Cheesy."

"And true. But that's not really what's bugging you."

I shifted again, always uncomfortable with how easily Mauro could read me.

"Nothing but a little guilt for robbing you of a vacation.

Honest. So . . . let's get back to work and make it worth it."

After a long look at me, he shrugged and went back to the laptop.

But all I could think about was Yo. Anyone looking at me and Yo together would see the ways we were the same. Both Latinas. Both from around this way. Except that she was good enough to get a scholarship to an amazing school, win awards, keep up with people like Mauro. Surpass him, even. Get into a program he couldn't get into.

She could do all that . . . so what did it say about me that I couldn't?

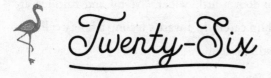# Twenty-Six

THE NEXT NIGHT WAS a rare Thursday night off.

The quince was three weeks away now. And then end of summer. End of everything.

The beginning of school and real life. For everyone but me.

Mami was out with Enrique and I had the house to myself. I turned on my computer and waited for the century to pass as it booted up.

The door buzzer went off. Mami must have forgotten her key. Despite her eternal warnings about traffickers, I buzzed her in without double-checking and opened the door, already braced for the same lecture I always got.

Mauro stood in my doorway, a fresh batch of daisies in one hand and a laptop under his arm.

I shifted my bare feet, suddenly very aware of how short my cutoffs were. I hadn't exactly been expecting company.

"I have something for you," he said. He shoved the flowers at me. "Two somethings."

I opened the door a little wider. "Mami and Enrique are out." I watched him carefully. I wasn't feeling a booty call. But he just nodded, still hesitant.

First test passed.

We went to my room. He'd never actually been in here before. Mami's voice drifted through my head. *Pick up that bra, Carmen, he'll start thinking bad thoughts.*

"So, this is where the magic happens," Mauro commented. I pulled out my desk chair for him and watched while he set up his MacBook next to my ancient laptop.

"You . . . came over to work?"

"What, you think I had another reason?" He picked up a perfume bottle and opened it, taking a big whiff of vanilla and honey. "Correction: THIS. This is the magic that happens. Bottled. Literally."

I raised an eyebrow at him.

That's when I took a good look at his laptop screen, the toolbar at the bottom showing off how tricked out the thing was—Final Cut Pro, PowerDirector, Pro Tools, Vegas Pro, Audacity.

Everything else was wiped. A picture of him was the wallpaper.

"I figured in case you got short on inspiration," he said,

gesturing to the screen. "Not because I think I'm hot." Here he smirked. "Although that's not a bad picture of me."

"I . . . don't understand."

He took a deep breath. "This. It's for you."

"It . . . like, the laptop?"

He nodded.

"You . . . have got to be freaking kidding me! Estás loco? I can't keep that!"

"Look, you said your computer can't handle the new software and . . ." He glanced at the ginormous laptop teetering on my desk, still straining with the effort of functioning. "I can see why. So . . ." His voice went soft, husky. "Why not?"

I waved my hands in the air. "Because! It's a MacBook that probably costs more than everything in this room! With thousands of dollars of software on it! There is NO possible way I could EVER accept a gift like that!"

He held up a finger and smiled. "Aha! It's not a gift! It's a loan! Much as it pains me to admit it, you might have more patience and talent for the editing thing than I do. And I want you to keep practicing. Who knows? I didn't find my thing in high school, but maybe you did. Maybe it's this. And maybe you can be the one to make the video for my next track." He paused, rubbed his elbow. "Plus, I figured you could always give it back to me, like, when you come visit me up in Boston."

We'd never talked about me going up there before.

"But . . . your dad. He's not going to be happy . . ."

He shrugged. "Truthfully? I doubt he'll notice it's gone. And a machine like this deserves some use, Carmen. It's like you'd be doing me a favor."

"No, it's not a favor."

"It is, though." He stared at the screen for a second, and then looked up into my eyes. His face was empty of any teasing, any flirting, anything besides rock-solid honesty. "My friends—they're not better than you, Carmen, not more creative, not more intelligent. But I knew telling you that wasn't enough, so I figured the only way to fix it was to show you how talented I think you are . . ." He stood up and looked at me, the truth in his eyes. "So take the MacBook, practice, and who knows?" He smiled without a single bit of smirk. "Maybe you'll end up at a college in Boston, too. And even if you don't . . . so what? You can still get better, learn, make things. College or not."

I looked at him, and again at the MacBook. Judging it, and myself.

Accepting it would mean that I believed him. And I wasn't sure if I did.

It would also tie me to him.

And unraveling us at the end of the summer was going to hurt more than I'd ever thought.

He watched me steadily the whole time, the light going out of his serious face. "Too intense, right? I told myself that I wouldn't—"

I could have leaned away, opened my mouth, and blasted away his gesture. It was the smart thing to do.

But I didn't want to do the smart thing.

I crashed into him. My mouth was on his, and his hands were tangled in my hair, and I fell all in.

There was no reason to stop. We slammed into the chair and I tore myself away for a second. "Óyeme, careful with the laptop!" I smiled. "It's a loan."

"What laptop?" he breathed. "All I see right now is you."

An alarm bell, dim and dusty, wavered somewhere in the back of my head, and the part of me on guard dog duty raised her head. But his hands were on my shoulders and then running down and up my back. His hips were pressed hard against me, and the feelings ran through me like a flood, and no way could my mind catch up with that.

We fell on top of the bed and I tossed his T-shirt toward my chair, where it landed on my perfume and tipped it over. Vanilla and honey filled the air with sweetness. He'd smell like me forever. Even after he washed it.

"Que símbolo," I muttered against his lips.

"Huh?" Mauro said, distracted.

I laughed and then I slid my hand down his thigh and I forgot why I was laughing.

Then we heard a sound, and it wasn't our intermingled breaths or the creak of my bed. The sound of a key, a door grunting open.

Mami. "Carmencita? You home, mija?" Her voice drifted closer.

Mauro and I froze, looking at each other.

This had never, ever happened to me before. I didn't bring guys home. How could I relax and hook up, knowing that at any moment the door could open and we could have . . . this?

What was happening to me?

"Carmencita?" Footsteps. Closer.

This was about to become a very bad teen movie.

Mauro had already gotten off the bed and was shoving his arms through his T-shirt sleeves. I pulled my pajama top back on, hoping she wouldn't notice my lack of a bra.

When the door opened, she saw: Me sitting on my bed, reading a copy of the preliminary schedule for Ariana's party. And Mauro sitting at my desk, typing on the MacBook, typing like his life depended on it.

Which it just might.

Her eyes moved from him to me and stayed there. For the first time in my life, I prayed to channel Junior. The hard, dead eyes that hadn't cared about doing illegal things.

"Why didn't you answer me?" She wrinkled her nose. "And what is that smell? Smells like a bakery exploded in here." She wasn't even trying to hide the suspicion in her voice.

"You didn't give me much of a chance. I opened my mouth and there you were. I knocked over my perfume." Good, I sounded normal.

"Oh, is that what that was?" Mauro added, teasing. He sounded like himself, too.

Maybe this was going to be fine.

"And here you are, Mauro, all chilling in my daughter's bedroom like I don't know what you guys must have been doing about five seconds ago."

Or, you know, not fine.

He started to stand up and then stopped and gave her his most charming, crooked smile. "You caught us, Ms. Mirella." He spread his hands out. "Working off the clock."

"Uh-huh."

His forehead got all wrinkled like he was confused. Then he just looked shocked. "Oh no. No, Ms. Mirella. We really are just working." Then he actually *winked at her*. "It wasn't for lack of trying. But you know your daughter."

Mami relaxed just a bit and I thanked past Carmen for having had some sense at least. She might have hooked up with Mauro, too (looked like every version of me had a little problem with that), but at least she got me the benefit of the doubt, because like I said, I never brought guys home.

Truthfully, by the time I was ready to come home, it was usually to leave them behind.

Everything was different now.

"Bueno . . . keep the door open, then! Air out that perfume. And Carmen, can you help me with the groceries, please?"

I slid my legs off the bed and followed her into the kitchen, leaving Mauro at the desk.

She pulled me closer to the sink and started to run the water.

"I never want to see that in our house, Carmen. Entiendes?"

"You didn't believe us." Not surprised.

She laughed. "Carmencita, I was eighteen once, too. And there isn't a trick in the world that Victor and I didn't know. Please. If I'd just asked that poor boy to stand up, he would have hurt himself." Then she got serious. "Still, just . . . please, *please* think and be careful. Believe me, getting pregnant is no way to hold on to a boy." Her face got a faraway look. "He's still gonna go back to school, and then where will you be?"

I thought about the MacBook, something external that connected us now. But at least I could return that.

"Don't worry, Mami. It's nothing like that."

"Uh-huh. Just remember what I said for when it *is* something like that."

When I got back to my room, Mauro groaned. "She didn't buy it, did she?"

"Not for a second."

"I'm sorry."

"Don't be."

". . . that she came home so early." He grinned.

"Oh, well." I put my arms around his neck. "You can be sorry for that."

Twenty-Seven

THE MORE I WORKED on the new laptop, the more it bothered me that Mauro had given up on his photography. He had access to this kind of technology all the time, he had a father who actually *wanted* him to go into a creative career, he had money. I didn't understand why he was so convinced that music production was his only path. Couldn't someone do multiple things, especially in college? Yes, his father was a star. That didn't mean that Mauro had to give up. He could develop his talent. He just needed to believe that it was possible.

Basically, what he needed was a kick in the ass. And that was something I could give *him*.

Plus, I'd gotten a bunch of information from FIU. So I was all about following your dreams and self-improvement and stuff right now.

"That is entirely too much moving away from me," Mauro said as he leaned back on the couch, lazily watching me bustle around the living room, connecting my computer to the speakers. After a hectic two days of parties and practices, Mauro and I were taking a well-deserved chill night. Mami and Enrique were blessedly out, so we had my whole place to ourselves for the night.

"Ta-da!" I pressed play and flopped down next to him.

But as the music came over the speakers, he didn't look as triumphant as I sounded. "These are some of my music files. From last year at Berklee. How did you get your hands on them?"

"Simone. And anyway, listen." Even my untrained ear could hear the weird volume issues he had. A few rhythmic skips that were obviously not planned. Abrupt shifts.

"Ugh," Mauro said, putting his arm over his eyes. "Is this about proving that Oscar is right about me?"

"Shut up," and then I played the next thing. Now he sat up. "This is what I've been working on—I sent you this."

"Uh-huh. And what do you hear?"

He cocked his head and closed his eyes. "Smoother. Brighter treble and intention." He opened his eyes.

"So, class, what have we learned?" If I'd had a pointer I would have tapped him with it.

"That I suck marginally less than I did last year? That maybe I'll overcome my late musical start and actually be less terrible in the future?"

There wasn't an eyeroll big enough. It was bad enough he had given up on his photography, but now he was shitting on his music also? He needed an intervention. "You know what? Sometimes you aren't effortlessly going to be the best at everything. Sometimes you have to try and screw up and try and STILL not be the best. Too bad. Sometimes people will be better than you are. Sometimes certain people will even be geniuses. Honestly . . . welcome to the world the rest of us live in, where we're trying our best and still end up just mostly OK, and somehow manage to get up in the morning in spite of that."

I could tell from the stubborn tightness in his jaw that my attempt at motivational speaking was falling flat. So I pulled out my secret weapon. The pictures he'd taken of us when we were together. I spread them in front of him. "Wait," he said. "What do these have to do with my music? I believe I've made it abundantly clear that photography is ancient history." I noticed that he could barely bring himself to glance at his old work. "I can't believe you kept these," he muttered.

"This has *everything* to do with your music AND your photography because they are both your art! In spite of what I just said five seconds ago, you *aren't* one of the mostly OK ones. You *are* talented. Why else would I keep your pictures, even though I totally hated you? You started music late, but you got good enough fast enough to land at the Berklee College of Music. And you'll keep getting better. Because you can't help yourself. But . . . if photography's your first love, you can have that, too. Don't give it up because your father is a jerk sometimes. Maybe you'll never be him, but so what?" His eyes were locked on mine, like he needed every single word I was saying. Drinking me in.

"Can I? Can I have my first love?" He took my face into his hands.

"All I'm saying, Mauro, is . . . love is hard to find. Don't give up on it," I whispered, my mouth suddenly dry.

"Sometimes it is. And sometimes it's right in front of you."

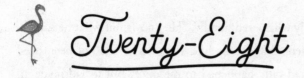 ## Twenty-Eight

IT HAD BEEN A while since we'd worked for anyone but my family. Thank goodness Simone, in her infinite wisdom, had booked a gig for us—part of her plan for Dreams World Domination. Waverly, Jessica, Matt, Mauro, and I were going to perform at a library story time. For toddlers.

"Think about what would happen if we got on the county's radar! We could end up going to schools, day cares, after-school programs. We'd have more work than we have hours in the day," she had said.

Toddlers, though. From what I'd seen this summer, that didn't always go well.

"Oh, Carmen! So young and such a worrywart! Don't worry! The library said that the kids were usually between four and five."

Usually. Key word.

When we got to the library, Jessica gulped.

Strollers. Parked outside, lined up as far as the eye could see.

Mauro looked around. "You all are overreacting. Babies are cute!"

Waverly whispered, loudly, "He knows not what he says."

I nodded. "He speaks like a man who has not been peed upon." It had only happened to me once. But it had made an impression.

"Hey," he said, holding up his hands. "I thought we decided not to judge our romantic pasts."

Jessica leaned forward. "We could just . . . keep driving."

We could have. But we didn't.

Oh man. It was like being at the beach, only the waves were the rising and falling sounds of babies crying. So. Much. Crying.

And the ones who weren't crying were crawling. Pulling themselves up on the shelves. Yanking books out. Hitting themselves with said books and wailing away.

The air was thick with the smell of rice cereal and diaper cream.

I was going to kill Simone.

Still. A job was a job and the sooner we got through this, the sooner we could leave.

I tried to crouch down to eye level (which meant I was practically sweeping the floor with the front of my dress). "Hi! I'm Belle!"

Let me tell you, it's hard to twinkle when you look like you are about to crawl into a foxhole.

Mauro terrified those poor babies. You could track his progress across the room by the sound of screaming. Finally, a librarian whispered something to him and he disappeared.

But not before his costume got baptized.

We read our stories to the parents (because let's be real, the kids weren't listening), we hoisted babies and their parents snapped cell phone pictures, Matt answered questions about his kingdom (and did a good job plugging Dreams Come True), and then, blessedly, thankfully, our slot was over.

At least the babies liked clapping.

Waverly wiped her face, still sparkle smiling. "Find Mauro and let's get the H-E-double-F out of here."

I tugged my skirt through a couple of the aisles toward the back, and then a hand pulled me into the business archives section.

"Is it safe?"

"Depends. You determined to wear that mask outside?" I asked him. "Because I don't think all the babies are gone—"

"I'll never doubt you again. You were right."

I cocked my head. "Ah, sweet words. Say it again."

"Come closer and I will."

I nudged close to him. My dress spread over his lap and glowed like spilled sunlight. "They might find us."

"Look, a baby just did unspeakable things to my fur. Help another one of my dreams come true."

Then he smothered my laugh with his lips. And the book smell mingled with the faint mint on his breath and the musky sandalwood he always wore, and wanting him and wanting that other thing got all intermixed. It got intense and I ached with it.

He cupped my face and kissed me. His hands lightly stroked my face, and the kiss deepened, until I pulled away a little. I had to, because I so didn't want to.

"This is very meta, Belle," he said, glancing at the bookshelves reaching past us to the ceiling. Sunlight slanted through the cloudy glass at the top of the wall and illuminated the motes of dust drifting in the air. The books smelled like paper and mustiness and school and made me want everything that I'd spent the whole summer telling myself didn't matter. A room full of editing bays, streaks of tinted sunlight shining through stained glass windows. The word *college* entered my mind and I pushed it out.

The fact of what was happening between us made other possibilities feel . . . possible. But that's the way these things always felt in the beginning. It had been so long that I'd forgotten, sometimes you had to edge into the wanting by inches, like into a freezing pool.

"Hey, hey," he whispered breathlessly against my mouth. "You OK?"

His hand slid past the satin of my dress to my bare skin. I shivered and strained closer to him. The only truth between us was right now.

I had to stop forgetting that.

And then we heard a voice. "Excuse me!" it said. "This is a PUBLIC library. For the PUBLIC. And CHILDREN."

An abuela type stood tall and huffing in front of us, holding a little girl's hand. The little girl was more eyes than face, she was so fascinated by us. The woman kept shoving the little girl behind her, but the girl always peeked right back out.

I opened my mouth to apologize, but she stopped me with a scornful glance. "Y una muchacha Latina! Que descaro! You should know better!"

Thank you, Abuela, for breaking the spell.

She pushed the little girl behind her firmly and hissed, "I like to cosplay as much as anybody, but there's a time and a place! You are the kind of people who make us all look bad! There's a CODE! Save the kinky stuff for Comic Con!" Then she flounced off, yanking the little girl away.

"Did . . . did that señora just tell us she liked to cosplay?" I wondered.

He snorted. "My only regret is that I didn't have my head on for her."

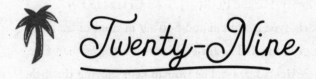# Twenty-Nine

MAMI ACTUALLY LET ME take the car to the next practice. Too bad the offer came with strings.

"Can't you go a little, you know, faster?" Ariana complained, flicking the edge of the seatbelt until I reached over and stopped her. Somehow, I'd been recruited to drive her to the tiara store. (Yes, we have tiara stores in Miami.)

"Stop twitching," I snapped.

"I should have waited for Mami," she grumbled.

"I should pull over right now and make you walk," I shot back.

She glared at me for a second, and then laughed. "OK, OK . . . if you made me walk, I'd melt into a puddle. And then what would be the point of all this?"

"Uh, a slamming party?"

"Without the birthday girl?" She put her hand on her heart. "I'm wounded."

"But not melted."

In spite of her teasing, I managed to get us there a few minutes later.

"This is so weird," she muttered as we walked inside to the happy tinkle of the door chime. The AC turned every bead of sweat on our bodies into ice crystals. Which meant we fit right in. Every shelf glittered with intricate Swarovski crystals and wrought silver and gold. From the most modest tiara to the kind that would have required a neck brace to hold aloft. Or possibly an extra head.

The salespeople bustled past us, sparing us barely a glance. Either it was peak quinceañera season or suddenly every girl and woman in Miami was crowning herself Miss America.

I hung back a little bit, my flip-flops sinking into the immaculate white carpet. The air was thick with rich-lady colognes, the kind they keep locked up at Macy's.

But Ariana was nothing if not Cecilia Lourdes Aguilar Garces's daughter, and I saw the exact moment her spine snapped into a rigid line and she channeled her mother.

"Excuse me? I'm Ariana Garces and I have an appointment to finish my tiara fitting and take it home."

Once it was established that we weren't just there to be blinded by the light, a young saleswoman, Tara, swooped down and got us settled. Then a hatbox was placed in front of Ariana.

"Go on," Tara said, smiling. "This is the best part. Open it!"

Ariana pried the lid off and gasped. Then took a tiara out of the box and almost hugged it.

It wasn't huge, but the braided crystals that would encircle her head seemed to catch every available light and spin it around her. It was the spotlight she'd always wanted. There were ribbons of stones, pink and green and blue and red, that looked like twirling fireworks.

"Mami was right," Ariana breathed out. "This will be PERFECT with my dress."

"It would be perfect with just about any dress," I said, running a finger over a red stone that looked like it could burn you.

"Let's make sure it fits perfectly, too," Tara said.

And then she crowned my cousin.

Just like that, she was a princess.

Or she'd always been one, but now it was official.

Ariana turned to me. "What do you think?"

I think life isn't fair. I think I'll never get this moment. I think maybe I'd like to smash this to the ground and turn it into diamond dust under my envious feet.

I breathed.

I think that this is my problem and it has nothing to do with you at all.

"It's beautiful," I said out loud. "Perfect. Just like you said."

———————

The boxed tiara was snug in the trunk as we drove to Palacio to celebrate with café con leche.

"You know . . . I'm really glad that you were the first one to see it. It makes up for the dress try-on day," Ariana said while we waited for our cafés to cool down (in Miami in August? Ha!).

"I'm happy to have been your Uber."

"No . . . Carmen, stop. Not like that. Just . . . I keep looking for ways to make up for lost time, you know? Which is super weird because I fought Mami on this so hard. She's two for two. Tiara and you. It's a real bummer."

"Yeah, well, don't tell her that. It will go to her head." I blew on my coffee. "And I can't believe I'm going to say this, but . . . I'm glad, too."

"Ooh!" She clapped her hands. "Does that mean you are finally going to agree to sing?"

"Ha! Hell to the no. But remember, I'm not not doing it in order to be mean, I'm not doing it in order to be nice. See . . ." I tapped her on the forehead. "Slight but important difference."

She rolled her eyes. "Hi. I've heard you sing."

"Ugh, not that song. Believe me. It wouldn't suit me."

"So . . . you've tried?" Her whole face lit up. "Which means it's a possibility?"

"Not so much. I did try it, but only because, believe it or not, Queen Quinceañera, yours isn't the only quince in the world. And since Simone wants to do other ones—"

"I thought the Simone thing was just for the summer."

"I'm hoping to stick around. So, I'll need to wow her with my awesomeness."

"You obviously already have."

"Not with that song, though. Let's hope every other quince wants to use the record. I sounded like a dying cat."

Her lips twitched. "I'm sure the cat was alive. Anyway." She gave an exaggerated sigh. "At least you'll be there. Let's promise never to let the grown-ups ruin things for us again." She held out a pinky finger.

"Except we can't exactly blame the grown-ups for my mistakes," I said, and stopped. I'd never referred to that time as "my mistakes." But . . . truth. Ariana was twelve. If I could barely hold things together at fifteen, it wasn't fair for me to put that on her. It had just always been easier to lay the blame elsewhere.

And easier had cost me a lot.

My cousin looked startled for a second, but then she said, "Nah. I screwed up, too. And then Mami and Papi and Tía Mira didn't exactly help the situation."

"True. I think they fought for a lot longer after we tapped out."

"Yeah, well . . . that situation between them had to explode eventually." She shook her head. "The sisters and Papi . . . it's not normal."

There it was. The thing we'd never allowed ourselves to say before.

"Well . . . I gotta be honest, Ariana . . . I've always wished that things had ended differently. Like, with them. Mami and Tío." I couldn't quite meet her eyes. "I'm sorry."

She pondered this. Then she asked, "So? Why are you sorry?"

"Um, because I've been wishing that Tío Victor had ended up with Mami, negating your whole existence?"

She peered into her cup for a second. "Did you slip something into this café con leche? Sprinkle some arsenic in my Cap'n Crunch when we were small?" She wrinkled her forehead. "There WAS the time you pushed me so hard on the swings that I almost flipped over . . ."

"Hey! You were the one who asked for that!"

She laughed. "So basically, you had, like, nine years, easy, to take me out. And you failed. So you must not have wanted to end me very hard."

"Maybe I'm just not cut out to be an assassin."

"Yeah, that's not what Alex says. And I've seen you with Louie."

"Louie would bring that out in anybody."

"True. Still, though. Here I am. Managed to survive almost sixteen years despite you. Conclusion: I'm too lovable to kill!" Then she got serious. "I always knew how you felt about Papi . . . and you know, I got it, even though it was weird. And . . . now it's my turn to confess. I used to wish that Tía Mirella was MY mom. She was so . . . glam, you know? Mami made being a woman look boring, but Tía Mirella made it look like it did on TV."

"Yeah, don't believe the hype."

"I think it's normal that we looked at each other's families and thought about what we felt like we were missing on our side. I mean, we should have appreciated that we had access to everything, I guess, but what kid thinks like that?" She stirred her coffee until the top frothed. "I'm glad we got through it. Did I already say that?"

"I think for the first time, maybe I am, too."

———————

On the drive back to her house, Ariana was so quiet in the passenger seat that I thought she'd fallen asleep.

Until she said, "I have a confession."

"That was the shortest truce we've ever had."

She didn't laugh, though. "I, um . . . I figured out pretty quickly that you liked Alex. And I feel bad that I didn't pick another chambelán after that. But . . . I really liked him, too, and I didn't want to give him up. And yeah, there was a part of me that liked that he chose me over you." She put her hands to her face. "I suck."

I gripped the steering wheel. I had not seen that one coming.

"But . . . you like Mauro now, right? Because anyone with eyes can see he's insanely in love with you."

"Don't try to flatter me into changing the subject," I said, even as her words burrowed into my heart. "And it's OK." As I said the words, I knew it was. "I did like Alex, but . . . it was mostly because he was so right to like. Understand?"

I glanced at her. She tilted her head, and then shook it. "Not really."

I allowed myself a little smile. "That's why he's better off with you." And then I added, "I wouldn't have expected you to drop Alex just because I liked him. That's not the relationship you and I have."

"But it's the relationship I want. Plus, you'd think the daughter of Cecilia Garces would know better." She shuddered. "That is definitely one thing that shouldn't run in the family."

I thought about Junior, and possibly some other things that shouldn't run in our families, either.

"And you know . . . if it was a choice between you and Alex, it's no contest," she said.

"Gee, thanks—what happened to sisters before misters?"

"No! I mean . . . yes . . . I mean, exactly. I'd choose *you*." She looked solemn. "From now on, I'll always choose you, OK?"

The road in front of me blurred a bit at her words. I'm an only child, but I always had Ariana. And even though she could be spoiled, could drive me crazy with envy . . . now that I had her back, I really wanted to keep her. Because it wasn't until she was gone that I had felt the lack of a sister.

"I choose you, too, Ariana."

"So, then . . . the song—?"

"Don't push it."

 # Thirty

IN HONOR OF MORE quince bonding, we were all spending the night at Ariana's house. Well, the girls were, anyway. We were a week away from the quince, and practice had just ended.

The rest of the corte had run inside and straight up the stairs, leaving Ariana and me to put the patio back together. When we were done, we headed in to join them.

The first thing I heard was a scrape and a loud thump. The second thing was giggling.

Tía Celia closed her eyes and pinched the bridge of her nose.

"Ariana Victoria! I am TRUSTING you!" Tía Celia called after us. "Y tú también, Carmen Maria!"

We got upstairs. Ariana knocked on her own door—three times, then twice, and two long ones.

"Nice code, James Bond."

Jessica opened the door a crack and barked out, "Password?"

"Because THAT'S not suspicious at all," I commented.

Ariana ignored me and said, "Salad."

"Salad?"

"It needed to be easy to remember, but hard to think about, in context."

Jessica nodded and a second later opened the door and yanked us inside.

Where we saw . . . absolutely nothing. Except a group of girls trying to look innocent and failing.

"Solo cup me, please," Ariana said. From the deep recesses of her closet, an arm came out, holding a Solo cup.

"OK, that's impressive," I admitted.

Olivia poked her head out of the closet. "Thanks. It was my idea." Then she came out, holding two more cups.

"So . . . OK? What now?" Ariana asked, after she took a long swig, wincing.

I raised my eyebrows at her.

"What?" she asked, all defensive.

"So . . . this is your thing? Like . . . are you the one who's a cautionary tale now?"

She laughed. "I just like to have fun! This isn't a THING."

"Actually, you have a point," I said. "Your THING is clearly getting caught doing it."

She flushed, but she didn't put the Solo cup down.

"Yeah, slow down there, slugger." Waverly stretched her

long legs in front of her on the bed and admired them. "Your brother will kick my ass, metaphorically speaking of course, if I sit here and watch you get trashed."

"To say nothing of your mother," I said, plopping myself next to Leila, sitting on the bed near Waverly's knees. "Or didn't you hear that incantation up the stairs just now."

Ariana took her last sip. "Otro más."

I glanced at Olivia, who shook her head.

"How much have you guys ALREADY had?" Practice had ended, what, ten minutes ago? I looked at them.

Giggles.

Waverly sighed. "Cesar is not going to be happy."

I laughed. "Wow, you are a goner. Every third sentence is 'Cesar this and Cesar that.' He got you good."

"He certainly has," Waverly admitted slyly.

All eyes were now on her.

"Please . . ." Ariana held up her cup. "I don't think I've had enough of this to sit through a discussion of my brother's . . . umm . . ."

"Don't worry, Ari. I don't kiss and tell."

Leila and I snorted at the same time. Waverly glared at us. "No loyalty."

Ariana's phone rang just then, and she leaped on it like she'd been waiting a week. She turned her head and hid her mouth with her hand. Probably Alex on the other line. So much for not having the boys around tonight.

"Let's play I Never!" Jessica said.

"What are we, twelve?" I said.

"Besides," Olivia said, glancing at me, "Carmen has DEFINITELY got us beat."

Oh, I'd like to have HER beat, all right. By professionals.

"Are you sure?" I asked, my voice honey sweet. "You've been spending an awful lot of time with Louie, haven't you? Emphasis on the *awful*?"

Ariana laughed, already off the phone. "He IS kind of awful, Liv."

"That surprises me, coming from you," Olivia snapped at Ari. "Considering he's your boyfriend's best friend."

"My boyfriend can have bad taste in some things," Ariana said. She slid down the side of her bed and onto the floor. "But I'm going to need another drink before I get into THAT."

Olivia went back to her favorite subject. "It's hard dating someone everyone else thinks is difficult. Not every guy is sweet like Alex or Cesar!" She looked at me for backup.

But it was Ariana who answered, sweeping her arm around. "Mauro's sweet—just pretty intense." I frowned. Since when was Ariana such an authority on Mauro?

And then we all stared in horror as her rum and Coke arced in slow motion out of her cup and splashed all over her rug. Her WHITE rug.

"I think I speak for all of us," Olivia said, "when I say oh shit!"

She certainly did.

Ariana just stood there, her hand over her mouth, terror swimming in her eyes. "I'm dead, I'm dead."

"You're not dead," I snapped. "OK, people . . . let's get to work. Olivia and Leila, get towels and mop up whatever you can. We just need to get some vinegar and baking soda on it, fast. Do we have any up here?"

Everyone shook their heads.

Yeah. Amateurs.

"OK, Ari . . . you need to go downstairs and get it, then."

"Me?" She shook her head violently from side to side. "I can't."

"Por qué no?"

"Because . . ." She held up her cup. "I think I'd rather face the music over the rug."

"How about you, Carmen?" Waverly asked me. "You haven't had anything. And you know this house."

"Please, Carmen," Ariana said. "Do it for . . . for sisterhood! For me!"

"Do it for your family," Jessica threw in.

"Do it for the rug," Waverly said, her lips twitching.

"OK," I said finally, standing at the doorway. "For the rug."

Tia Celia looked up as I came barreling down the stairs. And she wasn't alone. Mami sat there with her, an opened bottle of white wine between them.

Looked like everyone had the same idea tonight.

"Um, I hate to interrupt you all, but . . . Tía . . . do you have any baking soda?" I prayed the vinegar would be close to it. But asking for both of them would be a dead giveaway.

"Baking soda? Yeah, in the fridge in the garage. Why?"

"Um, I think someone has an idea for a T-shirt craft." Way to call on that princess training.

Mami's eyes pierced me, but she didn't say anything.

I had to cross the side yard to get to the garage. As I got to the garage door, I heard a noise. Probably a stray cat or something.

Until I saw the shadow.

You have GOT to be kidding me. Every horror movie cliché ran through my head. Doesn't the brown girl usually get taken out first?

"Hello? Who's there?" I stepped forward. "Everybody's home, you know. And we have an alarm."

The figure said, "I know. That's why I'm here. Ari said I wouldn't trip it over here."

"Mauro?"

He came out then, blinking in the lights that had suddenly blazed on. "Where is your cousin?"

"Wait . . . were you were the one on the phone?" Acid flooded my stomach, independent of my brain, which shouted that this made no sense.

"She said she was going to come down here and give me the

code and then send YOU down with your stuff." He shook his head. "Amateurs," he said, his voice disgusted.

"Send me . . . my . . . stuff?"

"This is a kidnapping."

I shook my head. "Uh-huh. Just let me get my baking soda, there, tough guy." I reached past him, and he shifted in front of me again.

"I'm not kidding."

"No, you're kidnapping."

"Exactly."

"So, how are you gonna get me to go with you?"

He gave me a melting look, and my stupid knees actually swayed a little. "How hard do you want me to work?"

"Well, it *is* a kidnapping."

Just then, his phone buzzed. "Ah, it's my belated coconspirator." He picked up. "So, yeah, this wasn't the plan." Pause. "Just throw the bag down, then."

I grabbed the phone. "Do NOT throw the bag down! You crazy? I'm not going anywhere. Mami is here!"

"Carmen! Oh, believe me, you want to do this." Ariana was giggling. "Just GO with him! I'll deal with Tía Mira! Now GO!" And hung up.

I looked at Mauro.

"If we get caught, my mother, my aunt, and possibly my uncle will kill both of us."

"It's a chance that we criminals have to take."

Right after he caught my bag, he got me into the van.

And that's all I knew because as soon as we got in, he slipped a blindfold over my eyes.

"Oh, come on. Considering that this has obviously NOT gone according to plan, don't you think you can forget the whole blindfolding me thing?"

"What makes you think it's not going to plan?"

"Uh, everything that has happened?"

I heard the soft ding of the turn signal. Happiness, as delicate as a soap bubble, filled me.

"So, where are we going?"

"Someplace."

"Really. No kidding." I stopped. "Ari stained her rug, you know."

"That was inspired of her. I just wish she'd warned me."

"Or, you know, me."

"Why would you need a warning?"

"Um, maybe to prepare myself?"

"And how would you have done that?" His voice was amused.

I hated not having an answer.

We rode in silence for a bit, broken only by the steady thrum of the wheels on the road. Mauro had the AC on, so I couldn't even tell from the street sounds where we were. We'd been in the van long enough to get almost anyplace, which didn't give me much of a clue.

Finally, finally, he pulled to a stop. I started to yank my blindfold off, but then I felt his hand on mine. "So close," he said softly. "Five more minutes."

He helped me up, helped me out of the van.

"Um," he said, his voice sounding a little unsteady for the first time. "I need to, um, put something on you . . ."

"You are insane. Also creepy."

"True. Now hold up your arms."

As soon as he draped it over my skin, I knew that this was a Dreams costume, but not my Belle dress. The chiffon whispered past my shoulders, my chest, my knees, and swirled down by my feet.

He stood behind me and started doing up buttons, and his fingers brushed against the back of my neck. I shivered and leaned back into him. The air between us felt like strings of firecracker lights connecting us.

And then he pulled off my blindfold.

"Welcome to your quinceañera," he said, his voice hoarse.

Thirty-One

WE WERE IN THE little cove on the outskirts of the bay. There were white fairy lights strung and curled around the edges of the fronds of the palm tree above us. On a table stood a pitcher of lemonade, a bottle of champagne with two flutes, and some books. A small picnic basket was tucked in next to it.

Chinese lanterns dangled above us on crisscrossed strings. And a few floated in the water lapping at the shore.

And absolutely no people. Just us.

He'd done all this. Somehow, in between working and practice and me, he'd done this.

"You don't like it." His smile wobbled a little bit. Mauro the confident, Mauro the arrogant . . . was nervous.

"I . . . don't know what to say."

"Thanks?" he suggested.

"No . . . I mean . . . why?"

"Because you wanted one." He put his hands in his pockets.

I hadn't even noticed that he'd managed to change into a tuxedo jacket at some point.

He was beautiful.

"But . . . it's not my birthday . . ."

He grinned. "That's how I knew it would be a surprise."

"But . . . how?"

"Do you want to know the but or the how?" he asked, smirking.

I took a step forward and felt the dress rub against my leg. I looked down at myself. Seafoam green and white swirled down to the ground, panels that moved like a wave that had just caught the shore. More chiffon drifted loosely past my elbows, medieval princess style. The bodice twinkled with sequins and flat opals and little pearls, and somehow the effect was like the glint of wet sand that sparkled with every step. "This isn't a Dreams dress."

He shook his head. "It's a gen-u-ine Doña Thomasina quinceañera dress."

I spread my hands over the skirt. I wouldn't have ever even let myself dream of a dress like this. And now it was on my body, like I was the kind of girl who was worthy of it. "How did you get your hands on it? Are we gonna have to go on the run from the law?"

"Won her over with my charm. She lent it to me. In the service of true love." Then, realizing what he'd said, he suddenly got really busy with the books he had propped on the table.

"So . . . my theme is old books?" I teased, trying to get myself out of this feeling like I was carrying an overfull bowl of water that I couldn't spill.

He looked at me over his shoulder and pushed one of the books in front of me. A photo album. Open to a picture I'd never seen. Me, sitting up in a little chair, flanked by Mami, Abuelo, and Abuela. And Junior. I stroked the plastic covering. "Where did this come from?"

"My bumbling coconspirator, your cousin. I told her what I had planned. She dug through all her mom's old albums and found . . . a lot of things."

I turned the pages, faster and faster. Junior carrying me in his arms. Junior and Mami each holding one of my hands.

"Looks like you guys definitely had some good times before it all went bad," he said softly. "You DID have a dad, Carmen. Look at the way he's looking at you." Then he glanced at me and said, "Oh shit. Carmen, I'm sorry."

Because at his words, it was like something had come undone in me, some muscle I've had clenched my whole life. It was easier to know what I'd always known. That he didn't care. That he didn't acknowledge me. That he went home and never came back.

"Then . . . why?"

"Because he was still young and stupid, and he still made bad choices, and probably listened to the wrong people, and went back to where he thought he might fix it. But that wasn't the only thing he was. Even if it was just for a little while, he was still your father."

I was still standing a little bit away from him, absorbing his words, absorbing everything about tonight like I always did. Alone.

Then I was in his arms and it made so much sense to be there.

After a few seconds of me snorfling onto his tux jacket, I pulled a little away, self-conscious.

"So, maybe I haven't learned that much from Simone about throwing a fun party," he said, mouth twisted. "I didn't do all this to make you miserable."

"So . . . why?"

He cocked his head down at me. "You really have to ask me that?"

"Um, yeah?"

"I could say that I did it because the whole quince thing ruined us the first time. Or I could say that I wanted to give you something that was all yours and had nothing to do with your cousin or anybody else. Or I could say that I wanted to get you alone in a beautiful dress, on a gorgeous night, and see what happened. Or maybe I just wanted to impress you. Again." He took a breath. "But . . . it's not those things. I mean . . . not just those things. I . . ." He looked fixedly at the water, spread before us with a bridge of moonlight connecting us to the other side. "I talk . . . a lot." He gave me a lopsided smile. "And when

I'm not talking, I text. Words come easy. But I wanted to DO something, I wanted to SHOW you, somehow." His voice was low, hoarse. "Because I was afraid that if I didn't show you, you'd only have the words, and you'd believe them. That it was summer, it was fun, and then it was done. But . . . it's not. It's not. Because—" He looked down and got busy with his phone. "OK, uh . . . yeah." He pressed a button that made soft music waft through the trees. "I would have played your 'Mi Niña Bonita' song, but that seemed a little, um, out of place."

And then I kissed him. I tried to make it smooth and hot and sexy and everything that it was supposed to be, but my heart kept replaying his words and stuttering over them, and I couldn't pretend to be cool-girl Carmen. I couldn't follow my own rules. Not tonight. So it was awkward and messy and full of who we really were. I was trying to tell him something, even if the words were locked back.

When we finally separated, we were both breathing hard.

I held out my hand and wordlessly, he took it. And we started to dance. It's funny; we'd learned all these elaborate dances together, but when you want to be together, there is nothing better than the basic sway.

It took a few seconds for me to recognize the song. "Hey, this is your stuff!" He ducked his head with a sheepish smile. "From the car."

"Yeah, but . . . something else, too . . ." I hummed along for a second, and then I started laughing. "'Tale as Old as Time'?

Seriously? And is that me singing it?"

"It seemed appropriate."

"And disturbing, so yeah. Fits us perfectly."

"I knew you would appreciate it."

"And I do," I said softly. "Seriously, Mauro, this is the most amazing thing anyone has ever done for me." I put my head on his shoulder and just . . . felt it. Felt everything.

The truth is scarier than any lie.

"What?" he asked me softly.

"I didn't say anything."

"Still, what? You want me to put my head on? Maybe that would make it easier to talk?"

"Let's stay off the clock."

"It took all summer, but I finally made a romantic out of you," he said, touching his forehead to mine. His hair tickled my skin.

I reached up and stroked the hair out of his eyes.

Another drop of water. But not from me this time. One crack and the sky opened, and Miami summer rain spilled all over us.

"Oh shit! The dress!" I grabbed his hand and we ran through the rain to the van.

We scrambled inside and looked at each other.

And cracked up.

"We didn't even get to have our Reubens." He stared out of the window forlornly at the picnic basket getting soaked.

"Give me a second." I pulled the chiffon dress over my head, Cinderella back to her tank top and jean shorts. Then I ran out of the van and grabbed the basket, the champagne, the lemonade, and those precious photo albums and booked it back inside.

"There," I said triumphantly. But Mauro wasn't listening. He was just staring at me.

"What?" I said, moving my wet hair out of my face self-consciously. "I didn't want to ruin the dress!"

He was still staring.

The rain thrummed on the windows of the van, steaming them up and sealing us off from the world. We were alone, with no Mami or Simone or anybody to interrupt us.

The food was forgotten. He cupped my face in his hands, fingers stroking the rainwater off my flushed skin.

I sat up and started to pull my tank top over my head.

His eyes got wide, and then hot. "Are you sure?"

I nodded, my eyes staying on his until my tank top covered my face, hiding him from me.

But only for a second.

———————

Afterward, I lay against him. It hadn't been like a lot of my other times, the times when I'd turn my brain off and just let my body move like it belonged to someone else. I wanted to belong to myself just then. To him. I wanted to memorize the exact way his fingers shook when they touched me, until they warmed on my overheated skin and grew bolder. My own hands stroked everywhere, marking him. Making him mine. I was there to hear the soft laughs when it seemed like we weren't quite sure what we were doing, or where we were, or what was happening. And that was before we fumbled with the condom, together. It was awkward and weird. Different. Perfect. Not my first time, but our first time together. The first time it's ever really mattered.

This was right around the time I usually went home. Tonight I wanted everything to stretch into forever.

Forever. Not a word I've ever used. Or wanted to.

"Those Reubens must be cold," said a sleepy voice by my shoulder.

"Doesn't matter. They are still God's most perfect food." I took a bite. "You know what I'm going to say next, don't you?" I said. "Just as soon as I finish this glorious sandwich?"

"Um . . . that I've ruined you for all men forever?"

The truth of that statement hit me like a bomb.

Holy shit. I loved him. I was in love with him. And all my terms and conditions hadn't been able to protect me.

I stared at up the ceiling and tried not to wince.

But then he sat up and ran a hand through his hair, and I was hit by how much I was going to miss that gesture. "I didn't mean for tonight to get all heavy. I just wanted to . . . I don't know. Give you something."

I raised an eyebrow. "Really."

He grinned, adorably sheepish. "Not what I meant. Just . . .

Look, I know this summer has been full of weirdness. Weirdness and people. And weird people." He smirked for a second, and then got serious. "I wanted to give you a night that showed you that surprises could occasionally even be good. And I wanted to give myself a night where I didn't have to share you with anyone else in the world."

Except now, I know exactly what I'm going to lose.

He was right here, in front of me. But soon, he wouldn't be.

Tomorrow, we'd go back to reality. To the weirdness and the people and the weird people, and I didn't know how any of it was going to go.

Tomorrow, I'd start to lose him to the world.

Thirty-Two

IT WAS FOUR A.M. when I finally tiptoed through the door. Ariana had left the key tucked into the dirt of Tía Celia's hibiscus and had made sure the alarm was off.

The house was finally silent, but it was a minefield of things that would creak, groan, spill, or shatter. Nothing was where it belonged—vases teetered on the edges of tables, making room for laptops charging and purses and people's phones. Boxes of favors were stacked on top of shoeboxes with our heels in them. Overnight bags were resting on the floor, their straps ready to catch any unsuspecting foot.

Finally, I reached Ariana's room. I expected to see a bunch of sleeping girls, heads barely peeking out, looking like human burritos.

But that's not what I saw. Instead, Tía Celia sat on Ariana's bed. Ariana herself was slumped away from her, face tear-streaked. And Mami sat by the desk, her eyes shooting daggers at me.

"Carmen Maria Aguilar, you have a LOT of explaining to do. Right now!"

———————

"So, that's it. He wanted to do something romantic before he left, and then the night got away from us. I shouldn't have stayed out so late. I am really sorry about that." I was proud of the evenness of my tone. I wasn't fifteen years old anymore. I could be an adult about this.

"The night got away from you? It's four a.m.!" Tía Celia hissed. "And that's not the only thing! I had young girls in the house, impressionable girls! ¿Y qué haces? You bring in alcohol? To serve underage girls in my HOUSE? I had to send them home!"

"No, wait . . . I didn't have anything to do with that! I didn't bring anything into the house!"

But the way she was looking at me—I knew she didn't believe it. Because I'd confirmed what she'd expected of me anyway. She'd been waiting all summer for me to screw up, and here it was.

I looked at Mami, but she was almost as angry as Tía Celia. "Four a.m., Carmen Maria! And just WHAT were you doing until then? No, don't tell me! I can read it on your face!" She shook her head. "I expected better. I've talked to you about this so much . . . Why would you—"

"Why? Because you've always let her do whatever the hell she wanted, because you had to be the 'cool mom,'" Tía Celia said, making angry quotes by her ears. "You told me she had changed! You told me that I could trust that she wouldn't be a bad influence on Ariana anymore!"

"I told you, Mami. You smelled it because I dropped it, on purpose, but I really didn't—" Ariana tried, weakly.

"If I were you, I'd stay very quiet right now," Tía Celia said, rounding on her daughter. "Unlike Carmen, YOU were raised to know better—"

Mami snorted. "Really? What do you think she was doing tonight, guzzling rum out of Solo cups! What, did Carmen funnel it down her throat?"

"She would know how!" Tía Celia shouted back, illogically.

A thump, and then a few seconds later, a sleepy Tío Victor at the door. "What's going on?" He looked at me and Ariana. "Que está pasando, Mirella? Who's sick?"

"Nobody's sick, Victor. Everyone's fine. Go back to sleep," Mami assured him, while Tía Celia seethed. Tío Victor had instinctively asked Mami first.

He looked at us again like he wasn't entirely sold, but then he shrugged. "Keep the fighting to the daytime, please. Some of us have to work to pay for all this." And then he padded back to the bedroom.

"Tía Celia, I swear on everything, I had nothing to do with

Ariana drinking tonight. Te lo juro."

"I barely had a sip," Ariana muttered. Everyone ignored her.

"And why should I believe you? You obviously lied about tonight!" Her face was twisted, and I saw a flash of the true Tía Celia. She wasn't Grace Kelly. She was just a pissed-off middle-aged Cuban woman who loved to hold a grudge.

"I didn't KNOW about tonight! Believe me, I wouldn't have planned it like this. I don't want to disrespect you."

I couldn't stop picking at the loose skin on my thumb. I looked down at my hands, at the blood beginning to blossom on my thumb.

And I could still see a hint of butter on that finger, from the Reuben I'd had at my quinceañera.

It felt like a long time ago.

She tossed her head. "That's all you've ever DONE is disrespect me! Acting like you are doing us a favor by being a part of all of this! Being nasty to your cousin and the rest of the corte, making everyone tiptoe around poor Carmen's big feelings—"

"Everything I've done has been for the good of the Dreams. Including this quinceañera." Still trying to keep my voice from cracking or shrieking. Still trying to prove something to her.

"The Dreams are NOT your family!"

"You're right!" I finally boiled over, done trying. "The Dreams are actually NICE to me, and they don't accuse me of things I didn't do!" I pointed at my cousin. "Tell her, Ariana!

Tell her that none of that had anything to do with me!"

She looked at me for a long second, and then she bent her head and said nothing at all.

Choose you, my ass.

"You know what, Tía? Tienes razón. This was all a mistake, but luckily, it's one that's easy to fix." I grabbed my purse and my overnight bag.

"I quit."

———————

As soon as we got in the car, I started in on Mami. "Can you believe that Tía Celia would actually—!"

From her seat behind the wheel, she held up a hand. "Basta. I really don't want to hear it."

"But, Mami—"

She whirled round to face me at a stoplight, and the red reflection only added to the fury in her eyes. "I can't believe you DID THAT! How could you do that to yourself, Carmen? To our family? Have I raised you to be so irresponsible?"

"Irresponsible to what? I told you, I didn't give Ariana the rum—"

"I'm not talking about that!" she said, waving a hand at me. "To go off with that boy, almost all night long, Carmen . . . I'm not stupid. I know what happened! He took advantage—"

"He did no such thing. We BOTH wanted it." Then I stopped. Realized what I'd just admitted.

I was no virgin. Mami knew that. But there was something about Mauro that scared her, that rang the same alarms I had tried to ignore.

"Oh, Carmencita. That Mauro—a boy like that, looks, money, talent, every opportunity—"

"Oh. You think I'm not good enough for him." I curled my hands in my lap. I didn't want to hear my own fears confirmed in Mami's voice.

"Claro que sí! Of course you are good enough for him! He should be thanking God that he even has a chance to make it up to you, considering how he treated you before!"

Well, I couldn't argue with that.

"But . . . that doesn't matter. He's worse than Junior! At least I thought Junior would stick around—"

"We used protection!"

"It can fail! Ask me how I know!" She took a deep breath. "And I had my high school diploma—"

"And I'll have mine, too, in a couple of weeks."

"Mauro's type is always gonna look out for Mauro, and you should do the same thing. You had all summer to figure out what was next, but instead you wasted it all on that boy. What's going to happen next for you, Carmen? You pretty much blew the Simone thing, because once she finds out about you quitting, she'll be done with you. Because Mauro knows what's next for HIM, and it doesn't involve you. Wise up! Protect *yourself*, because he's damn well protected. By his money, by his school, by his father, by the fact that he's a man. And what he says to get what he wants . . . you can't listen to that! You have to trust what he does—not what he says or what he supposedly feels—"

"OK! God! You think he sucks! I get it!" I put my hands over my face. "Why can't you be on my side?"

We got home just then, and Mami pulled over and took a deep breath. "Yes, I am on your side . . . more than you are yourself, obviously. I know you don't get it. Because I didn't. And I've always wanted more for you. But . . . you gotta want more for yourself."

And with that, she slammed the car door and went inside without waiting for me.

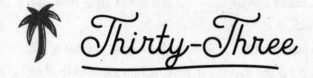 *Thirty-Three*

WITH LESS THAN A week to go, the next night's practice was the first I'd missed all summer.

I sat outside on the steps, breathing in the cooler night air, still tinged with a hint of lightning from a storm earlier.

My mind was a black hole, a maze without an exit. No matter where my thoughts ran, they always ended up right here. Tía Celia's accusations. Ariana's complicit silence. Mami's disappointment.

Everything was over.

Somehow, the most perfect night of my life had turned into a total disaster. And I couldn't blame anyone but myself. I should have known better than to sneak out of Tía Celia's house until four a.m. I should have found a way to keep Ariana from drinking, or at least from getting caught. What the fuck; hadn't she learned *anything* in the last four years?

No. I'd screwed up by staying out late, but I'd had nothing

to do with the drinking. If this whole quinceañera was about Ariana coming of age, she was failing fucking miserably.

Which didn't exactly make me feel better right then. But nothing could.

"Is this step taken?" I looked up. Alex stood in front of me, his bulk blocking the streetlight, making him a haloed shadow.

In response, I nudged myself over.

He sat down and put an arm around me. "Tonight's practice was . . . tough. Ariana kept bursting into tears. She told her mother they should cancel everything."

I rolled my eyes. "Yeah, and I'm sure she meant that."

"She's really upset, Carmen."

"Then she should join the crowd."

After a second, he said, "Wanna talk about it?"

"I'm sure you've already heard everything from your girl-friend."

"Yeah. But I want to hear everything from my friend. So talk."

"She lied, Alex! She let Tía Celia believe that I was the one who got her alcohol last night!"

"She said she tried to tell her mother the truth, but her mother didn't want to hear it."

"Oh right. She tried to send her telepathic messages maybe, but she didn't actually use her words like a big girl."

"Cut her some slack, Carmen . . . Her mom is scary."

I stiffened. "If you are just here to defend her, you can go the hell away."

"I'm just here to tell you that . . . she's as miserable as you are."

"Somehow I doubt that." Tía Celia's voice entered my mind again, and Mami's eyes when she reminded me that Mauro was leaving and that I should have known better. I *should* have known better—

And Ariana and me in the car, when we said we'd always choose each other.

I put my head on Alex's shoulder and really started to bawl.

He didn't say anything, just stroked my hair and let me cry.

"Do you run around knight-in-shining-armoring for every girl, or is this a Carmen special?" Mauro stood in front of us, arms crossed, a bitter twist to his mouth.

"Calm down, Reyes. This isn't about you."

"Last I checked, *Sharma*, this isn't about you, either. But you keep that seat warm next to my girl. Counting down the days until I leave and you can take a cousin sister wife? That plan might have worked better if the cousins in question still got along—which, let me guess, is why you are here? Checking on your backup?"

"God, Mauro, shut up!" I said.

Alex stood up. Mauro had a few inches on him, but Alex was an athlete and it showed.

"I'm her friend, you dick—believe it or not, she doesn't just exist for your pleasure and convenience. This is her life, her family—and she's gonna have to live with the consequences long after you go back to school and end it with her."

Mauro shook his head. "So, *so* sure you know everything."

"You don't have to be psychic to see you won't be able to keep it in your pants for five minutes after you get back to school. Luckily, she has people here who care about her."

I expected Mauro to come back with a smart remark. What I didn't expect was the crack of Mauro's fist connecting with Alex's cheek. Alex touched his cheek, already reddening from the impact, and launched himself onto Mauro.

When the hell had my life become a bad telenovela?

I glanced at the window upstairs. All I needed now was for Mami to come out and see this.

I got between them, pushed them apart. "OK, seriously? This is bullshit! What the hell was that?"

"That," Mauro said, "was a long time coming." He balled his fists, like he wasn't done yet.

"Damn straight," Alex agreed.

"Well, congrats to both of you idiots! Hopefully none of my neighbors called the cops—"

"Don't worry. I'm leaving," Alex said, brushing himself off. "Carmen . . . some people are worth fighting for." And then he looked right at Mauro. "And some people aren't."

With that, Alex turned and got into his car.

———

Mauro and I stood, facing each other in the darkness. I could hear the soft whirring of people's ACs in the background. Humidity hung heavy in the air, dragging down the palm fronds and pressing everything closer to the ground. I wished I could sink into the concrete.

"That was stupid," Mauro said finally. "I'm sorry. I just didn't expect to see Alex here with you . . . especially after I hadn't heard from you all day."

"He just showed up after practice. Wanted to check on me."

"Yeah, what a prince—" Mauro began sarcastically, and then stopped. "Fine, sorry. How are you?"

He sat down and I did, too. He didn't touch me and I didn't move any closer.

"I'm— This sucks, Mauro. All I've wanted all summer was to get the hell out of this quinceañera, but . . . not like this. Things were finally getting better. Ariana and I were getting along. Mami and Tía Celia were getting along, even me and Tía Celia . . . We were all one big happy family again," I said, choking on those last words. "And now everything is ruined, and even though it wasn't my fault, it FEELS like my fault, again."

Mauro sat silent for a moment, and then said, "I'm sorry that me doing something nice for you made such a mess." More silence. "I feel like we've been here before. At least this time I actually did the thing."

I touched his shoulder, for just a moment. "It was perfect. None of this is your fault."

"It's not yours, either." He paused. "Can you talk to your aunt? Like, tell her you are very sorry and you won't do it again?"

"Do what again? Give Ariana rum? I didn't do it the first time!"

"Just . . . look." He faced me and took my hands in his. "Your tía wants this to be over, she wants you in the quince, believe me, but she doesn't want to have to blame Ariana."

I stiffened. "So . . . you want me to lie?"

"I'm saying . . . think about how this affects everyone. You, Ariana, your mami, your tía, Simone . . . me."

"So . . . lie."

He threw his hands up. "You keep putting words in my mouth!"

I mean . . . he wasn't wrong. It would be so easy.

All I had to do was let everyone keep believing what they already thought they knew about me.

"Yeah . . . I'm not doing that."

"Fine."

We sat for a while in an uncomfortable silence, while I kept arguing with Mauro in my head.

Why is your first instinct to lie? You wanted to lie to Alex about you and me. You lied to me about your father. You just lied about my relationship with Alex to make me feel like shit. What does it say about me that I think about the quince you threw me and I want to believe everything you've said to me this summer, everything you've made me feel? Maybe it's because . . . why would you lie? You know we're over in a week. And I know it, too.

"I mean . . . *we're* not doing that," I burst out. "We've been honest about everything. Even when a lie would have felt better."

When he looked confused, I clarified. "Terms and conditions, remember? Four weeks of fun, friendship . . ." I choked on the last word.

"Feelings," he finished. "But . . . the truth can change. And then if you hang on to the old rules, doesn't that become a lie?"

"What are you saying?"

"I'm saying . . ." He looked down, took a deep breath, and then met my eyes. "I don't want to break up in a week, Carmen. I don't give a shit about our terms and conditions . . . I want to be with you. I want to try."

My hollow rasping breath sounded like static in the quiet.

I want so much. I want to believe that it's possible.

The Mami in my mind shook her head. Why couldn't I learn this basic thing?

Because I was her daughter.

"That . . . that was never our deal."

"So we change the deal!"

I shook my head. "We had rules for a reason. For THIS reason."

He jerked back like I had hit him. "Is this . . . is this about Alex?"

"What?"

He tapped his chin, like he was solving a riddle. "No . . .

355

wait. It makes a sick sort of sense. Maybe *I* was your convenient lie all summer . . . Maybe you took me up on my offer and neglected to tell me?" His voice got gravelly. "I'm an excellent actor. I would have been convincing. I promise. The perks, after all—"

"How could you say that?" I said, my voice getting high-pitched. "You know that's not true!"

"Do I?" He looked at me like he'd never quite seen me so clearly before.

I turned away. He turned me back toward him. His eyes shone with starlight. I saw my tearstained, blotchy face reflected back to me there. "Then take a fucking risk, Carmen." He stroked my cheeks with his thumbs. "Hey, hey . . . I'm sorry. I know you are hurting right now . . . I'm so sorry." My skin hummed in his hands. "This isn't the time. I get it—"

I covered his hands with my own and gently pulled them off me. Unlike Mauro, I was going to go with the truth. Even if it broke me inside. "It doesn't matter when we talk about it. Nothing has changed—"

"Everything has changed! For me, Carmen, absolutely every-thing has changed! But . . . that doesn't mean shit, does it?" He shook his head, a rueful expression on his face. "Come to think of it, you never actually ever said you forgave me . . . for the party, for the pictures, for the pole. You say you don't think your family thinks you can change, but that's bullshit. *You* don't trust . . . *you* don't forgive . . . and me and your cousin and your family . . . we just keep banging against your walls and nothing changes, because *you* refuse to admit it *can*. If I hadn't been leaving at the end of the summer, you wouldn't have touched me with a ten-foot pole."

"You know what?" I said, flinging my hands up. "Probably not! Just like I wouldn't have worked on this quince unless somebody forced me! Because . . . I was right! You . . . my cousin . . . you don't change! You agree to one thing and then you do whatever the hell you want anyway. Convenient lies . . . that's the way you live your life! And I'll be damned if I let myself stay here, miserable, wondering what the hell you are doing in Boston, and knowing that I can never, never trust you!"

"Don't do this, Carmen," he said, moving toward me, his voice broken. "I'm not Oscar and I'm not Junior—"

I moved away from him. "It doesn't matter who you are," I said tearfully. "Because I know who I am. I'm not Mirella. This is done. This was always going to be done. We're over, Mauro."

And I tried so hard, just then, to force myself to remember every bad moment between us—the receipts that would prove I was doing the right thing. But my traitor brain replayed the shy look in his eyes when he'd shown me my quince. The way he'd given me the photo albums. Us in my bed after he gave me the MacBook. The way he'd held me after Alex rejected me. All the times our eyes met and no words needed to be said. The way I'd always been able to tell him everything—even this.

Once he got back to school and was free of me, he'd thank me . . . well, in his mind, anyway, because no way we'd ever speak again after this—

My control was slipping fast.

He ran his hand through his hair, and the gesture was like a stab. "You know what? Fine. You're right. We were always gonna be temporary. I thought we'd just get it out of our systems. Closure." He shook his head and smirked through the bleakness in his eyes. "Idiots. But at least I'm smart enough to know that I'm not free and neither are you. And your stupid rules didn't work after all." He started to walk away, and then turned back. "Because I most definitely have hard feelings."

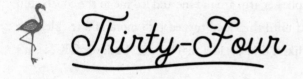# Thirty-Four

I HELD IT TOGETHER as I watched Mauro get into the Dreams van.

I held it together as he peeled away without looking back.

I held it together as I leaned my forehead against the door after I'd let myself inside. The only sound in the hallway was my shaky breath.

I didn't expect any sympathy. Mami had made her opinion of me and Mauro abundantly clear. If anything, she would be happy that I'd finally cut him out of my life.

I'd done it. I'd proved I *had* learned from her example, right?

Mami barely glanced at me when I walked in, but then she did a double take. "Carmen Maria, qué te pasa?" I covered my face with my hands, and my tears started again, leaking through my fingers.

I could tell she was still pissed about Tía Celia and everything else. But she was my mother. I needed her. This was just . . . triage.

Mami put her arm around me and led me to the couch, and then waited until the flood turned into more of a trickle. She patted me like I'd just had a nightmare. "Shh, it's OK . . . it's OK."

"No, Mami. It's not OK." And I told her about everything that had happened, from the beginning. She sighed when I told her about my quince, winced when I told her we broke up, shook her head, and cursed under her breath.

But—I don't know. I kept waiting for the flight of her own fury, because at least we could do that for each other. Mami would explode and I'd catch fire from the sparks, and I could burn all the pain of tonight away.

She was silent as I finished, hiccuping my last words. "See? I'm not a lost cause. I listened to you, what you said last night. You know, always protect yourself. Keep a part of yourself separate. Know that what they say and how they act is not who they are. Remember that they leave, and they don't come back."

She held up a hand. "First of all, I have to remind you again that I am still PISSED AS HELL about you staying out all night with Mauro, and believe me, that will absolutely have consequences. I want that on the record." Then her face softened. "Oh, Carmen. Talk about 'do as I say, not as I do.'" She shifted so that she didn't have to look at me. "Last night . . . the things I said to you . . . I was talking out of my own fear.

360

I haven't been the best example." She waited for my response. When none came, she shook her head and said, jokingly, "No, no . . . don't argue."

"You haven't been so bad."

"But I have . . . I let my own bitterness teach you the opposite of what I believe. Because, Carmencita . . . what they say and how they act is all we can really know. About anyone."

I shook my head. "People can pretend all sorts of things—"

"And I of all people should know that, right?" She shifted on the couch like it had gotten hot. "Mi amor . . . I've always worried you were like me. That you would think the whole force of a relationship was on you—that you were the only one who had to fight for it. Because you didn't believe that you were worth the risk. I was afraid that you would throw away your whole future for a boy who didn't deserve it, or you. But tonight makes me realize I don't have to worry about that at all."

Mauro's words came back to me. *Take a fucking risk, Carmen.* I leaned my head into Mami's shoulder. "Don't worry, Mami. I know maybe you can't tell right now, but I *do* have dreams in my brain, not just romantic crap. And those dreams are more important to me than crying over something that is obviously doomed." I wiped my eyes. "I got over Alex, and I'll get over this."

Except . . . this didn't feel anything like what happened with Alex. That was bubble-gum pink and my own shallow ego. This was . . . black and red and lightning, bone-marrow deep.

Mami pulled away and looked in my eyes, and I remembered how she could always read me. "Oh, mija. I'm sorry I made you think that I don't believe you have anything in your brain but 'romantic crap.' I've walked past your room at any and all hours, and I've heard you in there, making your videos. And I know you love it." She paused. "So, no, despite what I said before, I'm not worried about you throwing your life away. And I'm not worried about you thinking the whole force of a relationship should be on you." I opened my mouth, but she held up her hand. "But . . . I *am* worried. Because the story you told me, about what happened between you and Mauro? It reminded me of Junior."

And even though I'd made the same comparison in my own head, I couldn't stand to hear her say that. Still defending him, like a tonta in love. "Mauro is nothing like Junior."

"Not Mauro. You."

Mami stared at me quietly. Waiting for me to, what, run away? Never. No matter how much it hurt, here it was, finally. Finally, she was going to talk about Junior. A pin falling on the ground would have sounded like a bomb.

"You know the start of the story. Junior was glamorous. He was rich. He was handsome. Reckless, exciting. He felt like my match—I wanted to feel like his. And when he was happy, it was incredible. But . . . Junior expected the worst in people, in things. He really believed that looking for it, and finding it, would protect him somehow. That was what he thought was the truth. And when he found it—and he always found it—that person was dead to him because it hurt him too much. He didn't want to be that way, I don't think, but he didn't believe he had a choice. I thought I could be enough . . . that you could. But he was too far gone by then. The drugs . . ." She sighed, hard, and took a minute. "And he threw away happiness with both hands. I tried to be like him for so many years, to protect myself from being hurt like that ever again. I put Victor on a pedestal and dragged Junior and any other man who wanted to get close to me through the mud of my mind. *You* remember that hit parade. Then when I was finally ready to be myself, to be open, I found Enrique."

"How did you do it? How did you change the way you thought for years?"

Mami gave a short laugh. "All those years I believed I was in control . . . but I was still living out of bad history. It wasn't until I could forgive Victor, Cecilia, and even Junior that I could see a way out. Because I could move into something new. Victor and I . . . we were so young, and I wanted something that wasn't in him. Something complicated. I thought Junior was complicated, but he was just . . . dark and lost. Victor is happier with Celia, and I'm happier for them than I am unhappy for my old self."

"And Enrique . . . he's complicated?"

Mami smiled. "Enrique is exactly what I want right now. And anyone who gets to be our age is automatically complicated."

"That explains Tía Celia."

"Oh, Celia." Her eyes looked past me, at something only she could see. "Celia carries a lot of guilt about the way everything went down, so she tries to highlight the differences between us so that she can see herself as perfect. She chose the light, I chose Junior, et cetera, et cetera." Mami winked. "I let her believe it. What's the harm? It's nice that somebody still sees me like the bad seed. It's cooler."

"Yeah, well . . . I don't *want* to be the bad seed, and nobody gave me a choice."

"Oh, mija. Don't let Celia's delusions define who you are. In her heart, she knows that Ariana's flaws are only Ariana's. I know she loves you—she's the one who pushed the hardest for this reunion. She's always felt bad about what happened with your quince, and in her own way, I think, she thought this would be a way of making it up to you. Helping you with your summer job, with your diploma. But she can't help putting her daughter and you into our old scenes. I'm sorry that you quit the quince. I wish with all my heart that it had worked out differently. But I'm not sorry that you stood up for yourself. And I support you . . . even if it means that I won't be there, either."

I nudged her shoulder. I'd missed this. Feeling like we were on the same team. "Wow . . . que enlightened!"

She laughed. "Hey, I actually listened to some of Tony's yoga talk. And let's not forget Dr. Phil."

Mami gently moved my chin up so I was looking straight at her.

"Mauro's not perfect, sweetheart. You definitely know that. But I don't think you are looking for perfect anymore. If you were, you'd still be hung up on Alex. And I know I've never seen you happier. Or fighting it so hard. What would happen if you stopped fighting it? Only you know what you've seen of Mauro's heart. Only you know if you can fight *together* for what you *both* want. If it's worth it to take the chance and trust your heart, even if everybody and your mami thinks you are crazy. And for the record, I wouldn't think you were crazy." She grinned, and then grew serious. "I just . . . I don't want you to lose any more. Because you are *my* whole heart, mi corazón entero. The best thing in my life. And in spite of everything, I'll always be grateful for Junior. Because he gave me you." Then she sat up very straight. "Ay, mi madre, did I just encourage you to get knocked up?"

"I get what you mean."

"Good." She stroked my hair, smiling through her tears. "Because Enrique and I are too young to become abuelos."

Thirty-Five

I PERCHED ON THE edge of a chair, sitting in front of Simone. Her eyes were icicles of disappointment as she listened to my story. I couldn't put off telling her any longer.

"... and that's why I can't be a part of Ariana's quinceañera performance," I finished up. "Unfortunately, there are irreconcilable differences between me and the Garces family." Automatically, I alphabetized one of the piles of invoices on the side table. I probably wouldn't be the one to file those now.

She tightened her mouth. "Carmen . . . it's two days before the event. It's beyond irresponsible to quit right now."

"I understand, but—"

"No, I don't think you really do," she interrupted. "Dreams Come True is a small business . . . we live and die on our word of mouth. And this is one of the largest and most elaborate events we've ever done. You are not only letting the client down, but your fellow Dreams as well." Her voice sounded like it was chiseled out of the sidewalk. My toes curled inside my sandals and tried to disappear. I wished the rest of me could do that, too.

"I'm sorry," I repeated for what felt like the millionth time. "I should have said something. I thought . . . I thought I could do it. I wanted to make it work. For you, for the Dreams, for my family. But I just can't."

She shuffled some papers on her desk. Probably not alphabetically. I thought about our afternoons here, working together, laughing and listening to music and chattering about the quinceañera. I hadn't even imagined work could feel like that.

"I see," she said finally. But it didn't seem like she did.

Maybe if I kept talking, I could make her understand. "I really am sorry—I mean, I know it's uneven now, and that Mauro might not be able to perform—"

"Of course Mauro is performing. He hasn't quit, and he's worked as hard as anyone." Simone's voice went from cement to chips of ice. "But this means I'll have to stand in for you, because we won't be able to get anyone up to speed on the dances on such short notice, and considering that I'm also the day-of point person, you will also be impacting my ability to do *my* best work. Which, again, hurts Dreams Come True."

The lump in my throat was Snow White's whole apple as I nodded. "Of course. I'm sorry—"

She gathered the papers into a pile. "I'll make sure to get all your paperwork to the school. I'm sure you can pull something together for your final project."

Well, there it was. I was done here. Nothing left to say.

I nodded miserably. "I understand." I knew how this would look to Velez. Bad. This would be the second internship I'd quit early, for "personal reasons." I'd hoped for a glowing report from Simone, and a job offer. That looked about as possible now as a fourth wish from Aladdin's lamp.

She sighed. "Oh, Carmen. What a mess."

I stared down at my ragged cuticles. No one who saw me right now would ever connect me to Beauty. "That's me. A mess."

"Now, I wouldn't go that far . . ." She hesitated, as if torn between the fairy-tale mentor she'd been all summer and the tough boss lady. Then she softened. "I have to admit . . . I was hoping we'd be able to continue our association after the internship ended. I've never had an actual assistant before, and . . ." She smiled ruefully. "I guess I got used to it. But . . . I can't overlook this, Carmen. I'm sorry. This isn't how I'd hoped our summer together would end."

Icy Simone hurt. But nice Simone was going to break me.

I stood up, and so did she. She moved closer, like she was going to hug me. She didn't, though. Instead, she patted me awkwardly on the shoulder. "Good luck."

Luck. The thing that had always betrayed me.

———————

I lay in bed for a long time the next morning, watching the shadows crawl up my wall and hoping for the world to pass me by for one day. Today was the last day of regular practice. Tomorrow would be the dress rehearsal, and the quince the day after that.

If I timed it right, I could spend the whole thing in my bed.

So far, Mami had let me be. I heard her trying not to bang cups in the kitchen, and then a soft curse when she didn't succeed. And then I heard the door close.

I was alone.

When the door buzzed, I put my comforter back over my head and willed whoever was there to leave.

But the buzzing continued.

If Mami was expecting any repair people today, they'd just have to come back.

And then the buzzing stopped, and I let myself breathe again.

Until the pounding started.

My first thought was that it was Mauro, come to plead his case or something.

He could stay outside, too.

But the pounding continued, and a voice joined it. Waverly.

Groggy, I opened the door. I knew my hair was in a snarled bun and my raggedy pj bottoms had a hole in the left leg. I just didn't care.

My best friend stood in front of me, her face wrinkled in confusion.

"What the hell, Carmen? Why haven't you been answering my calls? And you quit the quince?" Waverly swept herself in. "When I texted Mauro two nights ago, he just told me that everything sucked and to ask you why. So . . . what's up?" She sniffed. "Wow, you haven't even made coffee? This IS serious."

I sat down at the kitchen table and put my head down. "Everything sucks, and you can ask HIM why."

She sat down directly in front of me. "Except that you're the one who is here, so . . . talk."

I kept my head down, and maybe I mumbled something about rules, and rum, and a surprise quince, and why did I even CARE that everybody thinks the worst of me, and realizing that I'd let the whole thing get way, way out of control, so of course I had to end it.

Waverly winced. "I think I understood only a third of that, but . . . ouch." She bit the edge of her finger. "But . . . OK, you kind of messed this up hard."

I raised my head briefly to shoot lasers at her, but clearly I missed because her head didn't explode.

"And don't look at me like that! Why didn't you just wait for your aunt to calm down and see reason? Eventually, she would have realized that you had nothing to do with the rum! I would have vouched for you. She likes me."

I snorted. "You don't understand my family at all. Tía Celia might like you now, but if Cesar ever gets a hangnail while you guys are together, she'll have you arrested."

Waverly laughed. "I'll make sure his manicures are one hundred percent safe." And then she frowned at me, like I was an amoeba stubbornly refusing to divide. "And you said you wanted no hard feelings . . . so you dumped Mauro less than a week before he goes back to school? After he threw you that amazing quince and showed you exactly how much he cares about you? I think . . . Carmen . . . you know I love you and I'm always on your side, but . . . girl. You played yourself here," Waverly said slowly. "It's really OK to change your mind, to change your plans. I mean . . . look at this summer! Look how well everything turned out. You didn't want to be a party princess. You thought the thing with Edwin had ruined everything."

She got up and started brewing coffee. "Look, I wasn't the biggest fan of you and Mauro getting back together. He'd really hurt you in the past, and I didn't trust him as far as I could throw him. And he's way bigger than me. But . . . ultimately, what I thought wasn't important. It was all over you both every time you were together, and it only got stronger over the summer."

"Like a disease. Or a tick."

"Or love," Waverly countered. She slapped two cups of coffee down.

"We never said that . . ." I started weakly, and then put my hands over my eyes. "You don't understand. This *can't* be real. How can it be real? It was so fast. It's . . . limerence. That's it. Gather ye rosebuds."

"Look, Carmen," Waverly said, taking a sip of her coffee

and closing her eyes. "Could use a splash of something. Rum, maybe?" At the look in my eyes, she grimaced. "Kidding, sorry, maybe not rum. But anyway, I know you think that if you love Mauro, you are repeating several variations of bad history. And maybe you are. But . . . so what? So what if it doesn't last forever? I love Cesar right NOW and I know that I want to try. As for everything else, we'll see. I mean, I'm terrified, Carmen! About everything! College and Cesar and the future and climate change and adulthood. I could go on. We can't protect ourselves from every single mistake! And statistically, neither the worst thing nor the best thing will happen to us."

"Then I must exist to break your statistics. I mean, look at this stupid quince. We were supposed to break the spell and instead—" Ugh. Even I knew I sounded melodramatic, but I also felt the truth of it. "It's just . . ." I continued in a low voice. "How can it be a good idea if it hurts this much now? Isn't the pain a sign that I need to quit while I'm already behind? How can I know?"

"Hey, idiot," Waverly said, getting up to stand by me so she could pull my head into her stomach. "You can't."

———————

Thanks to Waverly's intervention, I was caffeinated enough to leave the house. I decided to go to the bookstore, to do some research on local colleges. Yes, I knew I could do it all online, but . . . I needed to leave the house. It made me feel like I was actually working on something. And the bookstore has a great café. I didn't have much left that made me happy, but I had coffee, damn it.

I was settled at a table with a pile of enormous slippery paperbacks that promised the secrets of a successful college application to the perfect school. I could use all the help I could get. I was still scared of this process, of committing to a choice that could be totally wrong. But . . . I was more scared of NOT doing it. Because Tía Celia's sneers showed me that I didn't want to live a life where she was right about me.

So . . . I flipped through the books. I'd do all the research, make all the lists, and then . . . probably flip a coin. And hope that the coin landed on FIU, because out of all of my options, that was the only one that felt both possible and exciting.

Maybe if I stared at the books long enough, the words would rearrange themselves and solve all my other problems, too.

"Carmen?"

The words were not moving fast enough.

I turned a little in my chair, pointedly avoiding Ariana as she stood in front of me. Petty, yes, but I think I've earned that. Plus, we really had nothing to say to each other. She'd had the time to talk, and she hadn't done it.

Now, as far as I was concerned, she could stay quiet forever.

"Please?"

I flipped a page of the book and took a sip of my caramel latte.

Despite the lack of invitation, she sat down at my table.

Which made it shake. Which scattered my piles of notes to the ground and made coffee spill on the very biggest of the slippery paperbacks.

"Shit!" I said, grabbing at my papers and mopping everything up as best I could. The whole side of the guidebook I'd been reading had a streak of caramel latte. Great. I was almost out of caffeine, and I was now the proud owner of *The Complete Guide to Your College Application*. Which, like most things attached to college, wasn't cheap.

"I'm so sorry!" she said. "Are your notes OK? Let me pay for the book! It's all my fault!"

"Your family paid me enough to buy the occasional book," I said, my words sharpened to points.

"Carmen—"

"Are you here for a reason?" I turned a page of my book like the answer couldn't have mattered less. The scent of caramel latte wafted up from the pages.

She shook her head. "Just . . . wanted to be near books." That was always Ariana. While other kids had slept with a stuffed bunny or whatever, she slept with a copy of *Anne of Green Gables* for, like, years. She might still, for all I knew.

I gestured to the rest of the store. "All the rest of the store is the right place. I only have a few of them."

She ran her fingers on the spine of the one she'd helped ruin. "*The Complete Guide to Your College Application*," she read. "Wow, you're applying? That's great."

"Don't sound so surprised."

"No!" She faltered. "I mean . . . can you at least look at me?"

"Why? Have you changed?"

"Apparently not," she said in a low voice.

"Then?"

She tapped her fingers on the book, like it was going to give her strength. "I told Mami you had nothing to do with it. I should have done it the same night but . . ." She shook her head. "I am a total chickenshit."

"OK. So what did she say?"

Ariana glanced down and away. "She said I was sweet and noble for trying to defend you," she muttered.

I snorted. "Wow. Shocker."

"But I told her it was absolutely true! I told her that one of Olivia's cousins scored the alcohol for us."

"And I'm sure she promptly fired Olivia." I put my face in my hand, like it was story time.

"She didn't fire you! She would never have done that! You quit!" A few shoppers glanced our way and then around, like they knew they'd stumbled into a telenovela and were wondering where the cameras were.

"Oh right. Because I should have just kept working for someone who thinks I'm out to corrupt you?" I banged my hands down on the table. Ariana saved my coffee before the rest tipped over. I snatched it back. I didn't want her to do me any favors.

"It hasn't been work for a long time. You know that. You are family."

"My paycheck still says otherwise, though." I thought about Simone wishing me luck, and added "find a new job" to my long list of shit I needed to get done.

"It was the only way to get you to do it!" she burst out. And at a look from me, she added, "And to get me to agree."

"It doesn't matter anymore."

"It does to me," Ariana said softly. "Please, Carmen. It's not the same without you. And I'm not the only one who feels this way. I know Mami does, too. Please." She leaned forward. "Don't you want to spend these last few days with Mauro before he goes back to school?"

"Not really. Because Mauro and I are through." *The more I say that, the less it will hurt. Right?*

She gasped. "You broke up? It's not . . . not because of me and the quince, right?"

"Don't flatter yourself. We were always done by the end of summer."

"Wow. That explains . . . a lot," Ariana said under her breath, and then started her cantaleta again. "So . . . now you have to come back! You have to fix this somehow." Ariana always did this, wore Tía Celia and Tío Victor down until she got her way.

It wasn't going to work on me.

"Nothing to fix. And you couldn't, quite literally, pay me enough to come back."

"I don't understand you!" she said finally, tearing up a napkin in disgust. "I did it! I told Mami that it was my fault and that was SO HARD—"

"You *finally* telling the actual truth isn't a favor to me! And good job telling her later, so that she thinks you're La Virgen de la Caridad del Cobre for defending me—" One sarcastic slow clap for the effort.

"I can't control that! Please, Carmen . . . this is going to be my only quince. You are my prima hermana. We just found each other again. It's about me . . . not Mami, not even the rest of the family. You *have* to be there! I *want* you there!" Her eyes brimmed with tears. "I'm sorry! Can't you just take that as Mami saying sorry, too?"

The words *convenient lie* flashed through my brain.

"Actually, no, because I don't believe Tía Celia *is* sorry, and I'm tired of pretending to make other people feel better about treating me like shit. So . . . thanks for the ruined book."

And then I left before she could see the tears in my own eyes.

# Thirty-Six

NOT HAVING A SOCIAL life was making me a very useful person around the house. I had dinner waiting on the table for Mami and Enrique after I got back from the bookstore. I did the dishes. Went to Publix and got the paper towels when we ran out. Folded the laundry. It had been a day.

"You are driving me crazy!" Mami sighed when she caught me folding yet another load in front of the TV. She and Enrique had taken a longer than normal Labor Day weekend, because of the quinceañera. I hoped that meant they were going, after all.

Someone I actually liked should enjoy the fruits of Simone's and my planning.

"Yeah, well, get used to it." I shook one of Enrique's T-shirts at her. "You said you always wanted a maid."

"Not one I gave birth to!" She stole the basket from me. "I'll finish this. You go do something FUN!"

After a miserable nap, I felt different. Not just because my neck ached from being stretched onto the edge of my desk. Not just because the tear-salt crust around my mouth and face had its own topography. No, I actually felt—I looked around the room, afraid and daring the universe to strike me down—better. I felt better.

It was over. And I knew how to live from a place of Over.

I clicked on my loudest playlist and began straightening up the piles of misery that had covered every surface of my room after The Event (which was what I was already calling it, the way politicians did when nature slammed another hurricane into our tropical zone). I changed my sheets, pulled them extra tight against the corners. I sprayed rose water room freshener.

Mami and Enrique were at the table, holding hands and making lovey-dovey eyes at each other. As soon as they saw me, they dropped their hands, guilty. Great, now I was officially The One Who Killed Love.

Mami narrowed her eyes at me. "You look different."

"I FEEL like the first day after mono."

"Is that what we're calling Mauro these days?" Enrique asked dryly. That got a surprised laugh out of me. Mami beamed.

"No, seriously, carry on. I'm just looking for the vacuum."

NOW Mami looked alarmed. "The vacuum? OK, now I'm back to worried."

I shook my head. "No worries. Just . . . it's time to move on, you know? Get back on the horse and vacuum that man right out of my carpet."

"But it's OK to be sad, Carmencita." This from the woman whose post-breakup bacchanals were legendary in our townhouse complex. I'm talking legit parrandas that could have had a cover charge, and people would have paid it.

"I didn't say I'm not sad," I said, locating the vacuum and starting to unwind the cord. "I'm just . . . done with the moping."

"Thank goodness," Enrique said. "I don't think I could have handled another night of Adele." Mami and I lasered him with serious eyes. You do NOT mess with Her Highness, Lady of Breakups, Adele. He held up his hands. "Too much? I'm still not used to living with two women." Then his face got bright red. "I mean, not LIVING-living, pero . . . I spend a lot of time here," he ended weakly.

"And that's actually a good thing," I said, rescuing him from drowning in his own awkwardness. "Keeps her happy and occupied."

"Happy or not, I have eyes in the back of my head, Carmen Maria."

"Don't worry," I said, hoisting the vacuum and heading back to my room. "You won't need them anymore."

I floated aimlessly online for a while, clicking away from any happy or romantic stuff like my hair was on my fire. There's a

LOT of that shit online. There are more important things than love, people!

And as soon as I figure out what they are, I'll be plastering them all over the interwebs. Because everyone could use a reminder.

Two hours later, I knew there was no way I was going to get to sleep tonight. There wasn't a concealer in the world that could help me camouflage the entire set of luggage under my eyes.

My eyes kept drifting to my closet door. Maybe if I just DID IT, maybe if I just looked, I could have a good cry, go to sleep, and be done with it.

Decision made, damn it. I strode up to the door like I planned to argue with it, but it opened easily enough. And there it was. My box. I put it on the floor in front of me, all careful like it was a bomb I was about to defuse.

I glanced at the pictures of me and Junior, Mami and Junior, the family. The ones that Mauro had somehow found for me.

And there he was, at the bottom of the box, in pieces. Painstakingly developed photos of downtown Miami streaked with rain reflecting color. A blur of me dancing by a pool. Pictures of us, me trying different sides of myself to see what the camera liked best. Mauro usually looking at me.

I'd kept every print he'd ever given me. My fingers traced the lines of his face, lingered on his mouth. I arranged them on the floor, rearranged them, like a puzzle that I couldn't quite make fit. Like if I could just fix THIS, carajo, I'd be free.

Inspiration struck.

I took my camera and started to take pictures of the prints, and even short videos, just panning over them like one of those Civil War documentaries on PBS.

Then I uploaded everything into Mauro's MacBook. I connected my phone to it, uploaded all the short videos Mauro and I had taken of each other, of quince practice, of us getting ready for the kids' parties. Of the Dreams and the corte being silly or serious. All the S-words. I cued up the playlists he'd made me of his own stuff.

And then there it was, laid before me, digitally. My whole history. Family. Junior. Dreams Come True. Waverly. Everything captured in some form. Which, amazingly, was still incomplete somehow.

Almost without realizing that I was doing it, I was editing— not deleting anything, just moving stuff, grouping it. Using all the past footage to deepen what we'd been doing all summer. I even played with GarageBand to weave my own vocals throughout Mauro's electronica.

The sun was rising through my window when I finally looked up from the screen.

I watched what I'd created, and even though it was choppy in some places (especially the sound, because I'd only ever watched him use GarageBand), it was me, my history, my family, bare. Bigger than me, too. It was Ariana also. It was the way time had snaked through the Garces and Aguilar families, warping us and making us clearer. I felt . . . hollowed and clean. It was the best thing I'd ever done, and it wasn't even all that good. But still, the best parts of me. Of us. And for once, I hadn't tried to change the story. I had edited to highlight the truth.

Then I uploaded it, sent Olivia the link, and blocked her. I didn't care what she or anyone else in the corte thought about the gift.

I realized that I needed to do this. To go to college and really learn this. Edwin was one person, with one person's opinions. Mauro had different opinions. I did, too. We counted.

And now to finish cleaning, like I said I would.

———————

Once I was done, my room looked magazine spotless and I felt better.

For those keeping score, I made it about two hours into "I Will Survive" mode without tearing up. And then I finally slept. For a bit, anyway.

———————

Five p.m., the day of the dress rehearsal. It bothered me that I was still so attuned to that schedule.

One more day, and then I could finally be fully in my own life, instead of having Ariana's calendar rule my time.

My phone beeped its upcoming death, and I went into my room to plug it in. Woo, charging my phone. See? Still taking Mami's advice. Having fun.

One missed call.

"Hey," the voice mail began in Mauro's voice. "So, this is weird, right? No texting? But . . . at least this way you don't have to respond. I just wanted to let you know that Olivia showed me the video for Ariana. I saw your changes, and if your goal was to gut me once again, congratulations! Way to dangle everything you are, and everything I want for us, in front of me, again. I should be used to it. I'd already made my peace with it until that day at the car dealership when you kissed me. And I knew . . . I knew right then that I was wrecked. Um, back to the video . . . I know your cousin will love it, and I know it will make her cry, and I know someday you'll be sorry you missed all of it. I know a lot, don't I? Except how to get you back. In both meanings. Because, yeah, there's a part of me that wants you to feel like I do. To hurt like I do. I know you don't want to hear from me. And it would be easier, wouldn't it? To just let you get your way again and disappear? Only this time, it's worse. So much worse, because I love you." He took a long, steadying breath. "Yeah, that's right—destroying our contract. Violating every term and every last fucking condition." His voice cracked, and he coughed. "I know I sound maudlin, but I am fucking maudlin, because I hate that I wasn't enough for you to take the risk, and I hate that you broke my fucking heart. I hate that I'll always know what this felt like, and know that I had to let it go too soon. I hate that you are probably right—I *do* lie when it makes my life easier . . . so this is how you should know this is the truth, because none of this makes my life easier, Carmen. In fact, it's all made my life suck. Anyway, that's all from me, for all the good it'll do. I let you go with a fact. Never let it be said that I wasn't an interesting conversationalist. Did you know that more people have died taking selfies than from shark attacks? Oh, and by the way, I meant to leave this message." And then my voice mail cut him off.

I sat there for a long time, hands still holding my phone. The end hit me all over again, exploding all over my room. His words clinging to the walls, to my furniture. Everywhere, and I couldn't get away.

I closed my eyes and pictured it, really let myself go there. Mauro and me fully together, not a summer thing anymore. Boyfriend and girlfriend. Me asking Simone for occasional weekends off so that I could fly up to Boston. Hell, maybe I'd even have a car and could drive it sometimes. Him waiting for me on the front steps of some marble building that looked like the White House. Spinning me around. Me lazing in his bed while he worked on something on the MacBook. Maybe going up behind him and resting my head on his shoulder.

We'd sit in the cafeteria and he'd complain about the food while I pretended it was delicious, better than a Reuben sandwich, and pretending would almost make it seem true. He'd joke about my ability to commit to a story, even if it was the wrong one.

He'd bring me to parties, and Ahmed and Dylan and Yo

would argue about the music selection, and David Foster Wallace, and where to go for spring break.

My own fantasy spit me out. It would never be true. And I didn't belong there.

I opened my eyes and debated deleting everything he'd said. But I couldn't bring myself to do it. Especially when I knew that this was probably the last time I'd hear from him.

I'd asked him for the truth, and he'd given it to me.

At least he'd never know how much it hurt. That truth was all mine.

# Thirty-Seven

THE MORNING OF MY cousin's quinceañera dawned gray (for Miami) and cold (ditto). I could imagine Tía Celia sitting at the kitchen island, staring into her phone and muttering about the weather. And everyone making sure to stay far away from her fury.

You could say I had succeeded more than anybody else.

Her sun incantations took a few hours to work, but by the time the girls were scheduled to show up at Ariana's house for hair and makeup, the sun was blazing triumphant in the sky.

Not even the weather would dare dampen Princess Ariana's big day.

And I was spending said day slouched over near Mauro's laptop, pretending to stream a movie. The truth, though? I was watching Insta Stories and Snaps and Facebook Lives and other assorted videos on my phone. There was a quick one of the chaos reigning at the Garces house. Olivia narrating while packing enough makeup to open a Sephora. One shot of the girls in line at Palacio, giggling as they juggled about five coffee carriers.

None of those coffees were for me.

It was only going to get worse. Soon they'd be dressed and waiting for the cars. Then the church service (which would probably be uploaded by some religious tía to rant about how at least THIS Good Cuban Girl was honoring El Señor on her special day). I knew exactly how it would go. Padre Teodoro droning on while the corte drooped with the combined weight of their boredom and their fancy clothes.

The boys in their tuxedos, looking mature and serious, until the very moment they started wrestling or something, and then Mami or Tía Celia or Simone would shout at them that if they ruined the tuxes, they'd have to take it up with the rental place.

The girls like flowers in their gorgeous dresses. Mine should have been hanging in my closet, but I'd already returned it to Simone.

The impromptu singing in the cars, combined with bragging videos about the night up ahead.

And I'd be a part of exactly none of it.

Mami bustled into my room, her hair in an elaborate updo and dangly diamonds in her ears. "Maybe we shouldn't go," she said when she saw me. "I mean, me and Enrique."

"Sure," I said easily. "And then you and Enrique can go to El Pollo Loco dressed like that instead."

"You are my daughter. That's worth a million Pollo Locos to me."

"Tía Celia didn't fire me, I quit," I reminded her. "Just me. Not the whole Aguilar family. And look . . . you got what you wanted. The family will be together tonight. I want this for you. Please go."

"How can you say that?" Mami said as she wriggled into the gold dress she'd bought for tonight. "The family won't be together. You won't be there!"

"You all have your own relationships that have nothing to do with me."

"Still . . . Carmencita. Are you sure you won't reconsider? Call a one-night truce and go be a part of your cousin's history?"

"One night doesn't make me more or less a part of it."

"Fine . . . but at least admit that some nights matter more than others. This isn't just any random Saturday!"

I stared into my screen, clicking on another post someone had put up of Ari laughing as the hairdresser said, "I have not even begun to curl."

"If you are just going to sit here and stalk the quince online, why not just admit that you're sorry for everything, and take your rightful place with the family?"

"Because I'm not sorry." Not the sorry they wanted, anyway.

Mami gave a full-body sigh and patted her updo. "Bueno. Maybe you are right. It's only one night." She glanced at me. "One night you've been working hard toward for the entire summer, one night that is a turning point for your entire family, one night that—"

"I get it."

Enrique came into the room, straightening his tie. He was more dressed up than I'd ever seen him, and for once, I could see what Mami saw. I gave him a thumbs-up. "Looking good, Enrique."

His whole head flushed with pleasure, and then his eyes ran over me, in sweat shorts and a stained T-shirt. "Carmencita, are you sure?"

I nodded.

"Too bad. I'm sure Ariana will be missing you."

"Yeah, well . . . I'm sure she'll be too busy remembering the steps to all her dances and achieving her coming of age." I started to shoo them out the door. "Now, you both look amazing, so hurry up and make sure the camera gets you on your good side."

Mami's eyes opened wide. "Call me if you see a weird angle or something."

"Don't worry. Your good side is safe with me."

———————

The only way I knew how much time had passed was that I had to move the laptop to avoid the glare of the sun as it crawled through the sky. I was like one of those gamers who move into their parents' basements and turn into Rip Van Winkle.

The group had just assembled outside the church, posing

for pictures and taking selfies and videos. I hunted those down with methodical precision, following every possible hashtag— #ArianasQuince #ArianasBigDay #QuinceDeAriana #Garces16th #ArianasFiesta #GarcesGala—pruning the dead ends. Mauro would have been proud (and THAT was a #thought I didn't want to follow). But it was like trying to unite puzzle pieces with big gaps in the middle. Nothing connected quite like I thought it would. I wanted to braid all the events together, to have the whole story in my hands already. But this was happening in real time, in pieces, and I couldn't control the story other people wanted to share.

People who I thought would be posting all over, like Olivia, were surprisingly silent, while Gus actually posted a ton, but mostly of the boys clowning around. And of my boy, standing a little apart, smiling and joking but with something in his eyes that hurt to see. Or maybe I was just projecting. He looked heartbreakingly handsome today, hair slicked back with a few strands that fell across his forehead. And my heart was already three-quarters of the way cracked.

I wondered if he was thinking about me, too.

#BadChoicesHurt #AguilarAgony #NotBlessed

I saw Waverly roll her eyes as Olivia shouted, "Sucks to be you, bitches!" into her screen.

Suddenly, I felt really, really old.

My phone buzzed, making me jump and look around the room like I'd been found out. If anyone could figure out how to watch the watcher, it was my once and forever ex.

"Carmen? Can you hear me?" Mami, probably in a corner, finger stuck in her other ear.

"Yeah. What's up?"

"Everything OK, mija?"

Nothing is OK.

"Sure . . . what's up?"

"Your tía is frantic . . . no one can find the tiara! Ariana swears you guys went to pick it up and brought it home, but no one can find the box. Can you think of where it might be?"

I frowned. We *had* brought it home. I remembered tucking it into the trunk, surrounded by a few towels Mami kept back there (for an emergency pool run? who knows?).

What I didn't remember was taking it OUT of the trunk.

"Let me look and I'll call you back," I told Mami.

They'd taken Enrique's new car to the quince, so our car was still parked in front of the house.

I opened the trunk gingerly, hoping not to see anything new.

Nothing new. Just the box we'd picked up at the tiara place. Shit.

———————

I opened the box, and after a moment, I took the tiara out. The sun reflecting off it almost blinded me, and for a second, I lost my grip on it.

I brought the box into my room, put it on the floor, and thought about what came next.

The crowning was an important part of the ceremony, but it wouldn't ruin anything to skip it. Hell, maybe it would shave ten minutes off the whole thing. Get people home before post-club traffic jammed the roads.

I wasn't the one who had left it in the car. It wasn't my responsibility.

My phone rang again. "Sorry to nag, mija, pero tu tía . . . did you find it?"

It's not like I could even get it to her in time.

I nudged the box with my toe.

"No, sorry. I thought I'd seen it, but . . . I was wrong."

———————

I couldn't concentrate as well after that. The tiara on the floor of my room was like a magnet, drawing my eyes every other second like I was afraid it would move. Or start to talk. I didn't want to think about what it would say.

People arriving at the Biltmore, long shots of the gorgeous Spanish-style exterior. In this area, the Biltmore was legendary.

It had been my dream for my own quince, back when I still dreamed.

(Mauro had made so many of them come true. And he didn't even know. No, worse. He gave me something better than dreams. Memories.)

Way too many videos of people's shoes, as phones got nudged or misaligned.

Lots and lots of hushed giggling.

The first dance was about to begin. The formal waltz with the entire corte, ending with Ariana alone, waiting for her prince, who would arrive with the heels that would begin her transformation from girl to woman.

You know, just in the case the calendar and the rum didn't do the job.

Against my will, I looked again at the tiara. It glinted back at me with a wink, like it knew I was up to no good.

It wasn't wrong.

The screen blurred, out of focus, and then I saw Alex in the middle of the dance floor, pretending to look for Ariana, while the crowd shouted instructions in English and Spanish. He started to ham it up a little bit, opening his eyes wide and holding his hand up to shield them from the spotlight. Finally, he found Ariana, dropped to his knees, and placed the heels in front of her with a flourish. She put her hands to her mouth and her eyes swam with laughter and panic.

The crowning should happen soon after.

But it wouldn't.

When I was younger, Mami got me a paper crown from Princess Burgers, a local chain by the beach. I wore it on every birthday, but I could also take it out on bad days and parade around the apartment with it.

It never quite lost that French fry smell and it helped.

I wove a whole bunch of stories around the crown . . . that it could fix bad grades, help a sunburn hurt less, make that girl who talked bad about you during lunch bite her tongue. It was magic that made the wearer (me) a princess who channeled the powers of a long line of magical fairies.

And the thing was . . . when I wore it, I could *almost* feel that all those things were true. That it was magic, that I was magic, if only I could screw my eyes up tightly and believe.

Not bad for something that came with the $1.99 kid's meal.

Ariana was fascinated by it, reaching for it and knocking it out of position whenever I wore it around her. Finally, when she was around five, she pulled it onto her own head, so hard that she tore right through the delicate paper.

She tossed the sides down in horror and burst into tears. "I'm sorry, Carmen! I broke it! It didn't do the magic for me! Why didn't it do the magic?"

I remember a white flash of fury that she'd broken my magical crown, before I remembered that I was a very mature almost-*eight*-year-old now, who knew that she could get the same effect from any Princess Burger crown.

Still. She needed to learn. "It wasn't your crown!" And then at the fresh tears leaking from her eyes, I relented. "When it's your crown, it will have its own magic. Because it will be yours."

I sighed, turning away from a tableside video that was showing close-ups of the flower arrangements, orchids and roses and draped crystal-strewn candelabras (Doña Sylvia approved; good job, Simone and La Playa Florists). Then I took the tiara out of the box and put it on my own head.

Was I expecting a flash of lightning, a deep voice telling me that I'd finally gone de niña a mujer?

Maybe.

Instead, it dug a little into my scalp, and quickly tangled in the snarls in my hair.

It wasn't mine.

It didn't have any magic for me.

Well, correction. It shot me through with remorse and guilt. I might be angry at my cousin, and I was definitely still pissed at Tía Celia. But I wasn't this person. I didn't *want* to be.

I looked at the clock on my desk. Depending on traffic and my own driving bravery, I could be at the Biltmore in thirty-five minutes.

Ariana's crowning might not happen when anyone expected it.

But it would happen.

———————

Of course I hit every red light from my place to the Biltmore, and thirty-five minutes became more like fifty. Plus, I'd obviously had to de-troll myself before I left, so now I was dressed in Mami's nice black chiffon dress and high-heeled sandals.

No fairy godmother for me. Then again, that wasn't my story.

So there I was, walking into the Biltmore, the tiara box in front of me like an offering.

The setting sun was washing over the golf course, staining

the low clouds blush pink, and the tips of the palm trees glinted fiery against the ombré blue sky. In the distance, I could hear the faint treble of the music and an occasional cheer. I wondered if the group was already doing their baile sorpresa. I wondered if anybody missed me.

My heels clicked against the cobblestones, and I concentrated on not getting them caught between in the cracks. I needed to get in there, drop off the tiara, and leave. Let them think whatever they wanted when they finally found it.

The music carried me toward the main ballroom like a magic carpet.

"Uh, excuse me, Miss . . . can I see your invitation, please?" A young woman in braids and a sharp black suit was standing in front of me, holding a clipboard and flashing a customer service smile.

I held up the box. "I'm actually just here to drop this off."

If this had been a fairy tale, someone would have pegged me as the bad fairy bringing curses. I was even wearing black.

"Oh? Do you have a . . . badge or a receipt or . . ."

So much for showing up without calling any attention to myself.

"Would you like for me to call someone?" she asked, already pulling out a walkie-talkie.

I definitely did not want her to call anyone.

"Uh—I should be on the list. Carmen Aguilar?" No way this was going to work. I'm sure Tía Celia had power-washed my name off the list as soon as she smelled the rum on Ariana's carpet.

She scanned her list and I held my breath, already planning my next try at getting this tiara to its owner.

But then she smiled. "Oh, there you are!"

"Uh, I am?" I squeaked before I got my swag back. "Of course. Like I said."

She gestured to her side like a flight attendant. "It's right through these doors. Dinner will be served in about twenty minutes. Welcome to the quinceañera!"

I nodded and followed her directions. No way was I going to press my luck further.

Once I got inside, I kept myself to the shadows, turning my face away from anyone I might know, which in this crowd was . . . everyone.

Eventually, I dared to approach Tía Celia and Tío Victor's table. They were out on the dance floor, so I was safe. I dropped the box on a chair and made my way back toward the door, my heart pounding.

Before the song even ended, Tía Celia was back to the table. Maybe she'd felt a disturbance in the Force or something. I saw her open the box, put her hand to her mouth, and practically run toward Ariana with it in her arms.

Mission accomplished.

Truth? I actually felt pretty badass. Like I was Carmen Sandiego.

Especially when the door of the Alhambra ballroom closed behind me and I could take a full breath.

I smiled at the woman who'd almost narced me out and started to walk toward the courtyard doors.

My phone dinged with a notification. Waverly had updated her feed with a photo of the tiara headlined with one word: *MIRACLE*. I grinned.

A cheer bled through the edge of the door as a server left, balancing a tray of empty champagne flutes.

I glanced back toward the ballroom. And through the crack in the door, I saw my prima sitting on a throne, Mami and Tía Celia preparing to put the Crown of Womanhood on her head.

I'd watch the video of the crowning online when I got home.

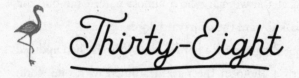

Thirty-Eight

AFTER ANOTHER COUPLE OF moments, though, I wasn't any closer to the exit. I wasn't going back into the ballroom. I *couldn't* (despite what the clipboard said). But I couldn't quite bring myself to leave, either.

I wasn't sure what I was waiting for exactly. A sign of . . . what? Something.

And then it happened. Music. Not just any music. The beginning of Mauro's remix of "Forever Young" that I'd laid my own vocals over. From the original video we'd worked on for Ariana.

Wait . . . what?

And then I heard the DJ's booming voice. "Bueno, y ahora para un momento muy especial. El baile de la quinceañera con su papá. The father-daughter dance. And the song they've chosen is one that is guaranteed to touch your heart: a beautiful version of 'Forever Young' sung by Ariana's own prima, Miss

Carmen Aguilar. And be sure to look around you, as a special video of the family will be shown."

My first instinct was to laugh. Typical Ariana. She was bound and determined to have me sing for her dance, and there I was.

But then, this wasn't the song that Ariana and Tío Victor had practiced to. This wasn't the song that Ariana had wanted me to sing. Well, she was learning one of the big lessons of adulthood, right? Sometimes, you have to settle.

Look at me, still teaching her the hard things.

Like how the people you love will disappoint you.

They'll hold grudges. They won't forgive.

God. I was the worst.

My fingers touched the ballroom door. I should already be out of here, on my way to the car. On my way home.

The quince was obviously going well.

But I opened the door anyway. Just a touch. And I saw Ariana's face as she looked up at her father. Loving, yes, but with a fake smile pasted on. She didn't look *truly* happy.

And I knew exactly why.

They weren't doing any of the right steps—in fact, they were barely moving.

Because the song was totally wrong.

It was really wrong.

I could feel my face burning, even though no one was looking at me.

Before I could talk myself out of it, I yanked open the door, ran to the DJ, whispering urgently, "Can you start again?"

He jumped like I'd fallen from the sky. "Start what? The song? The video? Why? It's going perfect."

"I want to sing. The song they really wanted. 'Mi Niña Bonita.' For them," I panted.

Can you blame him for looking skeptical? "Without music? And we'd have to restart the video, too!"

"You wouldn't. Just turn the sound off on the video! It'll be fine."

He shook his head. "I'm sorry, but that's not—"

"It's OK," said Tía Celia, who was suddenly standing next to me. "It's actually better than OK. It's perfect. She's perfect. It's my fault that she's late. It's all my fault. And . . . I'm sorry." She smiled at me, tears that mirrored my own in her eyes. Because she of all people knew what this meant.

The DJ still looked dubious. He glanced at Tía Celia and then at Simone, who nodded, a smile dawning on her face. "A cappella?" he asked me. I nodded. I knew that Ariana and Tío Victor knew the rhythm enough to be able to dance to just my voice.

If I could pull off the song, of course.

After another second, he shrugged and paused the video, killing the sound. Tío Victor and Ariana had been mid-step, and sort of stumbled out of the moment. Tío Victor glared at the DJ, who leaned into his microphone and said, "Well, it looks like this is a night for surprises! The quinceañera's prima, Carmen Aguilar, has made a special request. She would like to be the one to sing the song for the rest of their dance. 'Mi Niña Bonita!'" He covered the mike, and muttered, "I'll restart the video with your first note. You better know how to sing, kid."

My throat tightened, and I wasn't sure I'd be able to speak, let alone sing. But I nodded anyway. I'd started this, and now I had to finish it.

Most of the guests knew me and the applause felt exactly like a million warm hugs. At least *they* thought I could do this. I still wasn't so sure.

Until Ariana looked at me, her eyes gleaming with happiness. I'd have to do it now. She'd never let me live it down if I didn't.

I took a deep, shaky breath and it was like the air couldn't quite make it all the way down, or maybe all the way up. My head was swimming in the sudden glare of the spotlight. The spotlight on ME, not as Belle, or Ariana's cousin, or Mami's daughter, or Mauro's ex-girlfriend. Just me, alone.

There just wasn't going to be enough air.

But I couldn't keep them standing there forever.

Another deep breath. And begin.

No lovely guitar solo to prompt me. Just me and the words. My first note shook but Tío Victor and Ariana had already started swaying again, more carefully this time, as if they knew how fragile this dance was.

I tried to concentrate on them, on their relationship, on how much I loved them both.

Junior kept creeping back into my brain, into my choky voice, and I realized I was singing it to him. And then I knew it. It wouldn't ever be this way for me. That story was over.

But I had other chances, other stories I could tell. Maybe not like this; maybe I would never know this precise feeling. Maybe the closest I'd be able to come to it would be right now, honoring what Tío Victor and Ariana had. But love? Love was available, and all around me. Love in the eyes of Tía Celia and Mami, standing together, weeping as they watched Tío Victor, Ari, and me. New, tentative love in Enrique, standing a little bit behind them, his eyes also suspiciously wet. Love in the guests, new and old in my life, bathed in the generous multicolored lights of my history, humming the tune in the background. Humming it along with the guitar, even as my voice struggled and snagged over some of the words.

Wait? Guitar?

I looked behind me, and there was Mauro, standing behind the DJ, somehow having found a guitar, keeping my rhythm so subtly I hadn't even noticed. Supporting me. Strengthening me. Just the way he always did.

It was all wrong, the video, played at the wrong time, and muted; no one could even tell how well the images married to the song I'd chosen.

Still, Ariana and Tío Victor looked around, amazement

reflected on their faces. Maybe they understood that it wasn't perfect, but it was just right. Just like my voice. It was the real version of us, of our history.

And I wasn't ashamed of any of it anymore.

I realized it all the way into my bones, even as I belted every word of this song that had been like razor blades in my mouth. This song was a celebration of being wrong. The father had been wrong about wanting a son, realizing that his "niña bonita" was the child of his heart. He'd been disappointed by life. But it had been his own mistake. Just like leaving us had been Junior's.

Tía Celia had been wrong about me, and I wasn't entirely over that. But . . . that was her own blindness. And the things she'd said before I started to sing, they gave me hope that maybe someday she'd see me clearly.

People do show you who they are. But that's only part of the story. You have to have the eyes to see who they are in spite of their mistakes. And maybe some people would never show you the same courtesy. Because they're scared, or maybe they like the lies rather than the truth.

But you don't have to be what they see. Not if that's not who you really are. And you get to choose that, over and over again. You get to choose where you place your faith. You get to choose love. You get to choose you.

Maybe Mauro and I wouldn't end up together. But that didn't mean I had to run away from love, like Junior had. Just because love wasn't everything didn't mean that it wasn't something.

I could forgive; I could overcome my own envidia.

I could change.

I could trust.

I reached the end of the song and held the last high note with conviction. And the guests began to shout and applaud, louder and louder. Ariana and Tío Victor walked over to me, both their faces wet as tears raced down my own salt-sticky cheeks. They crushed me in a hug, and I felt it.

Tío Victor whispered, "Tú también eres mi niña bonita." For one brief second, I felt like the kind of treasured daughter the song was about. Except that I'd been the one to give myself that moment. I'd been so focused on what I didn't have from birth that I had ignored how much I'd found along the way. And how much I could give.

I'd been wrong about everything. But I didn't have to stay wrong.

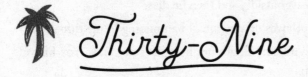# Thirty-Nine

FINALLY, I DISENTANGLED MYSELF from my family and went outside. So self-sacrificing. Coming of age, just like my cousin, and at a fraction of the cost!

I'd given my cousin the gift she'd wanted from me. And I'd given it to myself, too.

I should have felt as high as one of the golden balloons nudging the ballroom ceiling.

So why did I still feel like an open wound?

I turned a corner, following a moonlit path into one of the Biltmore's gardens, where the cut grass smelled like a green blessing. It was a good place to be alone.

Except I wasn't.

Mauro sat, his back to me, slumped forward on a wrought iron bench. His tux jacket sat balled up next to him.

Everything in me wanted to run to him. Everything in me wanted to run away and keep running.

With one foot facing in each direction, I couldn't move at all.

He didn't turn around. "So, we've gotten to the end. Belle finds the Beast outside, and then he dies."

My mouth was dry, my heart hammering in my throat, but my eyes still rolled. "That's not how the story ends. You know he doesn't die."

Mauro turned toward me and shrugged. "Semantics."

I reached for the words I needed, the ones to break the spell. But they were jammed like Miami traffic in my mouth.

"You're the worst thing that ever happened to me" was what I blurted out.

"Wow. I'm already aware of your high opinion of me."

"Mauro, I think—"

He leaned away from me and narrowed his eyes. "Wait. I know that voice. You want to give *me* the 'let's be friends' speech. Tonight's the perfect night for it. You've got your cousin back, your family, your beautiful song. I'm the last loose thread, right? Well—"

"It was easy, before you. I didn't want to end up like this. I knew the right things to do to avoid it. Especially after our first attempt at this."

He stood up and shoved his hands into his pockets. "Sorry I came back to disappoint you. Don't worry, I won't do it again." He started to walk past me, back toward the party. I grabbed his arm. He stilled, watching me. Giving me nothing to work with.

The old Carmen would have stopped at that. I was awesome at endings. Beginnings were new. Raw.

"Once upon a time, let's say, oh, around three years and nine months ago, a girl turned a boy into a beast. She didn't have to do much work to make it happen—I mean, he was kind of a jerk."

He snorted. "Ouch."

I plowed on. "And then he left the kingdom and disappeared, and she told herself she was glad. Until one day, the Beast came back, and he made the girl look in the mirror. And she saw a beast looking back at her. And, man, she really hated the boy for showing her that version of herself, but it was what she was, and she thought she couldn't be different. But then she realized, if he wasn't a beast anymore, maybe she didn't have to be, either. Maybe they could just be in a new story."

My words just hung there, and my face flushed with embarrassment. I wasn't sure where those words had come from, but I wasn't going to take them back. I needed him to know how I felt, even if nothing changed.

After another millennium of silence, I turned to go back into the ballroom. "Wait," he growled. "How do I know that this isn't just you on some high from your amazing success in there? And that you won't change your mind in five minutes or five months or five years?"

"Five *years*?"

"I'm being optimistic."

I looked at him, his white tux shirt almost glowing in the garden lights, tie undone, hair rumpled, and I couldn't imagine not loving him as much as I did in this moment.

"I don't have any guarantees, Mauro. Being a beast this long is gonna take some detox."

"Quit trying to steal my part," he said. "You're Belle. You keep forgetting that."

That's when I took the final step. Right into his waiting arms.

"You made me sweat for a bit there," he said into my hair. His arms shook around me.

"Same."

"Only fair." He cupped my face. "Carmen Maria Aguilar, I absolutely love you." He paused. "You can jump in at any time now."

I laughed. "Jump in? I do believe I'm the one who started this, and I demand full credit and an amendment to the terms and conditions."

"Duly noted. But—"

"I love you, too."

"Even the Beast parts?"

"Well, certain people believe you are hotter as the Beast." I looked him up and down. "No offense."

He jerked his head toward the parking lot. "I can always go get the head."

I pretended to be thinking about it. "Good idea. Although

the head makes certain things more difficult . . ."

"Good point," he said immediately. "Not that I'm unwilling to be creative and hardworking for you. I know this isn't going to be easy." And then he grew serious. "I have to ask, though. Am I really the worst thing to ever happen to you?"

"Obviously, YES."

He smiled. "Same."

 # Forty

IT COULD HAVE BEEN five minutes or five hours later when Ariana found us, her tiara securely on her head, but wearing the sparkly catsuit that she'd picked for the baile sorpresa.

"Finally, I found you!" she gasped. "I held off Simone as long as I could, but she said any reunions could wait . . . It's time for the dance!"

Mauro looked down at himself, still in what was left of his tux. He would need to change into his jeans and black T-shirt.

I squeezed his hand. "I'll be right here when you get back."

Both Ariana said, "Uh, what? This is THE dance we've been practicing for months! Get inside and get your outfit on! I *know* Simone brought it—I saw it!"

"Don't let that crown go to your head," I warned.

"Yeah, and Mami's already lighting a candle to your glory about *that*, but right now we have to DANCE!"

_____

"Yo, people. It's time for the surprise dance! So . . . surprise!" Ariana put her hands up and started jumping up and down.

The guests let out a collective "Ohh!" and moved to the edges of the dance floor.

The lights started to wash and pulsate over us, and the guests started to clap in rhythm. We all got into our opening position, frozen there for a second. Letting the anticipation of the music and the future build until the right moment to move. Mauro held me close against him, mirror images of the rest of the corte. Of the rest of our quince family. Then he spun me off in perfect time to the beat drop. Step, step, swivel, heel, toe, turn—and even as everyone moved in perfect unison, I could see our ghosts stumbling over the same moves just a month earlier. I could see us crashing into each other until our fateful game of Twister. The hours of repetition, sweat, fights, laughter. I arched myself into the backbend and grinned, remembering Alex's phone call and Mauro's reaction. And then, finally, the lifts—every dama balanced gracefully, effortlessly by her chambelán. I caught a glimpse of Waverly blowing a kiss to Cesar while we were floating. Of Ariana, smiling, with her face tilted up and her eyes closed, like she was in a dream and wanted to stay there. And I looked down at Mauro, into the eyes that had seen so much of me, and I knew without words that he'd always do his best never to let me fall.

So we were feeling it, we were having fun, and the guests were, too. Maybe we missed a step or two (OK, we definitely did) but it didn't matter. Because . . . if I watch this in fifty years, I'll remember exactly how I felt at this moment. Like I was light and music and energy, all on my own, and like I'd be that way forever. Like nothing would ever, ever have to change.

We did it all, bachata, reggaetón, hip-hop, disco, cumbia, and if anyone had a voice left when we were done, I swear it was not our fault.

Tía Celia had been right so long ago. Even if she'd gotten the emphasis wrong.

It was sweet, beyond sweet, to shine bright around certain people. And to watch them shine right back.

 _Epilogue_

SOMETIMES HAPPILY EVER AFTER has to take the interstate. In my case, I-95 from Miami to Boston.

Through the whole Catholic rosary and all the santos' blessings (and Alex's special traffic app), I didn't miss a single sign while I white-knuckled it up there, talking to and arguing with the Mauro in my head before every merge. I was beginning to see the appeal of this whole driving thing. For starters, the bus would have taken way too long to reunite us.

I parked about a block away from the school. Mauro lived off campus, but he wasn't the one I needed. Yet.

Dylan charged out of the kitchen, an oven mitt in each hand, and threw his arms around me. "Carmencita! You made it!"

"Barely."

He pulled me toward the kitchen. "Come taste my latest creation."

Ahmed rolled his eyes. "When are you just going to transfer to culinary school?"

"I am on the vanguard. Culinary sound production."

"Yeah, Mauro couldn't explain that, either," I said, laughing.

"Apparently, though, sound production and photography are a match made in heaven. Like one school isn't enough?" He rolled his eyes. "Mauro Reyes, overachiever."

Yo squealed and tackled me. "It's SO good to see you! Man, I've never had the guts to drive all the way up from home to here. You are my heroine!"

I grinned. "Thanks. It was terrifying."

"Maybe sometime we can do it together? And you can teach me some stuff about video production." She linked arms with me. "We can work on something together . . ."

"She's on a love mission, Yo!" Ahmed called out. "No work talk!"

Just then, my phone began to buzz. I held up a warning finger before I answered.

"It's been a whole forty hours since we last spoke. Is this the beginning of the end?" Mauro's voice, closer than it had been since the day after the quince. Only he didn't know that yet.

"Yes. I'm one step away from changing my number and living under an assumed name."

"I'd always find you."

"That's creepy."

He chuckled. "I was going for romantic. Clearly I'm out of practice."

Practice was exactly what I was looking forward to.

"I called you at work, but your boss said you were taking a few personal days?"

Oh shit. I had told my boss at FIU that I was driving up to Boston. I grimaced at Ahmed, who literally clutched a necklace he was wearing.

"You still there?"

"Yeah," I squeaked, and cleared my throat. "Everything is fine. Work is fun, class is busy but fun, and all of us Dreams are busy, you know Mami is crazy with the wedding, y Tía Celia no se queda atrás, but she and Tío Victor and Ariana are fine—"

"Yeah, I know. I figured the last forty hours were not THAT momentous."

Oh, he had no idea.

I kept anxiously telling him shit he already knew. "Waves and Cesar are fine, Ariana's a little nervous about Alex. I mean, now that the quince is over—"

"Yeah, they should try being a thousand miles away from each other." Mauro sighed. "Damn, hearing all that makes me miss Miami so much."

"You'll be back soon, though, right?"

"Not soon enough. Never soon enough." Something happened in the kitchen just then and Ahmed yelped loud enough for Mami and Enrique to hear back home. "Um, hey, I have to go. I think Waverly's ringing the bell."

"But isn't Waverly in—"

"Love you, bye!" I crashed the red end button on my phone twice for good measure.

Dylan came out, sucking his pinky. "Skin to hot metal is usually bad news. Especially when you aren't prepared." I could hear Ahmed whimpering in the kitchen. Dylan smiled. "Want to take some snacks with you? You might need sustenance."

I crouched in the gray hallway diagonally from Mauro's front door. Dylan had already texted to let me know it was time to put the next phase of my plan in motion. I put the laptop about two feet from the doorway (to make sure he walked out a bit) and knocked on the door. Then I scooted out of the way and waited.

When Mauro opened the door, this is what I hope he saw.

A video. Scenes from the summer, the quince, long shots of his photos from high school and some of his newer work, and even a few clips from my road trip of love and terror, interspersed with moments around Boston that his friends had taken. A shot of my newly framed high school diploma, the screen announcing that I'd just finished my application to FIU, and then a time lapse to the screen declaring that I'd been accepted. All set to music. His.

He stood still, staring at the screen. Too busy to notice me creeping up behind him and putting my hands over his eyes.

"What—?"

I couldn't keep the smile out of my voice. "What this is, mi amor, is a kidnapping."

ACKNOWLEDGMENTS

People say it takes a village to raise a child. I think it's safe to say that it took a small country to raise my book.

Being chosen to be a part of the Pitch Wars class of 2018 was one of the greatest experiences of my life. Thank you to Brenda Drake, Kellye Garrett, Sonia Hartl, Sarah Nicolas, and everyone in the organization and in the community! And to my writing heroine/mentor, Rachel Lynn Solomon—thank you for seeing the potential in my story and for your literal hours of editing and conversation. I'm so lucky to have you, not only as a wise fairy godmother, but also as a friend. I'll never really be able to thank you enough for changing my life, but I'll keep trying.

To my incredible agent, Jim McCarthy. I've learned so much about writing from you. Thank you for your brilliant editorial ideas, your creativity, your tenacity, and your humor, and for always knowing exactly what to say. You are a magic person and I'm forever thrilled that I get to work with you!

To my wonderful editor, Kristen Pettit, and her amazing assistant, Clare Vaughn—thank you for the care you've taken with Carmen and Mauro, your enthusiasm, and your patience with my occasional bouts of writerly anxiety. Somehow, you managed to take a book that I've been editing and re-editing for years and help me see it with new eyes. You've truly made this debut experience a joy.

Thank you to the meticulous copyeditors and production people: Vivian Lee, Ivy McFadden, Lindsay Wagner, and Caitlin Lonning. To Isabela Humphrey for my utterly adorable cover illustration. And thank you to everyone working in editorial, design, production, publicity, sales, and marketing at HarperTeen and HarperCollins—you are truly the dream team and I appreciate everything you do to bring books like mine into the world. Endless gratitude to every single one of you.

Thanks to all the current and former members of my writing group: Kristin Walker, Meg Gaertner, Jonathan Hillman, Amanda Moon, Claire Forrest, Katrina Soli, Ashley Larson, Eva Langston, Bethany Johnson, Lynda McDonnell, and Emily Shore. Thank you for reading my earliest drafts and pointing me toward the good stuff, especially when I couldn't see it myself. You are all crazy talented, and I'm so lucky to have had the chance to read your words. I can't wait until your books join mine on the shelf. My bottles of champagne are ready!

To everyone at Barnes & Noble, Calhoun Village, past and present: Kelley Bren Burke, Jill Boschwitz, Erin Fremouw, Pete Ritchie, Sarah Hamer, Martha Jo Cavanaugh, and all the booksellers I was lucky enough to work with. Thank you for geeking out about books with me, and for believing that some-day my stories would be on the same shelves that I was zoning. May our literary conversations never end.

I'm so grateful for my fantastic friends Colleen Onstad and Joy Shimmin-Olson, their families, and their daughters, Annika and Clara Onstad and Jana Olson. Thanks for the venting sessions, the walks around the lake, and taking this transplanted East Coaster under your wing. It's been a privilege to watch your daughters grow up, and I'm very glad I get to hang out with them and celebrate all things Teenage Girl.

Thank you to my lovely next-door neighbors, Matt Murphy, Leah Vergara, Ava Murphy, and Oreo the wonder puppy. You are a shining example of the true meaning of Minnesota Nice, and I'm so glad I get to celebrate with you!

To my college besties, Nina Pinsley and Jamila Mayo-Schragger—you convinced me that our adventures can continue even now, and that the voices in my head deserved to live on the page. I promise to keep a closer eye on my backpack at our next reunion.

To Lindsay Duke and Ashley Ouellette—thank you for SDCC, DragonCon, fanfic, Allonsy, and reading so much of my writing and letting me read yours. I'll always be grateful to Spixie and the fandom for bringing us together. Texas Forever. And to Gail Ebert, for her creativity, sense of humor, and being there when I needed her.

Thank you to the online writing community—on Twitter,

on Instagram, and on YouTube. You taught me that every writer, at every level, has things to contribute and things to learn. Thanks for your generosity, inspiration, openness, and memes.

I'm also grateful to Kelsey Rodkey, Andrea Contos, Joy McCullough, Jessica Sinsheimer, Sarah Jane Freymann, Susan Lee, Carol Wichers, Stella Jang, and las Musas for their wisdom and inspiration.

This book would not exist without my best friend, Sherry Saab. Thank you for the hours of patient brainstorming, the intricate dissection of soap opera plots we've loved, and for sharing the brain. There are no words for how much I love and appreciate you.

To my wonderful extended family, the Hiras, the Raichandanis, the Alimchandanis, the Karams, the Sujans, the Guwalanis, the Tejwanis, the Sharmas, the Chhatlanis, the Hemrajanis, the Gomezes, and the Velezes—we are scattered all over the globe, in California, Colombia, St. Thomas, New Jersey, Maryland, Miami, Mumbai, Dubai—but you are never far from my thoughts and from my heart. Thank you for keeping me connected to what matters.

To my parents, Laureano and Elvia Gomez, for absolutely everything. Thank you for the endless trips to the library even when you were bone-tired and knew I already had a million things to read. Gracias, Papi, for always remembering to pick up the latest Sweet Valley High book at the beginning of every month. Y gracias, Mami, for listening to all my stories and always asking how the writing was going (even when I didn't want to tell you!). You both gave me space to think and to dream, and taught me to always make space for joy. Estoy tan orgullosa de ser tu hija. Los quiero mucho!

And thank you to my siblings, in-laws, nieces, and nephews—Edua, Leo, Eddy, Natalie, Muñe, Maria, John, Alejandro, Sebastian, and Ariana. You never lost faith even when I did. I'm so grateful to share a history and a future with you all. Thanks for always showing me where the party is. I love you all so much.

To my beloved Hira, who knew I was a writer as soon as he met me, and never let me forget it. I write love stories because you made mine come true. Te adoro.

And to my darling Anjali—from the moment you were born, you made me better. You made me braver. You are my whole heart.

Last, but certainly not least, thank you to all the readers, especially those who've had a harder time seeing themselves in the pages of their favorite books. You are all stars.